A SUGGESTION OF DEATH

Also by Marianne Wesson

Render Up the Body

A Suggestion *of* Death

MARIANNE WESSON

POCKET BOOKS
New York London Toronto Sydney Singapore

This book is a work of fiction. Names, characters, places and incidents are products of the author's imagination or are used fictitiously. Any resemblance to actual events or locales or persons, living or dead, is entirely coincidental.

POCKET BOOKS, a division of Simon & Schuster Inc.
1230 Avenue of the Americas, New York, NY 10020

ISBN: 0-671-03559-2

POCKET and colophon are registered trademarks of
Simon & Schuster Inc.

Printed in the U.S.A.

for Jed Mattes

ACKNOWLEDGMENTS

I am grateful to Mel Lockhart for thoughtful reflections about recovered memory, to Stan Gerk for help in understanding farm life, to Wayne Gazur for advice about estate taxes, to Jim Palmer for the many insights he shared with me, and to Ben "Freshmouth" Kaplan for linguistic consultation. I was also, while writing this book, blessed with the friendship of several gifted writers who managed to serve as both sharp readers and kind critics: Kerry Palmer, Juliet Wittman, Tom Lamarr, Tim Hillmer, Janis Hallowell, Jeanne Winer, Clay Bonnyman Evans, and Sarah Krakoff.

Judy and Larry Wesson and Ben Cantrick inspired, cheered, and loved me: thanks, I needed that. I thank Susan Novelli for excellent and good-natured assistance with permissions and other lawyerly matters. Jason Kaufman displayed loyalty, patience, and sheer editing talent in large quantities, and pulled off a rescue operation as well, for all of which he has my gratitude. For sturdy support and friendship during the storms of this writing season, I am indebted to Susan Appleton (model for The Lock), JoAnne Arnold, Barbara Bintliff, Shivaun and Michael Black, Ann Estin, Rebecca French, Jerry Frye, Glenn George, Ellen Gault, Judge Carol Glowinsky, Nan Goodman, Carol Heaton, Mary

Hey, Lynda Leidiger, Hiroshi Motomura, Christopher Mueller, Lisa Penaloza, Justice Nancy Rice, Mark Roberts, Victoria Routledge, Mike Sandrock, Jeanine and Guy Saperstein, Larry Schiller, Susan Tixier, Jane Thompson, Jan Whitt, and Anne Williams.

I know I have failed to keep a sufficient account of David Mastbaum's many contributions to the enterprise of writing, not to mention living. For all the help I remember, and also all I've forgotten, thanks to David.

Jed, this one's for you.

Law, say the gardeners, is the sun,
Law is the one
All gardeners obey
To-morrow, yesterday, to-day.

Law is the wisdom of the old,
The impotent grandfathers feebly scold;
The grandchildren put out a treble
tongue,
Law is the senses of the young.

Law, says the priest with a priestly look,
Expounding to an unpriestly people,
Law is the words in my priestly book,
Law is my pulpit and my steeple.

Law, says the judge as he looks down
his nose,
Speaking clearly and most severely,
Law is as I've told you before,
Law is as you know I suppose,
Law is but let me explain it once more,
Law is The Law.

Yet law-abiding scholars write:
Law is neither wrong nor right,
Law is only crimes
Punished by places and by times,
Law is the clothes men wear
Anytime, anywhere,
Law is Good-morning and Good-night.

Others say, Law is our Fate;
Others say, Law is our State;
Others say, others say
Law is no more,
Law has gone away.

And always the loud and angry crowd,
Very angry and very loud,
Law is We,
And always the soft idiot softly Me.

If we, dear, know we know no more
Than they about the Law,
If I no more than you
Know what we should and should
not do
Except that all agree
Gladly or miserably
That the Law is
And that all know this,
If therefore thinking it absurd
To identify Law with some other word,
Unlike so many men
I cannot say Law is again,
No more than they can we suppress
The universal wish to guess
Or slip out of our own position
Into an unconcerned condition.
Although I can at least confine
Your vanity and mine
To stating timidly
A timid similarity,
We shall boast anyway:
Like love I say.

Like love we don't know where or why,
Like love we can't compel or fly,
Like love we often weep,
Like love we seldom keep.

—W. H. AUDEN

SPRING 1994

Your Vanity and Mine

Never ask a witness a question unless you already know the answer. It's one of the first things they teach you in law school, but I already knew it anyway. Everybody knows it, from television. This advice is not really meant to apply to a discovery deposition, but even there you're at least supposed to know what it is you're trying to discover.

They also taught us *A surprised lawyer is a bad lawyer.* Then there's another good one: *Don't get emotionally involved with a client.* Sterling principles, really, although I admit I never put much stock in the second. Even lawyers aren't so dull as to wish for lives devoid of surprise.

It was my law partner, Tory Meadows, who induced me to violate the first one, but although I broke it at Tory's behest, it wasn't on her behalf. It was for Mariah.

As for the last rule, I broke it on my own. I'd broken it at least once before. I suppose that makes me some kind of recidivist.

Our first meeting was unpromising. Inside the Hygiene Cafe the air was close and warm, a contrast to the windy March chill outside. Fog condensed onto my glasses as I stepped in. It was disorienting, and so was the slight but unmistakable lowering in volume of the ambient conversational buzz: the regulars turning to survey a newcomer. This breakfast spot was not on the tourist circuit.

A freckled waitress in red jeans smiled and came toward me, a menu in each hand. "You want breakfast or lunch?" she inquired.

"I'm supposed to meet someone," I said. "Mariah."

"Oh." She turned and looked at an older woman who was sorting checks behind the cash register. "Martha? You seen Mariah today?"

Martha shook her well-permed head without looking at me and took a deep drag off a cigarette that had been burning in an ashtray. "She works on Thursdays. She won't be coming in here."

I started to take a deep breath, then thought better of it. The fog that I had taken for steam had a large component of cigarette smoke, I now saw. Smoking is not allowed in restaurants in Boulder, not even in bars, and like most Boulder types I have gotten used to smoke-free environments. But I gathered that the rules were different here in Hygiene, its name notwithstanding.

I smiled back at the waitress. "Suppose I just have coffee and a cinnamon roll. I hear you make really good ones."

"Betcha life," she agreed. I followed her through the first room of the cafe into a larger room at the back, empty except for one couple smoking and eating eggs and bacon at the same time. "Joe and sugar," she called out as we passed the service window. "Black?" she asked me as she gestured toward a worn Formica table with two tubular-steel-and-vinyl chairs.

"I'm sorry?"

"What are you sorry for? Do you want your coffee black?"

"Oh. No, cream, please. If you have it."

She smiled crookedly. "We have it."

"And if you see Mariah come in, will you tell her I'm back here?"

"You heard Martha, didn't you? She won't be here."

"Well, just in case."

She shrugged indifferently. "I s'pose."

I couldn't believe I had neglected to bring anything to read; I never travel without a book or at least a magazine. Abibliophobia, Sam calls it. Fear of running out of reading material. He went to one of those schools that makes you study Latin.

There weren't many other customers in this back room. The bacon-and-egg couple seemed absorbed in their breakfast and their smokes; they paid me no attention. I looked at the photographs of prize bovines and rodeo scenes on the walls for a few minutes, then gazed out the west-facing window. There was no opportunity for eavesdropping, because the room was too noisy. In the corner of the room an ice machine made loud ka-whump sounds, like it needed a visit to the small-engine repair shop I'd seen on the corner.

I could have used a tune-up myself. For days I had been suffering from Impostor Syndrome, certain that the confidence that had carried me through fifteen years of practicing law was in retrospect a delusion, that I did not have the slightest idea what I was doing, and never had. I believe it may have started with the dream, which would mean it really started when I agreed to be on the radio.

It was one of those anxiety dreams: I was back in law school, carrying a crushing load of casebooks in a backpack as I banged about through the dim corridors, trying to locate the room where my exam was to be held. I couldn't find it, even though I knew it would be the same room where the class had been meeting all semester. That knowledge didn't help because (here I could feel my armpits dripping and the blood buzzing through my arteries like a swarm of furious flies) I hadn't been to class all semester. Not once. I flew around a corner, but there was nothing there but the door to the law library, full of all the unobtainable answers to the examination I was certainly about to flunk. I couldn't even remember the *subject* of the exam, I realized with sickening clarity. It could be anything: torts, criminal law, civil procedure, contracts. Commercial paper. Regulated industries, first amendment, administrative law...

I don't know why my dream self didn't just give up, didn't simply drag the hopeless pack of books back out to the parking lot, and drive the rattletrap Opel I had in those days away from the school and the law forever. But she didn't, and I pounded those corridors in a fever of anxiety and shame all night long. Then, somehow, my waking mind must have suspended the memory of the dream. I didn't think about it all day.

It wasn't until the evening, when I was on the radio and the whispery voice asked its question (*What if it happens to a child?*), that the memory of the dream blew into my head like a chinook ahead of a cold front, and I knew I was about to be unmasked as the impostor I was.

But I was on the air and I had no time for dream analysis. And since simply saying "I don't know" is not good form when you are on the air, even if it's God's truth and in fact the only accurate answer, I used the skills I had. For despite the dream, I had passed all of my law school exams, graduated successfully, and even passed the bar exam, all many years ago. So I did know something useful. I knew how to make it *sound* as though I knew the answer, or that I *would* if it weren't such an ignorant and ill-formed question. And that's what I did. For which sin, utterly common in my profession, I am punished on various unpredictable nights by a recurrence of the dream.

Okay, sometimes I get ahead of myself; I never seem to know where to start. Let's go back to the radio show. The thing was, it never occurred to me that a radio appearance could be very difficult. Radio and I were old friends; I was into radio long before I knew anything about law. Twenty years ago, when I was in college in Poughkeepsie, New York, I used to deejay a folk music show: *The Flower Power Hour.* Folk music was old hat by then; everyone else was into disco—*Saturday Night Fever* and all that—but I'd always had an unaccountable infatuation with the 1960s. I'd line up those big old vinyl platters on the turntable and fill in the spots between Leonard Cohen and Mimi Fariña with innocent jokey patter left over from the sixties: Woodstock, the Chicago

Seven, and Senator Roman Hruska saying that even mediocre people deserved representation on the Supreme Court. At the time, I imagined that being mediocre was about the worst fate a person could suffer.

I loved being on the radio because I had been told I had a sexy voice. Although our little collegiate broadcast station didn't have enough power to reach far beyond the campus, like an idiot I imagined lonely bachelors all over Poughkeepsie, and scattered through Cold Spring and Red Hook and Wappingers Falls, listening and imagining the slender, witty, lovely, but somehow melancholy girl talking away into the microphone on a Friday evening. At the time I weighed about two-ten, and probably hadn't had a date for eleven months. I believed that being fat was nearly as disgraceful as being mediocre, if perhaps not quite. My radio show comforted me immensely.

I don't know why I was always so hungry then, but the hunger left me without warning or explanation during my junior year. I lost eighty pounds and graduated from Vassar in a white size-eight minidress; in the photographs my mother took, the dress barely covers my crotch. Almost everyone else in my class was wearing floppy polyester and pointed collars, including my roommate, Susie (The Lock) Wheelock, who graduated magna cum laude in philosophy, but I remained true to my chosen style. My final radio show was broadcast the night before graduation; the last song I played was "Fire and Rain." "Goodnight, and peace," I whispered as Sweet Baby James hummed out the last measures. "This is Cinda Hayes, signing off. Hope your life just grooves along."

There was no student radio station at the University of Colorado, where I went to law school. Over time all the skinny hippies had turned into jocks: rock climbers, runners, swimmers. So I started running myself and now, in my forties, I get twitchy and weepy if I can't run for three days in a row, and I eat almost everything I want to. Like most prosperous cities today, Boulder is bursting with astonishing food—tender croissants spread out in glass cases, pearlescent smoked salmon in the grocery deli, cappuccinos and lattes with foam bubbles tiny as nanoseconds. I am almost prosperous enough to buy whatever treat catches my eye without hesitating over its cost. Unlike cars and boats and Manolo Blahnik shoes, food is so cheap in this country that even the best of it is affordable to a middle-class lawyer with a mortgage but no kids—if she doesn't like fish eggs, anyway, and I don't.

Business had been a little sparse lately, however, and the nest egg with which my law partner Tory Meadows and I had bankrolled our new law practice was beginning to dwindle a bit. Tory was getting snappish about the cost of copier paper and bicycle messenger services; the week before my radio appearance, she had insisted on delivering a motion to the courthouse in Fort Collins herself, on her motorcycle, despite the circumstance that her time is worth one hundred fifty dollars an hour, and the messenger service would have charged us fifteen dollars for the delivery. But I think it was the footnote instead of the motorcycle trip that made me realize how slow things had gotten.

"What do you think of this motion?" she had asked me that afternoon, flapping a page in each hand to dry them as they emerged from our office ink-jet printer.

"What is it?" I asked inattentively. I was looking over our billing records.

She shrugged. "Routine. Motion for return of items seized as evidence. In that violation of custody case I did in Fort Collins."

I took the two-page document from her and looked it over. Probably she saw me trying unsuccessfully to suppress a smile.

"What?" she said.

"Nothing," I said back. "It looks great. Excellent."

"Give it up, Minnie. What's the smirk about?" Tory called me Minnie Mouse when she was annoyed at me, or wanted to annoy me. Together these circumstances accounted for about sixty percent of the time.

"What smirk?"

"It's the footnote, isn't it?"

"It's an excellent footnote," I said, squinting at it again. It described a skirmish between two Supreme Court justices concerning the proper view of how *another* footnote, in an earlier Supreme Court opinion, should be read.

"So?" she said.

I handed it back to her. "It's very impressive. But without wishing to disparage the experience of being a judge of the Nineteenth Judicial District Court of Colorado, I doubt that any member of that worthy bench has ever seen a footnote in a two-page motion before. Not," I added hastily, "that there shouldn't be a first time for everything."

She turned away from me scornfully. "You talk like some professor, but you're one of the most anti-intellectual persons I have *ever* met, Minnie Mouse." Ten minutes later, I heard the subdued roar of her Kawasaki as she turned it out of the alley behind Pearl Street, heading north toward Fort Collins to file her motion. She had left without saying good-bye; I guess she was really fond of that footnote.

It was ridiculous. Fort Collins is forty miles away, and even March days that start out sunny and mild can turn out very iffy in Colorado; March is the snowiest month here. I knew Tory's burning need to carry the motion to the courthouse herself by motorcycle had more to do with her own demons than with any need for us to economize. Tory had been kidnapped and hurt—hurt badly, I thought—by a thuggish police officer in 1989, in part because she knew something that might have proved the innocence of my client Jason Smiley. Jason was dead now, executed three years later because his innocence hadn't mattered enough. I thought I had come to terms with my failure to save his life, and Tory seemed to have recovered from her ordeal. But she wouldn't talk to me, or to her lover, Linda, about what had happened to her that weekend. Linda and I agreed that this wasn't good, but it had been a long time since either one of us had brought the matter up with Tory. Constant motion was one way she kept her memories at bay.

Both the retreating whine of the bike's engine and the footnote made it clear we just weren't busy enough. Boulder had too many damn lawyers for us to sit around drinking lattes, decorating routine motions with footnotes, and waiting for clients to walk in; I needed to drum up a little action. So when Marta Tafoya, president of the Boulder County Bar Association, asked me later that week if I would take a turn hosting the legal advice call-in show on the local NPR affiliate, I said yes. I won't say I didn't worry at all about not knowing the answers to the inevitable landlord-tenant and marital dissolution questions. I've been a criminal lawyer most of my life; I only started handling civil cases when Tory and I began our partnership last year. But I did a quick brushup from Continuing Legal Education outlines and thought I was ready. Other people did this kind of thing all the time, I told myself. I was smart; I had graduated in the top five in my law school class. Why shouldn't I be able to answer a few legal questions on the radio?

That was my conscious mind talking. Not the other part, the one that houses the ones that Stephen King calls the boys in the basement. Probably those boys were at work on the dream already.

It wasn't that I would be paid for appearing on the advice show; it's a volunteer service sponsored by the county bar association. But I had heard that sometimes people would listen to a lawyer on the radio show and decide that she sounded smart and easy to talk to, and later call the office and ask for an appointment. Marta had assured me I would be allowed, even expected, to strew mention of my name and our law firm, together with our specialties and location, liberally through the broadcast. And I had thought that being on radio again would be, as I would have said in my earlier radio days, a trip.

I arrived at the station about six in the evening, half an hour before the broadcast would begin. Darkness had fallen, but the March evening air did not have too much bite as I walked across the parking lot to the drab warren of offices that housed KGNU.

Fergus O'Shaughnessy, the station's programming manager, met me at the reception desk in a pair of spectacularly ragged overalls. He showed me to the glassed-in room we would use for the broadcast and introduced his assistants Shawna and Siobhan, a pair of University of Colorado students doing their internships. The place was like a Gaelic Woodstock; it made me quite nostalgic. Siobhan had a headful of ferociously red hair so spiky I made a whimsical mental note not to get too close, for safety reasons. She would be handling the technical end of the broadcast and providing introductions and transitions. Shawna, her shoulders under a Phish T-shirt at once slim and sturdy, like a dancer's, would get coffee and water and provide general assistance. This was way more help than I was accustomed to having with anything, so I luxuriated in it as they spaced the mikes, checked the sound level, and coordinated with the telephone operator, who would be answering the incoming calls and transferring them in to me and Siobhan through our headphones. I fiddled with the headset and leafed through the notes I had brought: a page of lawyer jokes in case things got slow, an index to the Colorado Revised Statutes, a list of legal resources to which I might refer a caller, the number of our nobly struggling local Legal Services office. I felt fine.

Six-thirty came, the red light went on, and I could hear a muted version of the perky music that always introduces the *Call a Lawyer* show. After a few measures, it faded away, and Siobhan began to speak. She had a great voice, I noticed, throaty but melodious; she was reading from the short written bio Fergus had asked me to bring.

"Our host tonight, in cooperation with the Boulder County Bar Association, is Cinda Hayes. Cinda is a graduate of the University of Colorado School of Law, former assistant district attorney here in Boulder, and after that director of the Boulder County Rape Crisis Team. She now practices law with the firm Hayes and Meadows, right here in Boulder, located on Pearl Street above Pour La France. Hayes and Meadows specializes in employment discrimination and personal injury litigation, especially intimate torts." Here Siobhan gave me a puzzled sideways look. The phrase was from my bio, and I suddenly regretted it. It had looked good on the page, but sounded weird when she said it. "We're lucky to have her with us tonight, and we encourage you to call in with your legal questions," Siobhan continued. "Ah, there's a caller already. Hello, this is KGNU *Call a Lawyer.*"

The first caller had put up her house to bond her brother out of jail on a drug charge. He'd disappeared and she was about to lose the house. She had no idea where he was, and he owed her five hundred dollars she had given him for the lawyer besides. He'd always been like that: rotten. And another thing, his dirtbag lawyer refused to tell her anything, even though he had to know where his client was. Can they do that? she asked.

Can they do that? How many times had I been asked that question in one form or another? It sounded like the name of a country folk song, of the sort that Robert Earl Keen could have written in a funny version, or Michelle Shocked in one of her seriously bitter moods. I tried to be honest with the caller (*Unless you have the money to pay off the bond amount, there's nothing you can do to keep them from taking your house*), while halfheartedly defending the tattered honor of my profession (*Your brother's lawyer is not allowed to disclose any confidences that he may have learned*) and offering a small amount of useful information (*You are allowed to bid on your own house at the sheriff's sale, and if you are the high bidder, you can buy it back*).

I sighed as she hung up, realizing that what I had really wanted to tell her was *Gosh, you need a lawyer.* I often had the same impulse with my own clients, and sometimes wondered what they would say if I yielded to it.

But... aren't you a lawyer?

Siobhan was motioning to me: hel-*lo*. Another caller.

"This is Cinda Hayes. Did you have a legal question?" I leaned into the mike.

Barely suppressed chuckles in the headphone. "I was, like, wondering. For a legal reason. Like, what is an intimate tort? Exactly?" Big snort. It sounded like a teenage boy, probably with a confederate on the extension. Shit. I'd never been a junior high school teacher. I didn't know how to handle this stuff. The Socratic method—answering one question with another—occurred to me because I had seen so many of my law professors use it to stall for time when they didn't know how to handle a student's comment.

"Why?" I asked. "Do you think you may have been the victim of one?"

More snorting, followed by some puffing. "Puhhh! I don't *think* so."

Of course, the Socratic method didn't always work. I repaired to the more traditional lecture method. "A tort is a civil wrong—it may be a crime, but not necessarily," I explained. "The law uses some quaint terms, like we call a person who commits a tort a tortfeasor. An intimate tort is simply a tort committed by a tortfeasor who is in a close relationship with the victim. Does that answer your question, sir?"

"Pfhhh!" He snickered again. "Tartfreezer?"

"*Fee*sor. Tort*feasor.* One who commits a tort." I was getting tired of this conversation. "Sir? Does that answer your legal question?"

"Okay," he said faintly, and hung up. I looked at Siobhan for guidance; she moved in smoothly, her well-modulated voice exuding competence.

"Do intimate torts pose any special legal issues, Ms. Hayes?" she asked, sounding profoundly interested.

"Well," I said with relief, "for many years, there were very few lawsuits based on these kinds of wrongs. Courts would say they were barred by family immunity, or victims just wouldn't want to sue the person who harmed them because they were too embarrassed. But family immunity has been abolished mostly, and victims have realized that civil suits can be a way to fight back. There's no reason why a victim of an acquaintance rape, or a woman who is beaten by her husband, can't sue for damages. My partner and I have handled several of those kinds of cases. They pose some special challenges, but we've been pretty successful with them."

I looked back at her, and she shook her head minutely. Still no caller. She pointed to my page of lawyer jokes.

"Now," I said in my best seductive radio voice, "for all of you who love to hate lawyers, a little joke. Do you know what lawyers use for contraception? No? They use…their *personalities.* Another one? What do you get when you cross a lawyer with the Godfather?"

Siobhan cut in. "Let's let them think about that one. Here's another caller, Ms. Hayes. Hello? This is *Call a Lawyer* with Cinda Hayes."

I could barely hear her at first, so soft was her voice, and like too many women she made every sentence into a question. "Those intimate torts you talked about? How long do you have to file them? You know what I mean? There's a name for it? But I can't remember…"

"Statute of limitations," I broke in. "That's what we call the deadline for filing a lawsuit. It isn't always the same, even for intimate torts. Depends on the nature of the claim, and possibly even on the intentions of the tortfeasor. One year to six years in Colorado, depending."

"Well, what if someone hurts you on purpose?" the small voice persisted. "How long then?"

"Ah, those are the shorter limitation periods. One or two years, depending."

"I see," she said. "Depending on—like, on what?"

I realized I wasn't really sure. *Tell her you don't know, you big fake.* I coughed delicately. "Well, it's complicated, actually. Probably too much so for a radio show."

One of the advantages of a really fine legal education is that you develop an unerring sense of when someone is about to ask you a question that you can't answer. Because I could hear the youth in her childish diction, I knew what Ms. Whisper's next question would be in the dread instant before she said it.

"Okay, then here's another thing? What if it happens to a child?"

That was when the memory of the dream broke over me like a wave, the hopeless chase around the echoing corridors looking for a test I was certain to fail. Worse, the dream had now acquired a soundtrack, an acerbic voice-over: *That's a good question, phonus balonus. And you don't know the answer, do you?*

The thing was, I sort of knew the answer. Sort of. I knew that in some places the statute of limitations doesn't start to run until a child reaches majority. And I also knew that in some places that's *not* the rule. So I knew quite a bit, actually, but I didn't know the really rather small detail about whether Colorado was the first kind of place or the second. This, too, was a result of having had a first-rate legal education. Even though I had gone to law school at the University of Colorado, my professors made a point of not teaching "local" law. We used to joke about it as students, dizzy from the relentless theorizing of our seminars: The really good law schools, we assured each other, will teach you in a way that is not limited to the law of a particular jurisdiction. And the *truly* elite schools, like this one, will teach you in a way that is not tied to the law of a particular planet.

If I'd had a few minutes I could have looked it up, but I didn't, and the unwelcome memory of the nightmare was expanding inside my head, crowding out everything else. It was fed by my terror of not knowing, but there was also the quaver of desperation in the caller's voice. I knew she wasn't calling out of curiosity. The headset started to feel hot and sticky on my ears, and I realized my hands were unsteady.

"Well, you know, that's also a rather complex question." I gestured ferociously to Siobhan. "I wonder if our caller could leave her telephone number with the operator, and I could telephone her in a day or two so we could discuss these particular questions further without taking up more air time."

"Yes, why don't you do that?" said Siobhan quickly into her mike. "I'll transfer you back to the operator. Thanks for calling. And now a news break from National Public Radio news. We'll be back at fifteen minutes after the hour for more of *Call a Lawyer* with Cinda Hayes of Boulder."

More peppy music. "Whew," I said, pulling off my headphones and wondering whether Siobhan saw right through me. "This is not easy."

"You're doing great," said Siobhan. "Just talk a little more slowly, if you can. Otherwise, you're fine. Water?" She gestured to an ancient-looking metal carafe.

"Sure," I said doubtfully, hoping the water was newer than the container. She started to pour a stream of it into a paper cup. "Shall I go back to the lawyer jokes when we come back?"

"Yeah, finish the one about crossing the Godfather and the lawyer. Then if we don't have any callers, I'll ask you some questions myself. I prepared a few." She smiled brilliantly and handed me the paper cup. I peered at the water inside; it looked all right.

"Do you think that last caller will leave her number?" I asked.

"DK," replied Siobhan, running her hands over her alarming hair, seemingly unaware of the danger of a puncture wound.

"DK?" I repeated.

"Sorry," she said with a smile. "Don't know. I don't know if she'll leave her number. That sounded like kind of a complex question she was asking."

"Um, yeah. Really not of general interest, I thought. Better to call her later."

"Sure." She smiled guilelessly. "Back on the air in five seconds."

I put the headphones back on and took a last sip from the cup.

Siobhan got me through the rest of the half hour. I finished the lawyer joke (*A guy who makes you an offer you can't understand*), a new caller had a zoning problem, a man asked about child custody evaluations. Someone wanted to discuss the Rodney King case. Finally, it was over.

Fergus shook my hand and invited me to come back soon. I stumbled across the parking lot to my Subaru, still preoccupied with the desperate dream and the feelings it had uncaged, then remembered I had left behind my briefcase and turned back. Shawna met me with it at the door. "You did great," she said as she handed over the battered leather pouch, gesturing toward a folded slip of paper tucked into the outside pocket. "I put that one caller's phone number in there. She gave the operator a little more information, too, and said she'd really appreciate a call back."

"Thanks," I said. "Thanks for everything, Shawna."

"No prob," she said kindly.

Back in my car I unfolded the slip of paper. *Wants to know,* the operator had written, *what if stat. of lim. is about to run but she can't exactly remember what tort feesor (?) did to hurt her. Because she was very young. But is sure something happened. Please call. 405-7522. Mariah.*

When Tory and I moved our newborn law firm into what had been Sam Holt's offices, on Pearl Street above the Pour La France espresso parlor, we flipped for choice of office. Tory won and chose the biggest, and I was glad: I liked the smaller one better, with its window overlooking the alley and an old stone cottage across the way. The alley represented the precise demarcation between downtown Boulder (business division) and the crowded, colorful *arrondissement* that is downtown Boulder (residential division).

I was supposed to be doing legal research so I could get back to my radio caller from the night before. Instead, I was watching the young woman who lived in the cottage water the colorful herb garden she had planted in pots that could be rolled outdoors on a sunny day; her green shoots glistened in silent rebuke to my dusty office plants. My interest was not exclusively horticultural. Although it was a little hard to tell from the distance, I was pretty sure the gardener was wearing nothing except a series of silken scarves tied strategically about her lithe body. Since I've never even learned the knack of keeping my underwear straps from falling down my arms, I have an inordinate admiration for women who can keep things from slipping down or flopping out. Watching her bend to tend a plant, I decided she was one of the best I'd ever seen.

"I thought you were straight."

I jerked around, startled, and banged my hip on the corner of my computer stand. It was Tory in running shorts, her copper curls dripping sweat. She must have parked her bike in the canyon and run the rest of the way down to the office; she did that sometimes.

"Ow!" I cried indignantly. "Haven't I told you not to sneak up on me that way!"

"Haven't I told *you* that if you're attracted to a woman, you should just tell her so? You don't have to resort to this pitiful voyeurism." She flopped down into my spare chair with a grin. "Or do you still maintain that you're straight?"

"It's not a matter of maintenance, Tory. Must you sweat on my good chair, where my clients sit?"

"I'd be more worried about that if you had any clients." She pulled up her tank top and wiped her face with the hem. "Straight, eh? Still mooning over Sam's departure? Not that he wasn't a prize, I admit. Remember what this office looked like the day he moved out? It'll never be that clean again." She picked up *The Colorado Lawyer* and started leafing through it.

"I admit he was the neatest man I ever met and I found that incredibly erotic. But I'm not mooning. He's in New York, I'm here, we do E-mail, life goes on. Will you put that down? I hate when you read while I'm trying to talk to you."

She looked surprised. "Are you trying to talk to me?"

"Yes!"

"Why didn't you say so?" She slid her feet out of her running shoes, sat back in the chair, and curled her legs into the lotus position as though it were nothing. "Shall we talk?"

"Remember that radio program I promised to do last night? *Call a Lawyer*?"

"Oh, yeah. How'd it go?"

"Okay except I got one call asking me a question I couldn't answer. Goddamn it, I hate that. So I faked it and said I needed to do some research."

"What faked? You needed to do some research, right?"

"Well, yeah. Because like a dummy I didn't know the answer."

Tory performed a perfect three-hundred-sixty-degree eye roll. "Cinda, nobody knows the answer all the time without doing research. And nobody but you thinks it's some kind of character defect. What was the question?"

"Something like this: A child is injured, tortiously. But she has trouble remembering it."

Tory nodded sagely. "Repressed memory."

"Maybe. Then later the memories start to come back. But she still isn't sure exactly what happened. So she—"

"—wants to know about the statute of limitations."

"How did you know?"

She shrugged. "What else? There are some cases on this question, you know."

"Colorado cases?"

"Yeah, I just saw one the other day, while I was looking for something else."

I reached for a legal pad. "Well, now we're cooking. What was the name of the case?"

"I don't remember the *name* of it. I think it's pretty amazing I remembered there is one. That's more than *you* knew."

"I know, that's what I'm telling you. Lately I feel like I'm about to get arrested for impersonating a lawyer."

She shook her head and stood up. "That's how you and I are different, Cinda. It bothers you that you're not perfect. That's very vain, if you think about it."

I threw a pencil at her as she turned to leave, but she evaded it easily.

"And another difference," she said over her shoulder. "Despite my imperfect memory, I don't tend to forget my sexual orientation. Now you just go back to watching the sweet little earth mother in her garden. I'm going down the hall for a shower, and then I've gotta get to court."

I turned back to the window. The scarf gardener was gone, so I swiveled my chair around to the desk. I almost bumped my hip on the computer stand again, and it reminded me. Westlaw. Computerized legal research. Tory and I had just started subscribing to it a month ago. It was expensive, but we got two hours a month free for the base price, and I didn't think either of us had used it at all since our business had slowed down. I double-clicked the Westlaw icon on my screen and listened to the modem stutter and chirp until I could see I was connected. I chose the "States" library and then "Co-cases." I considered how to formulate a search request, then hesitantly typed in:

```
"statute of limitations" AND lost OR recover! OR
repress! W/S memor!
```

I watched the little hourglass blink on and off to indicate that the program was working, looking for Colorado cases that had the phrase "statute of limitations" and one of the words "lost" or "recover" (or "recovery" or anything else that started like that) or "repress" (ditto) in the same sentence as "memory" or "memories."

Come on, girl, I urged it silently; I always think of Westlaw as a very efficient female librarian.

WESTLAW has found ONE case at Level One, she informed me.

There was not a button for *You go, girl,* so I clicked on the one for "Cite," and almost immediately saw:

```
1.LYNN K. CASSIDY AND SUSAN K. BALL, Plaintiffs-
Appellants, v. EARL DEAN SMITH, Defendant-
Appellee, No. 88CA1754, Court of Appeals of
Colorado, Division Two, March 28, 1991.
```

I clicked on "Full" and started to read furiously. By the time the printer was spitting out a hard copy of the case Tory reappeared. She was looking very professional in a black suit, the effect marred only slightly by her wet hair and bare feet. I was ready for her.

"*Cassidy v. Smith,* Court of Appeals, 1991," I said smugly.

"Huh?" she said, toweling her head strenuously.

"The case. *Cassidy v. Smith.* I found it on Westlaw. The statute of limitations for outrageous conduct, of which childhood sexual assault is one variety, is two years. The statute does not begin to run until the plaintiff turns eighteen. And the statute does not begin to run even then unless the plaintiff has discovered, or reasonably *could* have discovered, all of the elements of her cause of action. So if she's forgotten what happened, the statutory two-year period doesn't start to run until she remembers. It's called the discovery rule."

"I'm impressed. You auditioning for the Alan Dershowitz role in some movie?"

I shook my head. "Not me, I'm too tall. So, you think that's enough for me to tell my caller?"

"I guess," Tory said. "There aren't any other decisions more recent?"

"That's it."

"How old was this caller, anyway?"

"She didn't say."

Tory stopped rubbing her head and threw the towel into the corner. "I suppose you can tell her about that case. But there's still something puzzling about that rule, isn't there? I mean, what does it signify to 'discover all of the elements of your cause of action'? From what I hear, this recovered memory business is very tricky. You remember things a little at a time, sometimes there are big holes in what you can recall. What's the precise moment when you've discovered enough for the two-year period to start to run?"

"I wonder about that, too. In fact, in this *Cassidy* case that's what the argument was about. The plaintiffs remembered this older guy forced them into sex when they were teenagers, but said they didn't realize they had been harmed by it until much later when they got into therapy. The court said that even if they didn't get the whole picture until later, they knew what he had done. So they knew enough to get the limitation period rolling when they turned eighteen."

"So each one had to file before she turned twenty."

I nodded. "Or lose the right to sue, ever."

"If this call-in person asks you about that I think you ought to explain the rule but be clear about the uncertainties. Just tell her that law isn't like science. At some point the law's going to say she knew enough to have to file in two years or forget her claim, but it's hard to know in advance what that point would be. A lot depends on who the judge is. Listen, I've gotta go. I'm off to county court to cover a prelim for Morris Traynor." She vanished through the door; I could hear her rummaging around in her office.

"Morris Traynor?" I called out. "OPM Traynor?" The letters stood for Outrageous Prosecutorial Misconduct. The defense lawyer was notorious among prosecutors for his easy resort to that accusation. When I was a prosecutor, I was OPM'd by Traynor more times than I could count.

She reappeared at the door, briefcase in hand. "Yeah, Morris Traynor. We had lunch last week and agreed to cover for each other when necessary. We need that kind of backup, Cinda," she said, seeing my expression. "In case you've forgotten, we aren't DAs anymore. Nobody's going to pay us to prosecute anyone. If we want to practice criminal law, it's going to have to be for the defense. I do, so I'm taking steps to become a member of the defense bar. You got a problem with that?"

She was right. "No," I lied. "I just made that face because you threw your disgusting wet towel on my floor." I gestured toward the sodden lump in the corner.

She retrieved the towel and threw it into my lap. "Squeeze it over that poor thing," she recommended, pointing to my wilted *Ficus benjamina.* She wheeled around on the Cuban heels of her glossy black pumps, and marched off smartly.

I reread *Cassidy v. Smith,* and dug the note with the caller's phone number on it out of my briefcase. As I was about to pick up the phone, I saw the fluorescent lights flicker on in our reception area and heard Beverly come in the front door. Beverly is our office manager, receptionist, and fairy godmother, another legacy from Sam. I knew she was late arriving because she'd had a conference at Boulder High with her son Duane's counselor this morning.

"Hi, Beverly!" I called out. "How was the conference?"

"I'm gonna kill that kid," she called back. "Will you represent me?" I could hear shuffling sounds and exasperated breaths, then she came into my office. Her mascara was a little smeary, but that could have been intentional; Beverly is big on experimental makeup. "Turns out he's been ditching his third-period English class to hang out in the computer lab. He's invented some computer game that all the other kids are wild about, and he tried to turn it in for his English term paper. When the teacher wouldn't take it, he went back and put some deal in the computer game where the teacher gets killed by some little knight or soldier or something. So the other kids love it more than ever but someone tells the teacher and he's very upset, says it's a threat, he wants Duane expelled. So this counselor tries to get snotty with me and I—there I go, running off at the mouth again. Sorry, Cinda. Anything you need me to do before I get back to those bills?"

"Beverly, it's okay. Is Duane in serious trouble? You need me or Tory to help out?"

"He's not in serious trouble yet, except with me. But thanks for asking. We'll get through this. I mean, we got through the firecracker incident, right?"

I grinned, remembering. "Yeah, that one came out okay. I don't need you to do anything right now except get those bills out. I'm going to run downstairs for a coffee. Do you want one?"

"No thanks," she said. "I'll get on those bills right away."

There was a line at the take-out counter of Pour La France, five or six persons just slightly too well turned out to resemble addicts lined up for their methadone. I waited long enough to decide on a cappuccino instead of a plain cup of coffee.

I could hear Beverly on the telephone as I reentered the office. "I'll ask her to return your call as soon as possible, then." A pause. "I'm so sorry, but I can't say exactly when that might be. She's"—here she glanced at me—"away from the office on business this morning." Another pause, and this time she held the receiver ever so slightly away from her ear, her customary unconscious gesture of distaste. "Of course I will. I'll be certain she understands how urgent it is. Yes, you're welcome. Yes. Good-bye."

"For Tory?" I asked after she put the receiver down.

"For you," she said, writing on a message pad. "Extremely urgent, according to her." She tore off the sheet and handed it to me. "But I don't know. She seemed really bossy, you know? One of those people who think everything they want is extremely urgent, because they want it. That's why I didn't just put you on when you came in. She said she didn't know you, except by reputation."

I looked at the slip. "Morgan McKay?"

Beverly nodded. "She said someone McKay's daughter. She acted like I should know the name but she was talking so fast I didn't catch it."

"Harrison McKay? His daughter?"

"That's it. Should I know him?"

I shook my head slowly. "No reason you should, except I think I've heard he's running for some political office. He's kind of a local hero."

Beverly nodded. "You see? Having that kid has made my mind turn to mush. I know who you mean now. He's a political science professor at the university."

"That's the one. I don't know him myself. And I really don't know why his daughter would be calling me."

Beverly shrugged. "Beats me. I'm just a secretary."

"Right," I said, heading for my office. "And the Beatles were just a garage band."

Morgan McKay got right to the point. "I'd like to come and consult you about a legal problem. As soon as possible, preferably today."

My appointment calendar, open on my desk, looked quite empty for the rest of the day, and in fact for the rest of the week, but I found myself reluctant. "What kind of legal problem, may I ask?"

"I'd rather tell you in person," she said. "This would be a highly confidential matter."

"I only work on a confidential basis, Ms. McKay," I said stiffly. "No good lawyer does anything else."

"Of course. So what time this afternoon would be convenient?"

It wasn't like I could afford to be choosy about clients. I capitulated. "What about two?"

"See you then," she said briskly. "I know where your offices are."

At first, the only thing I could find to dislike about her was the hair. It was both perfect and indifferent, a buttery silken drape that would slide through your hands like water but always fall back into shape, the curved tips cupping her chin. She was charming and breezy, and even tried to redeem herself with Beverly by apologizing for her abruptness on the telephone. "Sometimes when I'm tense I act like a jerk," she said disarmingly. "I'm sorry if I was too pushy."

"Not at all," said Beverly, without looking up from her spreadsheet.

After she settled into the client chair and declined a soda, Morgan McKay told me she wasn't really there on her own behalf. "It's my father. Perhaps you know of him—Harrison McKay?"

"I don't think we've ever met, but I know who he is."

"He's a professor at the university, and is about to declare as a candidate for the state senate," she said.

I nodded. "I've heard that."

"He gave the University Distinguished Lecture the year before last," she added. "About the rural roots of populism. It was written up in all the Denver papers; perhaps you remember."

"I was a little preoccupied at the time," I said. "With—a piece of litigation." I pushed away the memory of my client Jason Smiley, executed by lethal injection in November of 1992. I'd spent the next year in a fog of sorrow and failure. I pushed again, harder, and asked, "Why didn't your father come in himself, Ms. McKay?"

"He's very, very busy," she replied. "Running for office these days is extremely hard. He's out every day, trying to raise money, putting together a campaign organization. He plans an official announcement very soon. I'm his campaign manager, and I handle everything that doesn't absolutely require his personal attention. So we agreed I would come see you today."

"And may I ask why he wanted to consult me? Since I've never met your father, I'm curious why you would seek me out."

"My father is a friend of Sam Holt."

This was unexpected. I had never heard Sam mention a friendship with Harrison McKay. "Really?" I said.

She nodded vigorously, the hair whispering as it shifted and fell back into place. "From Big Brothers. Sam used to play tennis on our court with one of the kids he mentored and he and Dad got to be friends. So when Dad decided we ought to consult a lawyer, he called Sam up in New York and Sam recommended you."

I couldn't quite identify what seemed odd in this. "Okay, Ms. McKay, why don't you tell me what the problem is? I don't charge for an initial consultation. I don't promise that I'll agree to take on the matter, whatever it is, until after we've talked, and maybe not even then if I need to do some research. If I do agree to represent your father, I'm going to need to meet with him in person. I have a standard fee agreement, and I'll give you a copy to take to him and then we can discuss its provisions—"

"Of course," she cut me off. "Of course. And I assume that even before you agree to represent Father, the usual rules of confidentiality and everything else apply as well?"

"The usual rules of confidentiality certainly apply. I'm not sure what you mean by everything else."

She lifted her shoulders. "It's not important. Sam said you were a very ethical and professional attorney." Here she looked uneasily at the door. Beverly was clicking away at the computer in the reception area. "Do you mind?"

I got up from my desk and walked past her to close the door. Beverly looked up at me as I reached for the knob, her face unreadable. I winked, but she just turned her head to the monitor again.

"Do you mind if I record?" Morgan said behind me; when I turned, she was pulling a tiny tape recorder out of her oxblood leather satchel. I'd never known a client to want to record our conversation before, but couldn't think of a reason to object. The recorder was a beautiful little machine, small enough to be concealed in a palm.

"If you like."

She inserted a miniature cartridge, clicked the diminutive machine on, and started talking.

"It's my sister," she began. "Her name is Drew, Drew McKay. I don't suppose you've ever met her?" She looked into my face searchingly.

"No."

She sighed. "Drew has had a very hard life. Our mother died in an automobile accident when she was only eight. We were all in it. Dad was driving, and we were coming home from a day up in the mountains. We were coming through Clear Creek Canyon and a car coming toward us was on our side of the road. Dad swerved to avoid a head-on crash, and our car skidded on the gravel shoulder and went into the creek. Dad pulled Drew out of the backseat and got her to the bank, and I was able to get out, but Mom must have been hit on the head. She drowned." Morgan McKay put her shining head down for a moment and massaged her eyebrows with her hands.

"I'm sorry," I murmured. I had no idea what this story had to do with Harrison McKay's legal problems, whatever they were, but it would have been mean to ask her to get to the point. "You talk like you remember this. How old were you?"

"Oh, I was twenty. I was going to the university at the time, living at a sorority house, but I used to come home a lot on weekends to be with them. We were really a close family, until the accident. But it changed everything. Drew and I were both hospitalized for a time afterward; she had a concussion and some memory loss and stuff. I'd just broken an arm, but I had terrible nightmares for a while. Dad was sort of overwhelmed; we didn't have any other relatives nearby, and he had his work to keep up. Mom was the one who had made everything work—the house, the horses, the trips, parties for colleagues. My father is a wonderful man and he did everything for us he could, but eventually, after Drew got back in school and was having a lot of problems, we saw it was impossible. So when Drew was eleven we found a really wonderful boarding school for her up in Carbondale, near Aspen?"

That lilting question mark, the one I could hear at the end of some of her sentences, plucked a string somewhere, but I ignored it. I was focused on her story, and on trying to discern the legal issue embedded in it. "Go on."

"Well, I know Drew is still mad at Daddy for sending her off when she was so young and still so sad about Mom's death. She kept crying and saying it wasn't fair that I got to stay when she had to go, but that was ridiculous. I mean, I was twenty-three years old. I was still going to the university. I just moved back home so Dad wouldn't be so lonely and so there would be someone to, you know? Someone there?"

An uneasy conviction was growing in me. I pulled open the top drawer to my desk and felt around inside, my eyes still on Morgan.

"So what did you do after you graduated from the university?" I asked. I hoped she wouldn't notice the irrelevancy of my question, or the movement of my hand in the drawer.

She shook her head impatiently, rejecting the opportunity to talk about herself. "Let me get to the main problem that brings me here," she said. "It's Drew. Drew kept running away from the school in Carbondale, and then the next one we put her into, and finally she dropped out altogether. She traveled around Europe some when she was sixteen or seventeen—Daddy gave her money for that, thought it would be some kind of education at least. But then about a year ago she came back to Boulder and got a job as a nanny on a ranch near Hygiene, out in east Boulder County. Or maybe it's a farm. There are some strange people out there, militia types. I'm afraid she's being used by them, or maybe she believes what she's saying. She says—"

Morgan McKay jumped at the peremptory knock on my door, but I didn't. "Come in," I called out.

Beverly looked flustered as she stuck her head in through the door. "I'm so sorry," she said. "But Cinda, Visiting Judge Carver just called from chambers. He wants you in court in ten minutes for a hearing in that matter you have pending before him. I told him you were in conference but he said it was urgent and I should interrupt you."

"You did the right thing," I said to her firmly. She looked relieved. I turned to Morgan. "Ms. McKay, I apologize, but you heard. I have to get over to the courthouse right away. This visiting judge who's here this month is really a pain in the neck, but when a judge calls, you have to go. Can we continue this conversation tomorrow?"

She was plainly annoyed, her lower teeth gnawing on her iridescent upper lip in an exasperated way. "Why don't you call me when you get back from court?" she said finally. "I don't mind coming back over then? I'd rather get this taken care of today."

"Okay," I agreed. "If I get back before five. Otherwise I'll call you tomorrow."

She looked as though she wanted to say something else, but then nodded. She clicked off her recorder and gathered up her bag and scarf, reaching inside the bag for a business card, which she handed to me. "All right. Please call," she said, then she stood and left.

Beverly watched her until the outer door of the office closed, then turned to me, her face clouded by doubt. "Did I do right?"

"You did great!" I assured her. "I was worried that buzzer wouldn't work."

"It's not very loud but it still scared the bejesus out of me. I'd forgotten all about it. After Sam installed it we never used it the whole time he was here. I had to think a minute about what I was supposed to say and I still couldn't remember the name I was supposed to call the judge. Did I get it right? Carver?"

"Close enough."

"No, really," she insisted. "What was it supposed to be?"

I smiled, thinking of Sam's grin when he told me about installing the buzzer and how he and Beverly would use it if necessary. "I think he suggested Crater. But the name doesn't matter. It worked like a charm."

"Judge *Crater,* Judge *Crater,*" she repeated softly, as if to fix it in her mind. "Next time I'll get it right."

"Tell Tory I need to talk to her when she comes in, okay?"

She nodded. "I didn't like that person," she added unnecessarily. "You going to tell me why you had to get rid of her?"

"I needed to stop her from telling me any more. At least until I look into something. But I couldn't think of how to get her to stop until I remembered the buzzer. If I turn out to be right about her, I'll tell you about it," I said. "Otherwise, she might end up being a client."

I didn't mean it as a warning about her behavior, but I think she took it as one. "Just because I don't care for someone doesn't mean I can't act," she sniffed. "Good as that Joan Collins, anyway."

"I know you can act, " I said. "I just had a demonstration. Listen, did you call the office supply place yet?"

"Not yet. Soon as I get these billings done."

"When you do, will you see if they have any of those little tiny tape recorders? You know, miniature?"

"Sure. Do you need one?"

I thought about it. "I think the true answer to that is no. But I *want* one. I'm sure once I have one I'll wonder how I ever got by without it. You know, like E-mail."

She made a face of elaborate indifference. "Your money."

I had never been much for telephone relationships, even in high school, when my friends were spending hours on the line every night. I remember some ferocious rows between my mother and my sister about tying up the phone; Dana had a string of boyfriends from one end of town to the other, and played them like an orchestra. The telephone was her conductor's baton.

But I never could find much pleasure in the disembodied voice, so I hadn't talked to Sam in more than a week. I had more liking for the new generation's favorite telecommunications tool: electronic mail. Just now, however, I needed a quick answer. I dialed the 212 number, imagining it ringing in his office, which I had never seen. It overlooked a tiny park, he had told me, two blocks from Bleecker Street. I closed my eyes while listening to the ring, and imagined his African masks and Yoruba carvings brightening a gray room, weak sunshine washing through the windows onto the battered walnut rolltop desk. After the fourth ring, a woman's voice answered.

"Law offices of Patterson and Holt. May I help you?"

"Hi, this is Cinda Hayes calling for Sam. Is he there?"

"No, he's at the courthouse, waiting for a jury. May I have him call you?" The voice was rich and musical, Caribbean, perhaps.

I considered. "No, thanks, I might be out myself. When he comes in, would you ask him to check his E-mail for a message from Cinda, and reply as soon as he can?"

"Of course. Cinda?"

"With an *a*. Thank you very much."

It was alarming, the way my heart sank merely from hearing the pronunciation of Sam's receptionist. He had left Boulder saying he couldn't figure out how to be a black man in such a white town. I didn't blame him, but missed him terribly, and sometimes would admit to myself that I secretly hoped that he would tire of the city and come back. There were no signs of it, however, although he returned often to stay with me for a few days.

In New York, Sam practiced law with his sister Natalie's boyfriend. He lived on the third floor of Johnny and Natalie's brownstone in the Village and spent many nights haunting the jazz clubs. This much I knew. What I didn't know was whether he was growing away from me in a way that would eventually become permanent.

Enough, I told myself. I took a deep breath and turned to my laptop. I called her Hypatia. She called me cinda@lawgrrls.com. Lawgrrls is, I am told, Tory's and my "domain." I'm not certain what this means, exactly, but we were told by the guy who sold us our E-mail setup that it is very cool to have one, so we got one.

I clicked the cursor twice on my E-mail icon, and the screen blinked and invited me to enter my name and password (respectively, cinda and louis, the name of my favorite nephew). I did, and Hypatia informed me that I had two messages: one from Dana (dmarker@dallaslink.com) and one from SHolt@nylaw.net. I skipped over Dana's and, using my little mouse, instructed Hypatia to show me the electronic traces of my erstwhile and unforgotten lover Sam Holt.

Dear Cinda,
Sorry I haven't written for a while. Actually I'm glad you talked me into getting E-mail. It's def, as Linc would say. Johnny and I just finished a federal jury trial: mail fraud, wire fraud, and RICO counts against our clients, and four other defendants too, including the one who's the real perp and set up our guy, or so we were explaining it just this morning to the jury. They're still out so we don't know how we did.

The City is still beautiful and ugly and exciting and exhausting and I still can't sort it out, so don't ask how I'm feeling about it. I will say it's some sort of bliss to be in a place where black people are as common as any other kind, and not to feel so damn different all the time. But we talked about that before, didn't we? And I still miss you like hell and wake up too early in the morning thinking about you.

I'll call you one night later in the week. I'd like to hear your voice.

I punched R to use the reply function.

Dear Sam
Hope your trial comes out right for you—I'm sending mental messages to the jury, over and

over again: "reasonable doubt, reasonable doubt." (Those messages have triple power when they come from a former prosecutor.) Miss you like hell, too. Although I have to admit that Boulder is rather a blissful Hell, with flowers coming up and fabulous spring skiing (those new telemark bindings make a huge difference) and enough blue sky to wallpaper the universe. Still, it seems empty without you.

Odd but urgent question: Did you give my name to Harrison McKay or someone in his family as a recommended attorney? If so, what do you know about him? I'll tell you more later, but for now just need an answer to these questions. Would you call me as soon as you get this? I'll be in the office until about 5:30 MST (yes, things are that slow), then home.

Soon.

Love, Cinda

It was only three o'clock, far too early to go home, and I didn't need any more coffee. I *was* a little worried about our lack of business. For myself, I didn't mind so much; I had been enjoying the late-season skiing and had started reading through James Lee Burke's Robicheaux books from the beginning. But Tory's manic energy needed an outlet or her ghosts would get restless. It was good that she was pursuing some business development strategies. Despite my hopelessness at self-promotion, I was going to have to do the same if something big didn't come along soon.

So there were lots of reasons I ought to have been happy to represent Harrison McKay, admirable and politically correct public figure, but I wasn't ready to agree until I heard from Sam. Morgan McKay's appearance had made me uneasy, coming so soon after the radio show. Nor was I ready to get back to my caller. I reached into my briefcase and pulled out a raunchy used paperback copy of *Black Cherry Blues,* purchased off the orderly used-book shelves of the Rue Morgue Mystery Bookshop across the street. I put my feet up onto my desk. Beverly called good night about five, turning out the lights in the reception area; I called back, but even before the door closed I was reabsorbed in the troubles of Cajun cop Dave Robicheaux, fleeing to Montana with his motherless little girl one step ahead of a band of ruthless thugs.

I might have read all the way to the end if I hadn't been aroused by the phone ringing simultaneously with the sound of a key in the outer door—Tory returning. "Hey," I called out to her, as I snatched the phone from its cradle. "Hayes and Meadows," I said into the mouthpiece.

"Hay, Hayes, and Meadows?" said a familiar voice. "You got a stutter now, or have you taken on a new senior partner?"

"Sam!" I said. "No, it's just us. Tory and me, and of course Beverly, the real boss. How are things with you? Did your jury come back?"

"Oh, yeah, they came back." His voice was laden with irony. "Found my client not guilty on all counts, and awarded him six million dollars for the trouble and embarrassment of being wrongly accused."

"Oh," I said. "Convicted?"

"Yeah," he said heavily. "It shouldn't have been that much of a surprise, but you know how you always convince yourself, even if you haven't convinced anyone else?"

"Yep," I assented. "I know that one. Sorry, Sam."

There was an awkward silence in which I wanted to tell him I missed him, which I did more painfully than ever now that I was hearing his voice. Damn telephones. The moment passed, and he spoke next.

"So, to what do I owe the honor? Rosalind said you called earlier. She said I should check my E-mail, but our system is down, like it is about half the time."

Rosalind. Such a reassuring name. "I'm really glad you called," I said. "I had a prospective new client come in today, a woman named Morgan McKay. Her father is Harrison McKay, and Morgan said she had come to see me to consult me about a legal problem of Harrison's. She's his deputy or something, the way she tells it. Morgan said you recommended me to him. What do you know about the guy?"

"She said I recommended you?"

"Didn't you?"

A pause, during which I could hear papers being shuffled. "I knew Harrison McKay when I lived in Boulder; he's on the board of Big Brothers, and I had a little brother for a while, a kid named Ricky. I was trying to get Ricky interested in tennis, and McKay let us play at his house. He has a big place off Baseline Road with a swimming pool and tennis court. I spoke to him a few times, and he seemed like a nice man. I don't know this Morgan. And I haven't spoken to any McKays since I left Boulder. But it looks as though one of them did call me this morning. I was in court, giving a stupendous summation obviously wasted on those jurors. Rosalind took the message."

"What did it say?"

"Just a minute, I'm trying to read. Damn, either I need new glasses or that girl needs to write better." More shuffling. "Okay, I think this is it. Harrison McKay called, old friend from Boulder. Can you recommend Lucinda Hayes as lawyer? If so, no need to call back. That's weird."

"What do you mean?"

"Saying I don't have to call back. And he didn't even leave a number, looks like. Unless Roz forgot to write it down, and I don't think she would have. Sounds like things in Boulder are as flaky as ever. Why would someone call to find out about a lawyer but then say I didn't need to call back?"

I didn't want to share my suspicions with him while they were still formless. "What else is going on, Sam? How are you?"

"I'm pissed off right now because of losing this case, but that's just temporary. Johnny's really good, but he's disorganized, so it feels sometimes like I spend a lot of time cleaning up after him. Literally and figuratively, you know? Like shuckin' and jivin' in front of some judge to get an extension or apologize when something doesn't get filed on time. I never used to miss a deadline, but Johnny just regards them as gentle advice. I think he'd let his car run outta gas on the Brooklyn Bridge if Natalie didn't look after all that stuff for him, and sometimes I think I'm just his office version of Natalie. But still, the guy's a genius with juries, and the work just comes pouring in."

"I thought you said a lot of the judges are black."

"Yeah, so what?"

"So you have to shuck and jive in front of them too?"

A small snort. "Most of all. Course it's a very brotherly shuck and jive, you understand. Cinda, when are you gonna come out here for a visit?"

It was not the first time he had asked. "You come here," I countered. "It's beautiful here. We can do spring skiing up at Eldora." I could not account, even to myself, for my reluctance to go stay with Sam in New York. "And then I'll visit you there. Soon, I promise. Listen, Sam, after what you told me about McKay, I need to follow up a little. Can I call you tomorrow, or send an E-mail?"

"Sure," he said. "But if you were in court I'd never let you get away with that answer. *Soon.*" He chuckled softly, probably imagining the waxing he'd give the hapless witness who tried to get away with such an inadequate response. "Listen, Cinda. There's a little place near the house, one of those cellar jazz clubs. Oh, man, it's just like Paris in the fifties. Sometimes I'll be there, just drinking wine and listening, and it seems real clear to me you need to be there too."

This was very romantic for Sam, so I don't know why I said what I did next. "You were in Paris in the fifties?"

"In my dreams, girl. You wanta hear about some of my other dreams?"

I did, but perhaps not over the phone, and anyway Tory was standing in the door to my office. "Maybe later, okay?"

"Sure," he said. "Someone else there?"

"Yeah, Tory."

"Terror of the Courtroom, Horror of the Slopes?" This last was a reference to Tory's new avocation, snowboarding. Sam, an elegant and accomplished skier, thought snowboarders ought to be confined to their own mountains, with patchy snow and rocks so they could acquire the concussions they courted without plowing into proper folks on two skis. "Give her my best. Let me know what goes on with McKay, okay? Do I need to return his call?"

"No," I said. "No." I was the one who had wanted to end this call a minute ago, but now I felt an unaccountable desire to prolong it. Even so, I couldn't think of anything else to say.

"Later, then," Sam said gruffly, and hung up.

"Well?" said Tory. She was unshod again, rising up and down on the balls of her feet, ballet-style. A few hours in court always infused Tory with an uncanny energy; she glowed as though from some internal sunburn.

"How did the prelim go?"

She shrugged modestly. "Cut him loose."

"Cut him *loose?* After a prelim?"

The shrug again, accompanied by more *relevés.* "The DA was new, and their case was pretty lame."

I knew there had to be more to it than that. The government's burden of proof at a preliminary hearing—probable cause—is so small that most lawyers don't even bother cross-examining the prosecution witnesses or putting on any of their own, and the rules of evidence don't apply so you can't object to hearsay or other stuff that wouldn't even be admissible at trial. I'd heard of cases in which the judge refused to bind the defendant over for trial after a prelim—like I'd heard of unicorns. I'd never actually seen one.

"What did you do? Cast a spell on the judge?"

She adopted a Hollywood Transylvanian accent for her reply: "I nevair tell, innocent one. You do not wisshh to know."

"I just hope Morris Traynor forgives you for making his case go away, along with, one presumes, his fee. But never mind that. Turn your brilliance in this direction. What would you think if a client came to see you, telling you she was relying on a referral from an out-of-town attorney, and when you asked the attorney about it, he said the client had just called him earlier in the day and left a message saying 'If you recommend Tory Meadows, you don't need to call back'?"

"Run that by again? 'Cause I didn't get it."

I ran it by again.

"I'd say the client is more interested in something else about me than in my legal abilities, since she didn't really try to find out anything about them, but she wanted to be able to tell me she had a referral so I would take the case. Or so I would at least talk to her."

I nodded. "That's what I think too. Now, on to the next level. What would the something else be that was her real motivation for talking to you?"

She didn't hesitate. "Conflict of interest," she said flatly. "There might be other possibilities, but I'd say the likeliest thing is she wants to disqualify me from representing someone else. She doesn't really want me to represent her, or she'd be more interested in finding out what kind of lawyer I am. But she thinks if she gets in to see me and tells me enough, then I'll be DQ'd even if she doesn't hire me."

"That's what I think, too. Now stay with me just a little longer. As you know"—I gestured to take in my empty desk—"clients have not exactly been thick on the ground around here lately. What case might my devious would-be client be seeking to disqualify us from?"

"Not that poor mope I just sprung, that's for sure. How about—no. I can't—wait! Your radio caller!"

I nodded. "That's what I believe."

"Wow. Have you talked to her yet?"

I shook my head. "The other side got to me first."

"And who might that be? The mom? The dad? The uncle?"

"Sister." I told her about Morgan McKay's visit.

When I was done, she said, "So you made poor Beverly your accomplice in fraud to get rid of this Morgan before she told you enough to disqualify you. Pretty slick, Minnie. But how did you know she was related to your call-in client? You said she called her sister Drew, but I thought you told me the call-in's name was Mariah or something."

"That's the name she gave," I agreed. "And I wasn't sure about Morgan. It was partly the story she was telling, but there was an inflection to her voice, the way it went up at the end of some sentences, like they were really questions. It struck me just a few minutes into her story that the call-in person had it too."

Tory looked unconvinced. "Practically everyone under thirty talks like that. You know?" She imitated the rising interval. "It, like, started with the Valley Girl thing?"

"I know. But this was more distinctive somehow. Anyway, she's not my client, is she?"

"Who, Morgan?"

"No, the other one—Drew. If she's the one who called me."

"Not yet," she said. "But let's try not to succumb to mural dyslexia here."

"What?"

"You know," she said as she rose to leave. "Inability to read the handwriting on the wall."

The phone rang only twice before it was answered by a sweet soprano voice. "Covington residence," it said.

"May I speak to Drew, please?"

"There's no—wait a minute, please." Her hand must have shielded the phone, as I could hear only hurried sibilants before she spoke to me again. "Just a moment."

Ninety seconds later, another voice said, "This is Mariah?" and I knew, but I asked anyway.

"Are you Drew McKay?"

"No. Not anymore. Who is this?"

"This is Cinda Hayes. Did you call me on—"

"Miss Hayes. I'm so glad you called. Can I talk to you?"

"I think it would be better if we met in person."

A small sigh. "I think so, too. Can you come here?"

"Where is here?"

"East Boulder County. Between Niwot and Hygiene. But wait a minute."

More whispered consultation, then silence on the line. I

heard Tory call out good night as she left, studied the square of sky through my window as it grew white at the bottom and dark near the top, shifted my feet onto the desktop. Finally she came back on.

"I can have an hour off work tomorrow at eleven in the morning, if you can meet me nearby. I don't have a car."

"Okay," I agreed. "Where is a good place?"

"There's a coffee shop in Hygiene. Right at the crossroads. They make these huge cinnamon rolls. Can you be there at eleven?"

"How will I know you, Drew?"

"Don't worry—I'll know you. You'll be the only one there I don't recognize, so it'll be easy. And I'm not called Drew anymore—it's Mariah. How did you even know what my name used to be?"

"See you tomorrow then, Mariah. I think we have some things to talk about."

In twenty years of living in Boulder County, I had never once felt the need to visit Hygiene. To locate it that morning I had to dig a county map out of the glove compartment of the old Saab Sam had left behind in my care. I spent several minutes at my kitchen table, trailing my fingers over the right half of the much-pleated paper, before I finally located the small dot in the northeast corner. I was surprised to discover that it was only about two inches from my house in North Boulder: sixteen miles, according to the scale.

I nosed the Saab north onto Broadway at about ten-fifteen, unsure how long it would take me to get there. The morning was cold enough to burn the breath, and bright enough to sear the eyes. A stiff chinook blew off the mountains, sending late-winter debris skittering across yards and streets and empty lots. Just north of the city limits, Broadway rejoins Highway 36, which runs parallel to the foothills to its west. After traveling that way about six miles, I pulled over to check the map again, then turned right onto Nelson Road and blasted east, toward Kansas.

As you head east from town, the foothills drop away behind you and the higher peaks of the Rockies, invisible from the city, come into view. In the side rear-view mirror I soon could see the summits of Longs Peak and Mount Meeker. Lettering on the silver ellipse informed me that the objects to be seen in it were much closer than they appeared, but I didn't believe it. The doubled white peaks shimmered in the mirrored sky like misshapen moons; my mind could not connect them to the flat carpet of brown earth I saw through the windshield.

It's not that easy to explain. How about this: The topography of Boulder County, Colorado, resembles what you'd get if you placed a number of objects of various sizes on a dinner table, then pushed all of them onto the left side of the table, reserving the far edge for the tallest (lamps, candlesticks), then the next tallest (casseroles, frog statuettes, books), finally the smallest (pencils, silverware, wadded-up napkins); and then, on the right half of the table, nothing, except maybe a few loose pieces of jewelry and a couple of small rocks. My point is this: The city of Boulder is right where the silverware and napkins peter out into uniform bare table surface; or, as the chamber of commerce would put it, where the mountains meet the plains. To the west of town, the foothills and then the Rockies jump up out of the earth, hiding steep canyons and old mining sites and the well-groomed slopes of the Lake Eldora ski area. But to the east the land runs flat, more or less, all the way to the state line and beyond. The farms start before you leave the county, and go on for days through the depopulated heartland of America.

The city of Longmont is the unofficial capital of agricultural east Boulder County, but there are a number of smaller towns with their roots deep in the stony soil, which still yields a living to a dwindling number of surviving farmers. Hygiene was one of those, and it was where I was headed, to meet my not-yet-client Mariah (née Drew) McKay.

The Saab had coughed itself to life roughly, but gradually began to run more smoothly as it warmed up, and I started to enjoy taking it around the curves. The first few miles of Nelson

Road were horse country—boarding stables, an Arabian breeding farm, a riding academy with a dressage ring. The next fields seemed from the distance to harbor a herd of very hirsute, hump-shouldered cows; as I drove nearer, I saw they were bison. A single brick prairie palace, all cathedral ceilings and gables, sprawled in windy solitude at the top of a hill on my right; two men were struggling to unload a garage-sized satellite dish onto a concrete pad beside it. But it was the only new building I saw. Not far away were raw neighborhoods of five-thousand-square-foot houses sprouting from quarter-acre lots, but they had not yet invaded Nelson Road. Most of these fields would be planted again with corn or pumpkins or alfalfa—at least this year.

Soon the road lost its dips and curves and the houses became smaller and farther apart, most surrounded by sheds and pens. Farm equipment crouched beside barns, waiting for the ground to thaw and be broken again. I was still in Boulder County, but it seemed a thousand miles from the glossy shops of the downtown Boulder mall.

Eventually I came to Seventy-fifth Street and hung a left for the two-mile distance to Hygiene, a town too small to have its own city hall, police department, or fire department. It did, however, have an elementary school, a small-engine repair shop, and the Hygiene Cafe, which shared a rickety wooden building right at the crossroads of Seventy-fifth and Hygiene Road with something called The Country Crow. I pulled in beside a very clean black pickup.

I was fifteen minutes early, so I went into The Country Crow to browse until eleven. I declined the offered assistance of a teenage girl who returned to watching *Leeza* on a tiny television set up in a back corner, and looked around the small shop. It seemed to sell principally scented candles, stuffed animals made of gingham, and potpourri. The mingled odors of fruit and flower were unbearably cloying, so I left again after about five minutes, stepping back out onto the wooden porch just in time to see a tall man in a denim jacket and cowboy hat climbing into the pickup. He gave me a hard look, then reached for a cell phone and started to punch the keys.

There was a sticker on the truck's front bumper: *The tree of liberty must be refreshed from time to time with the blood of patriots and tyrants.* No gun rack, however. Lose that paranoid city attitude, I instructed myself. Probably just a farmer who admires Thomas Jefferson and uses a cell phone to call in for the crop price report. I opened the loose wooden door and stepped into the cafe for my encounter with the freckled waitress, Martha, and Mariah.

"Here you are, miss." The waitress put down a mug of coffee, which smelled excellent, an aluminum pitcher of cream, and a cinnamon roll the approximate size and appearance of a cowpat.

"Thanks." As I tackled the roll with a flimsy stainless steel fork I looked back at the window and saw a child ride by on a bicycle, struggling against the wind. She wobbled to a stop and placed the bike under the window, then disappeared in the direction of the front door. In less than a minute she stood beside my table.

"Miss Hayes," she said, but I would have recognized her as Morgan McKay's sister even if she hadn't recognized me. I could see now she was no child, but a painfully thin young woman, white skin stretched taut over bony wrists and a jaw made prominent by the lack of cushioning flesh. Still, there was a likeness to Morgan. But it wasn't any resemblance to her attractive sister that prompted some hungry invisible fingers in me to reach toward the girl. I think now it was that initial impression that she was a child, reinforced by the tentativeness of her gestures as she pulled off a worn fleece jacket before settling in the chair across from me. That and the claim of the maternal, an account that my life had not to that point presented. Perhaps the events of that swift moment could be made to explain much of what followed.

Shocked by the unexpected lurch of emotion, I swallowed to steady myself. "Sit down," I said, gesturing.

"Thanks," she said. "Did you order something?"

"One of those cinnamon rolls you mentioned," I said, pointing. "You were right, it's enormous, but it's very good. Will you have one?"

She shook her head and turned to call the waitress. "Terry?

Could I have some black coffee, please?" Her jeans were loose on the jutting hips, and a hectic flush stained her cheeks. It was the hair that made up a large portion of the family similarity: Mariah had Morgan's corn silk grown two feet long and braided into a rope so sturdy and symmetrical it looked as though it might be useful in one of the events depicted in the rodeo photographs.

"So, are you sure you want to talk in here?" I asked after the waitress had brought her coffee. "It's not very private."

"You're right, but it's about as private as I can manage right now. I work as a nanny about two miles from here. The Covington farm. They're really nice people; in fact, Ginny let me off this morning for an hour so I could come see you. I live there, but the kids are always in my room or tugging on my shirtsleeve, you know, even when it's supposed to be my time off. I didn't think we would have any privacy there, and I don't have a way to get to your office. There's not much public transportation out here."

"I can see that. And I guess nobody is likely to overhear us in here, anyway." I inclined my head toward the noisy ice machine.

She smiled and nodded. "Do you remember the question I asked you? On the radio?"

"I remember. And I might have an answer for you, but of course it depends on some things."

She squirmed a bit and shot a look toward the next table, where the bacon-and-egg couple had been joined by two other men in gimme caps and windbreakers. "How does this work, Miss Hayes? I've never had a lawyer before. Would I have to pay you first? Because I don't have very much money. And then what if I paid you and there was nothing you could do because of that—what did you call it? Statute of limitations?"

"Will you call me Cinda?"

She nodded. "And I'm Mariah." That seemed to remind her of something. "Why did you ask for Drew when you called the Covingtons'?"

"First, let's get this on the table. What we're doing here is what's called an initial consultation. I don't charge for those. So no matter what we decide, you won't owe me anything for today.

After that, we'd have to have a fee agreement if we both agreed that I was going to represent you. There are ways of arranging that I'd be paid only if we collect something on your claim, in which case I'd get part of that. I'm not sure I'd be willing to work on that basis without knowing more, but it's a possibility."

She nodded. "I've heard of that. I hoped you might think about doing it that way. But the part about Drew? I haven't used that name for a long time."

"Did you change your name legally?"

"Yes," she said, looking around the room rather than at me.

"Yes, but what?"

Her eyes met mine. "But nothing. I changed it legally."

"In county court in Boulder?"

"No, somewhere else. Does it matter?"

"Probably not," I said, but made a mental note to ask about the name change again later. "I can't tell you why I thought you might be Drew McKay. But I had a reason to think so."

She pulled the braid over one shoulder and fingered the end of it, as though consulting a string of worry beads. "I don't really get that. Why can't you tell me? That really bothers me."

She looked so distraught I was afraid she might cry. Cursing the thoughtless impulse that had prompted me to ask for Drew when I called her, I reached across the table and took her hand in mine. "Listen," I said softly. "One of the things about being a lawyer is people tell you secrets. They have to, so you can help them. It's really important that anyone who confides a secret in me can trust that I won't tell it. So lawyers have to say 'I can't tell you that' a lot. It doesn't mean you can't trust me. It means the opposite. It means that you can be sure that anything you tell *me* won't be told, because I wouldn't betray you any more than I would betray someone else."

She pulled her hand away and whipped her head from side to side with her eyes closed. "You have some other client who knows who I am but I can't know who that is? How can I trust *that?* There are a lot of people who are not on my *side,* Cinda. If you're representing some of them..."

"I'm not," I said firmly. "Not everyone who consults me ends up being a client. But even if they don't, I have to respect their confidences. Do you see?"

"No," she sniffled. "This was a mistake. I'm sorry. I don't think I can trust you." She stood up quickly, almost overturning the chair, grabbed her jacket, and ran out of the room. Two seconds later I could hear the front door to the cafe bang closed.

Terry the waitress poked her head through the door leading from the kitchen, spotted me, then turned around and disappeared again. I smiled weakly at the four people at the next table, but they looked back at me sternly, as though I had committed some dire breach of Hygienic etiquette. I was ready to bolt myself, but wasn't about to leave without paying. As I rummaged in my purse, Martha of the cash register approached me, the Mickey Mouse emblem on her denim shirt bumping and rolling over her large bosom as she walked.

"Judge wants to talk to you," she informed me.

"Excuse me?"

She jerked her head toward the front room. "He's out there. I'd talk to him I was you."

"Which judge is it exactly?"

"Judge Sayers."

I knew all of the judges in Boulder County—muncipal, county, and district courts—and I'd never heard of one named Sayers.

"What kind of judge is he?" I asked Martha. "And may I have the check?"

She waved away my five-dollar bill. "He's our'n, that's all. Our judge out here. Go on, now."

He was standing near the outer door: the tall man with the bumper sticker on his truck. When he saw me, he gestured for me to follow, and walked out to the sidewalk. "C'mon," he said, and pointed to the passenger door of the truck.

"No," I said. "If you want to talk, do it here."

He shook his head slowly, managing to convey weary acceptance of my obstinacy. "Your way, then," he said heavily, and sat down on the wooden bench that rested on the porch between the cafe and The Country Crow. "But it's cold out here."

I sat down, too. "Then make it quick. I'm not having a very good day, and I've spent all the time I want to out here in Opryland." I regretted it as soon as I had said it. What a bitch.

But the man didn't respond to it. He took off the cowboy hat and ran a hand over his unruly salt-and-pepper hair, then looked toward the mountains. My gaze followed his. The snow on Longs threw off light like a sun.

"That little girl has a hard time because she doesn't know who she can trust. You just made things a lot worse for her," he said. "What'd you say to her, anyway?"

I knew I had made a mistake, but I wasn't eager to be criticized by this ersatz jurist.

"Do we know each other?" I asked. "Do you know something about me? Because I don't remember that we've ever met."

"I know some things about you. I've made it my business to."

"Are you really a judge?" I asked.

He nodded. "That's right."

"I have my doubts about that. But if you are, and if you know who I am, you'd know I can't tell you what she said to me. Or what I said to her. It's confidential. It's privileged. Not even a *judge* can make me tell."

He looked at me directly then, his light hazel eyes narrowed against the gritty wind. "I'm not tryin' to *make* you tell, Miss Hayes. That wasn't an order. I thought we were having a talk."

The man wasn't exercising any quality that could remotely have been described as charm, but nevertheless I could feel my resistance softening. "Tell me what bench you sit on," I said conversationally. "Or are you retired?"

"It's not one of the courts you're acquainted with, I imagine," he replied.

"Municipal court of Hygiene?" I suggested. That brought a little smile to his weathered face.

"Hygiene doesn't even have its own police station," he said. "We're an unincorporated county out here. Sheriff's department takes care of policing, county judges take care of enforcing the laws of the state of Colorado."

I said nothing, merely raised my eyebrows expectantly.

"Tell you what, I'll show you my courthouse. No"—he held up his hand to stop my protest—"it's safe. You can follow me in your car. We don't even have to go inside. *Can't* go inside, for that matter. I don't have the key with me."

I looked at my watch: nearly noon. I visualized my appointment calendar for the rest of the day: nearly empty. "Okay," I said. "How far is it?"

"Ten minutes," he said. "We'll be heading south on Seventy-fifth." He rose and swung nimbly into the truck, replacing the hat as he did.

He roared off without waiting and I didn't have time to get my sunglasses out of my bag before backing the Saab out to follow, much less ask myself what I was doing following a strange man to an unknown rural location. I squinted as I followed the truck past the crossroads and back toward Niwot. The rear bumper had a sticker, too, but I couldn't get close enough to read it. At first I thought it said NRA, but there seemed to be two letters after NR. I gave up and concentrated on keeping up with him as the truck careered around a corner, skidding on gravel. He drove like a man who thought himself immune from the operation of both the laws of the state and the laws of physics.

Judge Sayers, I said to myself, shifting down to keep the Saab on the road. Sure.

He turned right onto Nelson again, then left onto Sixty-third. In a couple of miles, he skidded into a left turn that led through rusty iron posts into a gravel parking lot. I pulled into the lot beside him, gravel dust enveloping us like smoke, as though the ground were on fire. By the time I got out, he was already walking through a chain-link fence toward a small stone building. I followed. *Ryssby Chapel,* said a stone marker. *Built 1875, Restored 1979.* And a discreet sign: *Property of First Lutheran Church, Longmont.* Sayers stood by the side door, which was secured by a padlock.

"I don't have the key, or I'd show you around the inside. It's the best courtroom I've ever had," he said. "No plumbing, of course, and no heat. But that's an advantage. Keeps things short and to the point."

"This is your courthouse?"

He nodded. "Sometimes."

"And—which court would this be?"

"It's a common-law court. I guess they didn't teach you about them in law school."

"No," I agreed. "What are they?"

"So I guess you never met a judge of one before."

"You," I turned to him, "are a very good guesser. I wish I were as good. I can't even guess why you brought me here."

He looked around. "Don't you think it's pretty out here?" The sweep of his arm took in the graceful stone chapel, the small graveyard behind it, and beyond that, to the east, a lake or reservoir screened by a copse of bare trees.

"Sure." But I turned involuntarily to look behind us for the peaks of the Front Range. They glistened at the horizon, guardians of a colder but more familiar country. Across the street from the chapel, two dogs circled and barked unhappily, chained to a hand-lettered "For Sale" sign in the front yard of a peeling wooden house. I turned back to him.

"Why don't you just tell me what's going on here? How do you know me, and what do you and your friend Mariah want with me?"

"I'll tell you. But first I want you to see something. Go back there and look for Lind Thorssen's grave. You'll find it. It's one of the oldest ones."

"Who was he?"

"I'll tell you when you come back; just go look for it now."

Shaking my head, but reluctant to abandon this encounter for the grim peace of my office, I trudged away from the road, toward the back of the chapel. The dried grass shuffled and sighed under my feet. There were only thirty or so graves in the cemetery, some quite recent, and I looked at every one. Many good old Lutheran names—Nelson, Halvorssen, even a Lindemann. But no Lind Thorssen.

When I found him again, back at the door to the chapel, he was just tucking something into the back pocket of his jeans. The padlock hung open.

"Look at that, I found my key after all," he said, his voice level as a cornfield. He pushed the wooden door and it opened easily, swinging aside to reveal a small anteroom with whitewashed walls and a floor of wooden planks. "Come on in."

I knew he'd picked the lock, of course, and I had no illusion that the company of this phony William O. Douglas would save me from a burglary prosecution if we were caught inside. I don't know why I obeyed him, but I did.

He followed me into the anteroom, then pulled the door closed behind him. It was immensely quiet inside the stone walls, and very cold. I peered into the chapel itself, a small room with the same stone-and-wood composition. The severe-looking pews were painted white, and the pulpit on the slightly raised altar looked homemade even from where I stood. But the plain windows framed the blue sky like a prayer for spring, and the wooden floor glowed softly in the midday sun.

He strode past me and down the center aisle, confident but not swaggering. When he reached the altar he stepped up to the pulpit, then spoke in a voice suddenly authoritative. "Of course, for court we have to move this aside for the bench. It's no problem."

"No," I said. "I'm sure not. When is your court in session, Judge Sayers?"

"Whenever we need it." He stepped off the altar suddenly and sat down in the first pew, motioning to me. "Come on, sit down. Overlooked old Thorssen's grave, did you? No matter. I'll tell you what you want to know, but you have to listen to the whole story or it won't make sense. Do you think you could do that?"

I nodded slowly, walking forward and hugging my leather jacket to me. I knew there was no water in Ryssby Chapel—hadn't he said there was no plumbing?—but that's what the place smelled like, cool clean water. He started his story when I was settled across the aisle from him in the second pew, my legs drawn up beneath me for warmth, my head full of the cold clean smell that I couldn't stop gulping down as though to quench some thirst I'd never known I had.

"What courts are you licensed to practice in?" he began.

None of your business, my mind responded automatically, but my voice, unbidden by my will, answered. "Colorado. United States District Court for Colorado. Tenth Circuit. What about you?"

"Some folks," he said, ignoring my question, "think that all those courts are illegitimate."

"I know that," I said. "In fact, I even prosecuted a guy once who wouldn't enter a plea. Claimed he didn't acknowledge the court's jurisdiction over him."

He looked at me with interest. "What was his reason?"

"He never told me, but the psychiatrist who examined him reported that the man believed he was a refugee from a parallel universe who had accidentally stepped through a—I think he called it a wormhole—and ended up in Boulder."

"Oh," said Sayers. "A nutcase."

"Pretty much, even by Boulder standards, which are rather loose. He was found incompetent to stand trial, anyway."

"Do you think you'd have to be a nutcase to think a court didn't have any jurisdiction over you?"

"Of course not. Defendants plead lack of jurisdiction all the time. In civil and criminal cases. Sometimes they're right."

"But suppose you had so little regard for the court that you refused even to make a plea. Or appear, if you had a choice."

"We're talking about, for example, one of the trial courts in the state of Colorado?"

He nodded. "For example."

"Then I think you'd pretty much have to be a nutcase. If you ignore a summons or an indictment or a complaint, sooner or later it's going to catch up with you. You'll be arrested, or your property will be seized. Why take that risk if you're rational?"

"Suppose you don't think the court will reach a just decision?"

This conversation was beginning to annoy me. "Listen, Judge Sayers, if you are a judge. I *know* the courts don't always produce justice. A year and a half ago the state of Colorado executed a client of mine, a *friend* of mine. He didn't do the crime he was convicted for, but they didn't care. They stuck a needle in him and he closed his eyes and died."

"I know," he said solemnly. "Jason Smiley."

I didn't stop to ask him how he knew; I was too angry. "You don't hear me advocating anarchy, burning down the courthouse, abandoning the courts for street justice. They're wrong sometimes, and I hate that as much as anyone. They killed my friend, but they're all we have."

"I'm not advocating street justice."

"What then?"

Sayers fell silent for a moment. I unbuttoned my jacket and slipped off the gloves I had been wearing, but didn't say anything. The sun outside had fallen away from the zenith and was slanting into the old chapel. Perhaps that was why it seemed so much warmer than before.

"Let me ask you this, Miss Hayes. Where did you grow up?"

"Texas," I answered. "You don't have to call me Miss."

"Ms. Hayes, then," he said seriously. "I apologize."

Somehow that sounded even more annoying. "It's Cinda," I said irritably.

"And what did your daddy do?" he asked politely.

"He was a lawyer," I admitted.

"Deceased?"

"No. But he doesn't practice law anymore," I said, seeing with my mind's eye the leonine figure sitting in his wheelchair, looking out the window of his room at the nursing home in Dallas.

"Did you grow up pretty much all in one place?"

"Pretty much. When I was born my parents lived in an apartment, I think, but I don't remember, of course. When I was two we moved to one house, in the suburbs. Then when I was a teenager we moved to a bigger one."

"Your parents still live there?"

I shook my head. "My mom is dead, and my father—has a small place," I said.

"Sisters, brothers?"

"My sister is married and lives not too far from where we grew up. Big house. Like some of the ones they're building out here now."

"Tract mansions, I've heard them called."

I grimaced. "Yeah." Then I leaned forward. "I thought you were going to explain something to me. Instead you're asking all the questions."

"See if you can imagine this, then, Cinda," Sayers said, his voice without accent or emphasis. "You were born in your parents' bedroom, in a bed that your grandfather built, in the *house* that he built, on the farm he tore out of the earth with nothing but his will and his back and a couple of mules and the love of your grandmother and your father and all of your uncles and aunts. You grew up on that farm with the smell of the hay around you. You and your cousins hid from each other in the corn when it was high, and raised your own calves and had your own horses that you rode in the rodeo. When your daddy died you grieved, but you expected to stay on the farm, maybe with your brother or brother-in-law and sister. But the estate taxes were high, and you had a bad year or two with the hail or the drought, and you had to borrow, and then there was a good year, a really good year. Except because it was such a good year all over the crop prices fell to the ground, and suddenly the banker and the farm agent and the lawyer that had been your friends all told you the same thing: You had to sell. No help for it. Sell the farm where you grew up and pulled calves out of their momma's bodies and put a new roof on the barn and fell in love and buried your parents. Sell it to a developer who wants to build a patch of those tract mansions so the yuppies who can't quite afford Boulder prices can still live like the folks on *Dynasty*."

"I know what you're taking about," I said. "It's regrettable. It's—" The crunching sound of vehicle tires on gravel sliced into my attention. Sayers looked back toward the door of the chapel, then stood.

"Best to tell you the rest a bit later," he said. His tone, solemn but casual, was the same as the one employed by a therapist I went to years ago to let me know that our time was up. But this was to be more eventful.

I was scrambling to my own feet when they strode into the chapel—two uniformed patrol officers with BOULDER COUNTY SHERIFF'S DEPARTMENT on their shirts. I still knew quite a few of the sheriff's department officers from my time with the DA's office, but not these two. The woman spoke first.

"Sayers, you *jerk,*" was what she said. "What did we tell you last time? And then go leaving your truck in the parking lot big as life. Apart from anything else, you make us look bad." She turned to me then, her eyes as hard as the buttons on her uniform shirt. "What's *your* name?"

Her partner bustled up to me watchfully, his heels loud in the aisle between the pews. He outweighed her by about a hundred pounds and looked at least ten years older than she, but he talked as though his job were to make sure she got what she wanted. "Didn't you hear her? What's your name?"

"Lucinda Hayes." I thought better of saying "What's the problem, officer?" I knew what the problem was.

"Get out." He jerked his head toward the door. "You're trespassing."

Sayers was turning his hat about in his hands again, his tongue pushing out the side of his face thoughtfully, his posture unconcerned. "Go on, now," he agreed. "We'll talk some more later."

I looked at the woman officer. She was so tiny I wondered if she had to have her uniforms specially made. Didn't they have minimum height requirements for police officers anymore? She bit her lip to arrest a smile that was forming there, and nodded at me. "You'd better go, lady," she advised. "The judge has issued his order. We'll just stay until court's adjourned for good."

I couldn't think of any reason to stay. "See you," I said uncertainly to Sayers, and left. I could hear the woman officer start in on him as I was walking out, reading him the riot act, but I thought there was as much affection as anger in her voice.

"Of all the stubborn, cockeyed..." was all I heard before the door closed behind me. The wind was still whipping the gritty air into a stinging froth as I climbed into the Saab for the trip back to Boulder.

We rent three parking spaces off the alley behind our building. When I pulled the Saab into mine, Tory's Bronco wasn't there, but Beverly's pickup occupied her own space and about a third of Tory's. I hoped Tory wasn't planning to be back and wondered if I'd have the heart to reprimand Beverly for her poor parking job. The pickup's bumper featured a display of assorted stickers, most of them appearing to be the selections of Duane, the delinquent genius. I didn't think Beverly would have chosen one with a picture of Einstein and a sphere surrounded by whirling electrons, bearing the legend *186,000 miles per second: It's not just a good idea, it's the law.*

"Where's Tory?" I asked cheerfully as I walked into the office, thinking this might be a way of working into a little discussion on the necessity of thoughtful parking.

"She got a new client," said Beverly. "Got a call from someone at the clerk's office in federal court in Denver. Something about she had to go down there and get sworn in to the federal court. So she could represent this new client."

I sat down on one of the wobbly reception area chairs and dropped my backpack onto the floor. "Cool."

She laughed. "You sound like Linc." Lincoln Tolkien had been an investigator for us for a time, but we didn't have enough work for him and he'd gone to work for some friends of ours in Colorado Springs. Everything I knew about generation X, I knew from Linc, but that word wasn't one of the things.

"For your information, Beverly, we used to say *cool* even when I was Duane's age. Even in Texas we said it."

"But not like that," she said. "Not like *kuhl,* all fast and offhand." Sometimes I forgot that Beverly was a lot smarter than she looked.

"You're right," I admitted. "Listen, on the parking places—" The phone rang. Beverly held up a hand to signal a brief delay.

"Law offices of Hayes and Meadows. May I help you?"

I raised my eyebrows, hoping to get her attention, but she ignored me in favor of listening intently to the caller.

"How very interesting." Catching my eye, she flicked her fingers at me in impudent dismissal, but then turned her hand around and cancelled the gesture with one of beckoning. "Well, of course I can check. Can you hold on for a moment?"

She covered the receiver with her left hand ostentatiously. "A gentleman who says he was responsible for your almost being *arrested* is calling to ask whether he can make it up to you. Would you be willing to see him about four o'clock? Cinda, you've been keeping secrets from me."

"The nice phone we bought for you has a mute button, Beverly. You don't have to make fun of me with your theatrical hand motions."

"You're changing the subject," she said, hands unmoving.

"I can't believe he got himself out of trouble so fast," I said, looking at the clock on the wall. "That was less than an hour ago."

"Well?"

"Tell him yes, but tell him he has to come here. No—wait." I thought of the way Sayers had made the Ryssby Chapel his own, and tried to think of a place where I would not feel that disadvantage again. "Tell him to meet me at the Trident," I said to Beverly. "Tell him it's good for me because it's right across the street from the office."

She nodded and repeated the words to Sayers, who must have agreed. After she hung up, she pulled out my appointment book and rested her red-tipped fingers on the empty page. "And what name shall I put here, at the busy four o'clock hour?" she said mischievously.

"Sayers," I said.

"First name?"

"Judge."

. . .

In the waning hours of the afternoon the wind had died down. Sunlight washed the sidewalks and teased the early crocuses coming up in the city's planters. I jaywalked across Pearl at a lull in the traffic, and pushed through the door on the coffee side of the Trident Bookstore and Cafe.

The Tri is a comfortable coffee-shop-*cum*-used-book-store whose amiable proprietor asks only that you pay for any used book you may covet before spilling his excellent cappuccino on it. Like many Boulder establishments, it's owned by a member of our local Tibetan Buddhist community, but that aspect of it is not especially visible to a customer. There's only a faint ambient serenity amid the chaos of the espresso bar, and one item hung high on the wall, over the "New Arrivals" shelf: six photographs, one after another in the same frame, stop-action style. A muscular bespectacled monk, his bare chest half swaddled in the crimson folds of his robe, takes aim at a distant target with a massive bow and arrow. The background is snowy tundra. In the first two frames the monk prepares to draw the bow; in the next two he pulls the arrow back against the tautness of the string; and in the last two the arrow has flown altogether out of the frame. The monk's expression does not change at all.

I was raised a Methodist in Dallas, Texas, although we were never more than holiday churchgoers. I have never studied Buddhism, and could not tell you what those photographs say to me that seems so important. I once overcame my shyness enough to ask the owner whether they were for sale. He smiled and said no. I look at them every time I visit the Trident, so I did that day too.

Then, pleased to have thought of a place that bore so little resemblance to Ryssby Chapel, I found an empty table by the front window, drank an almond latte that gradually infused a pleasant buzz into my skull, and watched the passersby. About ninety percent wore shoes, I estimated; this percentage would decline as the weather grew warmer. About forty percent had at least one pet on a leash (mostly, but not exclusively, dogs). I next examined the denizens of the coffee shop. The most frequent hairstyle was the dreadlock and the predominant headgear was the knitted Rastafarian cap. The footwear contest was a tie between high-tech hiking boots and black ballet slippers.

I looked at my watch: four-twenty. As I watched people come and go through the door that led out to the sidewalk, Sayers not among them, I realized that I was puzzled and faintly alarmed by the way his story and Ryssby Chapel had cast a spell on me earlier in the day. But I didn't think the common-law judge and I would occupy the same situations in this place as we had in that one. Whitewashed walls, silence, flat plains: That was his place. But here in the Trident I am at home. Bob Marley music, Buddhist photographs, the buzz of conversation over the hiss of cappuccino steam, the sight of the foothills in the window like a postcard—there is no place, including in the solitude of my own home, where I feel a greater sense of belonging.

It took me about fifteen more minutes to decide that Sayers was not going to show up. Surprised by my disappointment, I rose to leave. I bused my latte glass over to the tray by the bar and got close enough to hear the youthful *barista* whistling something familiar—"Claire de lune." His lips produced the intricate melody and rhythms effortlessly as his hands worked the pistons and nozzles of the big espresso machine. When it comes to whistling and archery, I have to admit the Buddhists have it all over the Methodists (although we have produced some excellent country musicians and football players).

On my way out, I decided to walk through the bookstore side of the Tri to check out whether they had any Sara Paretskys I hadn't read yet. But as I passed through the door that connected the coffee side to the book side I saw Sayers standing there, looking through a book.

"Hello," he said gravely, looking up. "This is a very good bookstore. I never knew about this place." His gesture took in the local history section, several shelves of assorted volumes. Then he held up the book in his hands so I could read the title: *Colorado without Mountains: A High Plains Memoir.* "Believe I'll buy this one. So, you're too busy to be on time, are you?" He pulled a well-used wallet out of the back pocket of his jeans.

"I was waiting in there," I said impatiently, pointing.

"Oh," he said with interest. "Coffee shop, is it?"

I suppressed a sigh of exasperation. "Why don't you pay for your book, then meet me back in there? I'll see if I can reclaim the table I had; it's getting crowded."

"Wouldn't you like to walk instead?"

I considered and shrugged. "Okay."

He refused a bag for the book, and carried it along as we walked, like a preacher with the Good Book close to hand. In his other hand he held his cowboy hat. "The fella who wrote this book grew up on a farm out in Logan County, near Sterling," he informed me. "Hardscrabble out there, especially in those days. You ever been out there?"

"No," I confessed. Never regretted it either, I thought.

"How long have you lived in Colorado?"

"Seventeen years."

"Ever been east of I-25?"

"I went to Greeley once."

"That's it?"

"I like to get out of town," I said. "I just usually go west, you know. I really like some of the little towns up in the mountains."

"Oh yeah," he said. "Like to ski, do you?"

"Well, sure."

He nodded. "That's the way with most Coloradans. They think the state starts at the Front Range and goes west to Utah. Never mind that nearly half the state is farm country."

"I'm not sure what you're getting at—do you have a first name?"

He smiled. "Everybody does, don't they? Only some folks, like that Cher, don't have last names."

"I think she has a last name. She just doesn't use it."

"Probably. Like I don't use my first one. Folks call me Judge Sayers and I think that's good, it helps them remember and respect. Not me, but the law."

"The law of Colorado?"

"The common law, Ms. Hayes. I know we discussed this before."

"I wouldn't say we exactly discussed it. Our little tour of your courtroom was interrupted by some officers of the law, as I remember it."

He nodded. "Mock me if you like. I don't mind."

"I'm not mocking."

"As you like."

We continued our walk down the Pearl Street Mall, a four-block pedestrian area that twenty-five years ago was Pearl Street, the main street of downtown Boulder. The day had grown mild and the buskers were out in force—jugglers, musicians, the man who twists balloons together into animals. The zip code man was halfway through his act with a good-sized crowd, asking people to name their home town and then telling them the zip code. Sayers stopped to watch him for a while. Presently he turned away and nodded, as though satisfied, and we walked on until we came to the giant animal sculptures at the east end of the Mall. They were built for children to play on but often, as now, they were occupied by a crowd of teenagers in bright baggy clothes.

As we stepped off the east end of the Mall and kept walking along Pearl Street, a real street now, we encountered a group of five adults laughing and struggling to stay upright on their Rollerblades. The women wore neon tights and one of the men, his face creased with the mild wrinkles of healthy middle age, had a row of braided yarn bracelets covering one arm from wrist to elbow. Sayers said nothing as we walked, only studied the passing scene gravely, but I started to feel defensive.

"You think we're frivolous, don't you?" I asked. "In Boulder, I mean."

He smiled. "Do you think so?"

"No. People stay young here, they exercise and take care of themselves and they're open to ideas that might seem silly, but they have that curiosity and—"I broke off, not sure where I was going. "I told you my first name," I said finally.

"So you did," he allowed. "Mine's Pike."

"After the peak?"

"Not exactly. The peak and I were both named after Zebulon. Where was I, anyway, before the interval?"

Interval. Not a usage you'd expect from a rustic. Who was this guy?

I turned my attention to his question, but it took a minute to remember. The cool chapel seemed much farther away than this morning. "You asked me to imagine," I said, "being told I'd have to sell the farm where I grew up for a bunch of yuppies to build their dream houses."

"Ah, right," he said, looking incuriously through the window of Phoebe Zen's Spiritual Body Piercing as we walked by. "To continue, then, suppose you went and talked to the banker, reminded him how he'd encouraged you to take out the loan. He said he didn't have any choice, it was the FmHA that had guaranteed the loan, and they were calling it. You went to—"

"Sorry, what's the FmHA?"

"Farm and Home Administration. A federal agency. It finances farms—land and equipment."

"Okay."

"You go to the local FmHA administrator and they tell you sorry, nothing they can do. You plead for some time but when you get home, your wife meets you at the door, some process server has just been there and handed her a bunch of papers. She gives them to you and you open them up and there at the top is the word that means the end of a farmer's world. Foreclosure."

Sayers looked at me to see if I was listening but it wasn't necessary. My attention was nailed to his story, which had stirred up some sympathy in me like the melody to an unidentifiable but familiar song. My half-formed plan to put him at a relative disadvantage by transplanting him to Boulder had not worked. His worn cowboy boots, his rolled-up long sleeves, and the indentation left by his hat on his hair now seemed the perfect signs of belonging on this level space with the hills rising up behind us. The zany garb I saw all around us (for we were approaching Penny Lane, the most antic Boulder place of all) now struck me as clownish and contrived.

"Let's turn around," I said hastily. "It's getting chilly." It was true that the sun was declining to the horizon, limned by the nearby foothills. "Does this all have something to do with Mariah McKay?"

"Oh, sure. Down the line a little bit. Are you finding this boring?" He stopped and looked at me in the hard way I remembered from my first encounter with him.

"No. Please go on."

"When you got to court you tried to explain to the judge about your farm, about how you were going to work it out, if you just had some time. The judge told you to shut up and let your lawyer talk. When your lawyer talked it was all about the Uniform Commercial Code and security agreements and articles this and that and it sounds very good but at the end the judge says, 'For the plaintiff.' You come home one day and a man wearing a jacket that says 'United States Marshal' is driving your John Deere away. One day you're at the feed store being told your credit is on hold, and the owner's wife comes in from the back and says your oldest girl is on the phone, she's crying. You take the phone and she tells you men are taking furniture out of the house, they've taken her bed and her bookcase, dumped her books out on the floor. You drive home like crazy and get there in time to see them trying to take the bed you were born in, the bed your grandfather made, out the front door, and you try to explain the bed was made in the house, there's no way it will ever go out the door, but they push you away and swear and someone drops his end of the bed and there's a huge crack and it's broken. A hundred and three years old and it's broken." He stopped then, and stopped walking too. Students and tourists and businesspeople in suits flowed past us on the Mall as we stood still, and I thought of the fellow who believed in the wormhole and the parallel universe.

"What then?"

He shrugged. "Many possibilities. You move to an apartment in town and work in a hardware shop. Your kids get laughed at in school and start taking drugs. You beat up your wife or your kids.

You drink. You put a gun in your mouth and pull the trigger. Or you find something else to believe in."

"Did this happen to you?" I asked.

He started walking again. He was a little ahead and I couldn't see his face when he said, "No. Not to me."

"So," I said, hurrying to catch up. "Mariah McKay? I don't think she grew up on a farm."

"She didn't. But she's gotten to know a lot of people who did. Who do. They're her family now. Family she had didn't treat her very well. To put it mildly."

"I'm sorry, Judge Sayers. I still don't know why you're telling me this stuff."

"Don't you?" he said. "Do you want to sit down for a minute?" He gestured to a curved wooden bench.

I looked around. We had walked back the entire length of the Mall. Across the way, Pearl resumed its identity as a street. A shiny red Jeep, vibrating to some rap song like an oversized woofer, careened around the corner and headed west, its occupants laughing above the boom of the radio. The display window of the Boulder Bookstore was filled with copies of something called *Everyday Warrior: Seven Rules for Enhancing Your Freedom, Success, and Power.*

I sat, and Sayers rested his worn boot on the bench beside me. The gathering chill had chased most of the sun lovers away, and many of the buskers were packing up their instruments and equipment. Here and there couples strolled by arm-in-arm, headed for the bars and restaurants, their fleecy jackets and confiding embraces promising to keep them warm through the evening to come.

"Remember I said I knew a few things about you?" he asked.

"Yes, I do. I'd be interested to know what your sources were."

"That's not important, but all of them told me you're a great advocate. Passionate, someone said. Unafraid. Go the distance for your client, even all the way to the execution chamber if that's what it takes."

"I was there when they killed Jason Smiley, if that's what you mean. But I didn't manage to prevent it."

"That's only part of what I mean. But here's what I want to ask you. Are you a good researcher, too?"

"Moderately," I said, remembering my recent success with Westlaw, somehow untroubled for the moment by the impostor feeling.

"Why don't you see what you can find out about common-law courts? Then we can talk more another time. In the meantime, I think you should see Mariah again. She needs some good advice. Disinterested, like."

"I don't think she wants to see me."

"Suppose she gives you a call later? Maybe tonight?"

I reached into my backpack and pulled out a business card and a pen. "Here's my home number," I said, writing on the back. "But the thing that's bothering her—I can't make it go away."

"Don't worry," he said.

The sun winked out altogether behind Dakota Ridge, and my stomach growled, reminding me that I hadn't eaten since the cinnamon roll. "Listen, would you like to have dinner somewhere?" I said, surprising myself.

He looked at the sky and shook his head. "I have some people I need to see back at the place. Anyway, I didn't mean to take this much of your time."

"Well, it's been a pleasure talking to you, Your Honor," I said.

He inclined his head before turning to walk away south toward Canyon Boulevard, as though to acknowledge the mockery, but I hadn't meant it that way.

It was nearly eleven o'clock that night when she called. I'd fallen asleep over a story in a magazine about two men—one was a blind lawyer and the other a housepainter—who ended a cross-country trip in a famous Memphis hotel that was home to a fleet of trained ducks who swam every night in a fountain. I know it sounds dumb, but it was a hell of a story and it deserved a better reader, one who wouldn't fall asleep before the end. The phone's trill disrupted the currents of my brain at some profound level, and I could barely speak after snatching the receiver out of the cradle.

"Dahh?" I said, my tongue thick as a washcloth.

"Is this the Lucinda Hayes residence? Miss Hayes, is that you?"

The familiar interrogative cadence awakened me a little, but also served to prompt some involuntary effort at imitation. "Yah, Miss Drew? I mean, Miss McKay? Mariah?"

"Mariah McKay," she said, with unusual emphasis. "I'm sorry to have called so late. I just got back from a meeting. Judge Sayers had a talk with me after."

"The good judge," I said, still groggy. "What did he have to say?"

"He said I could trust you, and I should call you and apologize for running away. I am sorry. I've just been such a wreck, you know?"

I was sitting on the side of my bed by then, shivering a little and hoping the chill would wake me up fully. "Mariah, we need to see each other again if you want to go on with this, but are you sure you do? What is it that you think happened to you?"

The whisper was so faint the first time she said it that I had to ask her to repeat it. "It had to be Harrison."

"Your father?"

"That's the one thing I'm absolutely sure about. Him covering my eyes up so I can't see who's doing the things, who's hurting somebody. Sometimes he pushes my face into his chest to keep me from seeing, and sometimes he puts his hands over my eyes. And I'm screaming. No, Daddy, no, Daddy! God..." The small voice broke away into a tiny sob.

"Mariah—"

"Sorry, sorry. I can't talk now, really. The kids are asleep; my room's just a kind of an alcove? I can't let them overhear any of this. Will you—would you come out here again?"

"The cafe?" I said skeptically. "Are you sure that's where you want to talk?"

"It's really the only place I can get to without a car."

"Okay. Tomorrow?"

"Nine o'clock this time? We won't have morning lessons tomorrow because Ginny's taking the kids to the museum in Denver. There's some dinosaur show. She said I didn't have to go with them."

"Nine o'clock sounds good, Mariah. I can have another one of those cinnamon rolls."

"Yuck," she said. "Make you fat." And she hung up.

I got into the office at eight, hoping to find that some lovely big checks had arrived in the mail from our overdue accounts receivable. Instead there were bills: a phone bill; one from Westlaw; one for the cellular service that Tory had insisted we needed; and one from what I have learned to call our Internet Service Provider. Staying au courant with the information age was costing us a bundle. I was working up to a small snit when Tory burst through the door, radiating energy like a cartoon character throwing off miniature stars.

"Yay," she said, kicking off her shoes and dropping her oversized backpack onto the floor. "I've got a new client. In federal court!"

"Word!" I replied with a smile, thinking of Linc.

"What?"

"*Word!* You know, it means, like, all *right!*"

"Cinda, it's so pathetic, your attempt to sound like a twenty-something. Do you want to hear about my client?"

"Of course. Tory, did you really spend three and a half hours on the cell phone last month?" I tried to hand her the bill from AirVoice.

She waved it away. "Who knows? Listen, this is going to be so much fun. My guy was indicted last week for being a felon in possession of a firearm. A federal beef. He just bonded out last night after being in custody for four days. He had a court-appointed attorney but yesterday he told the guy he was fired, then he wrote a letter to the clerk's office and he said he wanted me! Me! Said he'd heard I was the best there was. So the federal magistrate grants the other guy's motion to withdraw and I go down to Denver and enter an appearance. I had to go to the federal courthouse to get the papers and get admitted to federal court. My first federal case, Mouse. *Our* first."

"This is great! So you're court-appointed? What do they pay now, seventy-five an hour?" I hated sounding so mercenary, but there were those bills.

"That's the best part. One fifty an hour, our standard fee. Some friend or relative of the guy came through with the money—to bond him out and to pay for private counsel. That's why the judge had to let him fire the other guy and hire me."

"That's very good," I said, avoiding *cool* so I would not sound like I was trying to sound like a twenty-something. "So what's the defense theory?"

"I don't know yet, of course. I mean, I just had a very short conversation with my client yesterday. He'll be coming in next week for a real intake interview."

"Well, is he a convicted felon?"

"Yes, I believe he said he was. Nothing violent. Tax fraud, I think."

"And, ah, did he have a firearm?"

"Several, I believe. He's a hunter. Can't shoot deer with a peashooter."

"Well, you could if you weren't bent on killing them," I observed.

"Typical white yuppie reaction to someone who's different from you."

"Gosh, Tory, that sounds like an excellent defense. I can't wait to hear you try that one out on the jury."

She gathered up her pack and shoes and went into her own office. "You laugh now, but just wait," she said as she went. "Who got a dismissal after a prelim two days ago?"

"That was you," I admitted, but she had closed the door. "And stay off the cell phone!" I yelled.

It was almost time to leave for Hygiene again, but I thought I should check the voice mail before leaving; the little red light was blinking. I punched in our code and listened to the eerily featureless female voice tell me that I had one message, left at seven-eighteen this morning.

"This is Morgan McKay for Cinda Hayes. I'd like to come in today to finish the conversation we were having. I believe Ms. Hayes was to have called me yesterday, but I didn't hear from her. This is quite urgent. Please call and tell me what time I might come in later today."

I could think of many things I'd rather do than return this call, like eating nine plates of blanched broccoli, but I knew I'd have to do it sooner than later, and sooner was better. I dialed the number.

"McKay campaign headquarters."

"Morgan McKay, please. It's Cinda Hayes returning her call."

It took several minutes for her to get to the phone, giving me an opportunity to eavesdrop on a varied background of clattering and shouting and one tremendous crash, followed by hilarity. The median age of the political campaign worker these days must be somewhere in the low twenties.

But there was nothing madcap about Morgan McKay when she picked up the phone. "Miss Hayes, I am rather concerned. I thought we agreed that you would call me yesterday to continue our conversation. Yesterday at the latest."

"You're right, Ms. McKay, and I do apologize. Sometimes events in a lawyer's life get out of control, and that's what happened to me yesterday. I should have called you, but I didn't think the matter we were discussing was terribly urgent, and I—"

"You found time to go strolling on the downtown Mall with an associate of known criminals, however."

"Excuse me?"

"Pike Sayers. You should know, if you don't, that he's part of a dangerous and violent militia with headquarters in eastern Boulder County. Not just a member, but a leader."

She had someone spying on me? That discovery stiffened my resolve in a hurry. "Ms. McKay, I think I should tell you now that I am not going to be able to represent your father in the matter we discussed. In light of your comments, I'm sure you and he would prefer to find someone else."

"Why can't you represent him? Did Sayers talk you out of it?"

"Of course not. We didn't discuss it at all. I told you our conversation would be completely confidential, and it was."

"Sure," she said, her voice edged with scorn. "I hope you remember what you promised when we talked before."

"What was that?"

"The usual lawyer things. Confidentiality, no conflict of interest. I have a recording, remember? You could not, of course, represent anyone else in the matters that we talked about. I'm sure you appreciate that."

"Whoa! First, we didn't get very far in our talk. I was summoned away, you will remember. Second, there would not be a conflict of interest, since I did not at any time agree to represent your father. Our conversation was preliminary only. I have never met your father, Ms. McKay. And third, I would certainly be obligated to respect any confidences you shared with me when we talked. I have, and I will." I hoped I sounded more assured than I felt. I didn't tell her, of course, that my respect for her confidences had already cost me some amount of her sister's trust.

"You're making a very big mistake, Ms. Hayes. You have no idea."

Being around Tory has had a bad effect on my attitude. I know I shouldn't have said what I did next. "Thanks for the advice. And one more thing. The next time you send one of your goons out to follow me around, have him introduce himself, okay? I'd like to adjust his glasses for him."

"Is that a threat?"

"As you like." Now, where did that phrase come from? I asked myself as I put down the phone. Realizing that I'd picked it up from Sayers did not improve my frame of mind. I gathered my briefcase and jacket slowly, wondering whether I really was in trouble.

Beverly came in as I was leaving. "Court?" she asked, surveying my bare legs with concern.

"You know better. See you later."

"Not so fast." She raised her eyebrows invitingly and directed my attention to a carton she was carrying. "New office supplies. I met the delivery man on the way in."

"Is that new little recorder in there?" I started rooting through the box while she was still holding it, burrowing under stacks of legal pads and packs of felt-tip pens.

"Jeez, let me put it down at least, will you?" She dropped the carton onto a chair. "I've never known you to get so infatuated with a gadget, Cinda."

"It's just so cool what these tiny things can do. Aha!" I pulled out a box the size of a slim paperback book.

"Next thing we know you'll be carrying around a dainty little pearl-handled revolver. You gonna take that thing with you?"

"Just in case," I said, dropping it into my bag. "Very James Bond, don't you think?"

"Righto," she said. Excellent British accent.

There was a much bigger crowd than there had been the day before, but of course it was nine instead of eleven. The cafe vibrated with the drone of conversations and the mild clash of crockery and cutlery. Martha, presiding over the cash register in a halo of smoke from her cigarette, nodded at me in a friendly way. "She's in there," she said, waving the smutty white cylinder toward the back room.

Mariah sat alone at a small table against the wall, her neat head resting in one cupped hand in a posture of exhaustion.

"Hi," I said.

She looked up and smiled, then waved me toward the other chair. "Do you want some coffee?"

"Sure. Is that all you're having?" Her thick cup was half full of brown liquid, but there were no plates on the table.

"I ate with the kids before they took off for Denver. Are you my lawyer now?"

The proper formalities—fee agreement, disclosures, waivers—seemed preposterous just then. So I just said yes. Her grin was reward enough.

Terry brought me some coffee, remembering that I liked cream. I cradled the cup, ordered a cinnamon roll, and looked across the table at Mariah McKay. "Where do you want to start?"

"God, I'm so tired," she said, resting her head in the crook of her arm on the table. "I really wanted to tell you all this, but I don't even know if I can."

"Can I ask you a few things?"

Her nod was almost imperceptible; her eyes were closed.

"Have you ever been in therapy to help you remember the thing that's bothering you?"

She sat up wearily. "No. How could I afford it? When I was sixteen, after I'd run away from the third boarding school my dad and sister had put me in, he gave me some money and told me to run away as far as I wanted to, get it out of my system. I went to Europe for a while, and before long I ran out of money, so I came back here. Working for the Covingtons is the first job I've ever had. Do you think I need therapy?"

"I don't know, Mariah. I'm worried about your physical health, for one thing. Do you know what eating disorders are?"

"I don't throw up anymore," she said firmly. "Once when I was living in Paris I vomited and there was blood in it. That scared me so much I stopped? But I got really fat when I was away at school, until I started throwing up. I don't want to get fat again."

"So you don't eat."

"I eat. Just not too much."

"What did you have for breakfast?"

As tired as she was, her pale eyes flashed with ang
thought you were a lawyer, not a shrink."

"We're not going to be able to do anything if you d
anorexia."

"I'm not going to die. And you don't understan
never been fat. It's horrible."

"I understand, Mariah. Better than you know." B
I'd better let that subject go for now. "Let me ask y
else. When did you change your name?" A name

of those acts that always looks funny to a jury, but that wasn't my only reason for asking.

"I think it was last year. Maybe a year and a half ago."

"And where?"

"I don't know what you mean."

"Where did you go to change it?"

"It was all done on paper. I didn't have to go anywhere."

"Well, do you have a piece of paper now that says your name is Mariah McKay?"

"Mariah Suzanne McKay."

"That's a pretty name. Who signed the paper?"

"Suzanne was my mother's name. Mariah is from the song. You know: *They call the wind Mariah?*"

"Yeah, that's a great song. Who signed the paper changing your name, Mariah?"

"I never did like Drew. My parents—I'm sure it was my father—named me Drew Connor McKay. And my sister is Morgan Hardy McKay. It was like he wanted us to have names like men who came over on the *Mayflower.* Yuck. It was one thing Morgan and I agreed on, that we hated our names? We used to talk about what names we'd have if we could choose our own. I always said Mariah."

I said nothing, just sipped my coffee. The ice machine lurched and rattled in the corner until she broke the imperfect silence and spoke again. "Okay. It was Judge Sayers who did it. Under the common law? I wanted to change my last name too, but he said the common law didn't allow that."

"Interesting."

"Next question." She said it with a little more energy.

"How old are you, and when is your birthday?"

"Nineteen, and August fifth. Are we too late to file a case in court?"

"I don't think so, but we don't have much time. Are you sure hat's what you want to do?"

"No," she said. "I'm not sure. I really would just like to let ıdge Sayers handle it, but he wants me to talk to you. So I am."

Sayers again.

"How did you meet him, Mariah? Or let's back up from that. How did you end up back in Boulder after your travels? Did you come home again to your father and sister?"

"I guess you need to know the rest of the story for that."

"Can you tell me, then?"

"From the beginning?"

"That would be best."

The fine eyes drooped so drastically that for a moment I thought she would put her head down on the table amid the coffee cups and crumbs. "I don't know. God, it makes me so tired."

"What about this," I said, reaching across to put my hand on her forearm. "When you have time, in the evenings or whenever, write it down for me. Here, I even have a spare legal pad you can use." I started rummaging through my briefcase.

"It would take forever to write it," she objected, her chin resting in her hand again. The attitude of her upper body reminded me of certain rock formations you sometimes see in the West, in which a large boulder has somehow managed to spend years balanced on top of a slender column without falling down. They look as though a single tap in any direction would plunge them into a shattering fall, and so did Mariah McKay's heavy head at that moment.

"Maybe this isn't a good idea after all," she said.

"Wait," I said. "There's another way. Where's my bag?"

After I got back to Boulder, Hypatia and I spent some quality time together. She has gotten very good at finding things for me. Like this article, from the July 3, 1993, edition of *National News Weekly:*

OUTLAW COURTS: THE MILITIAS' JUDICIARY
by SVEN TEEGARDEN

They convene in people's homes. In trailers, even. Sometimes in barns, or abandoned churches. Often there is a flag next to the man in the robe, but it never has fringe; fringe is a corruption of the authentic flag of the United States, they say. In the same way, they will tell you, much of what passes as the law of the United States is a false, manufactured, and evil parasite on the body of a pure and noble document: the Constitution.

Take, for example, the widespread belief that a person may become a citizen of the United States by being born on American soil, or by being born to a parent who is a citizen, or by naturalization—and that all these citizens are equal. An attractive woman named Frannie tells me this is a grave error. A former junior high school social studies teacher, now in her thirties, Frannie belongs to the women's organization attached to a militia group in this Midwestern state. (I am required by promises to Frannie and others not to name the state.) She frowns as she recounts the events that led to her dismissal from the school district. It's a complicated story, but it seems she was teaching her views of citizenship and the law. When I offer this interpretation, she corrects me: They are not her views, they are the truth.

The truth about citizenship, according to Frannie, is this: People who were born on American soil are citizens—Constitutional citizens. This means they are citizens of the state in which they were born, and (unless they had the misfortune to be born in District of Columbia, or Guam, or a similar place) they have no obligations to the federal government. A genuine Constitutional citizen of this type is a sovereign—free from any obligation to obey the federal government or its minions, to pay federal taxes, to obey federal laws and regulations. Many people don't realize this, Frannie tells me seriously, and foolishly surrender their sovereignty by trafficking with the federal government. They get a Social Security account, she tells me, or join the military. Or get a marriage license, or register their vehicles.

I argue with her for a moment. It's the state, I say, that gives you a marriage license, not the federal government. Same for vehicle registration. She shakes her head at me sadly, as if I were one of her slower pupils. Soon we are joined, at her kitchen table, by Luther. I've seen him before—he's one of the men who frisked me as I entered the compound. He seemed unfriendly then, but now he's genial. Gettin' educated, eh? he says with a wink.

Luther, Frannie tells me proudly, is their judge. One of a couple hundred men (there are no women) who understand and enforce the real Constitution and the real law—the common law. Go on, he encourages her as he sits down with us. What were you tellin' this fella?

She tells me that there are some people who are citizens, but not natural ones. They got citizenship from the Fourteenth Amendment. They have entered into a compact with the federal government, which has granted them a privilege of citizenship and that's fine but then they aren't sovereigns, of course. They have to pay taxes and serve in the military, whatever the federal government tells them to do, because they made a contract to get citizenship. This would include immigrants who have been naturalized (only there's nothing natural about it, she says). People born in D.C. and Puerto Rico. People who weren't born here but one of their parents happened to be a citizen. And some others, she says, this time looking uneasily at Luther.

Luther puts down his coffee cup and looks me straight in the eye. Some people aren't ready to hear this, he tells me, and you may be one of them. Probably are. But there's no way in hell a colored person, or a person of color, as they call themselves, can be a sovereign citizen. That's not the foundation of this country and that's not the Constitution, the real, original Constitution. They can be Fourteenth Amendment citizens if they want to, but not the other. And I don't care what you think about it because it's the truth whether you like it or not.

So this is the law you enforce in your courts? I ask him. He tells me they enforce every law there is. Contracts, personal injuries. Divorce: They try to discourage it, but sometimes there's desertion involved. Crimes. We have a grand jury that considers serious cases, like treason...

"What the Kama Sutra is this?"

I jumped when I heard her voice at my ear, hitting my still-sore hip on the edge of the printer tray. "Damn it, Tory, you did it again! Do you have to sneak around here like an alley cat in heat?"

She burst out laughing. "Even for you that's a lame metaphor. Do you know what an alley cat in heat sounds like? Sneaking is not what they do!"

"I believe it's a simile," I said stiffly, rubbing my hip.

"Whatever. What is this stuff?" Her bright eyes were taking in the last screen of Sven Teegarden's article.

"Just some research I'm doing. I figured since we're paying for all this Internet wizardry we ought to use it sometimes."

"And which paying client's affairs require you to acquaint yourself with the wacko fringe?"

"It's not for a client, exactly. More for general background."

Tory folded her arms. "The radio girl? Is she mixed up with some of these losers?"

"It's just she lives out in the east county, where there are a lot of farmers who are being pushed off their land and that kind of thing."

"What does that have to do with blowing up buildings?"

"Who said anything about blowing up buildings?"

"Well," she said, peering at the screen again, "it doesn't sound to me as though Luther would say no if someone offered him a few blasting caps and some detonating cord."

"Look, I'm just doing some general reading to educate myself about a social phenomenon—"

"Okay, Mouse. Listen, Linda wants you to come over to dinner. She says she hasn't seen you in way too long and she's making some killer paella. Our place, six-thirty."

The invitation brought me an alarming rush of pleasure and something like relief. I must be getting really lonely, I thought. "I'll stop by the Boulder Wine Merchant," I said. "Does paella call for white or red?"

The sky was doing a Georgia O'Keeffe number as I nudged the Saab around the last curve before the driveway to Linda and Tory's house outside of Nederland. The altitude was nearly three thousand feet higher here than in Boulder, and I felt for the window control as the temperature dropped; the window went up, but not without a worrying whine. I've got to tell Sam that his car needs a trip to the shop, I thought, as I signaled a left turn for the benefit of nobody in particular and rumbled over the cattle crossing into their yard.

Tory and Linda had exchanged their smaller separate houses on Sugarloaf and Four Mile Canyon for the spectacular double A-frame that loomed ahead of me. In the seventies, it had belonged to a folk-rock musician who used it as a hangout when he was recording at nearby Caribou Studio. The studio had gone belly-up in the eighties, and the county had bought the surrounding ranch, so the house enjoyed solitude as well as splendor. From their living room you could see the Divide, watch the hawks soar, and sometimes witness the comings and goings of a herd of elk that liked to forage through Linda's vegetable garden in the fall. The house was still a little drafty for me, and I thought they ought to get rid of the macrame that the rock star had left behind, but I loved the tile floors and the fireplace, almost big enough to stand up in, and the way Tory's Melissa Etheridge records came blasting out of about fifty speakers all over the house.

"Hey, Cinda. Great to see you." Linda threw open the big carved front door while I was still getting out of the car. She was barefoot, wearing knee-slashed jeans that threatened to slide off her slender hips and a white T-shirt that would have fit me when I was nine. She looked every scant inch the triathlete she was, but few who didn't know her would have taken her for an M.D., Ph.D., or county medical examiner, although she was all of those things as well.

I hugged her and handed over the wine on my way in. "Good thing I brought red. Aids the circulation. A girl could get frostbite up here. Don't you ever wear clothes?"

Linda smiled and hustled me past the darkened living room into the kitchen beyond, where a fire blazed in the smaller fireplace at the far end of the room. The windows here faced east, and they were already dark against the warm yellow light that suffused the room. Tory lay on her back on a Navajo rug in front of the fire, trying not very hard to fend off the attentions of their

Bouvier, Astarte. The dog looked up as I came in and immediately romped in my direction, jumping a low table and knocking over a vase of daisies.

"Arghh!" yelled Tory, jumping up in a vain effort to catch the vase. She did manage to soak up some of the water when it splashed onto her shirt. She looked down at the mess with disgust. "See what I mean, Lin? She's nothing but trouble."

"What?" I said indignantly. "It's not my fault Starry likes me." I stroked the huge animal enthusiastically, taken as always by its resemblance to a fairy-tale beast of my childhood imagination.

"She doesn't mean you," said Linda, puttering around the stove. "She means the dog. She really loves her, but every time she causes trouble Tory's like, look what *your* dog did."

"I still don't know why we didn't just get an unneutered male husky like everyone else in Nederland," Tory grumbled, picking up flowers and pieces of glass from the floor. The water had spattered the large collection of magazines that colonized the table. Looked like everything from *Mountain Bike Action* (Tory's, I knew) to *Journal of Forensic Entomology* (Linda's, I was pretty sure). "But anyway, hi, Cinda. Did you bring some wine?"

"Not two but three bottles," I replied. "Taking into account the effect of the elevation here, I think we may cross the border between consumption and abuse before the evening is over."

"None for me," said Linda, lifting the lid of a huge pot to stir. Astonishing odors drifted out. "I have to do ten in the morning before work, or I'll never be ready for that triathlon in June."

Tory and I exchanged glances. "What does she mean, do ten?" I said. "Does she mean run? Ten? Miles?"

"'Fraid so." Tory nodded sadly. "That means one and a half apiece."

"That's a big responsibility," I said.

"I know you're up to it," said Tory.

After dinner we sat in the darkened living room with candles and watched for shooting stars. Iris DeMent, her twangy voice issuing from about eight speakers placed around the room, recommended that we Let the Mystery Be. In a state of post-paella ecstasy and wine-induced sedation, I was happy to acquiesce.

"Wow, there's one," said Linda, pointing toward the window with the glass in her right hand.

"Linda, what is that stuff?" I said. Even in the semidarkness it looked gross.

"Wheat-grass juice. It's great, Cinda. You should try it."

I looked at Tory, who mimed a shudder. "Don't listen to her, Cinda. This is a woman who cuts up stiffs for a living. She has no capacity for disgust. Lately I catch her reading a magazine—you know what it's about? How you can figure things out about stiffs from the *bugs* that are eating them. I'm sure this can be useful to a person in her line of work, but *please.* A whole *magazine* about this subject? I mean, it comes out six times a year!"

"Oh," I said, awareness breaking feebly through the fumes of Pinot Noir, "that reminds me. There's something I needed to ask you about, Linda."

"Yeah?" she said, idly doing yoga stretches with an infuriating lack of effort. "What's that?"

I struggled to sit up straight against the yielding cushions of the big sofa. "Do you know anything about the recovered memory thing?"

She shrugged. "Some. Tons of literature out there."

"Is it real?"

"What do you mean?" she said, performing the Plow, or maybe it was the Bow; I always get those mixed up.

"I mean, does it really happen that someone can be hurt or assaulted in some way, and be so scared or freaked that they forget all about it, and then later remember it?"

She was silent for a moment, holding the pose. Another meteor streaked by in the dark sky. "I don't know," she said finally. "People have such strong feelings about this question. Some are sure it happens all the time. Some are sure it never happens, couldn't happen. There are committees and task forces and foundations, they bring out these reports. There's one group called the False Memory Foundation that's very aggressive with its claims that all recovered memories are bogus. But most of the professional organizations say we don't know for sure."

"But what do you think yourself?" I asked.

She was silent a long minute. "As a scientist, I'd have to say I don't have enough data to form an opinion."

I could hear Tory's snort from her dark corner. "Jesus, Lin, this is our friend Cinda, remember? You're not under oath. C'mon, live dangerously, tell us what you think."

"This isn't really my field," she protested.

Tory turned toward me and spoke with elaborate formality. "Will you remind me never to take up with another scientist after I kill this one?"

"All right!" said Linda. "I think that a certain number of troubled people are persuaded by bad therapy to remember something that didn't occur. I also believe that there are authentic memories that get lost or pushed aside and are later recovered. But I haven't read anything that shows how you can distinguish, clinically or in a courtroom, between false memories and genuine ones. It's like that prayer they say at A.A.—the hard part is telling the difference between the two. There's a researcher that the False Memory Foundation relies on a lot who claims to have shown that false memories can be induced or implanted. But even she admits that she can't prove that all recovered memories are false."

"What's her name?" I said, wondering if I would be able to remember any of this conversation in the morning.

"Um, give me a minute," said Linda, jumping up. She vanished through the archway leading to the kitchen and back room.

I looked over at Tory, whose eyes were soft. "Isn't she a piece of work?" she whispered.

"Here it is," Linda said, gliding back into the room with a journal in her hand. "There's an article by her in here. Dr. Martha Trefusis. I think people call her Marty. Psychology professor—used to be at the University of Oregon, but I think she's at

Washington University in Saint Louis now. She's gotten very famous over this stuff—on TV a lot, testifies all over the country. Seems to be good at persuading juries that what someone says she remembers didn't really happen. You can borrow this if you want to."

"Thanks, Linda." I held out my hand for the journal.

"That's not one of the bug ones, is it?" said Tory lazily. "'Cause I like to scare myself with those."

Linda looked at Tory with affection, then laid a small hand on her head. "Don't worry, Bugface," she said, stroking the nape of her neck so tenderly I had to turn away.

"Hey, Starry," I called out, bringing the big beast lumbering through the door. "Come kiss me good-night. I need to go home. Gotta do ten in the morning."

"You?" Tory said. "Ten?"

"Silver," I said. "Dollar. Pancakes." And I rose to leave.

"Cinda!" Tory's voice was firm. "You are not driving home in your present state. The guest bed is made up. Get into it."

Resistance was bootless when Tory hauled out that voice, and anyway she was right. "Okay," I said meekly.

Their guest bedroom was spacious and comfortable, a room where, according to legend, Grammy-winning songs had been composed and famous partnerships both musical and romantic had been made and broken. But when I awoke in the middle of the night it wasn't to ghostly guitar picking, but to the wail of the wind across the Continental Divide. I couldn't get back to sleep, so after a wakeful half hour, I stole out the front door and drove down the canyon toward home, sober and thirsty and lonely. Back in my own dark house, I turned on the lights just long enough to drink two glasses of water as a hedge against the hangover, then burrowed under my quilt until the sun awakened me for the second time.

The clemency of the morning, although pleasant, didn't do much to alleviate the fog inside my achy head. Probably that's why my old Subaru's broken window didn't really register when it caught my eye as I went out to get the newspaper. I thought at first look that I'd gotten a parking ticket, although there was no reason a car parked quite legally in front of my house should have been ticketed. But when I drew closer I saw that the white rectangle taped to the driver's-side window was no ticket, and that the window behind it was shattered. As I reached for the paper and tugged against the clear tape that held it on, the window collapsed, pieces of it falling in a greenish rain onto the seat and out onto the sidewalk. One of the rounded shards struck my bare foot but bounced off harmlessly, its smooth perimeter a tribute to the engineering genius who invented safety glass.

I might have written the whole event off to random mischief if it hadn't been for the paper stuck to the tape, the one I had thought was a ticket. It was my car registration, containing my name and address, as well as information about the car. It was no mystery how the vandal had gotten the statement: I always kept it in the glove compartment, and I never locked the compartment, or the car when it was parked at the house. But why?

I reached for the door handle and gingerly opened the door, peering in. The glove compartment was open, all right, its contents—maps, flashlight, tire pressure gauge—spilled onto the floor and passenger seat. But resting on the driver's seat was an item I was sure had never been mine, a key chain. The ring was empty, and at the other end of the chain a metal ornament glittered against a black leather tag. I had seen such ornaments before, on bikers' jackets and in museums and tattoos worn by misguided teenagers. An Iron Cross.

I didn't touch it, left it there, and went inside to telephone the police. A 911 call seemed unnecessary—this was hardly an emergency. As I looked through the phone book for the nonemergency dispatcher's number, I thought of Morgan McKay's reference to a right-wing militia, and it occurred to me that the broken window and Iron Cross might have something to do with Mariah. Some disgruntled acquaintance, maybe, afraid she would tell me things about the common-law courts. I thought about Mariah, heavy head resting in her narrow hand, being questioned by police officers.

I put the phone down slowly, considering, and when I picked it up again it was to call the auto-glass repair shop. My insurance company would have insisted I file a police report, and anyway the whole window replacement would probably cost less than a hundred dollars. Hardly worth the trouble of filing a claim, with the deductible. I showered and dressed in haste, tossed the Iron Cross into my kitchen junk drawer, then drove the Subaru to the shop, broken glass crunching underfoot every time I depressed the brake or clutch.

I was planning to call Beverly to come get me, but another customer was kind enough to offer me a ride back home, where I got the Saab. Wasted nearly an hour, and still had a headache. But then things started looking up: I hit the Boulder Trifecta.

"I hit it, Beverly!" I said triumphantly as I came through the door. "I hit the Trifecta! How much is in the pot?"

She looked at me suspiciously. "One, there are two hundred and ten dollars in the pot. Two, are you sure? You don't look like your vision is too keen this morning."

"I know, my face always gets puffy when I drink too much. I had dinner at Tory's last night and we got carried away by some nice wine. Or, it seemed nice at the time."

"Yeah, she doesn't look too good herself. Barely nodded when she came in. So, you hit it? I assume you recorded license plate numbers so we can double-check?"

"Beverly! It's always been the honor system, ever since Sam started it."

"Yeah, well nobody ever hit it before. Claimed to hit it. How do I know you're not just making it up?"

"Beverly," I said patiently. "I was *driving*. I couldn't write down license plate numbers at the same time. But I definitely hit it."

"In the right order?" she said stubbornly.

"Yes! First, *Visualize World Peace*. Then, about two blocks later, right at about Mapleton, *Visualize Whirled Peas*. Then, just as I was turning into the alley back there, the last one. *Visualize Using Your Turn Signal.*"

"What kind of cars?" she insisted.

"An Audi," I said. "Silver with a sunroof and a crystal hanging from the mirror and an NPR bumper sticker. Then some funky four-wheel drive painted black and white like a cow. And the last one on some kind of an American car like Buick or Chevy. Sedan."

"Sounds like it might be right," she said grudgingly.

The contest had been an invention of Sam's. Every month, all participants put five dollars into the pot; it started out with me, Sam, Tory, Beverly, and Lincoln, but of course Sam and Linc had stopped throwing in when they left town, and for the last few months Duane had joined the pool. The first to see each of the three bumper stickers in a single day won it all. To Sam, the three slogans described a sort of Boulder trinity: the New Age, the surreal/anarchic, and the old-timers who were grumpy about what had happened to their pleasant small town. Each sticker was common enough, but nobody, until now, had ever claimed the pot.

"It's yours," said Beverly. "I've got the cash box locked in the supply closet; do you want it now? What are you going to buy with it?"

"I'm thinking about some travel," I said. "Will you see if the travel agent can find a low fare to Saint Louis?"

"Agent?" she said dismissively. "I'll find you the best fare on the Net. Duane just showed me how last night. When do you want to go? Can you stay over a Saturday night? Window or aisle?"

"Let me think about it," I said. "And I need to make a phone call."

I got passed around a bit from one public relations flunky to another, but finally got one who saw no reason not to tell me everything she knew. "Professor Trefusis came to us in 1993, from the University of Oregon. She was appointed to the Bernard and Alice Lowenthal Distinguished Chair in the Behavioral Sciences after a nationwide search identified her as the most outstanding researcher in the world in the field of memory.

She holds a joint appointment at the law school, where she teaches a course called The 'Scientist in the Adversary System.' Her many publications include..."

"Excuse me," I broke in. "It sounds as though you're reading from something."

"Well, yes," she agreed. "The press release from a dinner honoring her last spring."

"You've been so generous with your time, I hate to waste any more of it," I said. "Is it possible you could fax me the press release?"

"What news organization did you say you were with?" she asked.

"Boulder, Colorado, ah...," I said, desperately casting about for a name but still preoccupied with having won the Trifecta. "Ah—*Visualize! Daily Visualize!* You can address it to me, Beverly Lockhart, City Editor." I gave her our fax number.

"Visualize?" she said. "That's the name of your paper?"

"Yes," I said firmly. "We're doing a feature story on Dr. Trefusis. Thank you ever so much."

I heard the fax machine whir to life a few minutes later, out in the reception area, and waited for Beverly's reaction. It did not take long. "Awright," she called out toward my door and Tory's, "which one of you is the joker?"

Toward the end of the morning, I went down the hall to use the ladies'. The fluorescent lights definitely did nothing to mitigate the puffy-face situation. I made horrible faces at myself in the mirror and drank several paper cups of water from the tap, trying to ward off the desire to fight poison with poison by popping downstairs for a double latte with an extra shot of espresso. As I trudged back down the corridor toward our office in the rear, a man in khaki pants and a checked shirt who had been walking ahead of me halted, and then turned around uncertainly.

"Would you happen to know where I could find Cindy Haynes?" He smiled shyly and thrust his arms out awkwardly ahead of him as if to free them of the weight of his shirtsleeves. His face was freckled and healthy and he looked like a young but worried thirty-five.

"That's probably me. Cinda Hayes. And you are?"

"Oh." He seemed taken aback. "Craig. Craig Covington. I have something to give you. Just a second." He dug his right hand into the front pocket of the shirt, which despite its newness seemed to have attracted a collection of paper, a pen, and a few other items. "Here it is. Mariah knew I was coming into town to the doctor and asked me if I'd bring this to you. She said if you have any more of the blank tapes. *Asked,* I mean. She asked." He looked at me expectantly.

"Sure," I said, taking the little object from him, "come on in here." I opened the door to the office. "I'm sure we can find one."

"Okay," he said reluctantly, "but I hope they don't tow my truck away. I don't think that was really a parking space where I left it. Where do people find a place to park in this town, anyway?"

After sending Craig Covington on his way with a couple of blank tapes, I spent the rest of the day working on a pair of wills and an estate plan for my neighbors Rick and Carmen Avila; they had wanted me to do the work despite my explanations that I wasn't really experienced in that kind of law, and I figured it would be good for me to learn. It wasn't hard, really, just required attention to detail. Never my strong point, but I was working on it. Tory was wonking away too, researching federal firearms offenses to prepare for her new client, who would be coming in the next day. I drank several more glasses of water before succumbing to the lust for caffeine about five o'clock, when I courted a night of insomnia by drinking a cappuccino.

Shortly after that I left, telling Beverly I'd let her know tomorrow about the Saint Louis trip. I made a stop at OfficeMax on the way home: I knew that the tape deck I kept around for playing old Grateful Dead tapes and recording odd bits off the radio would not play the tiny cassette that Mariah had sent me, and she still had the recorder. I found its twin in a corner of the huge store and headed for the checkout stand, resolutely ignoring such distractions as a stack of boxed CD-ROMs labeled *Virtual Husband.* Don't even *think* about it, I commanded myself as I pulled out my credit card. The cashier looked to be about eleven years old. "Have a nice evening," she lisped as she stapled the receipt to the bag.

I had almost forgotten about the Subaru's broken window, but when I got home there was a message: The window was fixed, I could pick up the car any time, and the bill would be $126.84. No problems. I rode my bike over to pick up the car and got there just before the shop closed. Tossing the bike into the back, I slid into the driver's seat and noted they had even vacuumed up all the broken glass. This time, I locked the Subaru carefully when I parked it in front, even though nobody would ever bother to burglarize such a clunker.

There was some clicking, then a long moment with nothing but the hiss of the tape. I was beginning to think she had failed to record anything when her cough jumped out of the box; I had the volume up so loud by then that it made me start. I turned it down as she cleared her throat again. "Here goes nothing," said Mariah's voice, the whisper of a magnetic ghost that had taken up residence in the small plastic box. I pulled my legs up into the old leather chair that had once been in my father's office, and listened.

I grew up in Boulder, in a pretty house on Baseline Road with a tennis court and a horse barn. When I was eight, my mother was killed in an automobile accident. My father was driving, but it wasn't his fault, everybody said. My sister and I were in the car, too, and we were hurt some, me worse. I don't remember too much about that time, to tell you the truth.

I got better and came home from the hospital, after a couple of weeks is what they've told me. But nothing was ever the same after that? I don't mean just that she was gone, but my father changed in some awful way, and my older sister too. Suddenly I was outside, and they were in. My sister had been living in her sorority house before the accident, but she came home to live. At first she looked after me, because I was still messed up from the accident. But after a few months she went back to her classes at the university during the day. She'd come home at the end of the day with Da—with my father. He worked there, too—he's a professor. I remember they'd come into the house all laughing and talking about their days. I'd be waiting for them there, in the quiet. They'd get quiet, too, like I had reminded them that Mommy was dead, and they wished I hadn't.

They'd hired a housekeeper so there would be someone at home in the afternoons, but she was the kind that didn't want any kids messing up her neat house, so before long I didn't have many friends. They sold my horse, because they said there was nobody to take care of him.

A long silence, some throat noises, then a click as if she had turned the machine off, then on again. Girls and horses, I thought, remembering my own desperate wish for a horse of my own when I was about that age.

She was a good cook, our housekeeper Shirley. She'd see me sniffling or something and ask if I wanted to bake some cookies with her? She didn't let me do much—I made too much of a mess—but I'd get to eat them after they cooled off. Before long I learned that looking sad would get me some attention, and something that tasted good. I started to get chubby. I don't know, is this too much stuff from a long time ago? I think it's part of the story, but I'm not sure.

Go ahead, I whispered.

Some time around then, I started to be afraid of my father. I don't know why. I don't remember him doing anything to me—he never spanked me or anything. But I'd wake up at night and think I could hear him and my sister downstairs, talking about me, about where they were going to put me so they could be alone in our house, and laugh and not have to be sad. But I admit I can't really say I heard that—I was just sure that's what they were saying. Maybe I just think so because when I was eleven they did send me away, to a boarding school in Carbondale, near Aspen.

I was so lonely. The other girls seemed so grown up—they all wore lipstick and talked about their diets, like teenagers, and I could tell they thought I was a baby. I cried every night for the first month I was there. I didn't even have Shirley to bake cookies for me, but I learned to steal food from the kitchen and hide it in my room, and there was a candy machine? My roommate Felicia would go over to the room across the hall, where some girls she liked better lived, and I could be alone with my candy.

One night after I'd been there about a year I ate so much candy it made me sick, and I was in the bathroom throwing up when my roommate and these girls came in. Ooh, look, they said, she knows how to do it. And they were all asking me how they could make themselves throw up too, to be thin. It was the first time they'd paid any attention to me so I pretended like I was doing it on purpose, even though I'd never heard of anyone puking on purpose. Later I seriously started to figure out how and you know what? It was easy! It was like the first thing I'd been good at since riding my horse. I taught all the girls at the school and finally one of the teachers heard and there was a big stink. We had an assembly and everything with doctors and they scared everyone so bad they stopped doing it. Except me. By then I couldn't stop.

I got thinner and thinner, and let my hair grow out long and Felicia taught me how to put on makeup. Some boys started to talk to me, and two of them would try to kiss me and stuff. Touch me. You know.

By then I must have been there for a couple of years. I was still rooming with Felicia, and I was throwing up almost every night. She had a steady boyfriend and one night after I'd been hiding out in the bathroom for a long time, waiting to have it to myself, I finally came back to our room and came in without knocking and both of them were there. He wasn't supposed to be there, but he was. They were lying on her bed and her skirt was all up around her waist. It was dark, but when I turned on the light all I could see were her white legs, like in the flash from a camera, almost. I think she screamed a little and then they started to laugh—they didn't mind, really. But something about the sight of those white legs—like—I don't know what. Like fleshy white scissors, somehow—was bothering me so much I had to run out of the room, and then for days every time I'd close my eyes I'd see them again.

Another click. She was learning how to use the recorder, turning it on and off easily now. I could only guess why she wanted to stop at certain points.

So. I had only been seeing my dad and Morgan—did I say that's my sister's name? I'd only been seeing them for holidays and stuff. They even had me in summer school. Morgan was working for a real estate company then, still living in the house with Dad. They'd come to see me on parents' day or something: He was always full of his stories about the university and how he got cited in some journal or was appointed to some government panel or something. She'd ask how I was doing and tell me I looked so great, praise me like crazy for having lost weight. She acted like she was my mother, or his wife. In between visits I was supposed to call them once a week, on Sundays, and I did. That was about it. I didn't think about them much, really.

Except after the thing with Felicia and the white legs I started thinking about my dad a lot. I mean a lot! Somehow those legs didn't seem to have anything to do with Felicia anymore. In my mind they had something to do with my father. And me. But I didn't know what? I kept thinking about it, waking up in the middle of the night, trying to remember, but I didn't get anywhere.

This one boy, he was older than I was, a sophomore, kept trying to get me to do things with him, you know? Second base, third base, that kind of thing. Do you know what I mean, Cinda?

Another click. Then she started talking faster.

Okay. Somehow I thought that if I let this boy get under my skirt, like Felicia did with her boyfriend, I might remember what the thing with the legs was about. So I did, and I thought maybe there was something, but then it was gone. Then another boy wanted to and I let him too, but still nothing very clear. Sometimes, just when I'd think it was coming back to me he'd say something and I'd lose whatever it was. I'd try to lie really motionless and concentrate on remembering. But I still couldn't. Next thing I knew, it was like half the boys in the whole school were coming around. I couldn't see any reason not to let them do what the others had. Felicia got mad at me for some reason and asked to move to another room. Then not long after that it was Valentine's Day?

I got a valentine; someone slipped it under the door. It was drawn by hand and it had two sides. On one side was a stick figure lying down with its little stick arms and legs all floppy, and its skirt flipped up over its head. "Fuck Raggedy Ann Quick Before She Pukes," it said. On the other side was a picture of the same stick figure throwing up into a toilet shaped like a heart. I can still see that valentine. The puke was coming out of the figure's mouth, my mouth, in curved dotted lines like a—what's it called? Like a parabola; we were doing them in geometry.

My hands were shaking so bad I couldn't even pack a suitcase. I took my backpack and parka—it was February, you know, really cold—and I ran, all the way out to the highway. I stuck out my thumb at the first set of lights that drove by and it was a cop. He took me back to the school and they called Dad and I went back home. I was thirteen. They let me stay home for a month before they sent me to the next school.

"Who are you talking to, Mariah?" This new voice was even wispier than hers, and sounded sleepy.

"Just a minute, sweetie," she said.

Another click.

I'm going to have to stop for now. Maybe I'll ask Craig to take this to you tomorrow—he has to go into Boulder. Send me another tape if you have one and I'll keep on.

I'm still not sure this is a good idea.

I finished off *Black Cherry Blues* and still wasn't sleepy, so I decided to check my E-mail, hoping there would be something from Sam. Hypatia was still in my briefcase, so I dug her out and fastened the various umbilici that enabled her to perform, print, and connect me to the rest of the virtual world. After the obligatory beeps and tweets, she disclosed that I had one unread message, from dmarker@dallaslink.com. Dana. The date was three days old, and I remembered with a twinge that I had seen the message earlier, but neglected to read it; I hadn't given it a thought since.

Dana and I were not close, although we tried to be good sisters to each other. Three years younger than I, Dana had been in high school during the time when Dad, an accomplished but underpaid criminal defense lawyer, had finally yielded to our mother's wishes and taken on several big companies and banks as clients. I missed most of this era, as I was off at college pretending it was the sixties and I was the last of the hippie princesses. But I gathered that Dad was very overworked and not at home much, although able to put a lot of money in the bank. Mother, I believe, considered this a good bargain, and she had been able to dress and groom Dana for aspirations in which she had never been able to interest me: admission to SMU, membership in Tri-Delt, and a marriage that coincided nicely with graduation. Our mother died of a stroke twenty years ago, just as she was on the brink of securing her own election, and Dana's, to full membership in the Dallas Women's Club (or so she thought—I sometimes believe they were just stringing her along, letting her give the teas and be on the committees with no intention of awarding the final prize). I used to imagine her arriving at the gates of heaven full of indignation, demanding to be permitted to go back and enjoy the flowering of her patient strategies.

Dana's husband, Jerry, had taken over as her social sponsor, and the resulting life of prayer breakfasts and country club dinners seemed to suit her just fine. I was crazy about her kids, especially her oldest son, Louis, now fifteen, and I needed to see Dad, confined to a nursing home near Dana and Jerry's home, from time to time. So the Markers and I spent Christmases together, and the occasional long weekend, always in Dallas. Dana and I had never been in the habit of exchanging letters, but since the advent of E-mail we did write back and forth a bit across the ether, and I thought it was a good thing. Guilt stung me as I commanded Hypatia to show me Dana's letter.

Hi! Can you believe it's already spring? I haven't even gotten my woolens bundled up for winter storage, and it's already time to pull out my linen things. Time does fly, doesn't it? Will you be coming for the Fourth of July? The club is going to have the most amazing fireworks this year, as they are bringing a Chinaman all the way from Beijing to do the show. The Chinese invented fireworks, you know.

Louis has been completely wrapped up in his science-fair project—something about acids and bases, which neither Jerry nor I understands at all and we have been unable to help him with it as neither one of us took many courses in science. He refuses to go to tennis camp this summer, which is making his father very angry because it seems awfully ungrateful, as not every kid has this chance and Jerry has already had to be disappointed by his lack of interest in football. But Woody did great this year and will be playing end on the fifth-grade team next fall, so he'll have a lot of practices to go to, plus he's going to Bible camp in July. Jerry says he can't get away over the summer because that's when the car business is really hot (I told him everything in Dallas is hot in the summer—my little joke), so I'm thinking myself of going to Green Canyon Spa for a week, just to relax and maybe drop a few pounds—do you think you might like to meet me there for part of the time? Honestly Cinda, I keep thinking of what you told me last Christmas about not being on any skin care program and it does make me worry about you. I mean, I've been on Lancôme for years, and you're older than I am!

I hope you can—let me know because we need to make reservations soon, as it is very popular. Also, if I see you I can tell you all the stuff I learned about our family's genealogy. Did I tell you I took a class at the Texas Heritage Center on how to trace your family tree? It wasn't easy for me because of Mother being dead and Dad being useless (well, you know what I mean!) but I talked to Aunt Lorraine and she told me a lot of stuff, although it seems our ancestors were not anything very interesting unfortunately, mostly just farmers. But still, we go way back!

Cinda, please think about the spa! I know you think we don't have very much in common and maybe you're right, but you're the only sister I have.

Hugs and kisses. Jerry says to tell you hello!

Love, Dana

Whew. As always, Dana left me stranded in some exasperating emotional territory where amusement meets despair. I ought to write back, I thought, but I'd do better in a day or two.

Still a long way from sleep, I rummaged through my CD collection, curled up again in the leather chair, and listened to Janis Joplin sing her guts out on *Cheap Thrills*. It was enough to restore my affection for Texas.

The Saab wouldn't start the next morning, just wheezed vigorously but to no useful effect. The Subaru started all right, but in the morning brightness its mechanical regularity did not make the cracked plastic of its dash any less depressing, and its pitted windows and torn upholstery seemed even more tawdry compared to the one extremely shiny new window. Especially dispiriting was the broken radio. I pulled away from the curb singing to myself (*Oh, Lord, won't you buy me a Mercedes-Benz*) and thinking of Dana and the extraordinary clarity of the sound system in the Lexus Jerry had given her last Christmas. I sang the song all the way through twice, and had moved on to "Piece of My Heart" by the time I reached the office. It's not that easy a song to sing, I discovered.

I meant to call Dana, but after greeting Beverly and settling down at my desk with a cup of French roast, I realized that Sam was the one I really wanted to talk to. When I asked for him, Rosalind recognized my voice.

"You are Cinda, isn't that correct? I have heard from Sam about you. I am sure he will want to talk with you; just a moment, please."

"Miss Hayes, how very nice to hear from you." Sam's voice was as sexy as the vibrating of a tenor sax, and brought me a memory or fantasy of my hands on his broad bronze shoulders, kneading away the tension in the muscles. He turned over on the bed and smiled, and... Suddenly I didn't know what I wanted to say.

"Should have called you sooner, sorry." Lame. "Thanks for your help on that McKay business. It probably kept me from making a mistake."

"So you're not going to represent him after all?"

"No. There is a case, though. Very interesting. Wish you were here for me to talk to about it."

"We could talk about it here. Next weekend."

Excuses flew into my mouth like a swarm of gnats. "I have to go to Saint Louis to speak to an expert," was the first one that got out. "About this same case."

"Good," he said. "That's almost halfway here. The client's paying your expenses, I assume?"

"No, I—listen, Sam! I forgot to tell you. I won the Trifecta!"

"Are you changing the subject?"

"Me?"

"Yes, you, but okay, let's talk about the Trifecta. Are you sure? Let me speak to Beverly. She didn't take your word for it, did she?"

"Of course she did! It was the honor system, remember?"

"The right order?"

"Yes! It was a clean win. I needed it, too. I haven't won anything in a while."

"Okay, I won't file a protest. You can take me out to dinner with your winnings. Cinda, you won't believe the restaurants here. Why don't you see this witness on Friday and fly in here Friday night? I'll borrow Johnny's car to come pick you up. We can have all weekend that way. Do you want to see *Rent*? I could try to get tickets."

"Let me see about flights. And I have to see if this expert is available on Friday." Or at all, I thought to myself.

"Wait'll you see the brownstone," said Sam. "I have the whole third floor to myself—you'll like it, Cinda. Natalie and Johnny are good people, and they want to meet you."

We talked some more, of people and places we knew, and of weather and books and the news. I explained about the Saab and he told me he'd call its primary-care physician—Dave at Scandinavian Motors—and arrange to have him come get it for repair. I can't say what it was about the conversation that made this so clear, but by the time we hung up I knew that if I didn't see Sam soon, it would be over between us. I also knew that I fiercely didn't want that to happen.

I tilted my head back to get the last of the coffee, and looked through the piles on my desk until I found the news release from Washington University. I took a couple of deep breaths and then dialed a number I'd memorized years before. It belonged to Susan Wheelock Madison, Vassar '78, University of California Law School '81, although I'd never think of her as anything but Susie, The Lock. She'd had a lock on success for at least as long as I'd known her. My college roommate was now professor of law at Washington University. I hadn't talked to her in more than a year and I hated to call her just to ask for a favor, but I knew she'd understand.

I caught her just as she was leaving for a faculty meeting. Unfortunately, she would be leaving for a conference in Scotland on Friday, but she promised to talk to Martha Trefusis about seeing me. "She's a very smart lady," said The Lock.

"Pot," I replied. "Calling kettle black."

"I'm not any smarter than you are, Cinda," she said, reviving an old conversation. "Just maybe less conflicted. Sorry I'll miss seeing you this time. Listen, I gotta go. I'll leave you a message about Marty, if I can catch up with her tomorrow."

"Thanks, love," I said. "I owe you one."

"You always were a lousy accountant," she said. "I believe you now owe me *three,* but don't worry. I'll collect some day."

I was feeling antsy that afternoon, reading yet another incomprehensible screed on a militia Web site, when Beverly stuck her head into my office to say she was leaving to walk over to the post office to get some stamps.

"No," I said, rising, "let me go."

"It's okay," she protested. "I like to go."

"Then let me walk with you," I said. "I need to get out for a bit, too."

On the way, we talked about Beverly's husband. Charley was getting to be a problem, she confided. He'd lately decided he should stop wasting his time trying to get a job, and had occupied himself with growing a thin mustache, telling people that he would like to be called Chico, and writing a screenplay about a man who discovers that his Harley-Davidson can talk.

"It's actually kind of good," she said as we stood in line at the philatelic window in the old stone post office. "But I don't know. It kind of pisses me off that he couldn't have a job and write in his spare time, but he says that serious writers have to give up other distractions and concentrate on their work."

"Well," I said thoughtfully, "Wallace Stevens worked as a lawyer and insurance executive while he wrote, and I think William Carlos Williams was a pediatrician."

"Yeah," she said, "but I don't think Charley's going to be

asked to be an insurance executive, and he doesn't know an aspirin from his ass. Plus, I'm pretty sure he's never heard of those guys. The question is, are there any writers he's ever heard of who have a day job making cold calls for a telemarketing company? That's the job he was offered last week."

"Ah," I said. "I see what you mean. No, I guess I never heard of one. Although I believe Hemingway drove an ambulance."

"Really?" She brightened a bit. "I'll tell him. 'Course, he lost his license after that last DUI. Despite Tory's efforts. I don't guess they'd hire him to drive an ambulance."

"Probably not," I conceded.

"Still," she said. We walked along the Pearl Street Mall in companionable silence, the scene quiet in the lull of a midweek afternoon. "Hey!" she exclaimed. "Why don't we go by the farmer's market and get some flowers?"

"Because it's not Saturday," I said reasonably.

"No," she insisted. "They've started having it on Wednesday afternoons, too."

So we detoured two blocks south to a tiny square of park between Canyon and Arapahoe. Sure enough, the street was closed and various vendors of fruits, vegetables, plants, and cut flowers had set up booths or were simply selling from the backs of their trucks. Beverly wandered off to look for flowers and I was eyeing a tidy potted cactus, wondering if I might adopt it and redeem my character vis-à-vis plant care, when I heard someone calling my name.

"Miss Hayes? Miss Hayes!"

I turned, but at first could see only strolling shoppers, clutching bouquets or carrying lumpy bags. Then the call was repeated and I saw that it came from a folding table that had been set up between a wagon selling bread and a flower stall. The table bore a red, white, and blue sign that said *McKay for State Senator,* and at it sat Morgan McKay and another, older woman.

"Please come over here," she called. "I want to introduce you to someone." A couple of passersby looked at me curiously as I crossed the street toward the table.

"Hullo," I said reluctantly. "How are you, Ms. McKay?"

"This is Angelica Moore," she said, indicating the other woman, who was blond and polished like Morgan, but perhaps twenty years older. She smiled at me tentatively before turning to speak with a couple who had picked up a piece of campaign literature from the tabletop. "A friend of my father's," continued Morgan. "Isn't this exciting? We're going to have a booth here at the farmer's market every Wednesday and Saturday until the primary. Of course, after today it will be Angelica and one of the other volunteers, but today's your lucky day."

I smiled, clueless. My lucky day?

"There he is," Morgan practically chirped. "Don't go anywhere," she cautioned as she stood up and moved swiftly twenty feet away to the side of a tall man who stood with his back to me, talking beneath a tree to a couple on Rollerblades. She touched his arm above the elbow and said something to him as I watched. He took his leave of the Rollerblades couple with a small bow and inclined his ear to Morgan while she spoke to him urgently, then turned to look at me. Immediately, he smiled broadly and gave me a small wave.

Harrison McKay, I thought. He was blond like his daughters, lanky and handsome, his broad smile saved from predictability by a slightly worried quality to the cast of his brow that conveyed the suggestion he was fretting about the health care system even as he shook hands. He moved like an athlete as he walked toward me, and I remembered Sam's description of the house with the tennis courts.

"Lucinda Hayes, Harrison McKay," said Morgan breathlessly.

"Ms. Hayes, what a pleasure," he said politely. "Morgan has told me about your conversations. Have you met Mrs. Moore? Angelica, did you meet the famous lawyer Lucinda Hayes?"

Angelica nodded in affirmation, and looked at me with more interest than she had shown before. "Morgan tells me that you were very helpful during our legal consultation," McKay said, a little too loudly for my taste.

I looked at him closely. "Sorry I couldn't be more helpful," I murmured, not wanting to get into a conversation that could be overheard. I couldn't account to myself for his politeness, given the last conversation I'd had with his daughter, but maybe he didn't share her vindictiveness. Or perhaps both of them had gotten over being angry about it; she was standing next to him, and her grin was just as big as his.

"Well," he said briskly, but he had dropped his voice as well. "Must get back to pressing the flesh, you know. Don't forget to vote in the primary."

"Never," I promised, mystified. I smiled by way of farewell, turning my head slightly to include Angelica Moore, but she was occupied pinning a McKay button on a toddler in denim overalls, whose mother stood nearby trying to take a photograph of the occasion. McKay smiled back at me, then walked over and held his hand out to the little boy, who looked at him shyly as his mother clicked the shutter. There's one McKay vote, I thought, seeing the delight in her eyes. I turned away and started looking around for Beverly. It was time to get back to the office.

I actually had a little work to do—a will and estate plan for another new client—before I left on Friday for Saint Louis. But first I called the University of Colorado to see what I could discover about Harrison McKay. My experience with Washington University had made me aware that universities have public relations officers whose job it is to publicize the achievements of their faculty. And sure enough, a single phone call secured me a copy of McKay's curriculum vitae, promptly faxed to our office. This time I didn't even have to lie about why I wanted it; nobody asked.

The document was lengthy, but there was nothing surprising in it. Mariah's father had enjoyed an unremarkable academic career, published quite a few of the usual jargon-plagued articles (but apparently no books), served as chair of his department for two years, given talks at academic conferences in Colorado and Wisconsin and Florida. I scanned the list of his published articles: "The Influence of Rhetoric on Party Registration Demographics, 1950–1975"; "The Agricultural Origins of the Conservation Movement"; "Term Limits and American Skepticism About the Professional Politician." He had won his department's teaching award in 1985. Apart from teaching, his professional activities seemed to have tailed off quite a bit in recent years, but I didn't think that was unusual for an aging academic. No mention of family, but I didn't know whether that information would have been customary. Nothing about the CV suggested that Harrison McKay was a child molester, but what had I expected? Didn't mean he wasn't one. Didn't mean he was, either, I reminded myself. Didn't mean a thing.

The new Denver International Airport is a long and inconvenient drive from Boulder, but I do like the moment when, driving in from the west, you catch sight of the buildings shimmering along the horizon. I've been told that the terminal building, with its peaky white roof, is supposed to provide a visual echo to the faraway summits of the Rockies, but to me it looks like a surreal schooner trying to sail its way across the empty prairie. In a classic Colorado weather reversal, snow flurries had started coming down on Friday morning when I was less than halfway there. I drove the last half hour with flakes sailing madly at the windshield and decided to park in the covered area, even though it cost a mint.

It was a long walk in the dank concrete structure, and I was still a minute or so from the terminal entrance when I heard steps behind me going fast, too fast. I swung around, every muscle tensed, thinking of the someone who had left me an Iron Cross as a message. But it was neither a skinhead nor an enraged farmer with a pitchfork hurrying toward me, only a worried-looking guy in a flight attendant's uniform. He broke into a jog as he passed me, calling out an apology that left me feeling both relieved and foolish. I tightened my coat around me against the chill, and went in to catch my plane.

Saint Louis was hot. Hot and moist, like a small bathroom after someone's just taken a long shower. I peeled off my trench coat before I even got out of the airport, and had shed my blazer and rolled the sleeves of my white shirt up to the elbows by the time I climbed into the rental car, scrutinized the map, and headed for Washington University.

I got off the highway at the Delmar exit, pulled over to check the map again, then followed the twists and turns of a street called Big Bend through a modest neighborhood that was nevertheless so spectacularly leafy that much of the time I could not see the sky. The Urban Forest, a display in the airport had called it. Each blade of grass seemed to burst with green, and the hedges and shrubs jostled against each other like an unruly crowd. It was enough to take the breath away from someone accustomed to the austerity of the high desert. So was the heat, and I turned on the car's air-conditioning. The immediate cold blast enabled me to roll up the window, but a glance in the mirror confirmed that the rushing humid air had had its way with my hair.

Washington University was easy to find but, as on every campus I've ever visited, parking was not. I wound up four or five ramps of a behemoth parking building before I found a section marked Visitors. Before leaving the car I dug through my bag to find a brush and a frayed rubber band, which I employed to braid my hair into a crooked plait. I rolled my sleeves back down and cursed my pantyhose as I found an exit from the parking garage and located the law school on a campus map.

The law school, it seemed, was about to move to new quarters. I stood between the two buildings, taking in the contrast. On my left, a squat concrete bunker had all the charm of a block of workers' flats in Chernobyl. On my right, a fairy palace emerged from the muddy earth, complete with flying buttresses, soaring vaulted ceilings, and leaded windows. Washington University was apparently prospering, which was perhaps how it had been able to attract a star like Martha Trefusis away from her former home.

I approached a harried-looking young woman in tottery heels who emerged from the new building holding a sheaf of papers attached to a clipboard. "Excuse me. If I were looking for a faculty member's office, would I look in the old building or the new?"

"Move-in's not until December," she said, huffing a breath upward to riffle her bangs. "I'd try this one." She gestured toward the bunker.

"And would you know where Dr. Trefusis's office might be?" I asked.

"Third floor. But she doesn't use her law school office much; she's usually in the psych building." She began to point across a large grassy quadrangle.

"That's okay, thanks. We have an appointment; she told me she'd be here."

The building was every bit as unattractive on the inside, with the neglected look and smell of a place whose denizens know they won't be there much longer. Glum-looking students shuffled through the halls; perhaps some of them were feeling they'd gotten cheated by arriving when they did and graduating without an opportunity to reside in the palace next door. I wandered around the twisting corridors a bit, fluorescent lights snapping and buzzing over my head, until I found her office. MARTHA TURNBULL TREFUSIS, PH.D., said the plastic plaque on the door, which was closed all the way. It must not have been very thick, however, because I could hear her talking inside.

"It's not that easy," she was saying. "You have to define what you *mean* by the term repression, Barney. It has no scientific meaning, it's merely a—"

I would have loved to hear more, but a short bearded man emerged from the office next door and looked at me curiously, so I knocked quickly.

"Barney, I have to go. Someone at my door. Yes. Yes. I will, I promise. Okay. Bye." Then she called out, "Come in!"

Not tall, but somehow nevertheless formidable, she stood up from behind her desk and held out a pale slender hand to shake mine as I entered. I liked her graying dark hair; the humidity had gotten to it, as it had to mine, and after she let go of my hand she ran all ten fingers through the portion that had fallen untidily over her eyes. Her dark eyes behind her glasses studied me frankly, and then she said, "Marty Trefusis. Why don't you close the door, Ms. Hayes? I take it this is a private matter?"

"You were very kind to agree to see me."

She waved a many-ringed hand in dismissal, and gestured toward the only other chair in her office, a molded plastic affair. Cardboard cartons full of papers covered almost every square foot of floor that was not occupied by desk, chairs, bookshelves, and a pair of filing cabinets. "Can't say no to a favor for a colleague. Not very gracious in here, I'm afraid. I rarely use this office, although I think I may use the new one more often." Her eyes narrowed in amusement at her own confession. "I'm not sure why you wanted to talk to me. As I explained, I am not taking on any more forensic work until my new book is finished. I can give you about forty-five minutes at the most. You weren't here to try to disqualify me from a lawsuit, were you? Because that's really not necessary. The book won't be done for at least two years."

"No," I said. "I'm familiar with that trick, but that's not why I'm here. I just need some advice, if you're willing to give it. I don't know how to explain this except by telling it straight. I have a client who is about to turn twenty. When she does, the statute of limitations for any civil suit based on a wrong someone may have done to her as a child may run out. While she isn't—"

"Excuse me," said Martha Trefusis. "I thought you said on the phone you were calling from Colorado?"

"That's right."

"And this case has to do with a so-called repressed memory?"

I nodded.

"So I believe you have the discovery rule in your state. The statute does not begin to run until your client discovers the injury. Her twentieth birthday would have no significance if she has not."

"That's right," I said, impressed. "But this case is not that clear-cut. She remembers some things, not others. I haven't even gotten her to tell me the whole story yet, because it's difficult for her to talk about and she has a hard time trusting anybody. But it seems possible she may know enough, or remember enough, for a court to say that the statute started to run when she reached majority at eighteen, and so would run out when she turns twenty. I'm afraid to advise her to take the chance of waiting until her memories become clearer. If they ever do."

"Ah. So your dilemma is whether to file a lawsuit when her memories are still incomplete, or to wait, hoping that she will remember more and it'll still not be too late for your lawsuit to be timely." The phone on her desk started to ring, and she glanced at it, then back at me. "My voice mail will get it," she said.

"That's right," I said. "But I don't expect you to solve that problem for us. I'm here because of your expertise in the processes of memory, especially memory loss and recovery. I've read some of your work." The phone, having rung four times, stopped.

She shrugged and reached into her top desk drawer, pulling out a pack of cigarettes. "If you've read my work, then you know that I am very skeptical about whether there is any such thing as memory recovery."

"I know you don't really believe there's such a process as 'repression' of memory."

She held the Gauloise between her lips as she lit it with a match, which she then shook impatiently as she exhaled. "It's all the same. After I discredited the idea of repressed memory, they started calling it recovered memory, but there's no difference. There's no evidence whatsoever that a memory can be mislaid and then much later found, like a piece of jewelry put away in the wrong place. In every case I've seen in which such a claim has been made—and I've seen many—it has emerged that the individual was persuaded by an incompetent or unscrupulous therapist to 'remember' an event that never happened."

"Why would a therapist be interested in creating a false memory?"

"It's an industry, Ms. Hayes. You have to have a diagnosis to persuade an insurance company to pay for treatment of a patient. Many people are simply unhappy, and I believe this has been true in every time and place of recorded history. During the early period of Freudian psychology, this was understood; Freud himself once advised a patient that his goal was to convert her hysterical misery into ordinary unhappiness. He appreciated that there was a difference. But in the late twentieth century, in a few places like Argentina and France and the United States, especially California, the belief arose that unhappiness was not an aspect of life, but a disease. It was useful for certain mental health professionals to encourage this belief, as they could not arrange to be paid for attempting to alter the nature of life. But they could for treating a disease."

The phone again. This time she just shook her head briefly.

"I don't understand. What disease?"

She pulled in a deep lungful of smoke, then blew it out thoughtfully. "Usually post-traumatic stress disorder. Sometimes multiple personality disorder—now they're calling it dissociative identity disorder. You see, they keep changing the names. But these so-called diseases all have one thing in common. Even according to those who believe in them, they must be caused by an assault, an event, some profound trauma suffered by the patient at some time in the past. But there was a problem with these diagnoses: Often, the patient could not remember any such thing."

"I see. So the therapist would have an incentive to persuade the patient that he remembered something."

"She," Martha Trefusis said, nodding. "The vast majority of such patients are female. Although it does happen with males."

"But even if you're right about the therapist, why would the patient suddenly start remembering things?"

"It's the power of suggestion, my dear. One of the most formidable powers in human cognition. We see what we expect to see. We remember what we come to believe must have happened. Let me show you something." She rose and walked around the desk, stooping to pull a thick file out of the bottom drawer of a filing cabinet. She was even smaller than I had realized. She returned to her chair behind the desk, and searched through the file until she had collected a narrow stack of paper—color photographs, they looked like, about 8½ by 10 inches. She beckoned me to pull the plastic chair nearer to her desk, turned the photos around, and laid them before me in a stack.

"This works better with a film, but since I don't have the equipment here, perhaps this will serve," she said. "Please look at each one of the photographs for five seconds—I'll tell you when to move on to the next one. Imagine they are what you see through the windshield of your car as you are driving down a country road. Go."

"But..." I seemed not to have any choice in the matter, so I looked at the first photograph. It depicted a lovely fall day, dappled sunlight shading the narrow road through the leaves of the trees that lined it. I could see the hood of the car, a blue-gray color, and the road rising beyond.

"Next."

I tucked the first picture under the bottom of the stack and studied the next one. A bit down the road, it seemed, and heading into a curve. Another car was approaching, some kind of sports car.

"Next."

And so it went. The photographs followed the road, always seeming to take in a panoramic view over the hood of the car. Various objects came and went: billboards, a stop sign, a collie sitting watchfully at the side of the road. There were about twenty shots in all.

"Good," she said when I had examined the last one. "Now let me ask you a few questions. What color was the car being driven?"

"Blue-gray," I said confidently.

"Was the day sunny or rainy?"

"Sunny."

"What time of day?"

"Um." I thought for a moment, and remembered that the

shadows were very short. "Around midday." I was feeling idiotically competitive; I wanted to get more of these questions right than any experimental subject ever had before.

"Good. Did you see a dog?"

"Yes."

"What kind?"

"Collie."

"Very good. When you got to the stoplight just past the barn, was the light red or green?"

"Green."

"Good. At the intersection with the stop sign, were there any other vehicles?"

"Yes. A truck crossing from the right."

"Excellent. What color truck?"

"Dark blue."

"Very good. Were there any other vehicles that you encountered?"

"Um, yes. A sports car approaching on the same road in the second photograph. Red."

"And did you notice the barn?"

"Yes."

"What color was it?"

"Dark red."

"You're certain."

"Of course."

"Excellent. Now please look through the photographs and find me the one that has the barn in it."

I reached confidently for the stack and went through it, but missed the barn shot. I looked more closely at the ones near the middle, where I thought I had seen it, but there was none. Finally, I went through the stack again from the first to the last. No barn. I looked up to see her eyes watching me.

"You see how easy it is."

My stomach was feeling very queasy. "Did you hypnotize me?"

"No, my dear. In that case you would have seen giant flying lizards—if I had wanted you to."

"How then?"

"I simply mentioned the barn in one of the first questions, as though we both knew it was there. You were so focused on pleasing me—no, don't be embarrassed, everyone does it—you took the path of least psychological resistance and incorporated the barn into your memory of the photographs."

I shook my head, disoriented. "But the color? I remember a dark red barn!"

She smiled. "Most barns are dark red, aren't they? Look, I hope you understand now how easily people can be persuaded to remember things that never happened. There was even a remarkable case in which some very coercive methods, tinged with religious suggestion, were employed to persuade a man that he had committed satanic ritual abuse." She stabbed out the Gauloise, and I was glad. The air in the office had grown gray. "Do you understand? Not that he had been a victim of it—that he had *done* it. He came to believe that he had subjected his wife and daughters to the most vile and despicable sexual torture, in service of the devil, and that he had then forgotten all about it! You see what I'm up against?"

It seemed like a moment to tread carefully. "I'm asking this because I really want to know. How can you be so sure that he did not do those things, that the things he remembered didn't ever happen?"

She looked at her watch. "It would take too long to explain," she said impatiently, "but it was simply impossible. Now, was there anything else?"

"Yes," I said desperately. "Please, I just need a little more of your time. I understand that you believe that only science, and not untested clinically based theories about behavior, can prove how memory works."

"Exactly so. More science, less magic. That's all I ask."

"So please tell me this: Has it been proven scientifically that every memory that a person experiences as having been lost and later recovered is false?"

"I don't know exactly what experiment could be devised to

prove such a proposition, but no, it has not been proved. It has not been proved scientifically that aliens from outer space have never landed on this planet, either. There is simply no evidence of it. Or none that would satisfy a scientist."

"Do you yourself believe it's impossible?"

She peered at me shrewdly thought the haze that hung in the air. "About the aliens?"

I said nothing, merely looked at her steadily.

She looked away first, examining her hand as if surprised not to find a cigarette in it. "The other, then. Of course, my opinion, being purely personal and not based on my scientific expertise, would not be admissible."

"That's okay. We're not in a courtroom."

"Will you promise not to quote me on this point? To anyone? I don't want to encourage the charlatans—you have no idea how many of them there are, Ms. Hayes, or how unscrupulous they are."

"I won't quote you. I'm just interested to know what you think."

She opened the drawer again, reached inside, then drew her hand out empty. "Damn. I've got to stop smoking like this." She looked up. "Your friend and my colleague, Professor Madison, did warn me that you were very persistent."

I smiled.

She ran her fingers through the tangled cloud of hair on her forehead again. "I think it's possible. That's all I can say. But I don't think I've ever seen a genuine case of it, and I don't expect to."

"If you were investigating a case in which someone believed she had recovered a lost memory, what features of the person or of the memory might push you a little in the direction of believing it was real?"

She looked up at the low ceiling for a moment. "It wouldn't be so much the person or the content of the memory I would look at. I would want to know what led her to recover the memory. Was she in therapy? What was the diagnosis? Does the therapist believe in recovered memories? Does the therapist claim to have had a recovered memory himself or herself? You'd be amazed how many of them do. Was it suggested to the patient that something terrible must have happened to her along the way? Was it suggested that she was 'resisting' the memory of it?"

I wrote a few notes on the legal pad I had brought along. "Anything else?"

"Was the patient ever hypnotized?" she said, with an expression of distaste. "Subjected to an interview with so-called truth serum, or sodium amytal? Those techniques, I must tell you, Ms. Hayes, are the absolute hallmarks of the recovered memory therapy industry. I could persuade you to remember anything, including a past life as Confucius or Mary, Mother of God—take your pick—with the use of those two tools."

"Suppose none of those things had happened?"

"Then my interest would be greatly aroused, as I have never seen a case of that sort."

"Never? None of those things has happened in my client's case, I don't think."

"But you say she also doesn't remember."

"She doesn't have a complete memory. She's sure it has something to do with her father, from whom she's estranged."

She nodded sadly. "Of course. Often the father, and often estranged. Typical, I am afraid."

"She is a troubled young woman. She has an eating disorder, for one thing, and I'm not too sure about the politics of some of the people she's close to. I'm worried now, because I think she needs some therapy just to support her efforts to live a decent life. But it sounds as though therapy might complicate things, might serve to discredit her memories if they ever become clear enough to be the foundation for a lawsuit."

"Ms. Hayes, psychotherapy, when practiced by a competent and compassionate therapist, is an excellent thing. Eating disorders can be very serious, especially in young women. I'd worry more about your client's life, and less about her lawsuit. And now, if you'll excuse me."

"Thank you very much, Dr. Trefusis." As I left, the phone was ringing again, and the woman for whom it rang was reaching again into the drawer.

I wandered around the bunker for a few more minutes until I found The Lock's office. I scribbled a note to her on the legal pad: *Thanks for the introduction to M.T. She was very helpful. Hope you're having a great time in Scotland, and that your lecture goes well (went well, I guess, by the time you read this). Hugs to you, and to Ben and Eliza. Call me when you can. C.*

I had to beg a piece of tape from a student passing by in the dingy hall; he obligingly dredged a roll out of his backpack.

"Are you a friend of Professor Madison?" he asked me as I stuck the note to her door.

"Old friend," I replied. "Since college. Are you in any of her classes?"

He nodded. "Scary," he offered. "Was she always like that?"

"Pretty much," I said.

The air was even heavier than before when I left the building and picked my way along the mud-caked sidewalk, where hard-hatted construction workers hurried by, pushing wheelbarrows and carrying crated windows. The sky looked bleached and tired, and thunder rumbled somewhere in the distance.

The first drops splattered on the rental car's windshield as I drove out of the garage, yielding to a steadfast downpour before I was back on the highway. I almost missed the exit for the airport in the swishing curtains of rain, and then nearly managed to drown before achieving the return of the car and the walk to the terminal.

They boarded us on time but the big jet sat on the runway for an hour, the storm raging around us, before we had clearance to take off. It was after eleven when I finally walked off the plane into the La Guardia terminal, my shoes still squishy, my hair having dried into a peculiar conformation encouraged by the clumsy braid.

Waiting just inside the terminal, Sam looked better than ever, his gray suit sitting precisely on his broad shoulders in a manner that suggested the ministrations of a Hong Kong tailor. I received his embrace gratefully, feeling that I had in some way come home, even while conscious that Colorado was many miles behind me.

I awoke the next morning to the pressure of Sam's lips on the side of my head; he was murmuring something about moving the car to the garage a few blocks away. This made no sense at all—who keeps his garage blocks away from his house?—and I went back to sleep immediately, conscious only of the shifting of the mattress as he left it, and agreeable faint residual sensations between my legs. We had not fallen asleep until four.

When I awakened again, Sam was sitting on the side of the bed, wearing a New York Knicks sweatshirt and jeans, and holding a mug. Coffee smells drifted out of the mug.

"You don't want to sleep all day, do you? Nat and Johnny have been up for hours, waiting to meet you. We've got some bagels and more coffee downstairs. Come on and take a shower, sleepyhead." He stood and waved the coffee mug under my nose, then trailed it along behind him as he walked toward the bathroom door across the room. I looked around groggily; this bright room seemed to occupy nearly an entire floor of the house. I felt around in the tumbled sheets, trying to find my underpants, than gave up.

"This looks like a very scary bathroom," I said as I followed him into it. In fact, it was quite nice, with brass fittings and black-and-white mosaic tile. "I'm afraid to take a shower alone in it. New York is full of psychos, I hear."

"Good point," he said, pulling the sweatshirt off over his head. "But don't worry. You'll be safe with me."

So, what with one thing and another, it was nearly eleven by the time we walked down the stairs to the first floor. Sam's sister Natalie and her boyfriend Johnny were sitting in a breakfast room—actually more of a nook. Newspapers were spread out everywhere, and some achingly sweet soprano aria was pouring out of speakers mounted near the ceiling. *Aida,* I thought, but I don't really know opera. Natalie and Johnny looked up from their papers as we came into the small room.

"Hi," I said shyly. "I'm Cinda."

"Well I'm sure as hell glad you are," said Johnny, holding out his hand, his eyes snapping with mischief. "Considering the racket I heard up there in the shower and the fact I knew Cinda was supposed to be coming in last night, I'm thinking that if you aren't Cinda she's entitled to be mighty pissed."

I took his hand and laughed despite my embarrassment, then turned to look at Natalie, a small woman with beautiful bones and a dancer's body.

"Johnny!" she said reproachfully, and then she surprised me by rising from her seat and coming forward to kiss my cheek. "Welcome, Cinda," she said with a gentle smile. "We're so happy you're here. Sam has missed you so much. He talks about you all the time."

"I'm so glad to be here," I said truthfully, liking her immediately. "Sam talks about you a lot, too."

"I'll bet," said Johnny, grinning at Sam. "Later, when we're alone, you can tell me everything he's said."

"She's not gonna be alone with you," said Sam. "But in case you're curious, I said you were a trifling fool but I put up with it because my sister had some unaccountable infatuation with you. Now please move over and make some room at this table for me and Cinda."

"Don't be buyin' their wolf tickets, Cinda," said Natalie. "They really love each other. Now we're gonna have some breakfast here, like civilized people. I'll go start the omelettes."

"Can I help?" I asked.

"No," said Natalie, looking at Sam meaningfully. "My big brother's going to help."

After they went through the swinging door, toward the kitchen, I supposed, I looked at Johnny and smiled. He smiled back hugely and looked at me expectantly, but didn't say anything. The soprano aria had given way to a chorus, very dramatic with a lot of percussion. I listened for a few moments, then turned to him.

"So," I said, desperate to make conversation. "What are wolf tickets?"

He laughed, then rose to his feet. He was very dark and slender, with beautiful hands. "So you're the woman," he said, ignoring my question, "that wants Sam to move back to that honky town and be the house nigger. He's not gonna do it, you know."

The adrenaline flew into my heart with such force it almost made my eyes water, but I think I was able to speak calmly. "Then I'm not any kind of threat to you, am I?"

He leaned his arms on the table and looked into my face. "You didn't come here to try to talk him into going back to Colorado?"

"I came because he asked me to," I replied. "I believe it had something to do with his wanting me to meet you and Natalie. So I would understand his life here."

"Uh-huh," he said, unconvinced.

"It looks like a good life to me," I said. "He seems happy."

"He is," he agreed finally. There were several more moments of tense silence between us, the voices of the opera chorus more and more frantic in the background. Finally, he spoke again. "In that case, I need to ask you something very important, Cinda."

"What's that?" I asked, apprehension clutching me.

"Do you mind if I turn off this caterwauling and put on some good music?"

I laughed and shook my head, giddy with relief. "Go ahead."

"What do you like?" he said, dangerously.

Was this a test of some kind? "Otis Redding?" I ventured.

"Ged outta here," he said, apparently satisfied, and soon we were smiling at each other uneasily over the truly excellent opening notes of "Try a Little Tenderness."

After we ate, Natalie shooed me and Sam out, refusing any help with the dishes. "Reservations at Calvin's at seven-thirty," she called out as we left.

I stood on the stoop and looked out onto the street—Leroy Street, Sam had told me—with pleasure. It was a lovely mild day, and crocuses bloomed in the small patch of earth between the town house and the wrought-iron fence that lined the sidewalk.

People were everywhere, pushing strollers and carrying shopping bags.

"Could we just sit here on the stoop and watch for a while?" I said, turning to Sam.

"Sure," he said. "Cheap date for me."

We settled down on the top step. In one quarter of a small park across the street a group of fifty-somethings dressed as though they were prepared to board the *QE2* played a stately game of croquet; in another, a *conjunto* band cranked out a raucous version of "Teresa La Panadera," complete with accordion riffs. An unending stream of people passed by on the sidewalk. A group of Puerto Rican kids chased each other down the street, yelling colorful oaths whose meaning I could only guess. A beautiful woman in a sari that bared her lithe waist walked hand in hand with a Chinese woman dressed in a severe business suit. A pale-looking couple dressed for what must have been their own wedding hurried by, he in a dark suit with a boutonniere and she in a short lacy white dress and white gloves; he shot his cuffs and checked his watch anxiously, like the White Rabbit. Where are *her* flowers, I wondered, and looked again, but they had disappeared around the corner.

I turned to Sam to speak and discovered that he was watching me. "So what did that jerk Johnny say to you?" he asked me.

"What do you mean?"

"I told him," Sam said unhappily. "I called him out on his shit at least a dozen times, but it was like talking to a tree. When we came back in there for breakfast I could tell he'd done a number. So which was it? The *He ain't leavin'* number, or the *He don't need to be with no white girl* number?"

"It was the first," I confessed. "But don't tell him I ratted him out."

Sam shook his head with disgust. "You know it's not personal, don't you? It's not that he doesn't like you. He doesn't even know you yet. He just doesn't want to bust up our partnership because it's going so well. For him."

"I understand. How could I not understand? I could sit here

and watch forever, Sam," I said, changing the subject. "There's everything in this place."

"No mountains," he said. "Think you'd miss them?"

I turned to look at his face, trying to discover his meaning. "Eventually," I said carefully. He smiled, the early afternoon light falling on his high cheekbones and broad nose. "What are we doing this afternoon?" I asked.

"Cinda," Sam said, moving closer on the stoop so his thigh lay against mine, "we could use another partner. Someone with criminal trial experience. Someone levelheaded and thorough. The New York bar exam isn't that bad, or maybe you could even be admitted on motion without taking it."

I looked at my hands, noticing my fingernails for the first time in weeks. They were ragged, no two of them the same length.

"I appreciate the invitation, Sam," I said. "I really do. But I don't think I can. Not now, anyway. I'm just not ready."

"Could you stop looking at your hands and look at me for a second? Why aren't you ready? You don't know me well enough yet?"

I shook my head. "It's not that. I just don't know what I want to be. I know I was a good criminal lawyer when I was a prosecutor, but I'm not sure I know how to go over to the other side. Tory's gotten right with the program, but I—I don't know. Seems like when you're on defense you're always trying to persuade someone to believe something that you don't believe yourself."

"Not always. But sometimes."

"Does it ever bother you?"

He looked thoughtful. "No."

I sighed. "I don't know why, but it bothers me. And I don't know if I could leave Tory, and Boulder. It's home to me now. I just wish it could have been home for you. Besides, what about Johnny? I can't imagine he joins you in this invitation."

"He would if we talked about it. But okay, Cinda, we can leave it for now. Still, I'm going to ask you again," he said, standing and brushing off his pants. "Now let's go uptown."

Immediately, I wished he hadn't given up so easily, but could hardly say so. "Let's," I agreed. "And then after, do you think we could find a place where I could get a haircut? I've been having a very bad hair week."

"Let Natalie do it when we get back. She's really good."

"Okay." I stood up and extended my hand.

We spent the afternoon wandering through museums and galleries, stopping to buy hot twisted pretzels and coffee from street vendors. Sam was both familiar and strange, and the strangeness attracted me as much as it worried me. Late in the afternoon, I was standing to one side on a sidewalk near Central Park, watching some kids fly a kite, while Sam bought pretzels from the street vendor. I saw them talking like old friends, and after the vendor turned a frankly curious gaze on me I heard him use the word "shortie," and then Sam say something that ended with *back in the day, you know what I'm talkin' about?* They both laughed, and brushed each other's right palms in farewell.

"You sound like a real New Yorker," I observed as he handed me the yeasty knot of warm bread.

"How is that?"

"I don't know. Sort of hip and borderline rude, with an attitude. You used to be very grave and polite, and you always talked in this very precise way, even when everyone around you was acting like Beavis and Butthead. Seems like you're more relaxed now."

"You don't know why?" he said.

"No. Why?"

He examined my face for a moment, as if to satisfy himself that I was serious, and then spoke in the old way I remembered. "Cinda, Boulder is a beautiful place, and a tolerant one, but surely you know that while I lived there I would always be typecast as the Race Man of the Flatirons. Mr. Negro Universe. Didn't you ever notice how I was always asked to explain the black point of view on this or that? And how everything I did was watched and judged to be sure I was still a credit to the race?"

"But you always were! People there think so much of you. It

wasn't like you were going to disappoint their expectations, Sam."

He shook his head. "It just got old, Cinda. That's all. Can we talk about something else?"

So we did. We walked around Central Park and Sam talked about music, about the jazz clubs of lower Manhattan and the extraordinary talent to be found there on any night, and about dance-hall reggae and Afro-Caribbean pop and some group called Pere Ubu. I always enjoyed listening to Sam talk about music, but this time I could listen with only half an ear. I felt as though an invisible fissure had opened on the ground between us—the sort that sometimes means there is a vast crevasse beneath the surface. And I was afraid of stepping on it and falling in, to discover that we were not, after all, tied together.

Long before his move to New York, nearly a decade ago, Sam had once before given up his law practice in Boulder. He moved to a small village in Nigeria for a while, looking for an answer to the questions that haunted him. He hadn't found it there, and had come back to Boulder after ten months unsure even of what he had been seeking. He had told me that many years later, after we had become lovers. At one time, the story had reassured me, but no longer. Now I was afraid he would discover that what he needed was some essence found only in the colorful streets of this city, in the smoky underground clubs where the names Bird and Trane and Prez were spoken with reverence and the music lasted almost until morning.

No, that wasn't it, really. My real fear was that he would find here a woman with coffee skin and a lilting voice and a body that carried the link he craved and needed: to Africa and the slave ships, to the struggles and triumphs of blackness, the aching blues of Robert Johnson and the elegance of Duke Ellington and all of the other things of which my childhood and youth and segregated public school education had left me innocent, and which therefore still seemed to me exotic and completely desirable and altogether terrifying.

So as we walked and talked, in a corner of my mind I began to block out and embroider an imagined life for myself with Sam in New York. I'd have to learn everything about jazz, have my hair cut short and chic like the women I saw around me, figure out the New York rules of civil procedure, toss out my cowboy boots and buy some platform pumps. Just at that moment, it seemed perfectly possible.

At six o'clock, we were back in the brownstone. Sam was upstairs having a nap while I sat on a stool in the middle of Natalie's living room with a towel draped over my shoulders, my hair dripping water as Natalie drew a long narrow comb through it. "I can see the problem," she said. "It absorbs a lot of water. I bet it's straight and shiny when the humidity is low, but gets funky when it's damp."

"Exactly," I said. "And then I get busy and forget to have it cut and that makes it worse. Maybe you should just cut it all off." I had been admiring her curly helmet and the way it showed off the back of her shapely neck.

She walked around to the front and looked me straight in the eye. "I think you're feeling reckless, Cinda. That's not a good time to make a major hair decision. Or any kind of major decision, for that matter."

"Okay," I said. "I'm sure you're right. Can you at least trim off the stringy ends?"

"Sure. And I can do something for tonight, if you like. Sort of a Greenwich Village Special."

"Does it involve the colors green or purple?"

"No colors, just some braids."

I peered into the big mirror across the room, trying to imagine. I thought I looked washed-out and puffy sitting under the towel next to Natalie's dark gamine figure. The phone started ringing in the next room and I gave her a questioning look but she shook it off. "Johnny will get it," she said.

"Okay," I said. "Go ahead."

She had just started trimming when Johnny came into the room, holding a cordless telephone. "For you, Cinda," he announced. "Your partner, she says."

I took the receiver. "Tory," I said into it, noting that Johnny was looking on with frank interest. "Is this business, and if so what are you doing in the office on a Saturday night?"

"It's still afternoon here," came Tory's voice, backed up by some racket on the line. "And I'm here because Linda had to go to some conference and it was too windy to think straight up there at the house. First there was that snow yesterday, then a big blow today. Crazy weather. I even brought Starry down here with me because she was so freaked by the wind. She's hiding under your desk. Listen, Cinda, what have you done to get the lawyer misconduct police upset? When I came in you had a certified letter from the Colorado Supreme Court Grievance Committee. Looks pretty official. Do you want me to open it?"

"Go ahead." Natalie was herding Johnny out of the room. "Maybe it's not about me," I added.

"Maybe," Tory said, unconvinced. I could hear the wind in the background, the kind of chinook that would tear limbs from trees and shingles from roofs all over town. "It seems," she said finally, "that Morgan and Harrison McKay have grieved you for violation of the rules of professional conduct governing conflict of interest, on the ground that you accepted employment representing Morgan and Harrison in a certain matter, then later agreed to represent one Drew Connor McKay, an adverse party, in the same matter. This is going to be a major PIB, Minnie."

"I knew it! I was worried about this for a while, but when I saw them just before I left, McKay and that Morgan, they were making with the smiley faces. Those hypocrites! They must have known this was in the works. But it's bullshit, Tory. You remember, we talked about it at the time. I never agreed to represent him, and he knows it. They certainly can't produce any signed engagement letter. I told Morgan two days after she came to see me that I couldn't represent her father."

"Hold on," said Tory. "I'm still reading. He says it was an oral agreement, with an agent of his. That would be Morgan, I take it."

"She's the one I talked to," I said glumly. "She even recorded the conversation. I remember thinking it was weird when she pulled out the recorder. See, all they ever wanted was to conflict me off of representing Mariah, just like we figured. But unless she tampered with the recording, it'll show I never agreed to represent him."

"No such luck. He says the agreement to represent came in a telephone conversation two days later. He also attaches an affidavit from someone named Angelica Moore, who says that you acknowledged the representation within her hearing. Just a few days ago."

"Who? I've never heard of her!" But even as I said it I remembered. "Shit! She's some campaign worker of his. I ran into her with Morgan in the farmer's market, and Morgan called McKay over to introduce me. That's the only time I've ever met him in person."

"Did you say anything to this Angelica about representing McKay?"

"Of course not. But maybe she overheard something she misunderstood." I tried furiously to remember what I had said on that occasion, but all I could come up with was McKay's and Morgan's weird cordiality. They had been setting me up, of course.

"Look, there's nothing you can do from there. Have fun in New York, give Sam a hug for me, then come on home and we'll deal with it when you get here."

"Those *creeps!*" I exploded. "I've never had a grievance filed against me!"

Tory, who had had three, none of them upheld, was unsympathetic. "I've never known anyone who put so much stock in being a virgin. Get over it, Mouse. People can't tell by looking, you know."

Calvin's was unlike any Chinese restaurant I had ever seen. When the food started to arrive, it was breathtaking. I don't remember all the dishes, but there was roast squab with frogs' legs, braised sea cucumber with duck feet, and something called Beggar's Chicken, which came enclosed in a baked clay carapace that had to be broken open. The fragrant steam that came out was intoxicating, or maybe it was the plum wine and the time difference that left me feeling so dizzy. Every time we finished one spectacular creation, another arrived. It was nearly eleven by the time we staggered out. I insisted on paying the check, saying it was from my Trifecta winnings, although it was probably about the fourth time I had spent them.

Johnny couldn't seem to get it about the Trifecta. "Whirled peas?" he demanded. "What's that shit about?"

"Fuhgeddaboudit, Johnny," said Sam. "Boulder can't be explained. You have to be there."

"Okay. Then let's hit Zinno," he said. "There's a hot new trio there."

Sam looked at me expectantly and I could tell he wanted to go, but I was so tired my legs were getting wobbly. He responded to Johnny before I had to say anything. "Time to go home," he said, taking my hand. "The sister needs some sleep."

Johnny, who had also taken a fair share of the wine, didn't protest, just looked at me closely and screwed his face up.

"If you wear those braids back to Colorado," he observed, "folks are going to think you're trying to pass." He looked startled; I think Natalie may have kicked his ankle. "Ow," he whispered.

Natalie smiled sweetly. "For a New Yorker, he means," she said.

My plane was to leave at 2:00 P.M. on Sunday; I kissed Johnny and Natalie good-bye just before noon as Sam stowed my suitcase in the trunk of Johnny's Mercedes. "Come back soon," whispered Natalie, tucking a stray hair back into one of my braids. My throat closed.

"Come to Boulder," I got out.

"Oh, we will," said Johnny. "Got to see it. You have to be there."

Sam insisted on parking the car and going into the terminal with me. I checked the bag and got a boarding pass, and we walked slowly to the gate. "Are you okay?" he asked me as we settled into the slippery bucket seats of the boarding area.

"Sure," I smiled. "Thanks for a great weekend. I wish I could stay longer."

"Why can't you?" he said bluntly. "What's so important you have to get back to Boulder so fast?"

"For one thing, you have a trial starting tomorrow. You need to work. And something's come up in one of my cases, too." We were sitting under an air vent; I started shivering slightly.

Sam took off his leather jacket and put it around my shoulders. It smelled so much like him that I had to close my eyes. "I figured something was up when Johnny told me Tory had telephoned. Tell me about the case," he said. "Is this the one that Harrison McKay called me about?"

"Yes, but he's not my client. I'm sure now that he had Morgan call me just to conflict me off representing the other daughter. Mariah." I was about to mention the grievance when Sam spoke again.

"I thought his younger daughter's name was Drew."

"She's alienated from her father and sister, and she's calling herself Mariah now."

"Changed her name legally?"

"I think so, but it's a little hard for me to get the whole story out of her."

"Couldn't you check the court records to see if there's a name change on record?"

"It's not that simple. She's mixed up with some people who live out in the east part of the county, not too far from your old house, actually."

"Good neighborhood," he observed. In Boulder, Sam had lived in a renovated farmhouse that had survived the subdivision of the accompanying farm into residential streets.

"Yeah, and I think some of your old neighbors are fine people, farmers struggling to survive and blue-collar folks with good values. But I think there may be some militia activity out there, and—have you ever heard of common-law courts?"

"Yes, I have," Sam said gravely, "and I hope you're not going to have anything to do with them. Those people are crazy."

"No, of course I'm not involved with them," I said quickly, deciding against telling him about the vandalism to my car. "It's just—apparently some phony judge is running one out there. She says that's where she had her name changed. That part's not a big deal. The main problem is she thinks her father may have done something awful to her when she was young, not too long after the mother died, but she doesn't remember much. Only some fragments. She thinks she might be interested in a lawsuit, but she's very skittish and hesitant. And the statute of limitations might run when she turns twenty, in August."

Sam was looking out the smeary window toward the runway; when I followed his gaze, I saw a big jet pulling up to the gate. He turned back to me. "Yeah, I see the problem. It depends on whether she remembers enough about what happened."

"That's the rub. What if she remembers enough that the statute could expire, but not enough for me to file a proper complaint?"

Sam sat back and rubbed his face with both palms. An amplified nasal voice announced that boarding would begin in five minutes. "That's a hard one. What does McKay's lawyer say about all this?"

"I haven't talked to him yet. I don't even know who represents him, since we haven't filed anything yet. But now *he*'s filed a grievance against me. That's what Tory was calling about. He claims I had a conflict of interest when I agreed to represent Mariah after talking to him."

Sam fingered his lower lip in thought. "Did you learn anything from Morgan you'll use against Harrison?"

I shook my head. "But he's a big shot now, running for the state senate. I guess he figures a little preemptive strike like this grievance may scare me off filing a lawsuit for Mariah. And I figure I can't even tell Mariah that Morgan consulted me. It's a mess, isn't it?"

"Yes it is." Sam was serious now in the way I remembered, his playful language gone. "The grievance doesn't sound very well-founded if you're not violating any confidences, but I didn't hear any grounds for a lawsuit in what you just told me. You don't have to stay with this crazy case just to prove to Harrison McKay that he doesn't scare you, you know."

I studied my hands again. "That's not why I'm doing it. Anyway, Tory says I shouldn't worry about the grievance. She's had three of them, you know, and all of them were eventually thrown out. I think she sees them as a badge of honor."

"Yeah, that's what I'd expect of the Terror of the Courtroom, but it may not be the same for you, Cinda. I think you'll beat this grievance eventually if you really didn't violate any confidences, but in the meantime it could affect your reputation. Tory's strong suit is her fearlessness, but what people respect you for is being meticulous and careful. Maybe you ought to try to settle this some way."

It isn't fair, I thought childishly, that she always gets away with so much more than I do, but what I said instead was, "I can't contact McKay directly now; it's gone too far for that. I'll have to wait until he hires counsel and his lawyer contacts me. Otherwise he'll claim I tried to intimidate him or something." The gate agent called for boarding of rows twenty-five through thirty-six. I looked at my boarding pass: 32A. I stood and handed Sam his jacket back, feeling the chill again and wishing I hadn't packed my trench coat in the suitcase.

"What do you and your client hope to gain by a lawsuit, anyway?" asked Sam. We had moved into the line for boarding. "Here, take this with you."

"What?" I said. "Your jacket?" I couldn't take his nice leather jacket, could I? I breathed its aroma in deeply.

"Yes," said Sam. "Take it. Wear it to bed, Cinda. Tonight." The line was moving me inexorably toward the gate. "Go ahead." He draped the jacket across my shoulders again, pressed the small of my back toward his body as he covered my mouth with his, then let go. I was pushed along toward the door by the line of people behind me. "What do you want?" Sam repeated, as he let go of my hand.

"Thank you," said the woman in uniform, looking at my boarding pass, then shooing me along into the passage.

I turned back to look at Sam. "She just wants to know the truth," I said. An older man whose pass was just being checked looked puzzled, thinking I had been talking to him.

"Excuse me?" he said quizzically, and I smiled and looked past him.

Sam stood just beyond the gate agent, a still figure surrounded by hectic motion. "That's okay for her, then," he said, his voice low but carrying, "but what about you?" But there was no time to answer; the line pushed me forward along the jetway, and I could not see him any longer. I put my arms into the sleeves of his jacket, one at a time as I walked along, and inhaled deeply to taste the scents of the animal and the man as I stepped into the stuffy airplane.

I settled into my seat, wondering what the answer to his question was. I thought I understood Mariah's need to walk back into the darkness that shadowed her past: Virtually an orphan, her roots damaged and torn, she sought the truth as a shelter. But why did her need exert its hold on me? I knew who I was and where I came from, didn't I? Thinking about Dana and her genealogical research, I fell asleep, and slept all the way to Denver, where I stumbled off the plane trying to remember where I had parked the Subaru.

I didn't take Sam's jacket off until I was home, and then only long enough to shower and slip into a T-shirt. If sleeping in a leather jacket sounds strange, all I can say is you should just try it once.

I awakened warm and content, pulled on some jeans, and went out to get the mail, hoping to find some more tape from Mariah. But there wasn't any, so I went back inside and called her. We arranged to meet the following morning in the cafe.

I did have a package when I got to the office, but it wasn't from Mariah. I couldn't tell who it came from, as there was no return address on the clumsy brown paper wrapping. "Lawyer Lucinda Hayes," said the printed address. The office address was correct, although without zip code.

"It came on Friday," Beverly told me. "We thought maybe it was a bomb of some kind, but it isn't ticking." Her grin belied any real concern.

I slit the string with Beverly's desktop scissors and tore open the loose paper. It was a doll, still in its pink-tinted box, with a cellophane window through which you could admire her tailored suit, her dark stockings and spiked heels, and the rectangular briefcase she held in her right hand. "BMR Perfectly Suited," said a label across the top of the box.

"It's a Barbie!" said Beverly. "Look, how spiffy!"

"What the hell is BMR?" I said, turning the box over. There was no card or identification of the sender, no explanation of why I needed a Barbie doll in my life.

"Barbara Millicent Roberts!" said Beverly. "It's her real name. But they only use it for the very most classy dolls, like this one." Beverly did not appear to find it at all strange that I should have received such a gift. Tory appeared out of her office, attracted by Beverly's exclamations.

"Look what Cinda got, Tory."

Tory raised her eyebrows at me. "Looks just like you," she said, peering briefly through the cellophane window. "Hair, suit, briefcase. Bust, as I believe it's known."

My chest is famously flat; I didn't even respond to the last. "My hair never looked that good on its best day," I said, inspecting the doll's brown wig. It was glossy and puffy and fantastically smooth, like an expensive chocolate mousse.

Tory had lost interest, except to say as she walked away, "Never looked that bad on its worst day." I started to open the box, but Beverly stopped me.

"No, don't. Vintage Barbies like this are worth much more when they've never been removed from their boxes."

"You think I could *sell* it?"

"You might. Could be worth hundreds if it's a rare one, in mint condition like this."

I shook my head. "I don't get it, and I don't really want this thing, Beverly. You take it."

"I couldn't," she demurred. "It was meant for you. And don't you want to find out who sent it?"

"No clues here," I observed, turning over the pristine box. I thought uneasily for a moment of the broken car window and the Iron Cross, but there was nothing to suggest a connection between that vandalism and this juvenile joke. "You keep it," I said, pushing the box toward her until it almost fell into her lap. The phone rang just then and as she reached to answer I took advantage of her distraction to get away, closing the door to my office so I could work.

By noon I had prepared my response to McKay's grievance, explaining the circumstances and denying any wrongdoing. Now there was nothing to do about it but wait to see whether the grievance committee would throw it out or set it for a hearing.

Mariah was sitting there when I arrived the next morning, talking to a waitress I had not seen before, who had taken a tentative seat at the table across from her. When I walked in, the waitress rose and smiled. "See you later, Mariah," she said, heading for the swinging doors to the kitchen.

"Hi," I said. "Who's that? A friend of yours?"

Mariah raised her thin shoulders, then dropped them again. She looked smaller than ever, the ruddy spots on her cheeks harsh in contrast to the pallor of her lips and forehead. "Sort of? Do you want coffee?"

"Sure," I said, and to my surprise she went over to a stand near the wall and poured me a cup from the burner there.

"Thanks, Mariah," I said. "How are you feeling?"

"Okay, I guess," she said listlessly.

"Thanks for sending that first tape. It was really interesting. I'd like to hear more. Have you recorded another one?"

She shook her head. "I—I haven't really had time."

I reached for the notes I had made for myself after listening to the tape, but when I looked back at her she was gazing indifferently out the window. "Mariah," I said sharply. "Are you sure you still want to go ahead with this lawsuit idea? Because if you are, I have to ask you a few questions."

She nodded wearily. "Go ahead."

"Okay, then," I said, turning back to the notes. "Is it possible the thing you remember is the accident that killed your mother? Maybe you saw her body, with the white legs? Your father was there, and you were too. Could that be the thing?"

"No," she said fiercely. "No. I remember that."

"The accident?"

She nodded.

"Mariah," I said carefully. "I'm not trying to mix you up, I just want to be sure I understand. I thought you said on the tape that you didn't remember much about the wreck."

"That's not what I said. I don't remember much about the time I spent in the hospital after. I remember the wreck just fine. Just fine," she said bitterly. I noticed that the waitress who had been talking with Mariah when I first came in was taking a long time to clear a neighboring table, polishing it minutely with a damp rag. Something about her back suggested she was listening.

I wanted to get Mariah out of that claustrophobic cafe, take her somewhere that allowed her to open up to me. I hoped some shared experience might shatter her resistance and lift her fatigue. At least that's how I explained to myself later why I said what I did next.

"Could you show me where it happened?" I asked. "Or would that be too painful?"

She twisted her braid with narrow fingers. "I can show you, if you can drive. I don't have a car."

I stood up. "Let's go, then. What time do you have to be back?"

"Ginny and the kids will be back about two. I should be there by then."

I looked at my watch: nearly ten-thirty. "We can make it."

"Is this your car? It's great!" It was the first glimpse of anything like enthusiasm I had seen her display.

"Are you kidding? It's a wreck. I've been driving a nicer car that belongs to a friend, actually. But I couldn't get it started the other day, so I had to revert to this rattletrap. It needs some work, too, but I don't know what kind exactly." Lately the Subaru was making many alarming noises, but I didn't know which were merely signs of age and which were harbingers of serious engine trouble.

"I think it's a great car," she said wistfully. "I bet Craig could tell you if there's anything wrong with it. He's amazing with any kind of machine."

"Craig Covington, the one who brought me the tape?"

"Yeah. Craig works for the Deere dealership in Longmont, but he can fix anything."

"Maybe I should have him look at it some time. Are they good people to work for?"

"Real good. And I love Marnie and Christopher."

"Their kids?"

"They're so cute. Marnie's eight and Chris is six. They're really smart, and Ginny wants them home-schooled so they aren't indoctrinated into the system. You know? So I help with teaching them math—I was always good in math—and art. I saw a lot of art when I was in Paris, and I know a few things about art history that I taught myself from books." She was almost animated now, like the teenage girls I saw talking their way down the Pearl Street Mall after ditching class at Boulder High.

"What do you mean, indoctrinated into the system?" I negotiated the curve where Seventy-fifth turns into Seventy-third, noting two signs by the side of the dusty road: "Eggs" and "Buddhist Tai Chi Lessons, Free, Saturdays." Each sign had an arrow, but, luckily, they pointed in different directions. I thought it would be disappointing to go in search of either one and find the other.

"You know." She looked out the window, chewing the end of her braid like a child.

"Can you go on with your story while we drive, or can I ask you some more questions?"

"Questions," she said decisively, turning toward me, drawing her feet up into the bucket seat and twining her legs together in a way that reminded me of Tory. "I'm too tired to put the story together anymore, but I can answer questions."

"Do you want to stop for some lunch in a while?"

She wrinkled her nose. "Maybe. I'm not hungry now. Ask real questions."

"What happened after you ran away from the first school, the one in Carbondale?"

"They sent me to another one, in Steamboat Springs. That lasted less than six months."

"You ran away again?"

She nodded. "From that one, and one more after that, in Connecticut. By then I was sixteen, and Dad just gave up on the school idea and sent me off to Europe with five thousand dollars. He said he hoped I would learn that you can't run away from yourself. I went to Amsterdam first, and it was great. Lots of lost kids, just like me. Then this one boy persuaded me to take the train to Paris with him, but after we got there he disappeared. I didn't speak French or know how to find a place to live, so I blew most of the money I had left on hotels before I found a little pension that was cheap.

"I spent all day at the museums, looking at paintings and drawings and sculpture. I think it was the only time I remember being happy since the accident. But I really was out of money by then, so I started turning tricks to make enough money for the pension and a little food." Her eyes grew hard as she turned to look at me. "So what?" she said, but I hadn't said anything.

"Go on."

"It wasn't immoral, since I had to do it to survive." This had the sound of a line she had tried out several times before. On others, or just on herself, I wondered.

"Okay," I said.

"Around then was when I met Kathryn."

"And who is she?" I had to slow down to twenty-five, to avoid getting too close to a swaying flatbed truck carrying a load of hay.

"I thought you knew. The judge's wife."

"Judge Sayers?"

"Of course. That's how I met him. Kathryn is an art historian, and she was doing research for a book about the architecture of the Marais—you know, the part of Paris that used to be a swamp?"

I shook my head. "You're ahead of me there, Mariah. I've only been to Paris once, for two days. All I remember is Notre Dame, and those boats on the Seine."

"*Les bateaux-mouches.*" She nodded with recognition. "Aren't they great?"

"Anyway, Kathryn?" I prompted.

"Oh. Well, she saw me hanging around outside this museum and came over to speak to me. I think she could tell I was turning tricks. I was really hungry and dizzy, and when she learned I was an American she took me to a cafe for some food, and then we got to talking. I was really tired and sad by then, and completely out of money, and I guess I ended up telling her the whole story. It turned out she had even been to Boulder. Her husband's family had a farm near Boulder, she told me, and she could even remember having been on Baseline Road and passing by the house where I grew up. I think hearing that made me feel pretty sad and I must have started to cry, because she offered to buy me a ticket home. But I told her that I could never go home to my family. So."

"So?" In desperation, I swung out to pass the hay truck, and barely got back into the lane in time to avoid colliding with an oncoming car.

"So she called up the judge in Colorado and she bought me a ticket back to Denver and when I landed at the airport he was there to meet me. He was the one who took me to the Covingtons'. And I've been there ever since. There!" she said brightly. "That's the whole story!"

"Well," I said. "It's a good beginning. Now here's the most important question of all."

She looked at me and then out the window swiftly. The braid went back into the mouth. "What?"

"What do you want, Mariah?"

"What do you mean?"

"What do you want to happen?"

She was still looking out the window, and at first I couldn't hear what she had said.

"Say it again, Mariah."

"I want him to tell the truth," she said, finally turning toward me. Her eyes burned with a bitter fire. "And then I want him to pay. For what he did to me. Look at me! You think your car is a wreck? *I'm* a wreck! I never finished high school. I'm fat and ugly and I don't have any friends my own age or a boyfriend or a car even a home, really! He took all that away from me." She put the knuckle of her right thumb into her mouth and gnawed on it.

I spoke carefully. "Assuming you can remember what he did, if he did anything, and we can prove it—then *how* do you want him to pay? Money?"

"What do you mean, assuming? He sent me *away!* He threw me out of my home when I was eleven and my mother had died and—" She broke into sobs. "Oh, God. I'm so *hungry.*"

I was alarmed now and pulled the car over to the side of Route 93; the shoulder was narrow and cars and trucks whizzed by only feet away. "Mariah," I said, and touched her shoulder, but she pulled away and drew her legs up into the seat, folding her body into itself in the manner of all threatened fragile creatures. "Mariah, I'm going to stop in Golden and we're going to get something to eat, okay? Will you eat something?"

She nodded, her body still seized by hushed spasms of grief.

We spent forty-five minutes at Pizza Hut, talking of paintings and train service in Europe and how smart Marnie Covington was. She drank two Diet Pepsis while we were there and ate less than half a slice of pizza, although she did nibble most of the green peppers and mushrooms off the tops of the remaining pieces. She literally wouldn't touch the pepperoni, even excusing herself to go to the ladies' room and wash her hands after she inadvertently rubbed a finger up against one of the greasy circles. I resisted an urge to follow her into the bathroom, and looked hard at her when she returned for any signs of recent vomiting, but her eyes were already swollen from crying and I couldn't tell anything.

She seemed livelier as we drove off toward Clear Creek Canyon, but her gaiety wore off quickly as the road narrowed and began to pass through the short stony tunnels that punctuate the route.

"Can you tell me what you do remember about the day of the accident?" I asked gingerly.

She gnawed on her knuckles, and put the end of her braid into her mouth again. "Black water and smashed glass and cold and that terrible current pulling me away, and Morgan screaming."

"And you're sure this couldn't be where you saw those white legs that bother you so much? I mean, could they have belonged to your mother's body?" It made me anxious to be asking her these questions when she seemed so frangible, but if we were going to pursue any kind of legal claim, she would eventually have to face far more difficult interrogations.

She answered calmly, anyway. "My mother's body wasn't recovered until they pulled the car out of the creek. They had taken me to the hospital by then."

"Is that what you remember, or what someone has told you?"

"I remember," she said stubbornly, pulling her knees up against her chest again.

We drove in silence for several minutes. "Will you recognize the place?" I asked finally.

She nodded. "After this next tunnel," she said. "The road twists to the right, and the shoulder is too narrow to park on. But if you go a little bit farther, you can pull off on the left. Just make sure nothing is coming toward you." She had wrapped her arms around herself, each hand hugging the opposite shoulder.

From experience, I knew to flip my sunglasses up onto my head as we entered the tunnel so I would be able to see in the sudden dark. As we passed through the entrance, a large oncoming vehicle blotted out the bright shape of the exit, five hundred feet ahead. It was a Winnebago or some similar recreational vehicle, I saw as we drew abreast. Its bulk edged the center line, and I pulled over as far to the right as I dared, the rough rock wall of the tunnel just inches from Mariah's window.

"Okay?" I said to her after we had gotten past the big camper safely, but she didn't reply. She was watching the road intently.

"Just up here," she said about two minutes later. "Go around this curve, then you have to cross over to the turnout."

The Subaru skidded, but not too badly, as it accomplished the maneuver onto the widened dirt shoulder, which was empty of other cars. There would even be room to turn around when we were ready to go back, I saw gratefully. Still, it didn't feel safe here. Cars whizzed by alarmingly close, many of them, I knew, carrying gamblers on their way back from a day at the casinos of Central City and Blackhawk. I didn't know whether the winners or the losers were likely to pose more of a threat.

Mariah opened the door on her side and stood uncertainly beside the car. Quelling an impulse to take her hand like a child's, I motioned for her to come stand next to me.

"Right over there?" I asked. The wind was blowing through the canyon like a banshee, and I had to shout to be heard.

She nodded, and put her mouth close to my ear. "A little ways back toward where we came. There's a barrier now, but there wasn't one then. I'll show you. Let's go!"

Without warning she darted into the roadway, even though we couldn't see what was coming around the bend. A forest green Range Rover careened around the twist, windows down, radio playing at top volume. The driver must have seen her because he hit the horn, but not, I think, the brakes. I could hear his curses, too, trailing behind as the California plates disappeared down the road. I looked across the road and saw Mariah standing on the narrow rocky verge of the creek bed, laughing.

I ran across myself, looking both ways anxiously. On the creek side, the roar of the water added more cacophony to the road noise. Mariah motioned me to follow her as she picked her way along the edge, then found a place to scramble down the steep bank. I proceeded after her, wishing as the thorny weeds tore at my bare ankles that I had worn boots and jeans instead of a skirt and my office flats.

She wove and hopped nimbly along the boulder-strewn edges

of the water, much faster than I could follow. When I caught up with her she was sitting on a big outcropping, swiftly removing her shoes and socks. "Let's go in!" she called out.

"Wait," I yelled, suddenly certain I had made a mistake to bring her here. "Wait, Mariah!" She continued to unlace her shoes calmly, but was still sitting there when I got to her.

"Talk to me first," I said, surveying the rushing water with dread. It was the purest snowmelt, I knew, a thousand gallons a second of pure hypothermia elixir. In addition, this stretch was so swift and rocky that anyone who took more than one step from the edge would surely lose her footing and be swept out of control.

Her voice was hoarse as she busied herself taking off her wristwatch. "What do you want to know? This is where it happened! There's where the car went in"—she turned her face up toward a sturdy-looking concrete barrier—"and right about there was where the car ended up." She pointed to a spot near the middle, where the foaming water tugged endlessly at a giant boulder and black broken tree limbs pointed crookedly upward like drunken sentinels.

"No, Mariah! It's not safe, sweetie! Don't go in." I took her arms firmly above the elbows, even in my terror shocked by their boniness. "We need to talk more!"

She shook me off with horrifying ease, then hopped off the rock onto the uneven ground and ran a few steps upstream before taking another step toward the water, her undone shirt flapping about her narrow torso. "Everyone's always trying to take me *away!*" she shouted. "Just let me *see* it for once!" She took another step, then another, and I ran toward her, but by the time I had reached the edge of the water she had already fallen to her knees, fighting the roaring scalding will of the creek as it tried to uproot her from the earth and make her its own. There was no point in screaming her name again, but I did anyway, over and over.

She was back on her feet now, trying to push herself away from the crushing torrent at the creek's center and toward the edge, understanding the force of the water at last. But she must have stepped on a sharp rock; her face showed surprised pain for a moment before she went down again, the side of her thigh striking a trapped tree limb. I searched frantically around the cluttered uneven verge for something to hold out to her but saw nothing long enough. I looked toward her and saw her struggle to gain her feet, without success, so I waded in. Shocked by the fierce temperature of the water, I turned upstream and leaned forward to compensate for the brutal push of the current against my knees. I was able to reach her as she floundered and fell again, her eyes as she turned her face to me finally registering an appropriate emotion: Mariah McKay was afraid. I put my arm under her shoulders, but we fell twice more before we finally arrived, gasping and weeping, on dry ground.

"Everyone," she wept, uncontrollably now, "is always trying to take me *away!*"

I struggled for breath, realizing how foolish I had been to bring her here, to think that I could accomplish some trick of amateur psychology without risk or harm. I turned to Mariah and forced her to show me her bruises and cuts. When she pulled up her denim shirt, her ribs stuck out through her torso so sharply I could count them, but her injuries from her struggle with the creek were remarkably minor.

"Thank you," I said silently, to someone, and helped her put her shirt and shoes back on. She was by then as docile as a doll, a state that I found almost as alarming as her mania. I hustled her back up to the car, and wrapped her in a burr-infested blanket I carry in the back. By then we were both shivering, but I turned on the heater and before long we stopped, although Mariah continued to hiccup softly until we were nearly back at the southern city limits of Boulder.

After that, she shrugged off the blanket and seemed almost content, offering to "think real hard" about the white legs again and see if she could remember more. But this faint cheer was brittle and unconvincing, and by then I was certain that Martha Trefusis had been right: Mariah McKay needed therapy more than she needed a lawsuit. The time for my clumsy psychology, if there ever had been one, was over. She firmly refused to entertain the idea of seeing a doctor for her scrapes and bruises, and it did seem to me they were the least of her problems. So I drove her to the Covington farm, following her directions to pull up in front of a neat two-story gray clapboard house. The Covington children, two towheads in dinosaur T-shirts, ran out to meet her, exclaiming when they saw her wet jeans. She told me she was fine and did not invite me to come in, so I let her out and promised to call the next day. Then I pointed my car toward the mountains and headed back to the office.

A strange beat-up truck was occupying one of our parking spaces, and Tory's and Beverly's cars were in the others, so I had to nose the Subaru out of the alley and cruise around downtown looking for a parking place. I managed to snag a space on Pearl Street by spotting a flash of brake lights on a silver BMW; I waited gratefully for it to back out, ignoring the engine-revving impatience of the line of cars behind me.

It was easier to go in the front entrance, past the Bob Dylan guy, who was on about the eighteenth verse of "Sad-Eyed Lady of the Lowlands." I slipped by him and walked up the stairs to our offices at the back. I told Beverly that there was a car in my parking space and she should call the towing company to remove it.

"Not unless you want to explain it to Tory," she replied. "That's her client's. She told him to park there because we weren't expecting you this morning, and then I guess he ended up staying a little longer than she thought." She nodded toward the closed door to Tory's office.

"The federal case?" I said. She nodded. "Then tell me when she's free, okay? Meantime, I have to make a few phone calls, and then I'm going down the hall for a shower."

"What happened to you?" said Beverly, taking in my muddy, soaked attire.

"Tell you later," I said.

. . .

Glenda's voice was just as soothing and inviting as it had been when I was in therapy with her after my marriage broke up. "How are you, Cinda?" she said, sounding as though nothing in the cosmos could interest her more than my answer.

"I'm fine, I think, Glenda. Thanks for asking. But this time I'm not calling about a tune-up. I need some advice about mental health resources that might be available for a client of mine who can't afford to pay. She lives in the east part of the county and has kind of an isolated existence. I'm sure she has an eating disorder and I don't know what else, and she seems really fragile. I'm afraid she may have some kind of serious breakdown soon."

"Just a minute," she said. While I waited I could hear taped music in the background, some mystical Celtic songstress subliminally urging me to experience my rootedness to the earth and yearning for the sky, but when Glenda came back on she was all efficiency. "This directory from the National Mental Health Association says there's a clinic in Longmont run by something called the NRHA, I think that's the National Rural Health Association. Sliding scale, free services available to the qualified. Um, let's see—this isn't for one of your court cases, is it?"

"Not exactly. I'm more worried about getting her some help right now. I'm not sure there even is a court case."

"Okay, that's good, because it says here no forensic referrals accepted."

"Do you think they'd talk to me if I called on my client's behalf?"

"Couldn't hurt to try." She gave me the number. "Are you sure you're okay, Cinda? You sound a little tense."

"Well, yeah, I'm a little tense. Isn't everyone? Have you tried to park in downtown Boulder lately?"

Glenda laughed, then bade me be well.

Tory was still closeted with her client when I went down the hall to use the tiny shower in the ladies' room. I showered, wincing when I touched a big bruised cut on my calf, then dressed in some khaki pants and a black turtleneck I keep stashed in the supply closet. Unfortunately I hadn't stashed any spare shoes, and the flats I had worn into the creek were destroyed. So I padded down the hall on bare feet, glad for once that there was little client traffic through the office lately.

I went on into my office and picked up the receiver, but put it down when I heard Tory's door open and her voice in the outer office. I got up and walked out there in time to see her shaking hands with a short man of indeterminate age, his russet hair graying but thick and full, his nose flattened at the bridge by an old break. He was wearing nondescript brown pants and a plain gray sweatshirt, which nevertheless hinted at something humorous, or perhaps it was just the comical alertness of his posture. He must have just said something funny, too, because both Tory and Beverly were laughing to beat the devil.

"Ah, then," he said as he turned to look at me. "This barefoot lass must be the senior partner, Missus Hayes."

"Mizz," I said irritably.

"Cinda, this is my client Seamus Kellogg," said Tory. "Seamus, my partner, Cinda Hayes. She's a little touchy, as you see."

He reached out a short-fingered hand and took my own to kiss it, so suddenly I had no time to decide whether I wanted to acquiesce in this form of greeting. "My respects, Mizz Hayes, and my apologies if I was inartful in my salutation. I must be leavin' now, as I believe I am occupyin' a precious parkin' space that could be put to better use." He bowed again, mischievously, and nodded at Tory and Beverly. "You'll be callin' me then, Mizz Meadows? I'd very much like to get this matter cleared up." And he was gone out the door, leaving behind a delicate whiff of men's cologne.

"That's the dangerous felon with a gun?" I said to Tory. "That—leprechaun?"

"He's so *cute,*" said Beverly.

"Unfortunately," said Tory, "my research indicates that is not a defense to this particular crime. However, he just paid us a large retainer and I am very motivated to find some Holy Grail of an argument for the wee lad. Cinda, I could use some help with this one. Buy you a latte?"

"All right," I said. "I'm just that easy, as you know. But next week I really am going to raise my rates. Do you have a pair of shoes around here?"

. . .

"It was a really long time ago," said Tory. "Nineteen eighty. But unfortunately, there's no time limit to this damn federal law—if you've been convicted of a felony, you can't ever possess a firearm." The usual occupants of the Trident flowed by our table, cups in hand, as we talked. At this time of day, they were mostly Trustafarians, just back from a bicycle ride or a workout at the gym.

"Seems like a good idea to me," I said mildly, stirring the white foam in my glass around with a straw. I gazed idly down at Tory's black high-heeled pumps below the hem of my khakis. It's a look, I decided. A weird look, but a look.

"Your antigun politics are not the *point,* Cinda," she said with annoyance. "As far as I can tell, the only way we could possibly get Seamus out from under this rap is to show that the old conviction was invalid in some way."

"The old conviction," I said. "Was it appealed at the time?"

"No, and that's a problem. Is it possible to bring a later collateral attack on a conviction if it was never appealed?"

I stirred some more, thinking. "I don't know. What was the crime? I think you told me before, but I've forgotten."

"Filing of false income tax returns. Two counts—I guess he did it for two years, 1978 and 1979."

"Why wasn't there an appeal?"

"Says he ran out of money, it was all gone after the trial."

"And nobody told him he could ask for court-appointed counsel on appeal if he was out of money?"

"He says not. We're toast, aren't we?" she asked gloomily.

Just what I was thinking. It was mere curiosity that led me to ask, "What did he lie about on the tax returns?"

"Oh, that." Tory bumped the heel of her hand against her forehead: *doofus.* "Check this out." She riffled through a file folder and brought out two photocopied 1040s, the bold dates 1978 and 1979 at the tops. "Look at this."

The first box said "Your Occupation." On both returns, it had had been filled in with a blunt pencil or very thick pen: "Carpenter."

"He's a woodworker?" I said. Tory nodded her head impatiently and pointed again, this time to the larger box labeled "Income." There were lines for various items: wages, salaries, tips; interest; alimony; business income or loss; capital gains; Social Security benefits. Each line was neatly marked with the symbol Ø, made by the same thick marker.

"I take it this means zero?" I asked. "Tough to live on no income, even if you're a leprechaun."

"This is the part that makes me crazy, Cinda. He admits he did have income both of those years. He just insists that he had no income in *dollars*."

"What, then? Pesos? Yen?"

"A lot of what he got was in trade—you know, barter. Food, clothing, machinery. A truck."

"Ah, and he thought that didn't count as income, but it did."

"Exactly. Moreover, he agrees that he did also receive some money from various sources during those years. But as he explains it"—here she consulted some notes, and began reading aloud—"'since they were all federal reserve notes, and not silver certificates, they were not legal tender and hence not dollars and hence not income.'"

"And what kind of lousy lawyer are you," I asked, "that you can't cobble together a defense out of those very promising materials?"

"Give me a break, Cinda," she said. "Anyway, he was already convicted on those charges. It's not like I'd be allowed to put on a defense to them, even if I could think of one."

"Well, what about the possession of firearms? How did they find the firearms in his possession?"

"It's hard to see a way out of that, either. He's a hunter, and he also goes out to shooting ranges all the time. There's no question that until recently he had a number of firearms in his possession. Someone must have ratted him out. Anyway, one day the ATF comes to his house and asks if they can come in."

"The ATF shows up without a warrant?" I said, sitting up straighter.

"Yeah, but don't get excited. They had consent to search his house."

"Had consent? Who gave it to them?"

"He did." Then, seeing my face, "Don't ask. Look, the guy is NRA all the way. He believes the Second Amendment prohibits any restrictions on the private ownership of firearms, including laws against felons having them. So why would he try to conceal his exercise of his Constitutional rights? That's what he asked me, anyway."

"Staying out of prison wouldn't be a good reason?"

"Who knows how this guy thinks? Don't even go there. The point is, he gave consent, they came in, they found the guns, and they arrested him and charged him. No question he has these two old felony convictions. And he's sure I can find a way to get him out of this."

"Sure and begorra." We smiled at one another ruefully before I went on. "Where does this character live, anyway?"

"A cabin outside Morrison," she said, naming a small town in the foothills west of Denver. "He really is an interesting guy. He was raised in Appalachia, the eighth child in his family. Irish immigrants."

"Irish, no kidding? Jaysus, Mary, and Joesus, Tory, I figured that much. Give me a little credit, will you? How did he get hooked up with the tax protest crowd?"

"He was in the army, stationed in Colorado Springs, and then in Vietnam. After he got out of the army in the seventies he came back to Colorado because, he says, he liked the way he could be by himself in the mountains. Rented a cabin in the hills west of Denver, but I guess he wasn't a complete recluse because after a while he got started talking to some of his like-minded neighbors. Their big issue was taxes. They all hated paying taxes. Eventually, Seamus started going to meetings of something called the National Tax Protest Forum. There was another group, too, something like the Trade and Barter Association."

"Did he agree with their stuff?" I asked. "Or were these associations just a flag of convenience for a guy who preferred to keep his money for himself?"

Tory raised her shoulders. "Who knows? What I personally think is that he agreed with some of the things that were said at the meetings, but he also liked the fact that there were a lot of women there—young, pretty women, who believed in the natural authority of the male. Seamus is very fond of women."

"So is he really a carpenter?"

"Yeah. He does carpentry and odd jobs for a living, but apparently he has at least one friend who's well-off and is paying his lawyer's fees. I hate to tell him there's nothing we can do and that he should just plead guilty."

"The only thing I can think of is possible ineffective assistance of counsel at those earlier trials. The fact that nobody told him he had a right to court-appointed counsel for an appeal suggests that. Even if he had to withdraw for nonpayment, the lawyer should have told Kellogg that much. I'd do some research to see whether you can attack those earlier convictions on that basis. Then if you can get them invalidated, poof! This new one goes away too. If he's not a properly convicted felon, he's entitled to own eight dozen guns, just like every other wing nut in the country."

Tory nodded. "I'll see what I can find, but I still think it's hopeless. What's going on with your case? The radio girl?"

"I don't think there's going to be a case. She doesn't really remember, it's not clear what she has to gain from a lawsuit, and most of all her mental health is just too fragile." I told her about our venture to Clear Creek, and its alarming denouement. "She's just not thinking straight, at least about some things. I'm going to try to fix her up with a therapist before we even think about going to court."

"I thought you were worried about being up against the statute."

"Yeah, that's true." I realized I had been gnawing furiously at a ragged cuticle, which was starting to bleed. "Damn it. But the main thing is Mariah's well-being now. She doesn't seem to have much of a life out there where she lives, but that's mostly because she doesn't have any transportation. I'm thinking of giving her my car."

"You're kidding. What would you do then?"

"Drive Sam's. It will be out of the shop in another day or two."

"What if he comes back and wants it again?"

"He's not coming back, Tory. If you saw him there you'd know it as well as I do."

"So—what then? A long-distance relationship forever? Phone sex?"

"Now *there's* an idea," I said. "Will you come to the phone store with me? Can you tell the boy phones from the girls?"

"Sure," she said. "The girls are better, babe. If you're going to switch species, you might as well switch sexes."

Pike Sayers telephoned me at home that night, having heard from Mariah McKay that I had offered to lend her my car to drive. "That was very generous of you," he said.

"She needs a way to get to therapy appointments," I said. "The Covingtons are being very good about giving her time off to see her new therapist in Erie, but they don't have an extra vehicle that she can use. And it's not a bad deal for me, because Craig Covington's going to fix up the car."

"Mariah also tells me you've advised against pursuing a lawsuit against her father for the present."

"That's right. I think she needs to get some help for her health problems before she decides on something as difficult and upsetting as a lawsuit. And there are other problems with it as well," I added obscurely, conscious of the need to maintain confidentiality.

"Aren't there problems with waiting?" he said. "Like the statute of limitations?"

"Judge Sayers, I don't really think I have any obligation to discuss this with you," I said, although truthfully the advice I had given

Mariah did make me uneasy. You just hate to let the statute run on a claim, no matter what. "It's a very puzzling situation," I added.

"Pike," he said. "You don't have to call me Judge. Like you said, I'm not a real judge."

"I don't remember saying that."

"Did you find anything out about common-law courts?" he said, ignoring my remark, and reminding me why I didn't like talking on the telephone. I wished I could see his face, try to figure out his reasons for taking such an interest in Mariah McKay and in my own edification.

"I did a little research," I said cautiously.

"Would you like to learn some more?" he asked me.

"Possibly," I said. "Do you have some materials I could read?"

"There's only so much you can learn by reading, Cinda. Why don't you come to court Friday night and watch for a bit?"

"Ryssby Chapel?" I asked.

"Not this time," he said. "We'll be meeting at my place. I'll send you a map."

On Friday morning, I arrived at the office to find Beverly looking anxious, one pink fingernail in her mouth. Her makeup was so inexpertly applied that her cheek color met her eye color high on one cheekbone, creating an effect like the Denver sun going down just below its brown cloud on a high-pollution day.

"What is it?" I said. "Duane again?"

"There is that," she said. "But it's more I'm worried about that doll you gave me, Cinda."

"What the hell," I said. I had not thought about the damned doll since giving it to her. "Just throw it away if you don't want it, Beverly. It's not important."

"No, listen," she said urgently. "Last night I opened the box, just to see if the doll had ever been removed. I was going to sell it to a collector Duane found on the Internet. It's worth more if—"

"I know," I said without interest, looking to see if the mail had arrived yet.

"Cinda, the doll was—it was damaged."

"Sorry, pal. Not worth so much, then?"

"You'd better see." She pulled a paper bag out from under her desk, and removed the Barbie box. She carefully opened the flap at the end, and drew the plastic tray containing the doll out of the box. "You couldn't see this until you took it out," she explained, reaching in to grasp the figure around its waspish little waist. As she raised the doll from the box, the doll's head, hands, and feet fell away and spilled back into the tray.

"The doll had been cut up like this?" I asked.

She nodded, chewing again on her forefinger. "I figure it's some kind of message to you, Cinda. Like, this could happen to you."

"That's ridiculous. Just some stupid joke." I didn't want to say that it made me feel squeamish, but I did sneak a look at my own sturdy wrists. They looked the same as always, a little knobby. I started toward my door.

"Cinda." I turned to look back at her, unable to walk out on the tremor in her voice. "There's more. This was under the doll." She was holding a piece of paper in an unsteady hand. I reached for it, but she let go too soon, and it fluttered to the floor. The paper was closer to her than to me, but she didn't move to pick it up, so I did.

It was a torn slip of what looked like the same brown paper that had wrapped the package, so dark that it wasn't that easy to make out the words. But the symbol that served as a signature was unmistakable: an ugly swastika.

We don't need your corrupt courts, and you don't need our kind of trouble. I read the words out loud, haltingly.

"What does it mean, Cinda?"

"Forget it," I said to her. "Nothing. Some wacko. What about Duane?"

At first, she was reluctant to surrender the subject of the cut-up Barbie, but after stashing the doll and the note inside the tiny closet in my office, I went downstairs and got a latte for each of us. As we drank the soothing milky coffee, I got her talking about a more familiar worry, her son. She was recounting her latest meeting with the kid's guidance counselor ("So she says to me maybe he's got Tourette's syndrome") when the fax machine beeped and then started to rattle. Without missing a word ("and I tell her much as I'd like to think so, he just has a trashy mouth, he gets it from his father"), she reached behind her for the paper and guided its exit from the machine. "It's for you," she said, glancing at it. Then, looking more closely, "Some kind of map."

"Yeah, thanks," I said, reaching for it. Beverly's eyes lingered on my face and I knew she was expecting an explanation. I offered none: I didn't feel like explaining to anyone why I was going to Pike Sayers's place that evening, even though it wasn't all that complicated. I didn't think I'd end up being Mariah's lawyer, but I still had to figure out where I belonged in my profession. And I wanted to know more about the common-law courts.

It occurred to me on my way out to the Sayers farm, with the sun setting behind my back, that nobody knew where I was going. Only an idiot, I reminded myself in an interior voice that sounded like my mother's, would drive herself to a deserted farmhouse for a nighttime meeting with a judicial impersonator and a band of his alienated constituents, especially after receiving what in the DA's office we had called a "threatening communication." Had Sayers or one of his followers sent me the mutilated doll, trying to scare me off of representing Mariah? But Sayers was trying to talk me *into* representing her. I couldn't think of any reason why he'd want to scare me.

Remembering that Mariah had spoken of the judge having a wife reassured me a bit. Somehow, the prospect of her presence seemed comforting. Still, if the twilight hadn't been so velvety, or the air so caressing, or my empty house so empty, I would have turned back. Instead, I stopped at a crossroads between Niwot and Erie and called Tory, but it was Linda who answered.

"She went to bed with a temperature right after dinner," said Linda. "Looks like the virus that's been going around; if it is, it probably won't last longer than a day or two. Do you want me to give her a message?"

"No, thanks," I said, wondering what a message would sound like: *I'm going to a farm out between Erie and Niwot, I don't know the address or the phone number, the guy calls himself Pike Sayers, he's not a judge but he plays one from time to time, you take a little twisty road off Isabelle just before 119th and look for the water tower. . . . If I never come back, good-bye and good luck.* "I'll see her Monday at the office," I said. "Tell her I said get better."

After leaving Isabelle Road for a well-maintained dirt road, I followed the map through two more turnoffs, each road narrower and more rutted than the last. Finally I guided the newly tuned-up Saab around a corner the map designated "Driveway." Now I was heading west again, back toward town, but the rising grade of the land blocked my view of anything ahead but the immediate road and the sky. I had an impression of fields on either side of the rocky passage, but it was too dark to tell whether they were cultivated or range. I stopped and turned on the interior lights to check my watch: five after eight, just a few minutes late. The night was moonless, and the sun long gone; without the headlights I would have been altogether disoriented. But after about a quarter of a mile, the car topped a ridge and I could see the lights of the house below. Several vehicles, mostly trucks, were gathered around it. It was an old two-story house, not very large. Perhaps two or three bedrooms upstairs, I guessed, kitchen and living room on the ground floor.

I drove slowly down the other side of the rise, still deciding whether I wanted to get out and join the gathering, but the decision was made for me. As I drew the car alongside a dark truck, its fenders crusted with mud, a man stepped out of the front door onto the porch and walked down the steps toward me. As he drew closer, I recognized him: Craig Covington.

"Evening, Miss Hayes. The judge said you might come."

"Good evening, Mr. Covington. I hope it's all right for me to be here." I half hoped he would express some objection that would enable me to make a blameless exit, but he only smiled and told me to come on in.

The front door opened into what must have been the living

room, but most of the furniture had been moved against the walls to make room for five or six rows of folding chairs. Almost all the chairs were occupied, by a group that included about twice as many men as women. The room was quiet but not silent, with an air of anticipation; those who spoke did so in whispers, to the persons next to them. I recognized Martha from the coffee shop, sitting next to the waitress that Mariah had spoken to when I had last met her there. Martha was holding an unlit cigarette in her hand, but making no move to light it. As Covington led me to a seat in the fourth row, I looked around for Mariah, but did not see her, nor did I recognize anyone else. I tried to imagine any of the sober-looking people in the room cutting up a Barbie doll with—what? A meat cleaver? It was ridiculous. I nodded my thanks to Covington, and he smiled back and went to join a narrow-faced woman with dark hair in the last row.

I surveyed the room, curious about Pike Sayers's home and what it might tell me about the man. The chairs had been arranged to face one end of the room, where a plain oak table and three chairs sat empty. One of the chairs faced us from behind the table, and the other two faced one another across the space between the table and the room. The rest of the room and its furnishings suggested a taste more rustic than stylish. There were several signs of interest in Native American artifacts and art: a case of arrowheads, a polychrome pot that looked like it might be from Zia Pueblo, or possibly Santo Domingo. A large rug hung on one wall—Navajo, I thought, although I didn't know much about Indian rugs. I only knew about pots from a course I had taken once, back when I was married.

The house itself looked to be about a hundred years old. The walls were brick, inside and out, the windows surmounted by arched patterns in the brickwork. Molded wooden cornices guarded the juncture of wall and ceiling. All was well maintained, but not meticulously so: I noted some cracks in the ceiling plaster, and the wooden planks looked pretty roughed up toward the center of the floor.

At length I gave up the visual inventory. The room and its air of solemnity turned my thoughts toward my last appearance before the Colorado Supreme Court, in that tribunal's courtroom in the Colorado Judicial Building. I had been trying to save my client's life that day, and I had not succeeded. Maybe that was why I found this room more comfortable than that rather chilly and antiseptic chamber. But I was still dubious about whatever proceedings were about to go forward here.

I realized that I had a headache; I poked gently through my shoulder bag, on the floor next to me, to see if I could find some Advil, but before I encountered any there was some commotion at a door behind us, which appeared to lead to the kitchen. Pike Sayers, dressed in jeans and a shirt and carrying a thin sheaf of paper in his hand, strode up the aisle toward the table. He was followed by two middle-aged men similarly attired, one burly, one slight. I suppressed a smile prompted by the resemblance to a wedding procession. This was serious; nobody else was smiling. The two men sat in the facing chairs, and Pike Sayers took the seat behind the table. After the rustling of their settling in subsided, Sayers nodded at a man in the front row, who rose and carried a small black book—it must have been a Bible—to the table, and placed it there.

"State your names," said the man, who appeared to be quite young, and angry about something. His eyes darted from one of the contestants to the other, as though daring them to depart from the script.

"Tad Conroy," said the slight man.

"*Full* name," said the young man reprovingly.

"Thaddeus Monroe Conroy."

"Warren Revere Hankerson," said the burly man, half standing, as though unsure what posture was called for.

The young man then faced the assembly and said, "This court is convened in this place under the authority vested in each citizen here under the Constitution of the United States, Article Three. This court sits to adjudicate cases and controversies arising under the original Constitution, and disputes arising from the contractual and other lawful relations between and among Constitutional citizens. Does any person here contest the authority and jurisdiction of this court over the persons of Thaddeus Conroy and Warren Hankerson?"

Everyone in the room but me, or so it seemed, murmured, "No."

The young man seemed satisfied, and motioned Tad and Warren forward. As they rose from their seats, he reached for the Bible, then placed each man's hand on the book, one atop the other. "Repeat after me," he instructed. "I hereby accept and honor—"

"I hereby accept and honor," the two men muttered.

"The power and jurisdiction of this honorable court..."

The men repeated it.

"And that of the judge, ordained and sanctioned by the original Constitution of the United States..."

"...the United States..."

"And bind myself to speak only the truth in these matters ..."

"...in these matters..."

"And hereby commit myself and my issue to abide by and honor its judgments."

"...honor its judgments..."

"In the name of the God of our fathers, Yahweh, who is our sole sovereign and *king*."

The young man stamped his foot at the end of this, and Tad and Warren did too, as they said the last word.

Glaring at all of us, the young man sat down, leaving the Bible on the table. Behind that table sat Pike Sayers, looking as though he had been somewhere else during the ceremony that had just taken place.

"You can sit down," he said mildly to Warren and Tad, who had been left standing and looking rather bewildered at the end of the oath. He then looked briefly through the papers, and spoke to Tad.

"Mr. Conroy," he said, "please explain your petition to the court in respectful and peaceable language."

Tad half rose again, but Sayers shook his head, and the small man sank back into the chair with what looked like relief. "I am asking," he began, then cleared his throat. "I am asking, Judge, for Warren, uh, Warren Revere Hankerson, this man here"—he gestured toward his opposite number, who was sitting rigidly in his chair, hands on his large thighs—"to pay for the trouble and damage he caused by sleeping with my wife, Mary Ann Conroy, who is the mother of my two girls, Lacey and Geraldine. Mary Ann sometimes don't know her own mind, which Mr. Hankerson took advantage of and hurt my family and me and ruined our last Christmas, not to mention a vacation to Mexico, plus which it was already paid for and we had to lose the deposit, which was more than we could afford in the first place. And all because of him. And now Mary Ann knows that she shouldn't never have had anything to do with him, but that doesn't turn back the clock, in my opinion. That's it, Judge."

Sayers nodded in a reassuring way, and then turned to the larger man, who was rubbing his face with both hands. "Mr. Hankerson? What would you like to say by way of introduction to this matter?"

"I don't know what to say," came out of Warren Hankerson's mouth, but faintly.

"Do you concede the truth of Mr. Conroy's account?"

Warren looked unhappy, and moved his hands about as if looking for some object to hold in them. "Pretty much. Except the part about her not knowing her own mind. She knew it pretty well, I believe. And I don't know nothing about any trip to Mexico. Neither here nor there, in my opinion. Your Honor," he added quickly.

"What is your attitude toward the relationship now?" asked Sayers in a neutral tone.

"It's over. She's shut a me and I'm shut a her. I believe it was a mistake, but a mistake on both sides." Warren Hankerson rubbed his palms up and down on his worn jeans. I have seen many uncomfortable witnesses over the years, but I don't think I ever saw one more eager for the end of the ordeal than Warren.

My head was starting to pound, with more than sympathy for Warren. A wave of dizziness hit me, and I thought of Tory and realized I must be getting the same virus that had sent her to bed. A little cold, I thought. Nothing. I straightened my back and tried to pay attention.

"Do you wish for the court to hear from any other witnesses?" Sayers was asking Warren. He shook his head, seemingly overcome with some strong emotion, although I could not tell whether it was regret, or anger, or something else altogether.

"How about you, Mr. Conroy?"

He appeared to reflect for a moment. "I think my wife could tell this court about whether she was in her right mind or not when all this happened." He looked toward the back of the room, and many others turned to follow his gaze. I realized that the dark-haired woman sitting with Craig Covington was not, as I had assumed, his wife, but Mary Ann Conroy. She shook her head in a panicked way and held up one hand in the traffic cop's "stop" position, as if to ward off the prospect of having to vouch for her own sanity, or confess its absence. Covington took hold of her elbow, whether to reassure or to restrain her I could not tell, and a slight rustling amid the rows of chairs suggested that the drama of the moment was not lost on the crowd. For the first time since I had arrived, I began to feel uneasy about the ugly possibilities of the situation, and I felt hot and chilly at the same time. I must be coming down with something, I thought.

Sayers's voice, no louder than before, turned every eye back to him. "The court does not find that Mrs. Conroy's statement would assist it in its task," he said. "Anything else, Mr. Conroy?"

Tad shook his head, defeated. "I don't think so, Your Honor. I'm just sayin'. That's all. She wasn't thinkin' straight at the time and everybody knows it."

Sayers then asked questions of the two men, back and forth, bringing to the task a kind of grave attention that subdued the more comical elements of their answers, although in truth it was a sad, if familiar, story. Tad recounted the events of the preceding autumn, when a broken arm sustained in a fall from a tractor had made him, he conceded, irascible and hard to live with. He mentioned that Mary Ann had a miscarriage about the same time, and that he hadn't had the heart or the patience to grieve with her, especially since he had been worried about how they would feed another mouth. He had bought the tickets to Mexico without telling her, he said, hoping that if the two of them got away for a holiday, even one they couldn't afford, it would put things right. He spoke of his disbelief when she told him about what had happened between her and his neighbor, and the sleepless nights, of the way his kids' grades had gone down in school, of the tearful Christmas and canceled vacation, and of his loss of trust in the goodwill and reliability of all his neighbors. He said he thought some of the fault might be his. Still, he argued, it wasn't right.

Warren, looking as though he'd rather be mucking out a cattle pen, responded to the judge's questioning in a low voice. He told about seeing Mary Ann at the grocery store looking sad, reminding him of his own wife, fled home to her parents in Minnesota after two bad years. He confessed to meeting Mary Ann at the coffee shop, and then at the little bar in Erie, and finally at the motel in Lafayette; to asking her to leave Tad and come live with him on his played-out farm, take care of his neglected house. He was sorry for it now, he said. He knew he had broken God's laws, more than one of them. He hoped his neighbors would forgive him.

Sayers nodded his head seriously and said, "The court will take this matter under advisement. The judgment of the court will be announced when the court next sits, which will be a week from this evening, same time, same place." He stood, and started to walk around the table, when the young man who had administered the oath rose and spoke in a loud voice, halting the hushed shuffle of the observers' preparations to rise and depart.

"When can we start meetin' again in the other place?" he said petulantly. "I don't like that we give up meetin' there just because the Talmudic law courts and their hired badges refuse to recognize our claim to it."

"I'm working on it, Jeremiah," said Sayers. "I'll let you know what progress I make." He said this as mildly as ever, but there was an air of authority and finality in his voice that caused the others to rise from their chairs, scraping them on the floor to punctuate the end of the proceedings. Jeremiah, however, was not satisfied, and he approached Sayers as the crowd was flowing toward the front door, placing a hand on his sleeve. I was not close enough to hear their conversation, but Sayers listened patiently. At one point he unobtrusively wiped his cheek where the oblivious younger man's heated words had propelled spittle out of his mouth. Finally both men nodded and Jeremiah turned and pushed his way through the crowd to the door.

Craig Covington and another man had started folding up the chairs and placing them against the wall. "Want us to put 'em back out in the shed, Judge?" asked the second man.

Sayers shook his head briefly. "No need. I'll get around to it later, or else just leave them here for next week. Thanks for your help."

I had not meant to stay on after the end, to find myself alone in the house with Pike Sayers, but somehow that's exactly what happened. The turning over of engines and the rumble of truck tires over the stony road was over in a minute or two, and I was left standing in the middle of the now-empty room, feeling that to leave would be rude and to stay unwise. As ever, my early training, which emphasized manners rather than wisdom, won out.

"Can I help you straighten up?" I asked.

Sayers smiled and shook his head. "Let's talk for a bit," he said. "Would you like to go out on the back porch? Nice view out there."

That was an understatement, I saw, as we walked out a side door onto the cantilevered wooden deck. This porch faced west, and in the moonlight the faint ragged edges of the Rockies bisected the sky like the tracings of a polygraph needle recording the worst lies of the century. The stars seemed not their usual pinpoints, but a field of fat glowing volcanoes. He must have heard the quick involuntary intake of my breath. "Yeah," he said.

It was cool out there, and that felt good at first; I sneaked a feel of my forehead, which felt hot, but so did my hand. When he inquired whether I'd like anything to drink, I asked for hot tea. I sat in an old metal glider, reeling a little from the stars and the fever, while he went back into the house. What he brought was just plain Lipton, from a bag, but it tasted good.

"So what did you think?" he said, sitting on the edge of the porch, while I pulled my legs up beneath me in the glider.

"I think you're a very good judge. Why didn't you study law and become a real judge?"

"You mean why do I waste my time refereeing penny-ante disputes between losers like Tad and Warren?"

"You know that's not what I mean. I just think your talents could be put to better use. What are you going to do in that case, anyway?"

"Make Warren pay some amount of money to Tad, of course. Probably a thousand dollars or so. I think that will make most everyone feel justice was done. They'll feel better about it, too, if I wait until next week, make it clear I need to give it a little thought."

I shook my head. "Every jurisdiction in America has abolished damage suits for alienation of affection. Don't you think this case treats the woman like a piece of property, a prize cow or something? You don't even know how she felt about the whole thing!"

"The law we employ in these matters is a little different, that's all."

"Yeah, different from—what did that one guy call it? *Talmudic* law? What's that supposed to mean? Is that what we're calling the law of the state of Colorado these days?"

"That's just the way Jeremiah talks, Cinda. You can't assume that one hothead speaks for everyone."

"Then how is it that you seem to speak for everyone? Who elected you, and where do you get your authority to be the law out here?"

"Let me ask you this, Cinda. What do you think would happen if Warren were to refuse to accept the judgment, refuse to pay?"

I thought about this. "I don't know. You don't have access to a sheriff or any other law enforcement agents to enforce your judgments. So in the end, if Warren refuses, there's not much you can do, is there?"

"That's right. You've noticed something most people never

do. Law depends on force, in the end. On violence, at least your laws do. Knowing that the force is there makes most people follow the law, pay their debts when they can and live up to the terms of the judgments that the courts make, even when they disagree with them. People put their kids on buses to go to schools an hour away, and walk through airports full of bald-headed people trying to hand them flowers and Bhagavad Gitas, and get licenses for their cars and even for their dogs, and pay over most of what they earn for taxes while they watch the TV and see kids in pants about to fall off their behinds burning the American flag, and they do this all because the law says it's required of them. But the law's just words on paper, and if that's not enough to compel them, then the sheriff and the United States Marshals and eventually the FBI and the ATF will come in with their guns to accomplish what the words could not."

"That's why it's important to have good judges. And good lawmakers."

"Why is that?" He turned sideways to the edge of the porch and leaned forward, his face illuminated obliquely by yellow light cast through the window by a lamp inside.

I fumbled for words, at a loss to explain the obvious. "So—so the laws will be made for the benefit of everyone, instead of for the selfish interests of some. And so judges who interpret those laws will be objective, instead of corrupt. I know it doesn't always work that way," I added hastily. "But that's the ideal."

"What do you think *objective* means?" he said.

"Detached," I said. "Not having a personal stake in any dispute or its outcome."

"Ah," he said. "You mean, in an unconcerned position."

"Yeah," I said. "That's one way to put it."

Then he said something I didn't understand. "Odden," it sounded like.

"Excuse me?"

"The poet. He said we're all looking for that in the law—someone in an unconcerned position."

"W. H. Auden?"

"Yeah. Just a minute." He rose and went into the house. I looked up into the inky bowl of the sky, but no answers were written there. No questions, either, and I realized I was less interested in a jurisprudential debate than in knowing more about Pike Sayers. I rubbed my hands up and down my arms, which were getting cold.

He was back in two minutes. "Here, read the whole thing," he said, handing me a worn leather-bound volume and snapping on the porch light.

"Out loud?"

"Only if you want to."

"I'll read it to myself, then."

He said nothing, but stood on the edge of the porch looking west toward the barely liminal contours of the Indian Peaks as I read.

I read it all the way through, then went back and read four lines out loud:

No more than they can we suppress
The universal wish to guess
Or slip out of our own position
Into an unconcerned condition.

"Those are the lines you were thinking of?" I asked him.

He nodded. "It's a very pessimistic poem, don't you think?"

"I don't know. Comparing law to love? Is that pessimistic?"

"Is love objective, Cinda? Besides, look what he says." He walked over, took the book from me, and read:

Like love we don't know where or why,
Like love we can't compel or fly,
Like love we often weep,
Like love we seldom keep.

"Okay," I conceded. "I guess he's pessimistic about law *and* love."

"Whereas you, Cinda, are optimistic about both."

"I wouldn't say that."

"At least about law, then."

"Compared to you, I suppose so. What makes you so cynical?"

"I don't think it's cynical. I agree with the poet—there is no unconcerned position. I don't care how much training and education and Socratic method he's been through, a judge can't put aside his own values and function like a machine. So why not acknowledge that, and have judges whose values are known and shared? Then their judgments don't have to be enforced with violence. They'll be accepted because the people have accepted the judge and voluntarily submitted to his authority."

"So how did you come to be accepted as the judge for the people who were here tonight?"

"Why do you ask?"

I stood and moved to the lip of the porch, but had to grasp an upright beam to keep from falling; dizziness overcame me and I sat down quickly, looking away from the vertiginous emptiness past the edge of the porch. "I really want to know," I said.

He shrugged. "I really want to know why you wouldn't file a lawsuit for Mariah McKay."

"We've already talked about that," I said.

"Well, if I answer your question, can we talk about it again?"

I thought about it. "All right."

He nodded. "Let's go inside, then. It's a long story, and it's getting cold out here."

He pulled a couple of pieces of the room's normal furniture back into its center and lit a fire that was already laid in the stone fireplace. I curled into the corner of a chintz settee, and he sat in a rocking chair.

"Are you feeling all right?" he asked, looking into my face in the light.

"A little wobbly," I answered. "I think I may be getting the flu or something. Someone else in my office has it too."

"Can I get you anything?"

"Will you hand me my bag there? I think I have some Advil in it." He found the bag and cast me a questioning look. Ordinarily I wouldn't have wanted anyone looking around in my purse, but my head was throbbing and I answered with a weary nod. He went through the bag until he found the small plastic container.

"Two?" he asked, shaking the tablets into his hand.

I nodded and accepted the pills, swallowing them with the remains of the mug of tea, cool by then. "Go on. I want to hear the story."

"I was born in 1942, right in this house," he began. "They wanted my ma to go to the hospital in Longmont because they knew there were two of us, but she refused to leave the farm and her sister midwifed the birth. My brother Gideon came out first, so he always claimed to be the oldest and I guess he was. We weren't real twins, you know, identical. We don't look alike. Didn't, that is.

"Our pa had this half section where we're sitting now and he ran a few cows and raised sheep, but he also grew sugar beets and alfalfa. My grandpa, Gunther, came here from Germany around the turn of the century."

I see, I nodded.

"My pa was the only boy in his family, so he got the farm when my grandpa died in 1938, and he didn't go off to war—he had a deferment because he was the only one could keep the farm going. We did real well when Gideon and I were growing up. In the fifties, Pa bought the adjoining half section and started a hog operation that was real successful.

"My parents were frugal people but we lived well; after the war was over, Pa hired on quite a few hands. Gideon and I played football for Erie High and when we were seniors Pa gave us an old truck for our own. To share—you can imagine the fights we had. We graduated number one and number two in our high school, and Gideon would have been number one except he was so stuck on this girl named Sally Nelson that he kind of neglected his studying during his senior year.

"Let me show you something," he said suddenly, and left the

room. I could hear him walking up the stairs. When he returned, he had a framed photograph in his hands. "That's me and Gideon." He pointed at two young men in suits.

I really needed my reading glasses to see it well, but it seemed too difficult to get them out of my bag. Still, I didn't need to be told which one was Pike Sayers; his lean face hadn't changed that much. His brother was much fairer, perhaps a redhead, although it was hard to tell from the black-and-white snapshot. Leaning against the brother was a blond girl, her hand raised trying to keep the wind from whipping her hair across her face. A tall woman stood between the two boys, squinting into the sun and holding a straw hat against her head.

"Our high school graduation," he said. "Nineteen sixty. See how all of us look shell-shocked? Pa had died that spring; he had a stroke when he was out in the beet fields one afternoon, and Ma didn't send the hands out to look for him until after dark. Then they just didn't find him in time. It was March, but it was wicked cold, and he didn't make it."

I shook my head, still looking at the picture. "How old was your mother in this?" I asked.

He looked toward the ceiling for a moment. "Thirty-four, I guess. About that."

Seven years younger than I was now. I tried to imagine having grown children; failed. It was too hard, and I was too tired.

"In 1931, the Niwot State Bank went bust," he continued. "My pa was a young man, just beginning to take over the farm as his sisters went off and got married. What he learned from that was never to trust banks; he always tried to teach us that. We used to worship right here in Ryssby Chapel, every Sunday; we were Lutherans, and my ma was a religious woman. But the real religion among the men in our family—Pa and Gideon and me—was never to trust banks, and never borrow money. We always knew he had a safe built into the back of the closet in his and my ma's bedroom; I guess I thought everyone had one. But that was where he kept the money instead of in the bank.

"I know Ma believed there was a lot of money in that safe. After Pa died and she went into it to get money for the funeral, she found out different. He'd spent almost everything to buy the new half section and get the hog operation started; there was less than a thousand dollars in the safe. But at least we didn't owe anything, because Pa had never borrowed a penny in his life. Still and all, it was a shock. Then on top of that there was another. Sally told Gideon she was going to have a baby. This was the week before we all graduated from high school; it's the second reason we have that blasted look in the graduation pictures."

"So," I said, still looking at the picture in its plain wooden frame. "Did Gideon and Sally get married?"

"Yep. Gideon and I both had football scholarships to the University of Kansas, but by graduation day everything had changed. Ma didn't think she could run the farm alone, and so it was decided that Gideon and Sally would manage the farm, and I'd go off to Lawrence and study agriculture and play football and come back after four years and we'd be partners. I didn't like it, not really, but everybody else thought it was a good plan, Ma and Sally and Gideon.

"I'd go home for holidays and everything seemed fine. I liked being an uncle—after Tommy, Sally and Gideon had a little girl, Gretchen. The farm was doing real well, the hog operation, especially, after the Montforts started the meat-packing plant out by Greeley.

"The only thing was, Gideon had to borrow money, which wasn't any big deal because all the farmers had been doing it for decades, but the Sayerses never had. Still, there wasn't any choice. It was the estate taxes that started it. When Pa died, everything was tied up in the farm. The estate tax rules were pretty harsh then, and even though half of the farm was Ma's without tax, we owed quite a few thousand on the other half. Then when Ma died of breast cancer in 1961, there were the hospital bills—farm folks didn't have health insurance back in those days—and then there was a real whopper of a tax bill on her estate before Gideon and I could own the farm. We could have sold off some of the land, but it seemed crazy when everything was going so well and the bank was more than happy to lend us what we needed against the farm and equipment."

"Did you come back after you graduated from college?" I asked.

"Nah. I was so mad about the way Ma's lawyer had screwed up her estate plan I decided to go to law school. Anyway, by then it seemed clear that the farm was never going to produce a living for more than one family. Sally was expecting again, and I had a girlfriend. Seemed better that way. Mom had left the farm to Gideon and me as joint tenants—you know what that means?"

"Sure," I said quickly, and it was almost true. And in a moment I did remember: When one joint tenant dies, the property automatically belongs to the remaining ones. Or one.

"You want some more tea?" he inquired. I shook my head. He stood up and walked around the room a bit, stopping to rub his fingers over a chipped spot in the brick above the fireplace. "I went to law school at the University of Illinois," he continued. "Had a knack for it, I guess you'd say. So a judge asked me to be his law clerk when I was about to graduate, and I couldn't think of a reason to say no. Then his old law firm wanted to hire me, and that seemed good. I was married by then, and Kate liked Chicago. We lived in an apartment on the lake, and she taught at a private school. We had a good life by most measures."

"Are you still married?" I asked.

He stopped and unfastened the wrist buttons of his shirt, rolling the cuffs up once or twice. The room had gotten quite warm with the fire going. "No," he said, sitting back down in the rocking chair.

I started to say I was sorry but didn't. Maybe it wasn't the right thing to say.

"This is a pretty long-winded story, isn't it?" he suggested.

I shrugged. "It's interesting. Is it going to explain what went on here tonight?"

He smiled. "Maybe. I guess you'll have to be the judge of that."

"Well then."

"Well then. I did pretty well at the law firm. It was easy work, really, and I was getting a little stir-crazy. Came a time there was a vacancy on the court where my judge had sat—he was retired by then. My partners wanted to put me up for it. That was the way it worked back then, pretty much. If a big firm decided one of its people ought to be appointed to the bench, it would happen. Katie was big on the idea—thought it was an honor. I said okay."

"So you really are a judge," I said.

"I served on that bench for ten years. Wrote more than a hundred and fifty published opinions."

"Why did you resign, then?"

"I needed to come back here."

"Why was that?"

"Gideon died, and since we were joint tenants it seemed I suddenly owned the farm."

"But you could have sold it, couldn't you?"

The scorn in his look caused me to turn away. "No," he said.

I changed the subject quickly. "How did Gideon die?"

"The insurance company said it was an accident; he got caught in the forks of a corn picker. It grabbed him and tore him apart. That gave Sally and the kids a couple of million dollars; it was a double-indemnity policy. He probably thought that would be enough for them to buy the farm from me, pay off the biggest debts."

"Thought? You mean you don't believe it was an accident?"

"My brother had been around farm equipment since he was old enough to walk. He wasn't going to walk into the business end of a corn picker. Not unless it was on purpose."

"So why didn't Sally and the kids keep the farm?"

"First off, it was mine. That's what joint tenancy means. But I would have let Sally and the kids stay on it. Hell, I would have let her *have* it. She and Gideon were the ones that worked it all those years. I'd become a soft city man, and living on a farm was about the last thing that interested Katie."

"So," I said, trying to imagine a paler version of those sunburned wrists sticking out from the cuffs of a bespoke dress shirt, "why not? Why didn't it happen that way?"

"Sally wouldn't have it. She knew, same as I did, what Gideon had done. He'd killed himself to keep the farm from being lost. The debts had piled up, they'd had a couple of bad years, first with hail destroying the wheat crop, then with sickness in the hogs that killed off every damn farrow that last summer. If he'd shot himself, the insurance company would have called it suicide and refused to pay, but an accidental death pays double. Every farmer knows that.

"So she hated the place; she knew it had killed her husband. She took the two million and bought herself a bed-and-breakfast place in Salida. Bought it outright, and put the rest in trust for her kids. The kids are happier to be in town, even a little town, and she's made a good life for herself, making beds and baking cookies for tourists who want to stay near the mountains. She's a good person, is Sally."

"So you and your wife came back to the family farm."

"Not Kate."

"Oh."

He didn't wait for me to ask why. "Kate's a complicated woman. After all those years of being a lawyer's and a judge's wife, all the committees and luncheons, she decided on her fortieth birthday to go back to school, get a Ph.D. in art history. She was admitted to the University of Chicago, and she was pretty much burning up the track there when we got the news about Gideon. That was 1987. She'd been offered a teaching assistant's job for the next semester, and there was some talk she might curate an exhibit at the Art Institute. When we first came out for Gideon's funeral, I could see she was uncomfortable. For the first time, I saw the farm through her eyes, how drab and dirty and ordinary it was to her. She flew back to Chicago after the funeral so as not to miss any more classes, while I stayed to help Sally and get the farm's business sorted out. By the time I realized I wasn't going to be going back to Chicago, except to close things up, I'd gotten a long letter from Katie.

"She was sorry, she said, but she wanted a divorce. I remember she said it wasn't just that she never had been able to interest me in Seurat or Frank Lloyd Wright—I seemed to have lost interest even in the law. Living with me had become like living with someone who wasn't there—that's the way she put it."

"Did you know what she was talking about?"

He nodded. "She was right."

"Well, why was she?" I asked. "What made you turn into the man who wasn't there?"

He stood up again and started walking around the room. "About 1980, I'd had to write an opinion in a farm foreclosure case. The bank's attorney had argued the case like it was a standard dispute about real estate and security and waivers of homestead exemptions and the like, and of course he was right. But the farmer's attorney had tried to argue about natural law and a man's connection to the soil that he'd tilled and where he'd raised his livestock and buried his kin. He didn't have a single scrap of law on his side, and I had to write the opinion in favor of the bank. But I couldn't stop thinking about it, and about the summers Gideon and I had pitched hay and helped cows give birth and patched up the roof of the farrow house over and over. I started doing some reading, about the origins of the law, property rights, the meaning of the Constitution. Quite a lot of reading, I guess. I think that's when I really left Katie, and she was smart enough to know it."

"Did you resign from the bench after Gideon died?"

"Oh, yeah. And the country club and the bar association and the condominium association board of directors. Katie kept the condo and the art we'd collected; I got most of the rest. She got married again before too long, to one of her professors. They still live there in our place on Michigan Avenue when they're not in Europe. I think she's happy, Katie. We're still good friends. She's the one who sent Mariah to us—Drew, as she called herself then. Found her alone and starving in Paris, selling herself to get food. When Katie found out where she was from, she thought of me. At first we thought we might get her back with her family, but that didn't work out in the long run."

I had just made this connection myself, between Katie and the Kathryn of Mariah's story. There was a lot more I wanted to know, but my fading consciousness told me it was time for me to find my way to a bed. "Listen, Judge Sayers," I said. "I want to hear the rest of this, and I don't mean to stiff you about the other talk you wanted, but I'm not feeling very well. I think I'd better go home now." I struggled to my feet. "Maybe we could find a time..."

"Hey," he exclaimed. "What's the *matter* with me? All this time I've been running off at the mouth and you really *are* sick. Are you sure you can drive?"

"Sure," someone said from a long way off, just before she sat down on the floor, pretty hard. It sounded like it might hurt, hitting the floor like that.

I woke up once in the darkness of the night, needing to pee. I sat up in the bed, my head vibrating, trying to make out where I was. After a minute or so, the light coming through a window across the room disclosed what I was hoping for, a lamp. I reached for it and twisted the switch, then had to close my eyes against the sudden light. When I opened them again, I blinked at the visual extravaganza; the small room was wallpapered in a faded but exuberant pattern of stripes, ribbons, and cabbage roses. The double bed was made up with a wedding-ring pattern quilt on which I was lying; another quilt, in a pattern I didn't know, covered me. There was only one door, which was almost but not quite closed. It must lead to the hallway, I decided; there were no attached bathrooms in houses of this era. I crawled out of the bed, almost tripping over my own shoes lying beside it on the floor.

I was relieved to see that I was fully dressed, except for the shoes. I pushed the door open slowly, and found myself in a narrow hallway. At the other end of it, I could barely make out a staircase leading down. Several other doors lay between, and I tried to walk quietly over the bare floorboards as I searched for the bathroom. The first door I passed, on my right, was another bedroom, even smaller than mine. My eyes growing accustomed to the dark again, I could see the outline of a person in the narrow bed, and hear his even breathing: Pike Sayers.

The next door was across the hall on the left, and I could tell it was a bathroom even before I could see it—something about the cold emanations from the floor tile, and the smell of water. I closed the door behind me quietly, grasping the faceted glass doorknob, found the light switch, and gratefully used the facilities. My stomach was queasy and my legs rubbery and I had a sore spot on my butt, probably from falling onto the floor, but the fever seemed to have lessened. My eyes looked back at me from the spotted mirror as I washed my hands, telling me I didn't feel as unhappy as I ought to at my predicament. I brushed the hair back from my face with ten fingers, turned out the light, and went back to bed.

The next time I awakened, it was to the muted hammering of metal on metal, followed by the protesting rattle of a large machine coming to life. I rubbed my eyes and slid out from under the quilt, testing the steadiness of my legs on the floor: not too bad. An elderly electric clock on the bedside table said it was nearly noon. Could that be right?

I walked over to the window and looked out. The sun was dazzling, reflected off the white sides of a shed next to the house. Just outside the shed, Sayers and Craig Covington stood together beside a tractor, talking. I couldn't hear them because the window was closed, and because of the tractor's noise. Tools were spread out on a stained cloth that covered a patch of ground beside the big vehicle. Sayers said something and both men laughed; then they shook hands, and Covington started to move tools from the tarp into a large silver-colored box. I scampered toward the bathroom as I saw Sayers turn and start walking back toward the house.

A thin towel and washcloth were sitting on the closed lid of the toilet. Very thoughtful, I reflected, but I searched the austere shelves of the bathroom cabinet in vain for an unopened toothbrush. I settled for a quick rubdown of my teeth with a smear of toothpaste wielded by my index finger, and a shower without washing my hair, which still got wet at the edges under the towel

I wrapped around it. The head pounding and dizziness were nearly gone, but I was weak and a bit achy in the joints.

Sayers was waiting for me in the kitchen, scrubbing his hands to remove the tractor grease. He poured me a tall glass of orange juice, then a squat mug of coffee. I sat at an old stripped pine table, where the day's *Longmont Daily Times-Call* sat next to the book of poems he had shown me the night before.

We cautiously alluded to my sudden expiration of the night before. He inquired politely about my symptoms, and expressed the hope I had slept well and had found the bath linens he had left out for me. I thanked him for his thoughtfulness and hospitality, and apologized for the inconvenience I had caused him; he demurred, saying there had been none. I did not ask, and he did not say, how I had ended up in the quilted bed.

After eating a piece of dry toast, I said that I really should go. "I've been in your hair for long enough."

"But we aren't through talking, are we?" he said reproachfully. "We were going to talk about Mariah McKay and her lawsuit. If you feel well enough," he added.

"I feel well enough," I said, sipping the coffee. "But there's not that much to tell, I'm afraid. In my professional judgment, there aren't sufficient grounds to justify a lawsuit at this time. A complaint has to specify the basis of the claim with some precision. If the basis isn't known, the complaint can't be put in proper form, and the suit would be dismissed by the judge. So filing it would be pointless."

He said nothing, only looked at me. His eyes were the most extraordinary light yellow color.

"Maybe it would be different in your court," I said. "I don't know about that. But in the courts where I practice, that's what would happen. Maybe Mariah should file her case in your court," I added, looking at him closely.

"Do you really think that would be a good idea?" he asked slowly.

"*I* don't know," I said, growing more annoyed by the moment. "How would I know? I only know *Talmudic* law, you know."

He got up from the pine table and walked over to the screen door, looking out casually, then came back to lean against the stove. "Remember what you said last night when I asked you what would happen if Warren wouldn't accept the judgment of the court?"

"Yeah," I said, beginning to feel like a sullen teenager in a quarrel with her infuriatingly reasonable father. "So?"

"So what would happen if Mariah filed a case in a common-law court, maybe in my court, and the defendant didn't acknowledge the jurisdiction of the court?"

"I don't know," I said. "What?" I really do have to go, I thought to myself with sudden longing for my own untidy house and unmade bed. I could floss and brush my teeth and go back to sleep until evening, I thought, then get up, wash my hair, and call somebody to go out to a movie. So I wasn't paying enough attention, but even so what he said didn't seem responsive.

"Do you remember a case of attempted murder in Weld County about ten years ago?" he asked. "Guy's name was Herbert Gohannon. The victim was the county clerk out there, Wanda Kersey."

I abandoned my nap fantasy and searched my memory, but without finding much. Weld is the county directly east of Boulder; the county line was probably less than a couple of miles from where we were sitting. But news from Weld County, even of serious crimes, rarely made it to the Boulder newspaper unless it affected Boulder. The last Weld County event I could remember clearly was the fire that started a few years ago in a tire dump in the little town of Hudson. It had sent into the air a column of oily smoke that could be seen all the way to the Divide, and prompted hundreds of worried calls to the Boulder police and sheriff's dispatchers. In contrast to this vivid recollection, the names Herbert Gohannon and Wanda Kersey prompted only faint stirrings of recognition.

"The names sound familiar," I said lamely.

He nodded, unsurprised. "Herbert was a farmer, and a member of what they called the Colorado Citizens' Republic. He and some of his followers decided they had been treated unfairly by the local courts in some foreclosure proceedings, and that the district judge out there, fellow name of Comerford, was to blame. They claimed the judge had impaired their legal rights, and that he owed *them* damages for it. So they filed some papers against him and prepared a bunch of documents, titled them liens, and filed them with the county clerk's office, against the title to the judge's house and ranch."

"Were they legal?" I asked. "The liens, I mean."

"Well, that's an interesting question," he said. "What do you mean by it exactly?"

"Were they properly enforceable?"

"Well, Judge Comerford certainly didn't think so. He ordered the county clerk, this Wanda Kersey, to remove the liens from the chain of title to his property. If she hadn't, then he would have had all kinds of problems, of course, if he'd ever wanted to sell or refinance."

"So they were bogus."

"The judge said so." Sayers's even tone was tinctured with a note of correction.

"So the judge said so, so they were."

"The same judge whose property was affected said so, Cinda. Do you see anything a little bogus, to use your word, in that?" Pike Sayers reached for the book of poetry, turned the pages until he found the Auden poem again, and read:

> *Law, says the judge as he looks down his nose,*
> *Speaking clearly and most severely,*
> *Law is as I've told you before,*
> *Law is as you know I suppose,*
> *Law is but let me explain it once more,*
> *Law is The Law.*

"Don't you think, Cinda, that Herbert Gohannon and his friends might have felt that they were being given the same runaround: The law is what the judge says it is?"

I thought for a moment. "I suppose it might have been better form for him to ask another judge to consider the matter."

"One of his *brothers* on the bench, you mean?"

"What are you saying?" I asked irritably. "That Herbert Gohannon and his friends were entitled to use any fraudulent scheme they could think up to make life miserable for a judge whose rulings they didn't like, and some poor county clerk who was just doing her job? That the courts are all *corrupt?*" I wanted to see if this word had any effect on him, but he just went on in the same unemphatic voice.

"I'm just asking you to see it from their point of view for a minute or two, that's all. I thought you wanted to hear this story."

"What story?"

"You said you wanted to know how I came to be a common-law judge."

"This is part of *that* story?"

"Are you always this impatient?" The dueling staccato rhythm of our questions must have suddenly sounded as funny to him as it did to me, because we started laughing at the same moment. He had a nice easy laugh. It didn't last long, but when we were silent again something had changed. I sighed and settled further into the chair.

"So," I said, struggling to recapture the line of the narrative, "then this Gohannon tries to kill the clerk?"

"Not much doubt about that part," he replied. "He was arrested by the state patrol next to a stock tank in the middle of the farm he'd lost to foreclosure. She was tied to a tree, and it appeared he was in the midst of trying to rig a rope so he could string her up. Fortunately, he was not very skilled at knots, and hadn't gotten very far when they caught up with him."

"Hang her?" I said in horror, but it came to me now that I had read accounts of this bizarre crime at the time. Still, not much of it had stayed with me. "He was tried for attempted murder?"

Sayers nodded. "He had a defense, of course."

"What was that? He didn't come close enough to the deed for his preparations to count as an attempt?" I guessed, thinking that line of defense might have worked in England in 1890 but was not a promising one in present-day Colorado.

"Better than that. He argued he was engaged in carrying out a public duty."

"Killing someone a public duty? Did he have a warrant of execution?" I asked, thinking this a rather good joke, but Sayers nodded soberly.

"Yes, he did. It was issued by the president of the Colorado Citizens' Republic, a man named Roswell Stark. Signed and dated, all official-like. I never saw it myself, but I'm told it had a nice purple wax seal on it."

"Let me guess," I said. "This defense did not avail Mr. Gohannon."

"Mr. Gohannon was held in jail while awaiting trial because he didn't have enough money to make bond, and he must have gotten some better with knots during his confinement. Or else he just had more leisure to pursue the craft. He managed to make a rope out of his underwear and loop it through the wire cage that covered the light fixture in his cell. If he'd a been any bigger a man it wouldn't have worked, I've been told, but he was skinny."

"He hanged himself?"

Sayers nodded, taking another sip of coffee.

"Was he just a follower in this Republic of Colorado business?" I asked.

Sayers shook his head. "He was a pioneer, really. Until Herbert Gohannon, there had been common-law courts and there had been militias, and they often attracted the same people, but they were different, sort of like the church and the chamber of commerce in a small town. But the Gohannon case was the first around here where a court enlisted a militia member to carry out its judgments. Roswell Stark held a kangaroo court one night with a lot of his people there and at the end of it he issued execution warrants against Judge Comerford and Wanda Kersey—Wanda just because she'd done what her boss, the judge, told her to do. Then he told old Herbert, who was a captain in the militia, it was his job to carry out the warrant against Wanda Kersey."

"What about Judge Comerford?"

"Someone probably carried out the warrant against him, too, but I don't know who. Comerford didn't show up for his docket at the courthouse the day after the warrant was issued. He lived alone on his farm, and when they went out there to look for him they found the back door unlocked, the house empty, and the livestock unattended to. He never turned up, and neither did his body. The FBI investigated for months, but they could never prove anything. It was pretty heavy-handed, the way their agents treated some of the people out here, threatening them, trying to turn people against one another. You can see why they'd be bitter about the federal government."

I reflected for a minute. "This president, whoever he was, ought to have been prosecuted too, if he ordered the executions."

Sayers nodded. "Except when Gohannon was arrested, Roswell Stark disappeared. I don't believe the FBI ever found him, either. But here's a question for a former prosecutor like you—what about all the people who were there the night he pronounced the sentence and ordered it carried out?"

I thought about it. "That's not so clear, is it? They don't become conspirators just by being there."

"What if the president went around after pronouncing the sentence and asked every one of the people in attendance whether they agreed with the sentence and wished to see it carried out?"

"Did he do that?"

"That's what a lot of people have told me. It would be pretty effective at keeping people quiet, don't you think? Understanding that they could be prosecuted themselves if they spoke up?"

I opened my mouth, then shut it again. "Do you *know* some of the people who were there?" I asked.

He nodded. "So do you, probably," he said. "I'd guess some of them were here last night."

At first, the buzzing sounded like a distant and slightly melodious chainsaw, or so it struck me at the moment, but when it stopped and then started again I realized it was the electronic ring of a telephone. "Excuse me," said Sayers, and walked through the swinging door, leaving me alone in the kitchen. I could hear his low voice through the door, but not well enough to make out the words, so I was left to reflect on his last disclosure. Some of last night's solid citizens had been at this grotesque event?

Sayers's voice continued to drone through the closed door. My feet twitched with restlessness and I got up to look for a bathroom, wondering if there was one on this floor. A wooden door beside the stove was cracked open an inch or so, and I pushed it in experimentally. The room inside was no bathroom, but a small study with clerestory windows along the ceiling, evidently added some time after the house's original construction. The pleasant little room was paneled in light-colored wood and lined with books. There were a few more pots, some in a glass case, but my eyes were held captive by another rug, this one much smaller, hung on the wall over the desk. A stylized cornstalk-like figure occupied its central vertical length, but it was the six symbols distributed around the borders that arrested me. Swastikas, four of them black against a white ground, and two white against black. I closed the door quickly as I heard Sayers returning to the kitchen.

"Sorry," he said. "Where was I?"

Still stunned by what I had seen in the study, I shot out my next words in a harsh stammer. "S-so," I said. "Your common-law court here, and everyone who comes to it, is a con-, a continuation of what you yourself called a kangaroo court, run by some half-assed cracker despot who condemned an innocent woman to death and then recruited some pathetic fool to carry out the sentence?"

He narrowed his eyes slightly, and spoke slowly. "That's right," he said. I realized I had been hoping for a different answer, some explanation that would take away the bilious taste in the back of my throat, and restore my conviction that I was merely curious, not a credulous simpleton.

"So." In my confusion I waded in further. "You're no better than he is. Was."

He looked at me steadily, then picked the dishes up off the

table and started to rinse them in the sink. "If that's your judgment," he said. "Now perhaps you'd best go. I think I may have been mistaken about you. Anyways, I have some matters to attend to, not to mention I've got to get some seed into the ground now that the tractor's running again."

The dismissal stung more than I could think of any reason for. "What about Mariah, then?" I said combatively.

He looked at me over his shoulder, then turned to face me again, drying his hands on a towel. "I gather you don't see any way you can file this case against her father in good faith. Seems like that's the end of it, then. She's free to seek other counsel, if she wants to."

My head was beginning to pound again. "I'm going now," I said unhappily. "Thanks for the breakfast."

By the time I got home, the wind was working its way up to a big-time blow. I pulled the Saab into the garage, then walked around the front porch, where I found two days' worth of mail stuffed into the metal box. Among the usual unwelcome collection of bills, catalogs, and notices from real estate agents letting me know that they had *Just Sold* (!) a house in my neighborhood and were now available to meet all my real estate needs, I found a more eccentric and less classifiable envelope. The address was typed in uneven and broken letters that could only have come from one of that vanishing breed, a genuine typewriter. It was addressed to Ms. Cinda Hayes, Esq., Counselor and Attorney at Law. I unlocked the front door and shouldered my way through, meanwhile ripping open the letter, which before the Barbie episode I would have taken to be a whimsically intended message from some acquaintance. The contents, on a half page of cheap lined paper, did not disclose their source. They hovered somewhere between alarming and amusing, like a ransom note in an old black-and-white B movie, irregular cutout newsprint letters spelling out a piece of advice, to wit:

Miss Lucinda Hayes if you attend E-Town
on Sunday evening April 14 you will see and
hear something to your advantage

Then, in the upper right-hand corner, there was stuck, like a collectable misprinted postage stamp, a dim photograph of me.

There was no mystery about the photo. About a year ago, when our law firm's team—consisting of me, Tory, and Linda—won the team competition in a local footrace to benefit breast cancer research, we had our pictures in the paper. This shot of me had been clipped from there. And *E-Town,* the radio show that is broadcast live from the old Boulder Theater, is a fixture on the local cultural scene; I had been to see New Grass Revival there just a couple of months ago. But "something to your advantage"? I turned the paper over, looking for signs that it was just a clever advertising device, but it was definitely hand-produced; I could feel the minute ridges where the cutouts overlapped the page, and anyway there was that photograph. I put the flimsy document down on my kitchen table, undecided what to do about it, and checked my voice mail for messages. The only one was from Tory, left at ten thirty-two last night.

"Where are you, Cinda? Linda said you called while I was crashed. Some virus from hell attacked me about five o'clock, but it must not be too bad because I feel better already. Call me in the morning, okay? Unless you're out dancing all night, in which case call me in the afternoon."

I looked at my watch: two-thirty. Call Tory, shower, sleep. In reverse order, I decided, heading up the narrow stairs to the pleasures of bed—in this case, my puffy down comforter. The wind was rattling the chimney as I pulled the cover over my achy head and tumbled back down into the dark.

When I woke up, the wind had died. It was eight-thirty by the garish green numerals of my bedside clock, but the light outside the window seemed too bright for that hour. I slipped out from under the comforter and almost retreated again—the room was cold. So I burrowed through my disorganized closet until I came up with a flannel shirt, and pulled it on as I went over to look out the window. There, lying on the ground, I found the explanation for both the cold and the strange light: snow. Fluffy oversized flakes were still coming down like tiny kittens, and a couple of inches blanketed the ground. April 13. Snow. I sighed at this equivocal blessing of life in the Mountain State, and undertook another toss of my closet in search of some leggings. The ones I found were not my nice black ones, but a spruce green color that disagreed with the purple of the shirt. Oh, well. After drinking a large glass of water and noticing that my head didn't ache anymore, I sat on the edge of the bed and called Tory. This time it was she who answered.

"Cinda," she began after hearing my voice, "if I didn't know you better I'd suspect you of having been out on a very hot date."

"But you do know me better."

"Sometimes I wonder. What were you calling about?"

"I got a very strange piece of mail," I said cautiously.

"*E-Town*? Tomorrow night?"

"You got it, too?" This put a new complexion on it. "Did yours have your photograph on it?"

"Yeah. Linda's too. I mean Linda's had her photograph."

"Linda got it too?"

"Oh, yeah. Mine came yesterday, but hers didn't come until today. Mountain mail service, you know. When did yours arrive?"

"I'm not sure," I said, too quickly. "I, ah, forgot to check my mail yesterday, so by the time I got it today, both nights, I mean both days, were in there. In the mailbox." I didn't want to explain to Tory that I'd spent the night, however innocently, at Pike Sayers's house.

"What?" she said suspiciously.

"Tory, do you think there's anything, like, sinister about these?" I was thinking of the amputated Barbie, and realized I wasn't sure whether Tory even knew what Beverly had found when she opened the box.

She laughed. "Sure, Mouse, let's call the po-leece. You call and I want to listen—I'd like to hear how you explain the need for police protection. *Oh, pleeeze, officer, there's someone out who knows my name and address and he's got a big...big...pair of scissors.*"

This last was rendered in a shrill and, I had to admit, remarkably mouse-like voice, and it really pissed me off. I decided against saying anything about the doll. "Okay, then, I assume we're going."

"Of course we're going. We'll meet you there at six. Tickets available at the door."

"Do we even know who's going to be on the show tomorrow night?"

"Yes, we *even* know. Artemis DiCastro—she's hot—and some other act. Wait a minute, I got it." I could hear the rustle of paper. "Tetanus Booster."

"Get out. You made that name up."

"I am not, as the man in the newspaper says, making this up. Look, we need to go and find out what this something to our advantage is. Besides," she said piously, "it will be good for you to have some exposure to contemporary popular music."

"I listen to popular music!"

She made an explosive noise with her mouth. "Popular with cowboys and current and former residents of Dallas."

"Those are not the same, Tory," I said heatedly, but she had hung up.

The snow had stopped coming down some time during the night, much of which I had spent awake, thanks to the weekend's various bouts of fever-induced oversleeping. I didn't mind; I lay under the comforter reading *A Morning for Flamingos.* Robicheaux was deep into some heavy New Orleans mob merde. From time to time, I'd put the book down and imagine sitting with Sam at a little table outside the Cafe du Monde, drinking chicory coffee and eating beignets. I also thought occasionally of Mariah, sleeping in her little alcove in the Covington children's room, and of Sayers in his narrow bed. Those thoughts exuded an aura of unfinished business, but I put them aside for another time and turned back to Dave Robicheaux, wondering if he and Bootsie would get together.

Anyway, it had been a long night, and a chilly day, and Sunday evening I was feeling both cold and tired as I stood around on the sidewalk underneath the art deco marquee of the Boulder Theater, waiting for Linda and Tory to show up. I passed the time by scrutinizing faces, looking for anyone that might be connected to Pike

Sayers's common-law court or the Colorado Citizens' Republic, but recognized only Boulder acquaintances—university types, lawyers, my gynecologist. Pacing around, nodding to the people going in, I shoved my hands deeper into the pockets of Sam's leather jacket and wished I had taken the trouble to find my winter gloves. I was about to surrender the opportunity to learn something to my advantage in favor of going home and firing up my woodstove when I spotted Linda and Tory strolling toward me along the sidewalk, chatting happily and clad like Yuletide revelers in immense wool sweaters, mufflers, boots, and woolly caps. Spare me, I thought grumpily, Christmas being a season I don't care to experience more than once a year, if that.

We exclaimed greetings and bought our tickets, with much exchanging of currency and negotiating of minor debts thereby owed and paid. Inside, people were milling around, jockeying for the best sight lines from the sea of tables and chairs that covered the floor. "Here!" called Tory, and we nabbed a decent table in the center section. I settled into my chair and shrugged off the jacket, still grumpy, while Tory and Linda went around kissing and hugging various friends and generally working the room like a pair of aspiring officeholders. I looked around me nervously, still thinking our invitations might be connected to the broken doll and the Iron Cross, but all I could see was a cheerful noisy crowd of well-fed solid citizens.

The Boulder Theater, in the most recent of its many lives, is a large cabaret-style venue in a 1930s-era building just off the Pearl Street Mall. *E-Town* being an earnest and politically correct program in the manner of one of those mellow National Public Radio productions, the crowd here was mostly over thirty, despite the expected appearance of angry young woman Artemis DiCastro. Looking around, I counted only two instances of visible body piercing apart from the ear area, and a shocking number of the earring wearers confined themselves to one per side. On the other hand, this wasn't North Dallas: Way more men than women had ponytails. I felt a hand on my shoulder and turned to find Linda, who handed me a glass of wine and favored me with a brilliant smile before vanishing again. I sipped morosely at first, but the tart liquid seemed to dissolve my bad mood. By the time the lights blinked and everyone scurried to their tables, my hands had thawed out and I was happy to be there.

Tory and Linda slid back into their chairs just as Nick and Linda Forster, the couple who created *E-Town,* took the stage for introductions and an opening duet. Then they exchanged a few rounds of George-and-Gracie-type marital humor (Nick playing the Gracie role) before inviting us to give it up for the hottest new band in Colorado, the bitchin', fly, slammin', and altogether apocalyptic (pause) *Tetanus Booster!* The crowd didn't exactly go wild, and I guessed that few in the audience had heard of this band any more than I had. The heavy velvet curtains swung open to reveal, not the amped-up bunch of punkers I expected, but a sort of bashful-looking collection of five guys—one on drums, one bass, one banjo, and two guitars. They started to play an instrumental number and I realized they were a bluegrass band; after about two minutes I finally placed the melody as a jazzy version of "Devil's Dream." They were good; people stopped whispering and the room gradually acquired a charge. They played one other instrumental before the lead guitarist stepped to the mike. "This next number," he announced modestly, "is one I made up myself. I hope you like it." I could swear I knew that voice from somewhere.

It was a good song, although I only remember part of it:

She never stops saying, your taste isn't mine
I bring her a beer, her palate craves wine;
She won't eat catfish or crayfish or chili,
Barbecue's greasy, and bangers are really
Too coarse and too crude, like my hands on her body,
She says, wash my face, my mustache is spotty.

I smile and I wash and I lie,
I think to myself, by and by
I'll watch that girl eat humble pie,

I'll feed that girl sweet humble pie.
I swear to you, lady, before I die,
You'll beg me for more humble pie.

It wasn't the song that was the tip-off, although I was haunted more and more by the certainty that the voice was one I knew. It was his smile, both shy and sly, and the turn of his shoulders as he stepped back from the mike to acknowledge the applause, that did it for me. I turned to Tory, who was staring, similarly transfixed. We said it at the same moment: "Linc!"

We didn't even stay for Artemis DiCastro; as soon as Tetanus Booster left the stage (having won the enthusiastic approval of the *E-Town* audience), Tory and Linda and I fairly flew outside to the stage door in the alley. We were importuning a couple of very skeptical-looking security guards when Lincoln himself stepped out onto the sidewalk, assuring the guards we were okay.

"So," he said shyly, "you got my invitations?"

We hugged him all around and made a tremendous fuss over him, until one of the guards came back out to shush us, whereupon Linc escorted us into the tiny backstage area and made us issue whispered promises to be quiet. We watched and listened while Artemis sang her heart out, and the Forsters and some other guests horsed around. Toward the end, Artemis and Linc and the other members of Tetanus Booster joined everyone else on the stage for a genuinely fine rendition of, to my astonishment, "Stand by Your Man." Artemis took the lead and sang her butt off, and I had to make very threatening faces to get Tory and Linda to pipe down, as they displayed a truly inappropriate inclination to sing along.

Afterward, Linc introduced us to his fellow band members, who insisted that their names were Adam, Ben, Joe, and Hoss. They declined an invitation to go over to The James with us, telling Linc they'd see him the next day. So the four of us staggered the two blocks to the bar, slipping on the icy patches and interrupting each other with questions and explanations.

. . .

When I first met Lincoln Tolkien, six years ago, he was twenty-one, working as a waiter in a snotty private club in Denver and living with his parents, who still called him Sonny. At that time he was in a band called Perestroika Pogo Stick, but it was coming apart and he was desperate to get out of the club and, even more urgently, the parental home. We needed an investigator to help us on a Colorado Springs angle of the Jason Smiley case, so we hired him, and the work he did there was so good that he ended up with a permanent job doing investigation for some lawyer friends of mine in the Springs. We thought it was permanent, anyway.

"Well, let me ask you this," he said, over a mug of Fat Tire ale in the back room of The James. "When you go to the hairdresser and get a permanent, how long do you expect it to last?"

"I don't get permanents," I said, fingering my professionally neglected hair.

"Well, if you did," he said, scratching his ear, "you'd understand that eternity is not what it used to be. Temporary means two weeks. Permanent means two months. I was with Connor and Connor *forever.* They're great people and I loved the job, but I missed Boulder. And the Cartwrights—that's what their band used to be called—I knew them from back in the day, and they knew I was money so they looked me up when they needed a new lead guitar for their band. They were ready for a new name and a new sound, they said. So I came back to Boulder. I'm living in a house up on the Hill, with the Cartwrights and a bunch of other people. It's okay, except it's noisy. Oh, and one guy raises ferrets. They're a pain in the ass, always running around underfoot and chewing up on everything. One of them crapped in my guitar last week. Do you need any investigation done? Because I could, you know, use a spare gig. The music doesn't quite cover the tab."

"Money?" I said with bewilderment, but nobody heard me.

"Were you the one who sent us those ransom notes?" said Linda, batting her eyes at him like a besotted teenager instead of a thirty-something lesbian with two advanced degrees. Linc had always been one of her favorites.

He nodded. "Weren't they all that? I knew they'd get you here."

"All that?" I said.

Linc and Linda exchanged glances, but it was Tory who broke it to me. " 'All that' means good, Cinda," she said helpfully. "So does 'money.' But don't worry. Nobody expected you to know that. Linc," she added, "please remember who you're talking to here." Just because she's four years younger than I am.

"Whose idea was the name of the band?" I asked him. "Tetanus Booster, what a name."

"It was mine," he said happily. "We had sort of a contest. You should have heard some of the other entries. I actually liked the second-place entry better, but Adam, he's the manager, nixed it. Nocturnal Emission, don't you like that?" He looked dreamy and turned his beer glass bottom up. "So," he said, "got any work for me?"

"Not right now," I said, "but maybe before long."

"I might have some now," said Tory. "Why don't you come by the office in the next couple of days?"

"Sam's old place?"

I nodded.

"How is Sam the Man?" asked Linc. "Happy in the big city?"

"He's good," I said. "He's—he's money."

This time all three of them laughed out loud, and I knew I still didn't have it right.

SUMMER 1994

Law Is Our Fate

It was a month later that I got my first look at Harrison McKay's television campaign—a month in which I hadn't seen much of Mariah. I had met her at the Hygiene Cafe a couple of weeks after our swim in Clear Creek, and had been encouraged by her cheerfulness. We talked about the Covington children and their baby lamb and the way the warming days were already bringing up green shoots of corn in the fields. She was happy about having the Subaru, and told me that as soon as Craig Covington relined the brakes she was going to drive up to Rocky Mountain National Park for a hike. We didn't talk about the lawsuit at all, and I had the impression she had given up the idea. I knew she was seeing the new therapist I had found for her through the National Rural Health Association, and that she liked him. Beyond talking about that and her placid life at the Covingtons', she had seemed guarded but contented. For the last week or so I had been meaning to call to make a date to see her again, even though it didn't seem as though she were really a client anymore, but then I had gotten busy with a lot of estate planning business that had suddenly arrived in the office. The campaign commercial started me thinking of her again.

The ad was a montage of images, each more appealing than the last: McKay at the front of a classroom, earnestly answering a student's question; McKay walking to the podium of some banquet to receive an award, shining faces upturned to him as he mounted the steps; McKay in shirtsleeves, talking to workers outside a plant or mill of some kind. The lettering in the last images, against the background of a fluttering flag, spelled out "*Harrison McKay for the Senate: Whether or Not You're for Him, He's for You.*"

A clever permutation of the famous Kennedy line, I thought. The brief paid spot had not shown much about the content of his platforms, but then most don't. He actually looked like an appealing candidate, and he certainly didn't resemble a child molester. But then, most don't. I clicked off the television and decided I needed a run. Upstairs, I burrowed through a dismal basket of aging athletic apparel before finding a good pair of running shorts.

The light was fading, a good excuse for a short run. I'd been a less than faithful runner this spring, and the hill that leads up from Wonderland Lake to the open meadow was wicked, a living force out of some horror novel trying to suck all the breath from my heaving chest. I paused when I finally achieved the top, gasping and bending at the waist to recover. But a few minutes after starting up again, I found a rhythm. I looked down from time to time, careful of the trail's irregularities in the waning light. When I did, my white shoes flashed across my visual field on the stony trail, still marshy between the rocks from the meltdown of the weekend's snow. My mind flowed gently into the disconnected state that is one of the chief pleasures of running.

Why, I mused as I ran along and admired the peach-colored clouds, would Mariah McKay be able to remember the terrible automobile accident that took her mother's life when she was eight, but not whatever later event she associated with the white legs and her father? And would it be good for her to remember that event? Since meeting Martha Trefusis, I had read some books about recovered memory, and there was no doubt that many persons, mostly (as she had said) women, had made terrible accusations, destroyed their families, and finally damaged themselves irrevocably after becoming convinced on the basis of very flimsy evidence that they had been victims of childhood sexual abuse. In many of these books, it was asserted with confidence that the accusations were false, but I didn't know how anyone could be sure they were false, any more than they could be sure they were true. Still, nobody would wish to be party to such a destructive exercise if there were any serious doubt about what had happened.

Would Mariah's new therapist be able to find a key into her bewildering memories? My ex-husband Mike, an English professor, had once told me that Kafka said a book should be an ax for the frozen sea within us. I could still summon a memory of Mike sitting on the futon in our little house, demonstrating the concept with a sidehand chopping motion to his own chest. Would Mariah's sea ever break up, allowing her a look into the depths? I didn't even know whether I ought to hope so, for her sake. If so, what would be the ax, and who would wield it?

I reached the trail's intersection with Lee Hill Road, the mile-and-a-half marker, and turned around, surprised at how quickly I had gotten there. The turnaround interrupted my train of thought, and it took me a quarter mile to recapture it. How does memory work, anyway? The ink stain I could see on my thumb, for example—how had I gotten it? It had to be from today, because ink stains wear off in hours. When did I first notice it? I looked up at the fading sky, sure that I couldn't say, and then caught a floating mental picture of myself in my office in the early afternoon. The phone had rung; it had been someone from my law school calling, asking whether I would contribute to the building fund. I listened to her pitch, trying to be patient. A bee was buzzing against the outside of the office window, frantic to get in. I had said yes to the caller, wondering if I really could afford it, meanwhile trying to get rid of an ink stain on my thumb by rubbing my forefinger against it. The sun was slanting through the window, lighting up a sparse school of airborne dust motes and the pitted surface of my old wooden desk.

A memory. Retrieved, recovered, or constructed?

I was home. I slid off my running shoes and went inside for a shower and, later, a solitary omelette. I tried to call Mariah, but the Covingtons' line was busy from eight until I finally gave up at ten. After learning on the news that the weather was due to change, I was about to click off the set when McKay's commercial came on again. I watched more carefully this time. His eyes glowed with conviction and goodwill. He'll probably win this election, I thought.

The next morning, I was studying a book called *Colorado Estate Law,* and gradually realizing that I'd have to go downstairs for a jumbo latte soon if I was going to keep it up, when Tory swept in. Every piece of paper on my desk fluttered in the energy she broadcast as she passed through the threshold into my office and deposited herself onto the chair.

"Cinda," she said urgently, and I could tell it was serious. "I really need some advice about the Kellogg case. He's driving me crazy."

"The leprechaun?"

"I've decided he's more of a troll. The first thing is, every time we talk, he insists on coming into the office. Phones make him nervous, he says. He's here twice a week, like clockwork, bowing and scraping and calling Beverly darlin'."

"Is that a problem?" I asked. "I can't see Beverly hitting us up with a sexual harassment lawsuit because we forced her to tolerate the unwelcome endearments of a leprechaun."

"No, she loves the guy. It just makes me crazy. So finally I decide that I can save myself a little grief by sending Lincoln around to talk to him to find out about the lawyer who represented him when he was convicted of those tax crimes, see if we can gin up some ineffective-assistance argument."

"Sounds like a good idea. Is Linc on the payroll now?"

She shook her head. "Just hourly. Independent contractor stuff. So he finally finds Kellogg's cabin, which is like way up in the mountains west of Denver, East Cowlick or someplace. But

Kellogg, the jerk, refuses to talk to him. Says Linc doesn't have proper ID, which I guess is true since he just went to work for us and his only business cards say Tetanus Booster. But when Linc asks him to telephone me to confirm that I've sent him, the little dork won't do that either—says he and I have an understanding that we don't do business over the phone."

"What a pain. So you have to ask him to come back into the office?"

"When Linc left his house, he drove on to Denver and requisitioned the court records, so I think I'll just wait until they come. They're so old they have to come out of a warehouse somewhere, so it's a large PIB, but we've got a little time. Trial date isn't until September. What are you working on?"

I shook my head. "Not much. Looks like I might be building up a little wills and estates practice—I did one for my neighbors, and now they've sent me some other clients. It's not bad—yuppies who've made enough money that they need some planning to save estate taxes. And a lot of them seem to be worried about medical stuff—living wills, durable power of attorney. It's interesting." I could hear the lack of conviction in my own voice.

Tory made a face that suggested she'd gotten a whiff of sewer gas. "How can you stand that stuff?" she said. "Wouldn't you rather get back into court? You're a great trial lawyer, Cinda. Jeez, I can get you some DUI clients right away if you want. They're thick on the ground in this town."

I shook my head. "I'm not sure I'm ready for that. Suppose I get some guy off and then he goes and does it again and kills someone?"

Gigantic eye roll. "Haven't we been over this? The Constitution? Right to counsel and all? You do your job and the jury does its job?"

"Just give me a little time, Tory. Anyway, what advice did you want about Kellogg?"

"Oh." She nodded. "Just this. You said something about some research on whether a prior conviction can be attacked because of ineffective assistance of counsel under this felon-with-a-firearm law. Will you show me how to use that Westlaw program to look? It will save me a trip to the law school library; I always get a parking ticket there."

"Sure," I said, turning to the computer. "Hypatia and I will be glad to show you. What's the question again?"

"Suppose a guy is charged under the federal felon-possessing-a-firearm law. He has a prior felony conviction; he has a firearm. It looks bad. But maybe when he was convicted of the prior he didn't have a lawyer. Or he had an incompetent lawyer. Can he use that as a defense to the possession charge? Because if not, all this work I'm doing may be barking up the wrong tree. For a red herring."

"Please," I said. "Mangling metaphors is my job. Let's see what we can find." I double-clicked the mouse on the solemn-looking Westlaw icon. Stars began shooting and globes whirling. I logged us on and entered the client's name before being invited to choose a database.

"See?" I said. "It asks you what library you want to use."

"I don't want to go to any library," said Tory. "That's why I wanted to do the research this way."

"Listen," I said. "We're logged on, so we're paying for this. If you're going to be a smartass, it's going to take twice as long and cost twice as much. Now look at this list and tell me what library we want."

"Federal materials?" she said meekly.

"Right," I said. "So we double-click here. Then we want 'Cases and Decisions,' here. Shall we see if there are any Supreme Court cases?"

"Might as well," she said, so I clicked on that file, and watched while a box came up on the screen.

"Now, this is the artistic part," I said. "We have to put together some combination of words and phrases that will turn up a case if there is one. What would you suggest?"

"Uh, 'felon,' " she said. " 'Firearm.' 'Felon with a firearm law.' "

"The search only turns up a document if the court used those words in its opinion," I said, frowning, "but they're more likely to have referred to the law by its citation. Do you know it?"

"Eighteen United States Code, section 1202(a)(1)," she said promptly. I typed in "18 w/3 U.S.C. w/3 1202(a)(1)" and stared at the screen, thinking.

"What's that 'w/3' stuff?" said Tory.

"That means each of the search terms has to be within three words of each other in the document we're looking for. Now shall we add 'prior conviction' and 'counsel'?"

"Sure, go ahead. I'm lost anyway."

I added the words to the search request, using the "w/p" connector to specify that all the search terms should be found in the same paragraph of the document, then clicked on the "Search" box. The icons spun again for perhaps twenty seconds, then informed me that Westlaw had found one document satisfying my request. I asked to have it displayed and there it was: *Lewis v. United States,* decided by the Supremes on February 27, 1980.

Tory was looking over my shoulder with interest. The reporter's summary was the first thing to come up. "Uh-oh," she said. Nobody could ever accuse her of not being a quick study. I scanned the screen myself, then clicked for the next one, and the next. The good news: We efficiently discovered that the United States Supreme Court had decided the exact question that interested us. The bad news: It decided it the wrong way.

"Can you print this?" Tory asked, sounding dejected.

"Sure."

She pulled the first page out of the printer as it rattled out its last line, and read aloud from the reporter's summary at the beginning of the case. " 'Even though petitioner's extant prior state-court felony conviction may be subject to collateral attack under *Gideon v. Wainwright,* it could properly be used as a predicate for his subsequent conviction for possession of a firearm in violation of §1202(a)(1) of the Omnibus Crime Control and Safe Streets Act of 1968,' " she read. "We're dead, aren't we?"

I read it over myself and nodded. "You ought to read the whole case to be sure, but yeah, I'm afraid so. A conviction that could be attached under *Gideon* would be one in which the defendant didn't have any lawyer at all. If a conviction like that could be used to nail a guy for felon-with-a-gun, I'm sure a conviction where the guy just had a bad lawyer would get the same treatment. It's a fortiori."

"On the premise that a bad lawyer couldn't be worse than no lawyer at all?"

I nodded, then burst out laughing at the same moment Tory did. "I'm sure there's a lawyer joke in there somewhere," I said.

"Well, shit," said Tory. "Busted again. I don't know how I'm going to keep that little guy's ass out of the slam."

I reflected on this while signing us off Westlaw to avoid further charges. "Does he have any information the feds might want?" I asked when I was done. "Maybe you could work a deal."

She shook her head wearily. "This guy's NRA, remember? No chance he's going to rat out any of his buddies in the gun trade."

"What about all that tax protester stuff? Maybe the names of some of the other people involved in those scams?"

"Too long ago. Whatever happened back then, the statute of limitations will have run a long time ago. Unless it was homicide, and one thing I never heard of those tax crazies doing was murder."

I shrugged. "Throw himself onto the mercy of the court?"

Tory snorted briefly. "We're before Judge Mason. I've heard stories about his mercy. It looks like a large porcupine in a very bad mood. It's not the kind of thing you want to throw yourself onto."

The first of summer's lightning storms was lighting up the sky behind the foothills in shocking strobes when the phone rang that evening. I had put down my copy of *A Stained White Radiance* and gone out onto the front porch to watch the light show when I heard the first muted growlings of thunder, and for fifteen minutes or so I had really been enjoying the approaching storm. In a few more minutes, I would probably have started conducting, like Mickey Mouse's sorcerer's apprentice character in *Fantasia,* but for the summons of the ring. Damn telemarketers, I thought, annoyed at the interruption. The screen door banged behind me as I walked back into the house.

It was Mariah McKay, her voice wavering even more than ever. "Cinda," she said, "will you come see me?"

"Where are you, Mariah?" I asked. There were others talking in the background, as well as some Muzak-type music.

"Longmont United," she answered. I had to think for a moment about where that might be.

"In the hospital?"

"I guess I'm pretty sick," she said. "I sort of stopped eating for a while, then I ate too much. Way too much. Ginny and Craig got worried. I won't be able to do that here. They pretty much feed me out of a spoon every few hours."

"I'll be glad to come see you, Mariah," I said. "Does your therapist know you're in the hospital?"

"Sure. He's here. Hold on a minute." A deep voice spoke before someone covered the mouthpiece, and then there was a shuffling before it spoke again, this time directly into the phone.

"Hello, Miss Hayes. This is Andrew Kahrlsrud. Mariah would like to see you very much, if you can make the drive out here."

"Of course, I told her I would. Do you think I should come right now?" A brilliant flash illuminated the window.

"I think it would be a good idea. If it's not an imposition." There was a boom rather than a crack, but the lightning was definitely getting closer.

"Give me half an hour," I said. "What room number?"

"Three oh nine," he said, with what sounded mysteriously like relief. "Thank you."

The electrical storm ripped and crackled overhead as I drove out the Diagonal Highway toward Longmont. I had to circle the town a bit before finding the hospital, but even so the rain had not started falling when I pulled the Saab into the dark visitors' parking lot and dashed for the door. It rolled open for me silently on rubber-sheathed wheels and admitted me to the reception area, where the greenish fluorescent overhead lights crackled faintly in mimicry of the lightning outside. An attendant pointed me toward the elevator, in which I was compelled to listen to a ridiculously cheery version of "Eleanor Rigby" while being lifted to the third floor.

I found the room and let myself in quietly. Mariah lay under stiff sheets, an IV tube in the crook of her arm. The contours of her body barely lifted the white covers off the mattress, and her wrists and hands, the only bare skin I could see apart from her face, seemed the appendages of a bird rather than a woman. She turned her face away from the person who sat in the corner and toward me as I came across the threshold. Hot red circles mottled her cheeks, and her teeth seemed too big for her hollowed-out face as she smiled. I smiled back, trying hard to act as though I saw nothing amiss.

"Hey, Mariah," I ventured, my voice catching on some sticky place in my throat. "I'm sorry you're not feeling well."

The man in the chair rose and stepped forward as Mariah held her free arm out wordlessly so I could take her hand. The inanity of my last words made me self-conscious as I turned to him. "Hello," I said.

He nodded reassuringly, a large man in wire-rimmed glasses and khaki pants with a plaid flannel shirt tucked in over a big belly. A few gray hairs glinted in his reddish beard, but the tight curls on his head were all russet. "I'm Andy Kahrlsrud," he said, not extending his hand, seeing that mine was occupied by Mariah's grasp. "Mariah's therapist. I'm going to the cafeteria now, and I'd appreciate it if you would come down and find me there after you finish visiting with Mariah. Would you do that?"

"Sure." I nodded, concentrating on keeping Mariah's hand in mine. She had loosened her grip, perhaps out of fatigue, and I was afraid that if I tightened my own grasp I would crush the bones beneath the papery skin.

"Thank you for coming," she said hoarsely, the first words she had spoken since my arrival. "I guess I look pretty bad, huh?" Andy Kahrlsrud went quietly out the door, pulling it nearly closed behind him.

I let go of her hand long enough to slide out of my jacket,

then sat down on the edge of the hospital bed. "What happened, sweetie?" I asked.

She shook her head. "I don't even know how to explain it, Cinda. I've been seeing Andy for about a month, two times a week, you know? I really like him and I was just beginning to try to explain the thing to him—you know, the thing with my father?"

I nodded.

"Then," she continued, "I don't know why I did this, Cinda, it's so awful. The Covingtons went out one night with their kids to a birthday party for a neighbor, and I said I didn't feel well and wanted to stay in, so they left me in the house. I was a little hungry so I made some dinner, and then I was still hungry so I made something else, and then I just started eating things right out of cans. I drank a half gallon of milk even though that meant there wouldn't be any for the kids' breakfast. I was"—here her brimming eyes overflowed, dampening but not quenching the angry spots on the skin below—"I was completely out of control. Then I had to get rid of all the stuff I had eaten, so . . . I'm so ashamed, Cinda."

"Shh," I murmured. "Shhh." I tried to comfort her by rubbing her shoulder, distracted again by the sheer absence of any palpable soft tissue between bone and skin.

"I clogged up their plumbing, Cinda," she said, eyes frightened as a rabbit's behind the wash of tears. "They came home and found me trying to clean up. Then I guess I fainted, and hit my head." She raked the lank hair back from her brow and I saw a patchy abrasion there, just inside the hairline. "They got disgusted with me. Who wouldn't? They threw me out. I don't blame them."

"Threw you *out!*" I was breathless with indignation. "You mean just put you out of the house?"

"I had your car, remember? They gave me some coffee after I woke up, but they said they couldn't trust me around their kids anymore. Not to mention I had eaten up a week's worth of groceries. They loaned me a suitcase for my things, and I drove over to the judge's house. I stayed there that night, and the next day he called Andy for me. Andy said I needed to be here, except I didn't have any health insurance, but the judge made it okay somehow. I'm scared, Cinda."

I nodded, thinking of the bedroom with the cabbage rose wallpaper and the double wedding-ring quilt. "I'm so sorry, sweetie. What can I do?"

"Talk to Andy," she said, her head turning sideways on the pillow. "I'm so tired," she added needlessly, and closed her eyes.

I sat quietly for a moment, studying the lines at the corners of her eyes and mouth, marks that no nineteen-year-old should bear. Then I rose as slowly and gently as I could. Mariah did not stir; her breathing was quiet but not, it seemed to me, very regular. I lifted the chart that hung at the end of her bed and took it with me over to the corner chair, shifting the gooseneck lamp so it shone on the top page.

MARIAH SUZANNE MCKAY/ F/ DOB 8-5-74
ADMITTED: 6-9-94

DIAGNOSIS:
DSM III, Axis 1:
1. Anorexia nervosa, 307.10;
2. Bulimia nervosa, 307.51;
3. Major depression, recurrent, 296.33;

Secondary:
1. Severe malnutrition
2. Severe digestive ulceration
3. Heart murmur

I carefully replaced the chart and went to join Andy Kahrlsrud in the hospital coffee shop.

It had been a long time since I had seen Jell-O, but that's what he was eating at a table by the window, putting garish yellow cubes into his mouth with a thoughtful expression as he read from a thick book that lay on the table beside the bowl. But then, the choices in a hospital cafeteria that time of night are limited, as I discovered when I looked for something for myself. I brought my cup of coffee over to the table and sat down opposite him. He looked up from the thick book and pushed his glasses up on his nose.

"She looks awful," I said. "How bad is it?" Just then the lights went down by half, either from the storm still gathering outside or because the cafeteria was closing.

"She almost died," he said flatly. "Would have died if a friend of hers hadn't brought her here this morning."

"Pike Sayers."

He nodded. "You know him?"

"I've met him. Was it some psychological crisis that brought her to this?"

He pushed the empty bowl away and looked around. There was nobody else in the darkened cafeteria except for the cashier whom I had paid for the coffee. She was stuffing bills and coins from the register into a zipper bag; it must have been closing time.

Andy Kahrlsrud reached into his breast pocket and brought out a carefully folded paper, which he handed to me. "I have the original in her file, of course. This is a copy you can keep."

It wasn't easy to read in the bruised half-light, but I could see that it was a standard release, authorizing Andrew N. Kahrlsrud, Ph.D., to disclose to Lucinda Hayes anything he had learned in the course of his treatment of Mariah S. McKay. Mariah had signed it and dated it today.

When he saw that I had read it, Kahrlsrud nodded and addressed himself to my question. "I could be wrong, I suppose, and I have considered the possibility that I'm trying to spare myself the knowledge that something our therapy stirred up may have led to this, but I don't think it has much to do with that. Mariah has been killing herself with food for a long time, starving, then bingeing. Her body is completely depleted from the way she's abused it. Her electrolyte levels are off the charts, but even after that's remedied here in the hospital, she may have done permanent damage to her heart. Her teeth are badly decayed from the purging—vomit is extremely acidic, and damages the enamel. She has an incipient stomach ulcer. She's a very sick young woman."

I thought of all the times I'd watched her starve, and was ashamed. "She told me not long ago that she'd stopped throwing up," I said indistinctly.

He nodded. "Almost all bulimics deny it. Sometimes they're proud of their ability to starve themselves, but purging is a matter of intense shame. I suspect she's been doing this on and off for years, most of the time trying desperately to stop."

I looked toward the window. Fat drops of rain were beginning to splatter the pane. "What's going to happen to her?"

"A lot depends on you, and on Mr. Sayers. She refuses to have anything to do with her other family. Somehow her sister learned she was here and came to see her this afternoon, but feeble and scared as she was, Mariah wouldn't talk to her. Called the nurse and told her to show her sister the way out. Pretty stubborn."

"What does Sayers have to do with this?" I asked, the phrase "other family" lingering in the air so palpably that I wanted to wave it away. "What do you know about him, anyway?"

Andy Kahrlsrud was silent for a long moment, and held up a hand for more time when I started to speak again, so I fell silent myself. Finally, he said carefully, "Sorry, I just needed a moment there. I see a lot of clients from eastern Boulder County, Lucinda. A lot of distressed farm families, displaced agricultural workers, even some worried bank employees and teachers who live with the consequences of the destruction of the farm economy. A lot of my clients know Pike Sayers, and I've heard a lot about him over the last couple of years. I just needed a minute to sort out what I know that I can tell, and what I know from confidential sources."

I nodded. "I understand."

Another pause, briefer this time. "I think all I can tell you right now is that he's offered to make a home for Mariah when she gets well enough to be discharged, and that he's paying for her hospitalization. She doesn't have any insurance, of course.

She's very lucky to have someone who cares for her that much, but I'm not sure it will be enough. She looks up to you a great deal and still hopes that you will be willing to represent her in this action she wants to bring against her father. She has a lot of issues about her family, as I'm sure you appreciate—abandonment, rivalry, grief. We're working on those, but at the moment her issue is survival. It's always going to be a struggle for her—there doesn't seem to be a cure for the kind of intense eating disorder she suffers from. I don't think it would be in her interest to try to mend fences with her father and sister just now, and I'm suspicious about their motives for wanting to. So—along with a place to live and some basic support, Mariah needs a reason to get better, to stay well. The Covingtons were pretty limited in their ability to understand her needs and tolerate her dependence—they have worries of their own, and after all they were looking for a nanny, not a patient. But at least there she felt she belonged, and she was very attached to their children. I'm worried about what kind of attachment or hope will replace that, now that it's gone."

I wondered if I ought to offer to let Mariah come live with me. I thought of my cherished small house and the grateful way I occupied every square foot of it; the idea of sharing it with someone was unthinkable. "What can I do?" I asked humbly, praying *not that, not that.*

Kahrlsrud leaned back in the flimsy chair and rubbed a hand over his round belly, exactly as if he had just eaten a Thanksgiving dinner instead of a bowl of radioactive-looking gelatin. Meanwhile, he studied my face so intently I had to resist the impulse to turn away. "Tell me," he said eventually, "about the lawsuit. Mariah said you told her it wasn't a good idea to go ahead with it now, even if that meant it would be impossible to file it later. Is that true?"

"Yes," I said. "That is true."

"Why?"

So I told him about Martha Trefusis and her remark, and about the day I had taken Mariah out to Clear Creek to the site of her mother's death. "Frankly, Dr. Kahrlsrud, it scared me. I realized she was in a lot worse shape than I thought, and I knew she needed you, or someone like you, more than she needed a lawyer and a lawsuit."

He nodded. "Will you call me Andy, please? And was that the only reason?"

"No," I said. "Far from it. The main problem is that she doesn't remember enough to even allow me to file a valid complaint. Remembering that something bad happened and it involved your father and some white legs isn't sufficient grounds for a lawsuit. And then there are some of the people she's mixed up with. Forgive me, Andy, if I'm insulting you or some of your friends, but I think it's possible that some of the militia people in Pike Sayers's community have an ulterior motive in encouraging Mariah to sue her father, no matter what it costs her."

"What would that motive be?" He removed his glasses and untucked his shirttail enough to allow him to wipe the lenses with it.

"Well, he's running for the state senate. I don't know exactly what his platform is, but it doesn't seem to me it's likely to encompass the freedom to own machine guns, discrimination against people of color and Jews, or the idea that the federal government is a giant criminal conspiracy."

Andy set his glasses back on his face with a bemused look. "What gave you the idea those are the predominant politics among her acquaintances?"

"I have reasons," I said darkly.

"When does the statute of limitations run out on any claim she might have?" he asked.

"That's not an easy question. It's possible a genuine failure of memory could extend it. But if there's going to be a complaint filed, the safest thing would be to file it before her next birthday. It's in August, I believe. Listen, what about this recovered memory business? What do you think about it?"

He turned over the book he had been reading when I arrived and pushed it toward me so I could see the title: *The*

Recovered Memory Controversy, edited by Martha Trefusis and Nora Demonica. "I believe in it, but I've been reading the skeptical literature lately, too."

"And?"

"And I don't know. Trefusis's experiments are very interesting—have you heard about them?"

"Better than that. I had a demonstration." And I told him about the red barn that I remembered but hadn't seen.

"Yeah." He nodded, scratching his chin beneath the beard. "Makes an impression, doesn't it? But it occurs to me that everything she says about the hazards of relying on memory applies just as well to ordinary memories as it does to recovered memories. Like that red barn. Did you have the feeling that you had at one point forgotten about the barn, then later remembered it?"

"No," I said. "My experience was that there was a barn and that I knew it from the first moment I saw it. The only problem was that I never had seen it. It was some kind of—of retrospective illusion."

"There, you see? Most of her work suggests that we ought to be very suspicious when anyone tells us that he remembers something, because he could very well be wrong. Whether or not the memory was ever lost and then recovered. And maybe she's right. But how much evidence could we ever receive in a courtroom or anywhere else if we declared that memories were too fragile to be relied on, and that nobody is allowed to testify to what he remembers?"

"Not much," I said, thinking. "Not any, in fact. Testimony always consists of someone stating what he remembers. Or what he believes, but that's about the same thing."

"See, that's my point. If we're going to have a justice system—and every civilized society does—it is going to have to rely heavily on people's memories. Without memory there's nothing—no history, no culture, no justice. That doesn't mean memories can't be disputed sometimes, and aren't sometimes wrong. But you can't ban them as evidence of what happened—there is literally no alternative. At least not until we institute universal all-points surveillance, heaven forfend, and replace trial by memory with trial by videotape."

"Trefusis told me that the worst cases of false memory occur when someone is hypnotized or given some kind of truth drug."

Kahrlsrud nodded. "I agree with her there. Those techniques make someone very suggestible, and there's a good chance that in such a state the client will remember what the therapist wants him to remember, whether or not it really happened—childhood sexual abuse, or a past life, or a satanic ritual. The therapist may not even realize how much he wants the client to come up with certain material that confirms the therapist's own beliefs, and he may be sure he's not suggesting anything—but he is."

"So I take it that you're not using any of those techniques in your therapy with Mariah."

"That's right. I'm not. And I'm working real hard on not forming any theories about what happened. But even so, I believe there was some event that she's struggling to remember, Lucinda, and I think it had the features that keep haunting her—her father's involvement, the white legs, trying to see and not being able to. Something scary and hard for an eight- or ten-year-old to understand."

"Do you think it's necessarily something sexual?" I asked. "I mean, is it clear her father committed some wrong that would be actionable, even if she could remember it?"

He shrugged. "The only clue, really, is the white legs. Mariah's own sexual behavior in adolescence and early adulthood included some deviance—promiscuity, and some acts of prostitution. But there was a cultural and economic context for them and I can't be sure they were pathological, much less that they resulted from a childhood event. Same for the eating disorder. Anorexia and bulimia are, unfortunately, pretty prevalent, even among young women who've never experienced any sexual abuse. But the legs, the shocking quality they seem to have for her—I don't know. Can you think of an explanation that doesn't have some sexual component?"

I thought, then shook my head. "Only some really implausible ones: someone being hung upside down, cartwheels. But what about the circumstance that she's apparently lost the memory, or some of it? Is it really possible to forget something and then remember it later?"

"It's a very common human experience. Haven't you ever?"

"I guess," I said. "Do you think she's ever going to remember more, Andy?"

He nodded. "I do. I think she's going to, if we can get her eating and keep her alive. But she needs something to look forward to. Everyone does. Tell me more about this statute of limitations business. You said she didn't remember enough for you to file a complaint now. Is there a way to keep the possibility of a lawsuit alive until she remembers more?"

"I don't know," I said. "The trouble is that the law isn't very clear on this point. I'm afraid that if we don't file by her birthday, a judge might say the statute of limitations ran out on that day because she did remember that something had happened and that it involved her father. Even though that much memory might not be sufficient to allow me to draft a valid complaint."

"That's not very fair, is it?" said Andy Kahrlsrud.

"No," I said. "It's not. The law often isn't."

He turned the plastic spoon with which he had eaten the Jell-O over in his hands, as though inspecting it for defects. "Isn't it your job to make the law work for your client?" he said softly.

"If there's a way, it is. I'm not sure there is a way." Just then his beeper sounded, a mild but insistent electronic summons.

"Everyone says you're an excellent lawyer," he said, reaching for the black box attached to his belt. "I know you can find a way. And it would give Mariah something to be involved in. Something to live for." He squinted at the beeper in the poor light, seeming to register recognition.

"Everyone?" I said.

"Mariah," he replied. "And some of her friends. Now I've got to go. May we stay in touch?"

"Sure," I said with more confidence than I felt, and I dug out a business card to give him. "Do I remember right that you're not allowed to do forensic work? I mean, you wouldn't be able to testify. Would you?"

"If you can work the other out, I'll work that out. Okay?"

"Okay," I said, uncertain whether I had agreed to something.

According to the radio announcer, it was already seventy degrees by the time I turned the Saab onto Broadway and headed for the office the next morning. A few white clouds drifted and morphed across the unquenchable blue canvas of the sky, but you could tell there was no more rain in the offing. Only sunshine and breeze and the intoxicating air of the Rockies—a day to make anybody giddy. Which it already had, in the case of a wild-haired Rollerblader who skated alongside me on the sidewalk for a couple of minutes before putting on a burst of speed, making a hard left turn, jumping the curb, and streaking across the street in front of me. He then jumped up the opposite curb and glided into the parking lot of the Ideal Market—the Boulder equivalent of beating the train to the crossing, I suppose. He disappeared with a flash of legs, leaving my heart jamming as though I'd just finished the Georgetown to Idaho Springs half-marathon. Nothing like a little cardiovascular workout before work in the morning.

Not to neglect the importance of mental exercise, provided this morning by the personalized license plate on a red BMW that cut in front of me at Broadway and Pine: KPASAMD. I would never have figured it out if I hadn't seen the Bugs Bunny doll hanging from the rearview mirror, chewing on a carrot. Ready for the day after these two workouts, I bounded up the back stairs to the office.

Beverly was looking rather flushed herself, although it could have been due to the very pink silk blouse she wore. She was sitting at the reception desk peering into a compact mirror when I came in. "Oh," she said girlishly, folding up the little case quickly. "Good morning, Cinda."

"What's up, Beverly? You look like the cat that ate the kittens. Have you rustled up some new clients for us?"

"Just the same old ones, I guess," she said. "And I believe you mean the canary."

"Whatever," I said. "What old ones, anyway? We don't have any old ones."

"Well," she suggested, tucking a piece of hair delicately behind her ear, "there's Mr. Kellogg. He's in with Tory."

"Ah," I said. "And I suppose he gave you the usual treatment—hand-kissing, darlin'-calling, flattery."

"He did say this color looked lovely on me," she confessed.

"And so it does, darlin'."

She shook her head. "No dice, Cinda. It's not the same when you do it. Anyway, Linc's here, too. In your office. He's studying or something."

"You're kidding. Studying what?"

She shook her head, disclaiming knowledge. "And now, if you'll excuse me, I've got some work to do." She turned to her computer and began tapping the keys industriously.

Linc was sitting behind my desk reading the newest copy of *The Colorado Lawyer.* "Hey, Linc," I said. "What did you do to your hair?" Its usual dark gloss had been replaced with a dull, roughed-up texture, and it was separating into small coils.

"I'm trying to do dreads, what do you think? It's not that easy, though. You can't wash it, and it gets real itchy." He gave me a demonstration, sending a small shower of flakes onto the desktop surface. "Oo, sorry, Cinda."

"So what brings you here, champ? Not that I'm not delighted to see you."

"I need your advice," he said earnestly, surrendering the desk chair and motioning me to it. "Career advice."

"I think if you keep writing songs like 'Humble Pie' you've got a real future," I said, sitting in the chair while he moved over to lean against the window.

"Naah," he said, rolling *The Colorado Lawyer* into a cylinder and whapping it against his thigh. "The music business is too crazy. It's a good hobby, but for real work I was thinking of something more like what you and Tory do."

"Law school?" I said in surprise. "You'd put yourself through that? It's not much fun, Linc."

"I was thinking maybe start with paralegal training, see how it goes."

"That might be a good idea. But isn't it expensive to go to those paralegal training schools?"

"Yeah, it's a bitch," he said. "That's why I was thinking maybe you and Tory could sort of point me at some things to read, like an independent study course or something."

"Sure," I said. "We could do that. You could start with some of the stuff we have here in the library. We could make a list that covers the basics. And I'll teach you to do computerized legal research—that'll be easy for you. The cyberspace generation and all."

"Cool," he said. "Thanks! Now I also have to ask you, do you have any work for me? I copied that old court file on the Kellogg guy and gave it to Tory this morning. About the time I do, he shows up and starts flirting with Beverly and Tory, and telling me I'm a *very foin lad.* I guess he's in there with Tory now. Anyway, that's done and I could use some more work."

"I don't know," I said. "Business is pretty slow here, Linc. I don't think, unless..."

"Unless what?" he said eagerly. "Anything, just let me do it."

"You want to use the PI skills you picked up in the Springs? See what you can find out about someone?"

"Word! Who's the someone?" He reached for a notepad.

I told him about Harrison McKay while he scribbled maniacally. "There should be tons of stuff on this guy," he said. "Academics are so easy, it's unbelievable. Every time they sneeze, they save the Kleenex and find someone to publish it and put it on their curriculum vitae."

I laughed.

"You laugh," he said seriously, "but it's true. So I can find copies of all the articles and books he's published, no problem."

"Actually, I already have his CV. It's in here somewhere." I pointed to the stack of paper at one corner of my desk.

"Good, I'll start with that. I'll see where his work has been cited, and by whom. Then I'll do a news database search, too, come up with any time this guy's ever been mentioned in a newspaper or magazine. So what's this guy supposed to have done?"

I told him about Mariah.

"Poor kid," he said, when I got to the part about her being hospitalized. "Should I go talk to her about her father?"

"I don't think so," I said. "Better for her to talk to her therapist about that stuff, and then he'll tell me anything that's useful. But she might like to meet you, now that you mention it. She could use some new friends right now."

"So—just go chill with her? That doesn't sound like work."

"It could be harder than you think," I said. "She's really sick, and even after she gets better I don't know how easy it would be to befriend her."

He made a small gesture with his hands, eloquent as sign language: *What's the problem?*

"Okay, then," I said. "And you could also keep your eyes and ears open and tell me about anything you come across that might help her case, if we ever file it."

"Don't you have to decide pretty soon?" he asked.

"Yeah," I said. "We do."

He shook out his shoulders, as though preparing for some undertaking. "Should I go see her today, in the hospital? Tetanus Booster doesn't have any gigs until the weekend, so I'm free."

"Sure," I said. "I'll call her and tell her you're coming. When you're done, phone in and tell me how she's doing; see if you can talk to her doctor and find out how long she's going to be in there. And keep your eyes out for a tall rancher-looking guy named Sayers, who's going to take her to stay at his house when she's discharged. Be nice to him, tell him who you are, but let me know if you learn anything interesting about him."

"Fresh," he said. "I'm outta here, then. Can I take a couple of your law books to study?"

I waved my hand. "Anything you want."

After Linc had left, I called the number that Andy Kahrlsrud had given me for Mariah's room and she answered on the second ring. She sounded tentative but less exhausted than she had the night before.

"How are you feeling, sweetie?" I said.

"I'm okay, Cinda. They made me eat so much breakfast! Two pieces of toast *and* eggs."

"You'll get used to it," I assured her. "That's just normal eating, even though it seems like a lot to you."

"I have to write down every time I pee."

"Well, that sounds like a nuisance. Listen, Mariah, I'm sending a friend of mine out there. Lincoln's his name. He wants to meet you."

"He does?" She sounded confused. "Why?"

"He, ah, just does," I lied. "I was telling him about you and he said you sounded like an interesting person, and he was going out that way anyway and so I told him to drop by." I winced as I realized how unconvincing this sounded. "He'll probably be there in a little while."

"Is he a lawyer, like you?"

"No, he's actually a musician, but he's thinking of studying to be a paralegal. He does a little work for me and my partner from time to time."

"Okay, I guess it might be nice to meet someone new. This isn't like a blind date or anything, is it?" She actually had a bit of a giggle in her voice. "Because I don't really look very good right now."

"No, it's not anything like that. Anyway, he's not looking his best lately, either. Just ignore the hair. And the dandruff. It's temporary, I'm sure."

"Cinda? I think I remembered something else."

"What's that, honey?"

A long silence, during which I realized what she must have meant.

"You mean you remembered something about what happened?"

"I think so." The voice was smaller now, shrinking perceptibly with each word.

"When are you going to see Andy again?"

"He said he would come here every Tuesday and Friday as long as I'm here. So, tomorrow, I guess?"

"Tell him, okay? And then we'll talk about it after you've told him." I was afraid of her memories now, afraid she was growing them like a prize crop to offer me as a basis for a lawsuit, a friendship, a life. Andy had to be wiser than I was about sorting this stuff out.

"Cinda, one more thing? My doctor here told me that I almost died from not eating right. Like, I could die any time, you know?"

"Oh, baby, we're not going to let that happen."

"But just in case? Will you make a will for me?"

Something from a pamphlet I had once read about suicide jumped into my memory, a list of signs about which one ought to be concerned: *Gives away valued possessions.* I tried hard to keep my voice casual. "Why don't you talk to Linc about it? Tell him what you have in mind. He's like, my paralegal assistant, you know."

"Good, I will. Bye, Cinda."

I hung up slowly, wondering what possessions Mariah McKay might have that were valuable enough to bequeath, even in her own mind.

"I thought you were never going to get off." It was Beverly, standing in the door with a pink message slip in her hand. "He held on for several minutes, waiting. But long distance from New York, you know? I told him you'd call him back, but he had to go to court. So he left this message."

She didn't have to say whom she meant. Beverly had worked for Sam before he left, and while she was loyal to her no-account husband and eccentric son, and a small hand-kisser-type guy with a funny accent might turn her head from time to time, as far as she was concerned there was only one real man in the universe.

"So, how is The Man?" I said, trying not to show how much I wanted that message slip.

"Misses Boulder, I guess," she said airily, and handed me the slip.

Beverly had very neat handwriting.

Big trial just settled, city getting too hot,
frequent-flyer miles burning hole in pocket,
arriving DIA Friday 3:30. Free for dinner
Fri. eve. abt. 7:30? SH

"Did he mention," I said to Beverly nonchalantly, "how long he would be staying?"

She reached over to take back the slip and studied it as though the answer might be written. Then she held it up against the open door and wrote a few more words on it before silently handing it back:

P.S. Must leave again Sunday night (unless gets better offer)

"That part in the parentheses, B," I said. "Did he say that, or is that your editorial comment?"

"You figure it out, Cinda," she said, before sweeping grandly back out to her desk. A few minutes later, I could hear her simpering like mad out there; the leprechaun had emerged. I tried to ignore their talk and get back into *Colorado Estate Law,* but the book had disappeared. After a brief exasperated search, I gave up and went to ask Beverly if she had seen it.

"...and to think that some lad would fail to appreciate the luck that would secure him the companionship of such a flower as yourself," or some such speech, was flowing out of Seamus Kellogg's mouth. Tory was standing next to Beverly; if a face could look like an itchy trigger finger, hers would have. Perhaps the prospect of adding my irritation to hers finally propelled him out the door, for he gave a courtly little bow, said, "Until next time, then, ladies," and departed.

"Can I talk to you?" Tory said, her jaw rigid, turning to return to her office.

"Sure," I said. "Be right there." And then, to Beverly, "Have you seen our copy of *Colorado Estate Law*?"

"Not unless it's one of the books Linc took with him. He had a couple under his arm when he left; said you'd told him it was okay."

"I bet you're right, that's where it went. Thanks." I headed for Tory's office.

"Sheesh," said Beverly, apparently apropos of Tory's bad mood.

"He's not so bad," I said as I entered, closing the door behind me. But it was not Kellogg's oily charm that had gotten under Tory's skin.

"He totally refuses to consider pleading guilty!" she said heatedly. "And he has absolutely no defense!"

"So," I said, "you have to go to trial without a defense. It's not like you'd be the first defense lawyer ever to be in this predicament."

"We'll lose!" she protested, running her fingers through her curly hair and shaking it into even more extreme disarray. "I've never lost a trial yet, damn it!"

I shrugged, eloquently, I hoped.

"Cinda! It's not just my ego at stake here. This is a guy who could end up serving a lot of years in federal prison because he's so damn stubborn."

"How good a deal are they offering?" I asked. "I mean, wouldn't he go to prison either way?"

"Maybe. For a while. But not nearly as long as if he goes to trial. And he acts like he's completely unconcerned about this prospect. Which is really dumb in his case because he's been through this before. He could have gotten a good deal on those old tax charges if he'd just agreed to pay up and plead to a misdemeanor. Then he could have owned as many guns as he wanted. But *noo*—he had to go to trial, and find some incompetent nutcase of a lawyer to argue that all those whacked-out things he put on his income tax returns, about federal reserve notes not really being money and like that, were really right. That the federal income tax laws were *unconstitutional.*" She waved toward a stack of paper on her credenza—must be the old court file Linc had copied.

"I thought the Sixteenth Amendment to the Constitution created the income tax."

"Cinda, that's my *point!* The lawyer was either completely incompetent, or some kind of ideologue. And now Kellogg wants an encore, only starring *me*—wants me to go into this felon-with-a-gun trial and do the same thing—argue about the Second Amendment and the right to bear arms and I don't, I don't know what else. Shit!" she concluded.

There didn't seem to be much I could say. I left her slumped in her chair, staring gloomily out the window. As I crept by Beverly's desk, I leaned over and whispered, "Let's give Tory a little space just now."

She nodded, not looking up from whatever she was doing. "Acres."

Sam insisted that I didn't need to go pick him up at the airport; he'd made a reservation on the Boulder Airporter. It turned out to be a good idea, as I used the extra time to clean up my house a little. I got around to almost everything, but never did clear off the tottery stack of books, magazines, and newspapers that cluttered my bedside table, just straightened them out a bit around the edges.

The limo let him off at my front door around six o'clock on Friday. For some reason, neither the margaritas that we drank at Zolo's, nor the dinner, nor the couple of hours that we spent in my bed afterward, put us to sleep. After midnight we were still awake, taking turns giving each other back rubs and talking desultorily about old friends of Sam's with whom he had lost touch.

"Sandy Hirabayashi?" he said. "She still with the public defender? Oh, that's good. A little farther down." The big muscles alongside his backbone shifted and flexed under my hands. Heat poured off his body and I felt warm despite the cool air of the room and the fact that I was wearing only a pair of bikini panties.

"Yeah, she is," I said as I pressed harder. "Got promoted to deputy chief of the appellate section not too long ago, but I think she'll apply for a judgeship one of these days. She may get it, too. She's really good."

"What about you?" he asked. "Did you ever aspire to be a judge?"

"No," I said. "I'm not sure why, but no. Doesn't appeal to me at all. Lately I'm not even sure I want to be a lawyer, except I don't know what else I could do. Masseuse, maybe?"

"You're good at that," he allowed. "But you're a great lawyer. Why would you give that up?"

"I don't know. Things get to me, I lie awake at night. Like this McKay case. Here's this young woman, I think she probably was harmed in some way by her father, and the statute of limitations is about to run on her claim, but she doesn't remember enough for me to prepare a complaint and file it in time. I can't figure out any way to file a claim before her birthday, or any way to ensure that she doesn't lose her claim if I don't. It doesn't seem fair, and I keep thinking a really good lawyer would be able to find a way around it, but I haven't."

Sam rolled over onto his back and looked at the ceiling. The candle beside the bed flickered as he flapped the sheets. "Sit right there," he directed.

"Again? So soon?"

"I just like to keep it warm. Helps me think better."

I shrugged and followed his instructions. Maybe it worked, because a few seconds later he said, "What about this? Take this uncertainty and put it off onto McKay. File a complaint that recites what she *can* remember and asks for relief in the alternative. Either he agrees not to move to dismiss, and to respond to the complaint in its vague and inadequate form, or he agrees to an extension of the statute of limitations until she remembers enough that an adequate complaint can be filed. Say that a refusal to order one or the other might deprive her of a claim without due process of law."

I looked at him in amazement. "Could that possibly work? I never heard of anything like that."

"Isn't that what creative lawyering is about? Doing things nobody's ever heard of before? Your problem, Cinda, is that you were a prosecutor for too long, where the emphasis is on dotting every i and crossing every t, and never pushing the envelope. Which is as it should be—we don't want people out there thinking of creative ways to put other people in prison. But you're in a different world now. Why not try it? Worst case is it gets dismissed, and then you haven't lost anything but your time, which you say you've got plenty of right now."

I reflected for a moment, drumming my fingers on his bare chest. "But what if he says okay, go ahead? We're still in trouble, because Mariah has to remember enough to testify to what happened by the time we get to trial."

"Sure," he conceded, catching my fingers with his own. "But how long does it take to get a civil case to trial around here? A year at least, isn't it? Seems like that gives the girl a chance to work on her memories with this therapist. Anyway, I bet McKay wouldn't go for that choice, he'd go for the other. He's got every reason to put his daughter's claims off, to agree to extend the statute for a while. Maybe it will all go away, would be his thinking, and in the meantime he just wants to get past this election. Of course, you'd have to agree to keep it all quiet, because any publicity before the election would destroy that incentive."

"I have to think about this, but it might be a great idea. You're amazing, you know that?"

"I hate it that you just love me for my mind."

"Only after I've used up your body. Listen, are you thirsty? I'm going to get some ice water out of the kitchen. Shall I get you some?"

"Sure," he said, pulling my face to his for a kiss. "Just don't bring me another one of those margaritas."

When I came back with two sweating glasses, he had turned on the bedside light and was sitting up against the pillows. His glasses rested down low on his nose the way I remembered them, and he was reading.

"What *is* this shit, Cinda?" he said, waving a section of newsprint he must have pulled from the bedside pile.

I looked at the tabloid-style top sheet, puzzled for a moment myself. "Oh," I said finally. "*The Jeremiad.* Some crazy newsletter I sent off for. You remember I said Mariah McKay was sort of mixed up with some patriot types. I thought I should do a little research to try to understand more about them. It's interesting, the connections among politics and religion and rural life. There's a pretty good article in there about agricultural price supports. And some of the people who are involved aren't so bad."

He cut his eyes at me, then cleared his throat and began to read aloud in what I recognized as his courtroom voice, very James Earl Jones.

> *"It is a common misconception that God looks on persons of all races the same, but the very words of the Holy Scripture belie this claim. Emanuel, that is, Jesus, repeatedly stated that he was 'only sent to the lost sheep of the House of Israel.' This means, sisters and brothers, that He is the God of the white race, the descendants of Abel, the Anglo-Saxon people, who are the real Israelites of the Scripture, and not the Jews, although they may try to claim it. In Psalms it is written: And the Word of God was given only unto His people and not to others: He showed his Word, his statutes and judgments, unto Israel. He hath not dealt so with any other nation; and as for his judgments, they have not known them.*
>
> *"All of the dark races, including Jews and so-called persons of color, are, as we know, descended from Cain, who murdered his brother, Abel. Cain's birth was due to Eve being impregnated with*

the seed of Satan, who took the form of a serpent. Thus the descendants of Cain, the Canaanites, are no better than the beasts and animals who lived outside of the Garden of Eden, and—"

"Okay," I said, "I know. Some of them *are* that bad. That stuff is gross, I agree. Some antigovernment people are like, neo-Nazis. But not all of them."

"Cinda, what have you gotten yourself into? This McKay daughter believes this stuff? What are you doing around someone like that?"

"She's not like that, Sam. Look, this is just something that I got in the mail. Mariah doesn't believe that stuff, I'm certain. It's just research."

"Well then why write off for it? Research for what, if it's not about her?"

"I don't know," I said, not quite truthfully. I wasn't sure how I could explain Pike Sayers to him.

He snorted in disgust. "Cinda, do you understand this? This newsletter is talking about *me.* Me! And *my* people. We're animals, it says. Do you know what happens to societies when they believe that certain people are the same as animals? Have you ever heard of the Holocaust?"

Suddenly I was tired of apologizing. "I can't believe this is you saying these things. You're a lawyer. Who do *you* represent? Thieves, child molesters, killers, that's who! And you want to get on my case because of this?"

"I wouldn't represent anyone who hurt some victim because he was a black person! Or because she was a white person, for that matter. And anyway, my clients have been charged with crimes. Without representation, they don't have any chance at due process. This girl has some civil claim, or thinks she does, based on some notion she's gotten about having been hurt. Bringing a suit is totally optional. You don't have any obligation to her, Cinda. Let it go."

"I can't do that. She's depending on me now. And I think you just gave me the key to how to represent her."

Sam climbed out of the bed. "Do you have any matches, Cinda?"

"Matches? Why?"

The skin around his eyes flexed dangerously. "Do you *have* any?"

I gestured. "In that drawer, I think." I went into the closet to find a shirt to put on, and came out to the stink of sulfur and smoke. I found him burning *The Jeremiad* in the bathroom sink. The basin was damp, and he had to keep lighting the last few scraps before the flame would consume them. Finally, he washed the entire mess carefully down the drain, then solemnly removed a can of Comet from beneath the sink and washed out the basin. I watched in silence, my stomach clenched with a numb despair.

"Burning books?" I finally said. "Is that your idea of a useful political method?"

"That crap wasn't a book. Now let's not talk about this anymore. Do you think you can sleep?"

"I don't know."

But I did before long, my cheek resting against his back, listening to his heartbeat. Whether he was asleep by then or no, I can't say for sure, but he was very still.

We didn't speak of Mariah McKay, or militias, or the practice of law, for the rest of the weekend. Instead, we went to the farmer's market, hiked the Mesa Trail from Chautauqua Park to Eldorado Springs, and went to the new Coen brothers movie. Sunday morning, we met Linc and Tory and Linda for breakfast at Dot's Diner, where Sam confided that nobody in New York seemed to understand how to make *huevos rancheros.*

On Sunday afternoon, he took the Airporter back to DIA. Beverly will be pissed at me, I thought gloomily as I watched the back of the limo recede from view, missing him already. I went back into the house to call Mariah.

The hospital was very quiet at about eight o'clock that night, the lone nurse at the central station on the third floor occupied with a copy of the newest Grisham, or maybe it was the one before that. I could hear low voices in conversation as I drew close to Mariah's room. I paused, not wanting to interrupt a medical visit, but recognized the second voice as that of Pike Sayers.

"...discharge you about ten o'clock," he was saying. "I'll be here then, or right after. I already got the rest of your things from the Covingtons. They said tell you they're praying for you."

I didn't hear her reply. I knocked softly on the doorjamb as I stepped into the room, in time to see Sayers's head near hers. "Oh," I said. "Excuse me."

He seemed not at all discomposed that I had interrupted their kiss. "Ms. Hayes," he greeted me. "Come in. I was just leaving." In the dim room his pale eyes flashed for a moment, like the scales of a fish that catch the sun as it breaks the water.

"Hi, Cinda!" said Mariah. She looked much, much better, her eyes clear, her face an even color, no longer blotched or wizened. "Guess what? I get to go home tomorrow. I mean"—the face fell a little—"home with Judge Sayers. To his house."

"Your home, too," he said, smiling down at her. "For as long as you want it to be. Look, I have to go now. I'll leave you with Ms. Hayes, and be back in the morning."

"Before you go," I said. "Could I speak with you for a moment?"

It was the first time he had looked at me directly since my arrival. "All right."

"Be right back, Mariah," I said cheerfully, and followed him out into the corridor.

His calm demeanor infuriated me for some reason. "What is your interest in her?" I asked. "Why would you pay for the hospitalization of a screwed-up teenager, then take her to live in your home, where there's nobody but you to look after her? You know she's going to be nothing but trouble. I'm warning you, if you have any ideas about exploiting her, I'll make you sorry." I was really getting warmed up, encouraged by the memory of my recent conversation with Sam. "She doesn't need any of your vicious politics," I continued, "or your crackpot law. And she sure doesn't need a boyfriend who's old enough to be her father!"

"Grandfather, more like," he amended. He seemed to be enjoying himself. "What vicious politics would that be?"

"You know your politics better than I do," I shot back. "What's Mariah going to do out there at your place? There's nothing for her out there!"

"She's going to eat," he said quietly, reminding me by his example rather than by his words that I ought to keep my voice down. "Eat regularly and sanely. That's her first job. Then there's useful work she can do if she wants to, just as there is on every farm, but that's not why I want her to be there. I have plenty of ways to get the work done without her. I ordered the materials she can study to get her GED if she wants to. And I'm not interested in being her *boyfriend,* as you call it. She may be almost twenty, but even I can see she's still a child, Ms. Hayes. Whatever else you think of me, surely you don't think I'm a pedophile." He gazed at me steadily, and my anger drained away.

"No," I said, defeated. "I don't think that."

"I gather you've provided her with a boyfriend, anyway. I met him here yesterday. Nice young man. You think she'd be better off living with you?" he inquired. "Then go ahead and ask her. She's of age, she can decide for herself."

A nurse hurried by pushing a medication cart, not too rapidly to give us a curious glance. I smiled at her in what I hoped was a reassuring way. When she'd vanished around the corner, I shook my head. "I—I can't do that," I said. "I don't have enough room where I live." Ashamed, thinking of my spare room upstairs, my refrigerator full of Häagen-Dazs, my new Calphalon cookware and Bose stereo system and queen-size four poster, and of the austere narrow bed on the second floor of Pike Sayers's house, where I had once seen him sleeping in the dark.

"Well then," he said. "Was there anything else you wanted to say?"

I shook my head, then changed my mind and spoke again. "I'm supposed to believe it was just a coincidence, her coming back to Boulder County, your finding a home for her?"

"What do you mean? Katie found her in Paris, starving and very nearly suicidal."

"But why did she call you? I mean, you weren't running some kind of rescue mission for wayward girls, were you?"

He smiled. "No. Not my line of country. But when Katie found out that the girl was from Boulder, she called me to see if I could help. I called her father and he said he'd be delighted to have her home, but that he was on his way out of town for a week-long conference. Was it possible I could pick the girl up at the airport and deliver her to their home? It seemed awfully cold to me, but I said all right, and I met her plane and drove her to their house. I left that little girl in a big dark house, with nobody there to greet her, and it bothered me, so I gave her my phone number and told her to call me if she needed anything. She didn't call me that night or the next, but she did early one morning about a month later. From the bus station. She told me she'd had to leave home, but she didn't say why."

"She never told me she'd been at home for a month. She made it sound like you picked her up and took her straight to the Covingtons'."

"I can't help what she told you. That's what happened." Pike Sayers's face grew taut at the memory, his jaws suddenly more prominent. "I didn't think it was suitable for a girl to be living alone with me out there—she was only seventeen at the time. I knew the Covingtons were looking for some help, so I arranged it. I'm sorry that didn't work out, but it lasted for nearly two years. I didn't know Mariah had this eating problem, that's what I blame myself for. I didn't know the signs, and neither did they."

"Yeah, yeah. But why did Katie call you about her in the first place?" I persisted. "I mean, from Paris to some farm in eastern Boulder County?"

"Because she knew I lived near the girl's home. Even then, Mariah refused to telephone her family, but Katie thought I might be able to effect a reconciliation if they were nearby. Anyway, it didn't last. She never told me why."

"So," I said. "That's all?"

He looked puzzled. "What else?"

I was silent.

He laughed then, a rich sound from the back of his throat. "I see. You think I was using Katie to run some kind of sinister recruiting scheme for, what? The Aryan Brotherhood?"

"Well, I don't know your Katie. And it all does seem a little too convenient. Are you trying to get back at Harrison McKay somehow, through her?"

"Back?" he said. "For what?"

"I don't know," I said stubbornly. "Some—old grudge or something."

"I didn't live in Colorado from the time I was eighteen until seven years ago," he said. "I'm not in a position to have a grudge against him, unless it's for the way he treated his younger daughter. As for Katie, she isn't mine anymore, we're just friends. She's married to someone else now, but she's gone back to using her maiden name. Shapiro."

"She's—"

He nodded. "Reform, mind you. Are we done now?"

My brain was seizing up like rusty machinery, unable to process this. "No," I blurted, "I want to know one more thing. What did Katie Shapiro Sayers think of the Nazi rug you keep in your study? Or did you get that after you and she divorced?"

"The..." He started, then a grin actually cracked his face. "Oh, I see. The Nazi rug."

"I saw it that morning I was at your farm," I said. "I was looking for the bathroom," I added, faintly aware that it was probably not morally necessary to defend oneself to a Nazi on a charge of snooping.

"You sure have a talent for indignation, Cinda, I'll give you that."

"I mean it," I said. "I want to know."

"I'll tell you some day," he replied, then turned and walked down the corridor toward the elevator. Infuriating man. If I hadn't known him, his back and gait would have suggested the body of someone much younger. I watched him until he turned the corner, then I slipped back into Mariah's room.

"What were you two talking about, Cinda?" Mariah clicked a button on the remote control and the television screen mounted at the corner of the ceiling gulped and turned dark. I realized with relief that she couldn't have heard us.

"Just making sure everything's arranged for tomorrow," I lied. "How do you feel about going to stay with the judge?"

"Great!" she said. "I'm going to raise some Angora goats, you know the kind with really, really fuzzy fur, and then harvest the wool and card it, and knit some handmade sweaters during the fall and winter, and show them at the county fair, and maybe start a business? If it goes really well he said maybe we could get a pair of alpacas, too—their fur is, like, the most amazing?"

I sat on the side of the bed. "You sure this is what you want?"

She looked away from my gaze. "What else is there, Cinda? I didn't graduate from high school, I don't have any skills, or at least not useful ones, unless you count getting fucked without feeling anything. I don't have a family. Where am I gonna go?"

I was sorry I had gotten her thinking along these lines. "You have friends, Mariah," I said irrelevantly.

To my surprise, she brightened. "Yeah, that Lincoln guy. He's pretty nice. Is he really a musician?"

"A good one. Since I've known him he's been in a couple of bands, but he's also a classically trained pianist."

"Do you think he'll come see me out at the judge's farm?"

"Sure, if you want him to. Did you ask him?"

She shook her head. "I didn't want to seem too—forward."

"I wouldn't worry about that," I said. This girl was a caution, one minute using the word "fuck" as though it were "hello," and worrying the next about seeming too forward. Her life hadn't afforded much opportunity for mastery of social skills. "Let me ask you something else. Are you still interested in the lawsuit we talked about?"

She nodded. "The judge says it's not a good idea to do it in his court, but I don't know why. Has something happened, Cinda?"

"Just I had an idea," I said. "Actually, it was another lawyer I was—consulting about it. There may be a way to go ahead and file it."

"Even if I still don't remember everything?"

I nodded. "Maybe. It might not work, but I'm willing to try it. If you're sure it's what you want to do."

She clapped her hands once, childlike again. Her wrists were still as slender and knobby as stems. "Did Andy tell you about the new stuff I remembered?" she inquired eagerly.

"I haven't had a chance to see him lately, but I'll give him a call tomorrow. I need to ask him about this lawsuit idea, anyway. We'll need his help if we go ahead with it."

She motioned me toward her, then kissed me on the cheek. "Thanks, Cinda," she said. "When will I see you again?"

"I'll telephone you at the judge's house," I said. "Do you know the number?"

"I'll call you with it," she promised.

Lincoln and Hypatia were getting on like a boy and his faithful dog. He'd brought me a few pages of new material he'd found on the Web about Harrison McKay, although it didn't look too useful, mostly printouts of some articles and citations and reviews of his academic work published in various journals. I thumbed through them and put them into my briefcase to look at later, put off by the tedious academic jargon and doubtful I'd find anything of use. I needed to know about McKay as a man and father, not as an academic.

I'd given Linc a new assignment yesterday, partly to keep him busy and partly to satisfy my curiosity about Pike Sayers and his friends. The kid was fast; this morning he had brought me a stack of paper in a folder labeled "Militias: Colorado."

"I didn't go back before 1950," he said. "Is that okay? Most of the stuff was from the seventies and later anyway."

"This is great," I said, thumbing through the pile. "Is it all from newspapers?"

"And magazines," he said. "At least, the ones that are on-line and go back that far. There's one thing, though." He came around the desk to my side and flipped through the printouts. "Here."

He had circled two words in the middle of one article, a name: Tyson Thornhill. "I just know that name from somewhere."

I looked more closely at the story; it was from the *Greeley Gazette,* dated March 11, 1986. It described an event I had heard about before, the indictment of Herbert Gohannon for the kidnapping and attempted murder of Wanda Kersey.

> *Mr. Gohannon's lawyer, Tyson Thornhill, has filed a motion to dismiss the indictment, arguing that Mr. Gohannon was engaged in the execution of a public duty at the time of the events described in the charges. This defense apparently rests on the claimed existence of a document issued by the Colorado Citizens' Republic, a militia organization.*

"See," said Linc, pointing. "That's why my search turned up this article, because it had the word 'militia' in it. But this guy Tyson Thornhill, I don't know...I wish I could remember where I know that name from."

I shrugged. "Does it show up in any of the other stories about this guy Gohannon? Like stories about his trial?"

"He never got to trial," said Linc, pointing to the next page of the printout. "See? He hanged himself in his cell before his trial date."

"Oh, yeah," I said, remembering Sayers's story.

Linc looked at me curiously. "You know something about this case?"

"I've heard a few things about it, that's all. It was a long time ago."

"Eight years. That's not so long, is it? Anyway, is this enough stuff? I could go back further if you want."

"This is fine, Linc. Thanks. Do you have some other stuff to do?"

"Just studying. Thanks for letting me borrow the books, Cinda. I'm learning the rules of evidence now. It's cool, the way they all go together. The hearsay rule? Phat!"

"It was good to see Sam," said Tory, tearing open her Lolita's sandwich as we sat out on the Mall, watching the passing scene. "Are you two, like, still together?"

"I don't even know what that means," I said irritably. "He's there, I'm here. How can we be together?"

"Well, you don't see other people, I guess is what I mean." She ripped her teeth into the rye bread with gusto.

"You mean are we having sex with other people?"

"Yeah," she said, her mouth full. "That's what I mean."

"Linc calls it *getting busy,*" I observed. "He told me he went into his room one night this weekend and found a couple getting busy in there. One of the Cartwrights, I guess, and his girlfriend."

"Oh, yeah? What did he do?" she said, tearing off another bite.

I chastely put a bite of yogurt into my mouth. "He left to get an espresso, and came back again after a while."

"Did you answer my question?"

"Which one?"

"Come on, don't give me that 'who's on first' bullshit. About you and Sam."

"I don't know the answer, and that's the truth. I'm certainly not sleeping with anyone else. Don't even want to, despite the separation. I don't know about him. I didn't ask."

"Well, are you using condoms?"

"Tory!"

"Sam is a good man. If he were getting busy with anyone else, he'd be using condoms with you."

"That's probably true."

"Well?"

"Is there anything at all that you think is none of your business?"

She gestured impatiently with her head. "Okay, be like that. Wow, look!" She pointed with her sandwich and I looked across the Mall but didn't see anything unusual in the swaying crowd of noon promenaders.

"What?"

She pointed again more urgently. "Beverly," she said. "And her new beau." And sure enough, there was our secretary with Seamus Kellogg, sitting outdoors at Old Chicago, conversing confidentially over a wrought-iron table. He said something and she laughed, her hands fluttering across her chest as though her fingers couldn't stop making typing motions even for an hour at noon.

I smiled. "She seems to be having a good time. Is there any reason she shouldn't let him take her out to lunch?"

"*I* don't care," said Tory. "But her taste in men is, as we know already, questionable. He's nuts." She crushed her sandwich wrapper and threw it toward the nearby bin; it went right in, a perfect field goal. "He insists on going to trial. And I'm still trying to figure out a defense, any defense."

"No ideas at all? That's not like you." I nodded and smiled as a couple of the paralegals I used to know at the DA's office walked by. One of them had on platform shoes so tall that she would surely break her ankle if she fell off them. She threw an unmistakable look at Tory: *traitor.* The DA's paralegals were true believers; they were much tougher than the lawyers on former prosecutors who had gone over to the other side.

Tory seemed not to have noticed. "I did have one thought, but I don't know if it's worth anything. I know that *Lewis* case says that an old felony conviction can count under the felon-with-a-gun law even if the guy didn't have a lawyer. And you thought that meant it would certainly count even if he had a *bad* lawyer."

"I still do."

"Okay, you're probably right. But what if he had a lawyer who was actually not on his side?"

"What are you talking about?"

"Like a lawyer who *wanted* him to be convicted."

"Why would a lawyer want that?"

"I don't know," she said with annoyance, shifting her position a few inches to get the sun out of her eyes. "I'll figure that out later if I have to, but don't you think the way this guy defended Kellogg in the tax case suggests a desire to lose? I mean, filing motions claiming that the income tax is unconstitutional, or that dollars aren't really money?"

"It's stupid, I agree. Incompetent, certainly."

"It's way beyond incompetent. What if I argued that those convictions have to be thrown out because Kellogg's lawyer was actually striving to get his client convicted?"

I thought for a minute. "If you could show that's what his actual goal was, maybe you could get around the *Lewis* decision. I suppose a conviction achieved with the connivance of the defendant's own lawyer might strike some judges as more invalid than a conviction against a guy who hadn't any lawyer at all."

"That's what I was thinking." The sunshine drifting through the leaves overhead lit up the freckles on Tory's muscular bare shoulders. "Otherwise, the little guy's going to do some heavy federal time. I think I'll ask Linc to see what he can find out about the lawyer. Maybe there's a disciplinary record on him."

"Good idea. But I doubt that even if you find him, he'll cop to trying to get his client convicted. Still, worth a try." I stood up and attempted the same trick with my yogurt carton that Tory had done with her sandwich wrapper, but with less success. "Who was the lawyer? Anyone we know?"

Tory shook her head as she bent to pick up the carton and toss it into the bin. "Some guy I've never heard of. You never played basketball, did you?"

"No," I conceded. "Not allowed where I grew up."

"Shows," she observed.

Andy Kahrlsrud said he was happy to make time to talk with me, but asked if I could come to his office. I agreed quickly, and so a few minutes before four that afternoon I found myself pulling the Saab up in front of a tiny and decrepit office building in Erie, a modest little town on the border between Boulder and Weld Counties. It would not be accurate to say that the building seemed as though it had seen better days, at least not much better. The cinder-block construction didn't look old, just cheap and streaked with rusty stains. The NRHA office was the middle of three, flanked by a video-rental shop and dusty pharmacy. Andy had told me he would be seeing a client until four, so I sat behind the wheel for a few minutes, listening to Linda Wertheimer delivering a classic NPR story about a composer who worked exclusively in the medium of old-fashioned player pianos, punching holes in rolls of paper by hand. At first I thought the tinkling sound was part of the story, but when I looked up I saw a plump woman in a sleeveless blouse and pink shorts leaving the pharmacy. A metal bell hung from the inside of the door and sounded again as the door struck the frame in closing. Almost simultaneously, a slight teenage boy in enormous falling-off pants, wearing a studded dog collar, emerged from the middle door, stalking across the street toward the corner service station in what looked like anger. He was followed very shortly by Andy Kahrlsrud, who paused on the narrow sidewalk. Andy spotted me, then nodded with a beckoning motion.

Inside, the building was not much more attractive, although posters and a large cork bulletin board covered most of the dingy pebbled wall surface. An air conditioner blocked most of the only window, and the ceiling fixtures hummed with greenish fluorescent bulbs, so the light had a quality that suggested the inside of a not-very-clean indoor aquarium. Still, the sofa and chairs matched and seemed comfortable, and Andy's steady presence was the most reassuring furnishing of all.

"Sit down," he suggested, pointing to the sofa and seating himself in one of the chairs. "I'm glad you waited outside. I forgot to mention there's no reception area, so my clients know to wait outside until I come out to the sidewalk for them. More of a hassle in the winter, as you can imagine."

"This office is funded by something called the National Rural Health Association?" I asked, settling myself into a corner of the plaid sofa.

He nodded. "As long as it lasts. It's one of those programs that gets less and less money every year, but usually at the last minute some farm-state congressman slips a little rider onto a price-support bill or something and we survive one more time. There's a well-baby clinic and an ob-gyn clinic in Longmont, but the mental health service providers all work out of here. It's just me and a woman who sees clients on Tuesdays and Thursdays now."

I looked around the bare room. "Looks like kind of a lonely gig."

He nodded, more in consideration than in agreement. "Not too bad," he finally said. "It's a different clientele than I see in my private practice in Boulder. Way different. I enjoy the difference, to tell you the truth."

"That kid I saw leaving looked angry about something."

Andy Kahrlsrud smiled. "Of course, I can't say anything about a client. But I think I can say that it's not easy to be a teenager growing up on a farm around here, or anywhere, these days. The life you're living is vanishing around you, but your family needs your labor to get through this season. Twenty miles away, kids are going off to tennis camp or shopping for five-hundred-dollar skis for next season, and you're pitching hay for your dad, who thinks you're taking drugs because you got a tattoo last winter."

"I guess being a teenager isn't too easy anywhere, anytime."

He didn't argue with me, just nodded. "Mariah?" he said, apparently by way of moving the conversation along. He reached for a notepad that was sitting on the battered desk.

"Yeah. How is she doing? Have you seen her since she was discharged from the hospital?"

He nodded. "Saw her earlier today. Pike Sayers drove her over for an appointment, then picked her up after. I'd say she's doing a lot better, and has every intention of beating this eating disorder."

"So is there a prognosis?"

He rubbed his hand over his beard a few times. "Wouldn't make one now. Eating disorders are remarkably persistent and very difficult to treat. And Mariah's facing a lot of challenges for so young a person, including the family issues and the memories, both the ones that trouble her and the ones she can't quite capture. You know, I tried to talk to her father last week."

"Tried to?"

"I wanted him to come in and sit down with me, maybe his other daughter as well, see if I could get a feeling for him and the family dynamic. Not family therapy, exactly, just an assessment of the family background. But when I telephoned their house I only got as far as the sister. She told me that her father's position was that nothing unusual had ever happened to Mariah except for her mother's terrible death, and that his attorney had advised him not to talk to me as long as litigation was contemplated. She had some harsh things to say about you, I'm afraid."

"Let's not even go there. Andy, Mariah told me a while ago that she had remembered something else about the incident."

"She did. Are you interested in the content of the memory, or how it came to her?"

"Both, obviously."

He looked briefly at his notepad. The extreme politeness of his manner was the only thing that made me aware of how unnecessary that "obviously" had been. "The content, then. It was night, it was partly outdoors and, she thinks, partly indoors, but not in a house. There were a lot of people about, and some shouting. And there was a large pile of stones or rocks."

I shook my head. "Like a stone altar or something?"

"I don't know. Remember, she was still pretty small then, so it wouldn't have had to be all that big to seem large to her."

"It's all sort of garbled, isn't it? No more about her father's part in it? Or what happened to her?"

"No. Only she continues to be certain that he was there and that he tried to keep her from seeing. That seems like almost the most vivid and frightening thing to her, the inability to see, to understand what was happening. But she's sure that someone was hurt."

"Just someone? She's not sure she was the one?"

"I've tried to work on that with her, but it's delicate because I don't want to suggest she must have been the one who got hurt. If that's the truth, she'll have to come to it herself. But it wouldn't be unusual for someone to dissociate herself from her own body during a traumatic experience, to remember that someone was hurt but not to remember who. Still, that possibility isn't the same as proof that it happened to her. And proof is what you have to worry about, isn't it?"

"In the end, yes," I agreed. "How did this new memory come to her?"

"During one of our sessions while she was in the hospital. We were talking, I asked her if she would describe the event to me one more time. She did, mostly describing the same elements as always. Her descriptions are very consistent. Only this time she came up with the nighttime setting, the indoor-outdoor feeling, the pile of stones."

"No hypnosis? No drugs, no suggestions from you?"

"That's right, Cinda. Not even a suggestion that she ought to remember more, or that whatever she was remembering really happened."

I smiled at him. "You'd be a very good witness, Andy."

"If it ever comes to that."

I thought for a moment, leaning my head against the stuffed back of the sofa. "Did she ever tell you about the time I drove her out to the place where her mother died? Right before her first appointment with you."

He nodded gravely. "Yes."

"She kept yelling, that time, about how they wouldn't let her see, how everyone was always trying to take her away. I think it was connected to not finding out what had happened to her mother, because she was taken off to the hospital. Do you think she's gotten the memories of the two events confused in her mind?"

"That's possible, too," Andy said. "There's even a name for it in psychology. Conflation, we call it."

"And something else bothers me. Her memories of that event seem to be pretty complete. Painful, maybe unbearably so, but not patchy or damaged. Why do you think she would remember that accident so well, but this other thing, whatever it was, with such difficulty?"

He shrugged his big shoulders. "I wish I could tell you that. I'd be in line for a Nobel Prize if I understood memory that well. Anything else, Cinda?"

Thinking about Martha Trefusis and her red barn, I tried to articulate my most haunting worry. "Do you think Mariah is finding these memories about her father, or creating them, or whatever you want to call it, to please me? Or to please you?"

"I don't think so. But the best insurance against that would be for her to be sure that you and I and the other people who are important in her life will care for her no matter what she remembers or doesn't."

"I understand," I said, but I was only just beginning to. Could I make room in my pleasant life for an unpredictable, needy, wayward young woman, too old to be my child and too young to be my friend?

"I take it you still think the lawsuit is likely to become impossible after her birthday?" inquired Andy.

"There is this one possibility." I explained Sam's idea.

Andy seemed skeptical. "I'm no lawyer, but I don't see how that gets you anywhere. Even if a judge allows you to file a complaint like that, and makes the defendant choose, wouldn't McKay just choose to file an answer and deny everything? Then you've still got the problem of proving something when the trial comes around."

"That's true," I said. "But I think McKay would agree to extend the statute of limitations, if only because that puts the matter off. Remember, he's running for political office. From his standpoint, putting this off makes the most sense. But even if he chooses the other, and files an answer, that buys us some time, because a civil case like this won't get scheduled for trial for at least a year, maybe a year and a half. That's a year longer for Mariah to remember, if she's going to."

"Well, then." He made a few notes on the pad.

"Andy," I said, getting up to leave, "would it be good for her to pursue this thing with her father? Or better just to forget it?"

He didn't answer right away, just flipped through his notebook in an abstracted way. "I don't know the right thing for her to do, but I don't think just forgetting it is one of the options. Forgetting might be the only thing harder than remembering." He hesitated for a moment. "Do you know that some people have suggested to Mariah that if you can't help her, she should file suit in a different kind of court?"

"You mean a common-law court?"

He nodded. "You've heard of them, then."

"Who is it making this suggestion?"

Andy looked at the place where the ceiling met the wall for a moment. "I can't say any more about that. Probably shouldn't say this much, but I will: I don't think it's a very good idea. Might be good if you could talk her out of it."

"How would I do that?"

"Give her an alternative," said Andy. "Other than forgetting about it. Something happened to this kid, despite what her father says. And it had something to do with him."

Typing is not my strong suit. I avoided learning it in high school as a form of guerrilla resistance to my mother's frequent reminder that secretarial skills are a great thing to fall back on. I didn't plan to fall back, but if I had to it would be all the way back into something romantic and desperate, like exotic dancing or growing organic vegetables. Now, every time I sit down at the computer to compose a document, the distracting squiggly red line that appears beneath each word that Hypatia deems to be misspelled or mistyped serves as a visible token of how wrong I was to resist Mom's well-meant suggestion.

I have also come to understand that exotic dancing is not a very romantic profession. Like law, probably, more or less.

So the squiggly lines plagued me as I labored over Mariah's complaint. I'd gotten past the necessary recitations about the parties and their places of residence and the court's jurisdiction, and now I was working on the hard parts. I was wearing out the delete button erasing all the false starts. The crucial paragraphs now read like this:

Plaintiff McKay asserts that an event occurred during the period of her minority in which her father knowingly caused her to be exposed to traumatic, harmful, and extraordinarily distressing events. This exposure led to many harmful consequences for Plaintiff, including nightmares, depression, and other psychological and physical diseases.

Plaintiff McKay is unable to specify the nature of these events with more particularity at this time because her memories of the event are clouded, partial, and to date uncorroborated, despite Plaintiff's and her counsel's diligent efforts to reconstruct the event.

Plaintiff's twentieth birthday will occur on August 5 of this year. If the relief sought herein is not granted by this court, Plaintiff justifiably fears that the passage of time and the operation of law will preclude her from maintaining any action filed after that date. Such a loss of a valuable cause of action, if not prevented by the relief sought herein, would deprive Plaintiff of property without due process of law.

Plaintiff continues to make efforts to remember more fully the events that form the burden of this Complaint, and these efforts have been to some degree successful. These efforts have been painstakingly and meticulously designed to ensure that any memories eventually recovered are accurate and reliable. It is possible that the passage of time and the further exercise of these efforts will permit the amendment of this Complaint and the specification of the proper particulars necessary to make out a cause of action in tort.

The interest of justice will be served by an order of the court granting the relief described below.

WHEREFORE Plaintiff prays that this court enter an order requiring Defendant Harrison Pierce McKay to elect one of the following:

1. that Defendant stipulate and agree that the statute of limitations on any claim or action held by Plaintiff shall be extended, and shall not expire on August 5 of this year or thereafter, unless by order of this court upon a showing by Defendant that Plaintiff should, by the exercise of diligence, have discovered the facts essential to the maintenance of such action at least two years prior to the making of such order; or
2. that Defendant agree to file an Answer to this civil action at this time, and waive the filing or urging of any motion or pleading that seeks dismissal of this civil action because of the vagueness, incompleteness, or other inadequacy in the recitation of the elements of the cause of action.
3. And for such other and further relief as the Court in its discretion . . .

Yadda, yadda, yadda. Even after going back and correcting all the spelling and typing errors, I was dissatisfied with this document. It had seemed like such a brilliant idea when Sam had suggested it, but on paper it just looked weird. Possibly that reaction was, as he had suggested, part of my conservative prosecutor's training. There was a time not so long ago, I reminded myself, when any action seeking damages against a family member for the intentional infliction of harm would have looked weird, but such suits were commonplace now. I named the document McKayComplaint, saved it, and hit the print command. Maybe it would look better on paper than it did on the screen.

I made four copies of the printout and left one on Tory's desk with a note asking her to take a look and let me know what she thought. I had meant to send another to Sam, for the same purpose, but after some reflection I was deterred by the memory of our conversation about *The Jeremiad.* I tucked two copies into my briefcase, one to take home to look at over the weekend, and one to deliver to Mariah. If all seemed well, I would file it on Monday, just before catching a plane to Austin. I had finally yielded to Dana's entreaties; I was going to spend four days with her at the fat farm.

It was late Sunday afternoon by the time I guided the Saab across the cattle guard and headed up the rise toward the Sayers farm. I'd forgotten my sunglasses, and blinked frequently to interrupt the piercing rays of sunlight reflecting off the hood of the car. Heat shimmered off the boulders alongside the track and supple rabbitbrush swayed in the breeze. I topped the rise, steering carefully to avoid a hungry depression just about the size of the front wheel, and looked down on the scene below as I started to descend. Instead of the collection of vehicles I had seen on the night the court was in session, I saw only Sayers's black pickup and, with a rush of affectionate recognition, my Subaru parked next to it.

Mariah ran out of the house as I pulled up in front, her hair in the long braid again, her tank top and jeans still slack on her thin body. But her skin looked healthier and less roughened, her shoulders were lightly tanned, and her smile was enormous. "Cinda!" she called out, and she wrapped her slender arms around me in a hug as I stepped out. "I'm so glad you came. You have to see my babies!"

She took my arm and led me around behind the house to a small barn, chatting away about the Angora goats Pike had bought her from a couple in Greeley yesterday. "Wait'll you see, they're the most adorable things you ever imagined." She pushed open the barn door and led me to a pen where a couple of dog-sized goats with wispy hair looked at us with placid eyes, then started butting their small heads up against the bars of the pen. "Cinda, meet Thelma and Louise."

"Oh!" I exclaimed, taken by surprise by the lump in my throat. The little animals' funny young-old faces, together with Mariah's obvious attachment to them, wrapped themselves around me like a filament of love and sorrow. "They're wonderful, Mariah. How old are they?"

"Just babies," she said. "Born this spring. But they're a breeding pair, so some day I can raise a whole flock. And by next summer I'll be able to harvest their fleece and make genuine Thelma and Louise sweaters. I think they'll sell real well in Boulder, don't you?"

"Yes, I do," I said. I was about to ask how a breeding pair could be named Thelma and Louise when some change in the shape of the light streaming in from the door behind us made me turn. Pike Sayers stood there, holding a bridle.

"Hello," he said. "Sorry to interrupt."

"It's okay," I smiled at him. "Mariah was showing me her goats. They're beautiful."

He started to speak again, as Mariah's face acquired a curious expression, first puzzled and then alarmed. "Oh, my God, the timer," she exclaimed. "The cookies must be done." She turned and ran for the door, yelling "Be right back!" behind her as she went. In the wake of her departure it was very quiet and I could hear the distant buzz that had summoned her.

Pike Sayers turned as if to go.

"It was very kind of you to buy those goats for Mariah," I said. "I know they're not inexpensive."

"Good investment," he said briefly. He turned away again, then back. "She tells me you're going to file that lawsuit after all."

"I think so," I said. "That's what I need to talk to her about today. I brought a copy of the complaint I've drafted to go over with her. And I need to be sure she still wants to do this."

He nodded. "She thinks you're going to stay and have supper with us."

"Oh," I said, taken aback. "I don't think..."

He shrugged. "Tell her. She'll be disappointed, though."

Mariah reappeared beside him in the door just then, walking with a side-to-side motion apparently dictated by the pair of dusty cowboy boots she wore. She carried a small stack of brown disks in her hand. "The cookies are fine," she said, smiling at him. "Oatmeal cinnamon. Here, want one?"

Pike Sayers looked at his own hands with rue. "I've been told it's not a good idea to eat horse manure," he said. "Maybe I better wait until later."

"Okay. Cinda, you want one?"

"Sure," I said, going forward. "Sounds like Thelma and Louise want theirs, too." The little goats' halting cries were coming in relays; as soon as one stopped, the other would start.

"Oh, you babies," said Mariah, handing me two of the warm cookies. "You know you can't have cookies! I'll bring you your dinner in a little bit." And then, to my astonishment, she raised the remaining cookie to her mouth, bit into it, and ate it. It was a perfectly ordinary gesture, but coming from Mariah it made my spirits mount.

"You're staying for supper, aren't you, Cinda?" she said, munching. "Because I made roast lamb. Way too much for me and Pike to eat."

"Sure," I said. "Love to."

The kitchen was as I remembered it: old-fashioned, but not faux old-fashioned, with the copper pots and carefully weathered wood furnishings seen in chic Boulder homes; it had linoleum floor tiles and a boxy white enamel Westinghouse stove sitting on them in the corner. Mariah bustled around energetically, peeling potatoes and sticking garlic cloves into a large mound of lamb while Pike Sayers and I sipped lemonade at the pine-topped table. She had declined an offer of help once already, but I felt guilty watching her work so hard. I concentrated on not looking at the door next to the stove that I knew led to the study.

"Sure I can't help?" I asked.

"Sure," she said cheerfully. "Why don't you two go for—a walk or something? It'll be at least an hour before all this is ready."

"I don't...," I began, but Sayers interrupted me.

"I'll show you the stables," he said, standing up. "We keep a couple of riding horses and a mule. You can curry the mule if you want to be helpful. He's full of burrs, and he bites."

"Okay," I said uncertainly, but Mariah protested.

"Don't make her groom that jerk Gabriel. Take her for a nice ride instead, why don't you?" She reached over to the cookie plate and broke a cookie in half before putting it into her mouth. "Then you can come back to supper all ready." She spoke this last through the cookie. Her attitude had undergone some subtle change; she seemed both watchful and slightly defiant.

"Good idea," said Sayers, and before I could say more he took me by the elbow and propelled me out the back door into the patchy yard. "We'll be back at six," he called out to Mariah. He released my elbow as soon as we were out of doors, but stood firmly between me and the door.

"I don't really want to go for a ride with you," I said. "I don't have the right shoes, for one thing." I pointed at my flimsy sandals.

"That's all right," he said. "Let's just walk down to the barn anyhow."

The path to the barn wound through a copse of cottonwoods that grew by a creek, then circumvented a small pond fed by the creek's noisy waters. I picked my way over the stones in my sandals, slipping once in a muddy slough, suppressing a scatological word.

"Sorry," Sayers said briefly, but he did not offer to assist me, to my relief. He looked back toward the house, out of sight now on the other side of the trees. "I thought it was important we leave her alone with the food," he said, turning back toward me as we walked. "I can tell that she's wondering if I'm wondering whether she'll do the same thing here she did the last night at the Covingtons'. I know she won't, and I want her to understand that I trust her. Sorry I pulled you out of there. I know you don't want to go for a ride with me. Or anywhere else, for that matter. I'll go tend to the horses and you can wander around, if you want. I'll meet you back there at six. There's a TV in the bunkhouse." He gestured toward a small stone building in the near distance.

I looked toward the uninviting little bunker, then sniffed the cooling air. "I'd like to go for a ride," I surprised myself by saying. "It's just these damn shoes."

"You sure? Because I've got a bunch of old boots in the tack room. I found a pair to fit Mariah, and I bet I've got some you could wear, too."

"What about socks?"

He looked at me with a grin. "How sensitive is your nose?"

I shrugged.

"Then no problem."

The boots were stiff from disuse, but I could tell they had once been good ones, the leather on the outside tooled in an intricate design. The old socks were stiff, too, and thin with age at the heels and toes, but not that smelly. Sayers helped me saddle up the gelding, Willie, but most of the steps came back to me from my childhood summers at camp. I put the bit into the big sorrel's mouth myself, forcing it between his large teeth. He didn't seem to mind. After I mounted and Sayers adjusted the stirrups, he saddled his Appaloosa mare Carla and swung easily up into the saddle.

"Watch your head as we leave the barn," he cautioned. "The overhang is low, and Willie's a tall guy."

We walked the horses out into the sunlight. Willie tossed his head once, but then settled down to a placid walk behind Carla's rump. We proceeded out of the corral and through a narrow passage between the stable and another outbuilding; then the path widened and Sayers moved Carla over to the edge to allow Willie and me to draw alongside. "I need to check on a fence out near the southwest corner," he said, pointing. "It's not quite a mile from here. All right?"

"Sure," I said, exhilarated by the barely remembered sensation of riding. I hadn't been on a horse in ten years or more. "Can we run?"

He laughed. "You don't do things by half measures, do you? Let's walk a bit, to warm the horses up and let Willie get used to you. We can gallop part of the way back if you want to."

So we walked for twenty minutes or so, Sayers pointing out various things to me: the fields of corn and sugar beets, the fallow fields and the purple thistles that dotted them here and there. "They're a bitch, those chokers," he said of the thistles. "Hard as hell to kill, and impossible to pull out. I have to come out here every once in a while with shears, cut off the heads. That keeps 'em from reproducing, at least."

About two-thirds of a mile from the house, he turned around in his saddle and said, "Do you want to take a small detour? See something might be interesting?"

"Sure," I said, and Carla bore right at a fork on the road and plodded up a small hill, her tail switching against the occasional fly. The bracing smell of baked earth rose up from the horses' feet with each step. A hummingbird whirred busily by, causing Willie to put his ears back for a moment. I saw that Carla and Sayers had stopped ahead at a low fence. On the other side stood five identical monuments of white stone, each inscribed "Sayers." I urged Willie up closer to the fence and looked more closely. Augusta, Gunther, Warner, Beatrice, Gideon. Each slab had an identical angel carved in bas-relief just below its arched top. My eyes clouded and I took a deep breath, reminding myself that I didn't know any of these people, and that they had left behind a descendant with extremely unattractive politics.

The quiet was stunning, a presence as palpable as soaring chords or blinding color. Even the flies seemed to have stopped buzzing. I started to ask Pike Sayers whether he expected to be buried here himself, but decided I didn't want to break the silence. Anyway, I was sure I knew the answer. After a moment, he pulled the reins over to his left and turned Carla around. We followed them back down the stony path to the fork.

When we reached the corner of the fence, he dismounted and pulled a set of pliers and some other tools from a saddlebag. Still sitting astride Willie, I watched him tighten a sagging section of barbed wire and replace another one. The fence ran alongside a road and I watched a dust cloud grow larger as it approached until it resolved into a truck. The occupants, a man and a woman, gave us a curious glance and did not respond to Sayers's raised hand.

"Is this fence the end of your property?" I asked.

He nodded, his teeth clenching a metal joint of some sort as he worked on the fence with his hands. I walked Willie around a bit, letting him nibble at the weedy green growth. It looked as though this field had not been cultivated in a long time.

"Ready to go back?" said Sayers. He was back on Carla, who danced with anticipation.

I nodded.

"Sure you want to run back? Because I have to tell you, Carla and Willie can get a little competitive once they get going. They're hard to rein in. Sure you know how to ride?"

In a movie, at this point a few bars of clever music would gently alert the audience, but not the oblivious fool on the horse, that things were soon to take a less idyllic turn. And I swear I was just about to confess that I had ridden mostly gentle old plugs and rescuees from the glue factory when Sayers said "All right, then," leaned forward, and whispered something in Carla's ear. I noticed, too late, that Willie was watching her alertly; in the next moment the mare bolted, and Willie thrust his head powerfully forward and shook it, nearly pulling the reins out of my hands. Both horses broke into a gallop.

"Oooohh SHIT," I yelled, forgetting my earlier restraint.

Carla's hooves just ahead of Willie's head carved a shower of divots out of the red earth, and his big neck strained against the reins as he followed the dirty cloud. I felt every muscle in his huge body grow taut to propel his pounding legs over the ground. The effort of holding him back was pulling and shaking my arms; I realized that if I let him have his head my balance would be much less difficult to maintain, so I did. I leaned forward, my weight in the stirrups, and gasped, my breath finally returning after the initial shock of our takeoff. Willie tried to pass the mare for a few moments more, then seemed to settle into a resigned second place just off Carla's rump. I let go of the saddle horn, which I had grabbed in my initial panic, and leaned forward into the rocking motion of Willie's long stride as we flew over the field. Something like joy settled in me and I thought, *I want to remember this.*

It didn't take long to get back in sight of the stable. Carla slowed, and immediately Willie did, too. I had to shift my weight to keep my feet planted in the stirrups as his gait grew rougher. I heard Sayers making soothing slow-down noises at Carla, and I leaned forward to whisper to Willie. "Good boy," I said, trying to sound like this had been my idea all along.

Sayers led Carla to a post in the corral and jumped off easily, looping her reins over the fence. "You okay?" he asked me.

"I'm fine," I said emphatically.

He smiled at me as he reached up his hand, which I ignored as I swung down. "Were you about to say something right before we took off there?" he asked me.

I looked at him closely, but couldn't tell anything from his expression.

He glanced at his watch. "Better tend to these beasts and then get back to Mariah and that supper," he said. "You think you can unsaddle Willie?"

"Of course," I said with dignity. When he turned away, I touched the crotch of my jeans surreptitiously. Thank God, I hadn't peed myself back there when the race started. I turned to my horse and flipped the near stirrup up over the saddle to loosen the cinch strap.

. . .

Supper, as they called it, was delicious. I ate two servings of potatoes, and a large piece of lamb. I tried hard not to monitor Mariah's intake, as I thought she would surely detect any such effort on my part. But it was hard not to take some notice. I think she ate a serving of everything, although her portion of salad seemed bigger than ours, and her portion of lamb smaller. She kept jumping up to go to the kitchen for things: the salt and pepper, more dressing for the salad.

As we drank coffee and ate more of the oatmeal cookies, I broached the subject of the complaint. "I have a draft of it out in the car," I said. "I've been over it with my law partner, and we think it looks good, but I want to go over it with you before we file it."

"Fine," Mariah said, but I thought her eyes looked alarmed for a moment.

"Also, I need to be sure this is still what you want to do," I continued. "It's not too late to change your mind. Not at all."

She looked at Sayers but his face showed nothing, at least not to me.

"It's what I want to do," she said slowly. "I saw him on television last night. It's such a huge lie, who he claims to be. Cares about *your* children, cares about *your* schools." She crumpled her napkin suddenly. "Excuse me," she said in a very small voice, then rose swiftly and ran up the stairs to the second floor.

I looked at Sayers. "Don't fret," he said. "Let her be for a few minutes. Sometimes she just needs to take a little time alone, I've noticed." I could hear a door being closed upstairs, but not slammed. "Anyway, there's something I wanted to show you," said Sayers. He rose and left in the direction of the living room. When he came back he was holding a book, which he set down in front of me.

"*A Century of Navajo Weaving, 1880–1980*?" I read from the cover.

"I think you might be interested in some of the material on page ninety-four," he suggested, reaching across the table to gather cups and plates.

"Why would I?" But he had passed through the swinging door into the kitchen, his arms full of dishes.

The illustration on page ninety-four was a photograph of a brilliant woven rug with a row of stylized figures in the central area and a border of swastikas. Not exactly like the one in Pike Sayers's study, but similar. The caption read:

> *This excellent* yeibichai *rug depicts the healing ceremony in four figures—the Talking God, the patient, and two other participants, one of whom may be a figure called Hogan God. Note the traditional elements of* yeibichai: *the prayer stick in the hand of the patient, the evergreens about the necks of all four figures, and the white deerskin shirt in which Talking God is inevitably dressed. The border of whirling logs is also traditional, and provides a method of dating the rug as one probably woven before 1930. Navajo weavers stopped using this centuries-old symbol in rugs at about that time, after it was appropriated by the National Socialist Party.*

I looked up as Sayers came back through the door and set a fresh cup of coffee in front of me. "Lifelong learning is a great thing, isn't it?" he observed.

"Sorry," I said briefly, for I couldn't think of anything else.

"Did you really think I was a Nazi?" he asked.

"I don't know." I hesitated. "I do think that some of your neighbors believe that certain people have less value than others. Along racial lines."

"I think some of your neighbors believe that their cats are reincarnations of Egyptian gods and that having their bodies pierced is a spiritual experience. Doesn't mean everybody in your zip code believes it, does it?"

"But some of them do. Are some of your friends racist?"

His head gave an impatient jerk. "Some of them. Out of ignorance, or fear, or because some demagogue has persuaded them that if we got rid of affirmative action and closed our borders to immigration they wouldn't have to sell their farms. When the subject comes up, I try to meet them where they are and lead them a little distance in a different direction. I've learned it takes time to change people's minds, and even more time to change their hearts. So sometimes I just listen and let it slide, until the next time. Does that make me a racist, too?"

"No," I said, faintly ashamed, thinking of things I had listened to my own sister say. "I guess I do the same, sometimes. Anyway," I added after a moment, "I admit it gave me a jolt to see that rug. Shortly after I met Mariah for the first time somebody broke one of my car windows, and left behind a Nazi insignia."

He sat down again and looked at me with interest. "And you thought I had done it?"

I shook my head impatiently. "That was before I was ever in your house. I don't know what I thought. Except that someone was trying to discourage me from helping Mariah."

"You were probably right about that. Have you had any other threats?"

"Maybe." I told him about the mutilated doll.

"I don't like this," he said. "I've been teaching Mariah to target-shoot, evenings. Maybe you should join us some time."

I drained my coffee cup and put it down, closing the book carefully. "Not interested," I said. "But let me ask you about something else. If what's really important to Mariah is getting at the truth, it occurs to me that she could file her case in your court. The common-law court. I think some people might even be encouraging her in that direction."

He nodded but said nothing, his eyes on the staircase.

"Well, why not?" I asked.

He looked at me, finally. "For starters, I couldn't sit on such a case. She's family now."

"So? Aren't there any other common-law judges around here who could handle it?"

"I imagine we could find one," he said.

"So?"

"I'd have thought you would have figured this one out, Cinda. There's no way in hell Harrison McKay would appear in a common-law court. He'd ignore any process it sent to him, and might get some investigation going of the court and its activities. If there were a trial, he'd default and there would be a judgment against him—say, for a couple million dollars, if Mariah convinces a jury he hurt her, which wouldn't be hard if there's nobody representing his side. Now, who's going to collect that judgment?"

I considered. "It's uncollectable. Like a gambling debt or an illegal loan. No court would enforce it," I admitted. "But at least Mariah would have that vindication."

"I'm not sure vindication is what she's after," he observed. "And people do pay off gambling debts and illegal loans, by the way."

"Well, sure, because otherwise they get their legs broken."

He was silent.

"Are you saying someone might break Harrison McKay's legs if he doesn't pay a judgment?"

Sayers's face registered the smallest moment of satisfaction at my tardy deduction, but still he said nothing, only reached for my empty coffee cup, rising to take it with him through the swinging door into the kitchen. I looked at my hands and tried to get my thoughts to march in a neat row, but they kept falling out of line like drunken soldiers.

"This's all there is, unless you want me to make another pot," he said, coming back into the dining room and handing me the cup.

"This is plenty," I said, putting it down. "I thought you told me the whole idea of common-law courts was that their judgments didn't have to be enforced by violence."

"There's not an idea in the history of thought that's immune from being perverted for evil purposes," he said. "Not God, not love, not common-law courts. Now I'm going to get started on the washing up. Maybe you should get that paper out of your car so when Mariah comes back down you'll be able to show it to her. I think she might be back in fifteen minutes or so, if this's like most times." He stacked a few of the plates together like a man who's cleared the table many times, and pushed the door open again with his back as he carried them into the kitchen.

I picked up most of the remaining dishes and glasses and followed him. "Then why would anyone encourage Mariah to think of filing the case in your court?" I asked. "If it would only mean trouble?"

"Some people like trouble," he said. "And some people find that trouble serves their interests."

"Like what interest?"

He squeezed a stream of liquid soap into the steaming sink basin and started scraping the table scraps into a pail. "I guess it's pretty common to be interested in seeing things happen that affirm our beliefs. Makes a person feel less helpless."

I started plunging the scraped dishes into the hot water, wincing at its temperature. "I have no idea what you're talking about."

"Suppose you believed in an apocalypse." He carefully sorted the bones to one side in the pile of scrapings. "That things would finally come to a shooting war between the forces of good and the forces of evil. When things were bad, you comforted yourself with this belief, but the years went by and it was just the same old grind, nobody ever seeming to win or lose or even come to terms. You might get tired of it. You might want to push things along a little bit, if you saw a chance."

I pulled my hands out of the suds and turned to him. "You mean some people see Mariah's lawsuit as a chance to start some kind of war?"

"Could be." He somehow moved me aside and took over the washing, so I took a tea towel from a neat stack near the refrigerator and started drying.

"Why would you want to be a part of something that's so destructive?"

"I don't, that's the point. Look, the common-law court had been out here for a long time before I came back to Colorado. It fulfilled an important function for some people who found very little sympathy or help in the courthouses in Boulder and Longmont. It gave them a feeling of community and a way to settle their disputes without paying money they didn't have to line the pockets of lawyers. But it was also susceptible to misuse by some unscrupulous people." He stopped talking for a moment while he maneuvered a big pot into the water. "When I was asked to become their judge, I thought I could help them keep the good parts and maybe discourage the others. If this thing with Mariah ends up in common-law proceedings, it's not going to do anything good for her, and it could hurt a lot of people. Could destroy some people. Your kind of court is better."

"Then who even gave her the idea of pursuing it there?" With my fingernail, I picked at a spot of hardened crust on the big pot.

"I don't know for sure. I let her change her name in the common-law court, so she got a look at how it works. Then she heard you talking on the radio about—what did you call them? Intimate torts?"

I grimaced, remembering my breezy rap that day at the studio.

"And then," he continued, "when she was living at the Covingtons', I think Craig—he's tight with Jeremiah and some other fellows who like to call themselves the Brotherhood of Colorado Militia—found out she had this thing about her father and encouraged her to start a case against him in my court. Craig's not a bad guy—he's more of a follower. But he tells me some of his buddies are starting to say I might be a traitor, might be a government spy. Jeremiah and his friends might have thought a big case against Harrison McKay in my court would put me in a jam, maybe give them an excuse to get out their guns and enforce any judgment that came out of it, maybe best of all bring down the wrath of the federal government on this community and give them the war they want." He reached down and pulled the stopper from the sink and the greasy water started to circle and drain. "All done?"

I nodded, put the last clean pot on the kitchen table and draped the tea towel over the refrigerator handle. "Thanks for telling me all this."

He turned away. "I'm going to see what Mariah's up to. Why don't you get that complaint out of your car?"

The overhead fan in the living room stirred the edges of the paper as I set the complaint down beside me on the sofa. As I rummaged through my bag for my reading glasses, I heard steps and looked up to see Mariah coming down the stairs. She approached me cautiously, her bare feet turned inward as she walked.

"Are you mad at me, Cinda?"

"Of course not," I said, surprised. "Why would I be?"

"Seems like I'm always running away from you."

I thought about this. "Do you know why?"

She nodded, shyly, sitting down in a chair opposite the couch. "Maybe. Andy and I talked about it last week."

"Do you want to tell me?"

She crossed her arms protectively across her slight chest. "Maybe not right now."

I smiled. "Okay, then. Mariah, I'm going to Texas for a couple of days. By the time I get back, we'll be right up against your birthday and the possibility of the statute of limitations expiring. Do you remember, we talked about that before?"

She nodded, her arms still clasped against her chest.

"Are you cold, sweetie?" I asked.

"No," she said. "Go ahead."

"If you want, I can file this complaint tomorrow before I leave. But if I do, I need to go over it with you tonight, make sure everything in it is right. Then I'll have Lincoln file it at the courthouse tomorrow while I'm on the way to the airport."

"Why are you going to Texas?" she asked.

"To visit with my sister."

"You have a sister?" She looked wistful.

I nodded. "Do you want to go over the complaint now?"

"Sure," said Mariah. "Then do I need to go with Linc to file it?"

"That's not necessary," I said. I thought her face fell a little. "But I can have him bring you a copy as soon as he files it."

"That would be good." She sat down next to me. "What do we need to go over?"

I arrived at the Austin airport about noon on Monday, where Dana met me and we drove the Cadillac she had rented an hour west to the Green Canyon Spa. After check-in, a late-afternoon nutrition lecture, and a dinner of poached fish, poached spinach, and poached tomatoes with cilantro garnish, Dana and I settled into the lounge of the Green Canyon Spa guest compound to read.

I was the one who had suggested the lounge; I was wary of the senseless quarrels that might arise if we stayed in our overdecorated two-bedroom cottage and tried talking like sisters. We had already had one spat before we left the airport, while we were waiting for my bags at the carousel.

"How's Dad?" I had asked.

"Oh, you know," she said, applying more lipstick while looking into her compact mirror. "The same."

"When did you see him last?"

She snapped the compact shut in irritation. "I don't know, Cinda. We've been very busy, with the kids and Jerry's business. He doesn't even know who we are, you know. There's nobody home behind that face."

"I don't believe that," I said miserably.

"Fine," she said. "Then you go visit him. I'm going to the ladies' room."

So, installed in our respective lounge chairs, I read *In the Electric Mist with Confederate Dead* while Dana leafed through an old copy of *Vanity Fair* with Tom Cruise and Nicole Kidman on the cover. I thought that Tom would look better in lipstick that was a little less purple, but didn't say so. It also occurred to me that we could have spent this time together at her home or mine at considerably less expense, but I didn't say that either.

The next morning I was the only one in the spa's luxurious gym in a T-shirt and running shorts. Everyone else was wearing Lycra in various luminous sherbet hues. The bright lights reflecting off all that metallic skin hurt my eyes, and that's not even to mention the fingernail factor. On the other hand, the exercises were ridiculously easy, and the gym was air-conditioned to a delicious chill.

After aerobics Dana went back to the cottage to shower and I wondered whether I might have to leave the artificial cool of the spa's compound and go running on the well-groomed trails, just to get some real exercise. I was drinking a grapefruit juice at the juice bar, considering this plan and wondering if the sign warning about rattlesnakes on the trail was to be taken seriously, when Dana came bustling in, a rectangular envelope in her hand.

"This just came for you," she said. "Some messenger brought it over from the office."

"Thanks," I said, puzzled. I ripped open the thick envelope with the spa's embossed seal on it and found one of Hayes and Meadows's fax cover sheets. Tory's note on the sheet suggested that she was sorry to interrupt my sweat idyll, but thought I might want to know there had been a motion filed in the McKay matter. I should call her if I wanted a copy faxed to me.

"Shit," I said, forgetting momentarily my resolution not to use what Dana called "curse words" in her presence. "I need to find a telephone."

"In the office," said Dana primly. I could tell by the set of her mouth that I had affronted her, as much by my failure to tell her what the envelope contained as by my language.

The office manager agreed that I could use the telephone and passed the cordless handset over the counter to me, but she continued to sit in her chair, filing her nails and humming along with the easy listening station on her desktop radio. I punched in a long string of numbers to invoke our credit with the telephone company before hearing a ringing at the other end.

"Hayes and Meadows," said a male voice.

"Linc? Is that you?"

"Cinda! Hey, what up?"

"Is Tory there, buddy?"

"Sure. Hold on."

Some clicking, then Tory's voice. "So, Mouse, looks like you stirred up a hornet's nest here." Tory sounded more worried than amused, which alarmed me in turn. "I've been fielding calls from the press all day, especially that Tanner woman from the *Daily Camera.* Someone in the clerk's office must have slipped her the word about the case. But we've also had calls from the *Denver Post* and the *Rocky Mountain News.* Dr. McKay's minions are going crazy trying to make sure the case file is sealed up tight so nobody can read the complaint. You want me to fax the motion they filed?"

"Just tell me about it," I said.

"Hold on, then. Let me go get it."

I waited, growing more unhappy with each second that passed. The office manager caught my eye and smiled in an ingratiating way before turning back to the application of some peppy pink polish to her nails. Finally Tory spoke again.

"Here's the deal," she said. "Jim Brant of Clyde, Mason, and Brink is representing McKay. He's filed a motion with the court to seal all the filings and documents in the case until it gets to trial. Which will be, you realize, after the election. He asked for the order to go into effect immediately, until there's time to schedule a hearing, and the judge granted that."

"Hold on a second," I said to Tory. The woman behind the desk was looking at me with unabashed interest now, even turning down the volume on her little pink radio to facilitate her frank eavesdropping. "Would you excuse me?" I hissed at her.

"I beg your pardon?" She looked offended.

"*Excuse* me!" I repeated, thinking this was the most inane conversation since man learned to speak. The woman got up, narrowed her eyes at me as if to ensure a precise memory of my face in the event she ever saw it on a "Wanted" poster, and disappeared without a further word through a door marked "Private."

"Sorry," I said into the phone. "I'm not really surprised they want to keep this quiet. Which judge did we draw, by the way?"

"Meiklejohn."

"She'll be fair at least. It's fine with me if the file is sealed. I don't want to try this case in the papers any more than they do."

"That's good, because in addition to sealing the files, Meiklejohn gave Brant a TRO restraining you, and Mariah, and anyone else who may have knowledge of the lawsuit from making any extrajudicial comment whatsoever about the matter while it's pending. Oh, man, the newspapers' lawyers are going to go wild on this one."

"Don't return their calls," I said hastily. "And don't say a word to anyone. Make this very clear to Beverly, okay? And would you call Andy Kahrlsrud, Mariah's therapist, and explain it to him? His number's on my Rolodex. He wouldn't talk anyway, but just in case. If the press wants to go into court and argue about the First Amendment, that's their privilege, but I'm just as glad the judge did what she did. I don't want Mariah to end up being a footnote in the history of this election, cross-examined by reporters and stalked by wackos. Did they file an answer yet?"

"Nope, they still have a few days before it's due. Like I said, the TRO is already in effect. The hearing on making it an injunction is in ten days. Let's see—Friday of next week. So go back to getting your bikini line waxed or whatever it is you're doing there. We've got plenty of time." At least she said *we.* "Oh, one more thing."

"What's that?"

"There's a hearing scheduled on McKay's grievance against you, but not until November 26th. They sent blank subpoena forms you can use to get your witnesses to the hearing. Do you want me to be a character witness?"

"You bet. I want you to wear your *Bitches from Hell* T-shirt, too, so be sure it's not at the dry cleaner on that day," I said, and hung up. I decided I was going for a run, snakes be damned. I was ready to bite someone myself, but I didn't see any snakes or anything else alive as I ran alongside the dry creekbed. Sweat ran into my eyes and down my arms to my fingertips, the searing heat momentarily overwhelming my other worries. When I returned, I canceled my massage and facial, and after a lunch of poached chicken I holed up in my air-conditioned room with Robicheaux for the rest of the afternoon.

There was to be a demonstration of skin-care products in the lounge that evening, and I assumed that Dana would want to go, but after dinner she surprised me by suggesting that we stay in and talk. "Sure," I said uneasily, standing by the door to my bedroom. "Anything in particular?"

To my horror, her blues eyes filled. "Sisters are supposed to *talk!*" she said, coming down hard on the last syllable in a way that reminded me of countless childhood arguments.

"Come on, sit down," I said, beckoning her into the self-consciously cozy living room of the cottage. "What's wrong?"

"Why don't you ever talk to me!" she said, sitting down hard on a slipcovered love seat. "I don't think you really want to be my sister."

"Of course I do," I protested. "Anyway, we are sisters, no matter what. Are you upset because I've been preoccupied while we've been here?"

"You're always preoccupied."

"I know. I'm sorry, Dana. Maybe it was a mistake for us to meet here. And that fax I got from my office today was about something that's bothering me."

"Tell me," she said, her face clearing. "I'd *like* to know about the things you do at work, Cinda."

I blew out a big sigh. "I wouldn't even know where to start. Why don't you tell me about what you've been doing instead? You said you were doing some genealogy? Tell me about that."

"It's so interesting, Cinda. Let me get the chart I've been working on." She went to her room and returned with a packet that she unfolded on the coffee table to reveal a genealogical chart with about half the blanks filled in. She motioned me over to look, and I sat down next to her on the love seat.

"You can see I have more about Mom's family than Dad's," she said. "Because he can't tell me anything, of course, and Uncle Webb and our grandparents are dead. But Aunt Cicely told me a lot about the Slidell side of the family. She had an old family Bible with a chart filled in showing a lot of their ancestors."

"Who were they?" I said, pointing. "Edward and Bertha Slidell?"

"That's Mother's paternal grandparents, see? Our Grandpa Slidell—his father and mother."

"So do you know anything about them?"

Dana consulted a spiral notebook. "They were just farmers. In Oklahoma. But look at these two," she said, pointing to a nearby entry. "Walter and Mary Isabel Torrington, see? Mother's mother's parents. He was a doctor, and they lived on a big plantation in Mississippi. Aunt Cicely says that the plantation was built by *his* grandfather, and that they had slaves and everything."

"Slaves? God."

"Yeah, he must have been very wealthy. Southern aristocracy, like. I wish I could find out more about that part of the family. I know we must have some long-lost cousins and things out there."

"What kind of farm was it?" I said, thinking of the lush towers of cornstalk lined up in one of Pike Sayers's fields.

"The plantation? I don't know. Wouldn't it have been cotton?"

"No, I mean the farmers. Edward and Bertha."

"*I* don't know what kind," she said impatiently. "It was just a farm."

"You don't know what they grew?"

"Honestly, Cinda, you are interested in the strangest things! Don't you want to know more about the Torringtons?"

"To tell you the truth, Dana, it makes me a little queasy to think of our ancestors owning slaves."

"Why? Everybody did in those days. Thomas Jefferson even did, Aunt Cecily says."

"I think that was a little earlier," I said, wondering if I would ever be able to introduce Sam to my family, or whether they would disgrace me.

"So what? Some very fine people owned slaves because in those days it happened to be legal. If we had lived in those days we would have, too."

"Not me."

She folded up the chart and snapped the notebook shut. "You don't know what you're talking about, Cinda."

She was probably right.

I spent our last day at Green Canyon trying to be a better sister; after lunch (poached *legumes de jardin,* according to the gold-edged daily menu), I even went with Dana to have my colors done. If that stuff has anything to it, I am going to have to throw away my entire wardrobe and replace it with items that display strong, clear, jewel-like tones. In the late afternoon, as Dana and I lay on adjacent massage tables and I succumbed to the insistent fingers of a Fabio look-alike named Ivan, I made her tell me about the only relatives I really cared about besides her and Dad, her two boys, Louis and Woody. She made me laugh with stories about their sayings and doings, and I got her to promise that she'd let Louis come visit me by himself during his school holiday next spring.

By the time we parted company the next morning at the Austin airport, I was glad I had made the effort to see her. But I was also happy to be going home, although it seemed likely that trouble awaited me there.

Harrison McKay won a decisive primary victory the third week of August—I caught a sound bite of his victory party on the ten o'clock news. Perhaps that's why he thought he could walk into my office the way he did one morning a week later. Through my open door, I could hear him arguing with Beverly out in the entrance area. He was an impressive guy, but she was evidently not impressed.

"Not a chance," she was saying. "Not without an appointment." What a woman, I thought, wondering if Tory and I could afford to pay her a bonus this fall. But she was caught behind the desk, I knew, and I doubted she could get between him and my door if he decided to ignore her. I decided to save her the effort, and strolled out there.

"Problem?" I said to her, ignoring him. She simply cut her eyes in his direction. I could have saved him a lot of trouble by explaining the hand-kissing technique, but he didn't deserve to know it if he couldn't figure it out for himself.

"Ms. Hayes," he broke in, "I would be very appreciative if you would give me a few minutes of your time. I believe I could preserve you from some difficulty. Will you do me the courtesy?" He looked flustered.

"I could not talk to you without your counsel present," I said, enjoying his discomfort.

"You could, I believe, if I initiate the conversation. At least that is how Mr. Brant explained it to me." His lawyer was Jim Brant, a partner in Boulder's oldest and poshest law firm. "And I hereby declare," he added with a little verbal flourish, "that I am initiating this conversation." He took in Beverly with a dip of his head, as if to designate her a witness to this ceremony.

I turned my back to him and walked back toward my office. "Do *me* the courtesy of making an appointment, and when you come back please bring a written waiver of your counsel's presence." I passed through the door and closed it firmly, leaning against it on the other side. It had been childish, probably, but the guy pissed me off. I waited a few more minutes, then cautiously opened the door to look out at Beverly. She was alone, her keyboard clattering away as she worked it.

"Two o'clock," she sang out without looking up. "Tough broad, aren't you?"

At two, he was sitting in the rocking chair in my office—the one whose caned seat has gotten kind of saggy. His khakis and polo shirt were unexceptionable, except perhaps for the rakish way he had turned up the collar behind his neck, as though to ward off a chill. It was about ninety degrees outside. He had handed me a carefully typed Waiver of the Presence of Counsel, signed and dated. I wondered what Jim Brant had said when McKay had asked him to prepare it.

"It really was most unethical for you to agree to represent my daughter Drew after Morgan had confided in you on my behalf," McKay said reproachfully.

"That's for the grievance committee to decide," I said, as though that prospect didn't worry me in the least. I carefully laid the waiver down on my desktop.

"Well, of course," he agreed, "unless we can arrive at some solution ourselves."

"What would that be?" I said.

Instead of answering at once he removed his horn-rimmed glasses and pulled a handkerchief from his pocket, beginning to polish the lenses. Without the glasses, his eyes looked tired, and it occurred to me that a political campaign must be an exhausting business. I had to restrain my impulse to offer him some coffee.

"Ms. Hayes," he said as he replaced the glasses. "Who are your people? Your ancestors, I mean."

I shrugged. "Farmers. Lawyers. Manicurists." I made up the last.

"My great-grandfather," he said, "was a governor of the Wyoming Territory." He studied me, looking for some reaction, I suppose.

"Oh?"

"And my grandfather, a justice of the Colorado Supreme Court. A portrait of him hangs in the court's conference room even today."

"Imagine."

He looked at me sharply. "Yes, it's common for young people to be sarcastic about the bonds of blood. Drew was that way too. I don't suppose it's occurred to you that it breaks my heart for us to be estranged in this way."

"Shouldn't you be having this conversation with her, then?"

"She won't talk to me. I imagine you've advised her not to. Might hurt the lawsuit, you probably told her."

"I haven't advised her at all on that subject."

"Well, someone has. When I call her up at that so-called farm where she's staying, she hangs up on me. Maybe it's that flea-bitten cowboy she's taken up with."

"What did you want from me, Mr. McKay?"

"It's Doctor," he said stiffly. "I am a professor, you know. I have a Ph.D. from the University of Chicago."

I said nothing.

"Tell her to talk to me," he said. "There's no need to allow our family to be humiliated in public, with journalists pawing over our troubles. Maybe we can work something out. And you would not have to face the grievance committee inquiries, which I imagine would be a relief to you as well."

"It's up to her."

"But I know she would take your advice."

"I don't have any for her on this subject."

He stood, his hands trembling slightly but otherwise composed. "If this matter goes forward, not only you but also that psychologist and Mr. Sayers will be exposed, in all of your pathetic lies and incompetence. You should all know better than to encourage this foolishness. My lawyer tells me you haven't a chance." The effect was marred, but only a little, when he stumbled slightly over a worn spot in our carpet as he turned to leave.

"Careful," I said, but he did not appear to hear.

FALL 1994

Thinking It Absurd

Andy Kahrlsrud looked at me across the table in the back room of the Trident. His broad face was as placid as ever, but he was going to be worried after I told him the news that had brought us here.

"Have you been bothered by reporters a lot?" I asked him.

"Not a one," he said.

"Good. I hope you won't be. Your name doesn't appear in the complaint anywhere, so if that's what got leaked, it wouldn't necessarily tip anyone off that you were involved."

"They must know I wouldn't talk to them anyway."

"Never underestimate the journalistic capacity for inappropriate behavior," I said. "But I think they're afraid of the judge this time, and of McKay. They haven't even challenged the gag order, and nobody's published a story about the case yet. My guess is someone in the clerk's office told a reporter about the complaint, but that no copy of it got out and the papers are reluctant to go with a story without any confirmation. It's pretty amazing how the guy has gotten the court to seal everything up. Of course, we didn't fight it, but even so, the newspapers didn't put up nearly as much of a fight as I would have predicted. I'm sure McKay's lawyers have threatened them with a suit if they print anything before the election."

Andy smiled. "Anyway, for Mariah it's good she doesn't have to cope with publicity just now."

"How do you think she's doing?" I asked.

"Really well," he said. "Her weight is back up almost to a hundred pounds, which sounds ridiculous but that's good, for her. She accepts that her target weight is about fifteen pounds more than that, and she's committed to getting there and staying there. I don't think there have been any more bingeing or purging episodes. She's happy with the life she has now, and she has a life plan."

"What *is* her life plan?" I asked. "Living on the Sayers farm? Raising goats, making sweaters from their wool?"

"Yeah, that's about it. Starting a small business to sell the sweaters. It's not surefire, of course, but whose life plan is?"

"Not mine," I said morosely.

"Not mine, either," he said cheerfully.

"What place does this lawsuit play in her life plan?"

"I don't know," said Andy. "Some days it seems very important to her, but on other days she's more preoccupied with the goats, and plans with her new friends. She's been seeing a young man you introduced her to, some musician?"

I nodded. "Lincoln. He's a great guy. He treats Mariah like a little sister, taking her around with him. She's been going along on the dates his band plays, so she's gotten to know some of the other guys and their girlfriends, too. They're sort of a ragged bunch, I guess, but good-hearted."

"It's healthy for her to have a social life."

"Andy, has she remembered anything more?"

He nodded. "One more thing, possibly. When she was out caring for the goats one night last week, it struck her that the barn was a scary place. She said she told herself that was stupid at first, because she's spent a lot of time in the barn, but she couldn't shake the feeling. It was related to the smell of the hay, she said."

I frowned. "Do you think she could have been in Sayers's barn when the thing happened?"

"Not necessarily," said Andy. "She just found it scary because of the smell. Smells are connected to memory in a very intense way, but they can be misleading, too. Possibly the barn, or the smell, reminded her of some other place, or possibly it's not related at all. She does have feelings of déjà vu from time to time, and those can be illusions of memory."

"Déjà vu? Like when?"

"Well, she was in a place with Pike Sayers one evening last week, where he was conducting some sort of community mediation. She thought she had been there before."

"What kind of place?"

"An old chapel, as she described it. It's a place the farm community uses informally for these things, I gather."

"Ryssby Chapel?"

He looked uncomfortable. "Well, yeah."

I shook my head slowly. "Sayers is going to get himself into trouble with that stuff. I happen to know he's trespassing when he uses that place."

"I wouldn't worry," said Andy. "I think he's been able to work out some understanding about that."

"No, Andy, I saw the police almost arrest him one day for being there. I was in there with him!"

"Cinda, the police know that Pike Sayers is not a bad guy. They aren't interested in busting him. He's useful to them."

I recoiled. "Do you mean he's a snitch?"

"I don't mean anything of the kind."

"How come you know so much about him?" I asked.

"I told you I have a lot of clients who work in the east county," he said. "Farmers, teachers. Law enforcement officers, maybe. That's all I'm going to say. I thought you wanted to see me about Mariah."

"Well, here's the problem, Andy. Mariah may have to testify about this stuff much sooner than we thought at first."

"Why? And how soon? This isn't good, Cinda. I thought you said it could be a year or more before the case came to trial."

"Yeah, that's what I thought. When the court allowed our complaint I was sure Harrison's lawyers would advise him to agree quietly to extending the statute of limitations. Since the case is under seal, and the seal seems to be holding, I thought they'd want to put off dealing with Mariah's complaint until at least after the election, but they didn't. Or else he wouldn't. Instead, he acceded to letting the case go forward with the allegations vague. He filed an answer denying everything. And now his lawyer wants to depose Mariah."

"What does that mean, exactly?"

"In an ordinary case, depositions are the way the lawyers find out what the witnesses are going to say at trial. They can make the witnesses come in beforehand and answer questions under oath."

"Like a trial before the trial?" he said skeptically.

"Not exactly. There's no judge at depositions, usually just the witness and the lawyers. And the parties can attend if they want to. A court reporter takes down the questions and answers. It's not as formal as a trial, but it can be pretty daunting. In fact, some lawyers try to use depositions as an occasion for some subtle witness intimidation."

"So you're worried that Mariah's going to be intimidated?" said Andy. "I think that's a pretty good worry."

"I'm a little worried about that, but there's more going on here. Ordinarily, depositions would come a little further down the line, in a few months, but McKay's lawyer got the judge to enter an order saying he could take her deposition next week, to make sure that no improper techniques contaminate her memory before trial."

"Does he mean me?" I had never seen him pugnacious before, but Andy Kahrlsrud's eyes had gotten the red-rimmed look I recognized from many cross-examinations as a sign of controlled anger.

"The lawyers don't know you, Andy, and neither does the judge. They're not accusing you of anything yet. But I'm sure one of McKay's lawyer's goals with this early deposition is to document how little Mariah remembers at this time. Then, if she comes to remember more before trial, they'll claim it's because you influenced her to remember it to serve the purposes of the lawsuit."

He shook his head. "I hate this. Have you told Mariah she has to give this deposition?"

I shook my head. "Not yet."

"Maybe we could tell her together," he said thoughtfully.

I considered this. "I think it's better not. In fact, it's best if we keep our distance from each other from here on in. I don't want to give them a chance to make you out to be a member of the litigation team."

"They will anyway," he said glumly.

"There's one more thing," I said, in unintended imitation of Columbo. "Once they depose her, they'll find out about you, and then I'm pretty sure they'll want to take your deposition, too. Not right away; they'll probably hire an investigator to see what they can find out about you. But before too long."

"But they've known about me for a while. I talked to Mariah's sister, remember?"

"Oh, that's right. Well, then they're probably looking into you already. Have you heard any strange clicking noises on your phone line?"

"Shit," said Andy. "You're kidding."

"Yes, I'm kidding. Just tell the truth, Andy. That's all that's important."

He looked away. "I don't know the truth yet. But I won't lie."

Jim Brant had wanted Mariah to give her deposition at his chilly suite of offices downtown, but I persuaded him to use the offices of the court reporting service, which occupied a turn-of-the-century Victorian building a few blocks from the courthouse. I had been there before, and thought its slightly seedy charm would be more comfortable for Mariah than the windowless conference room at Clyde, Mason, and Brink. Brant could have gotten a court order requiring her attendance at the place he designated, and knew it, so in exchange for yielding on this point he got me to agree that he could videotape the deposition. I didn't like it because I thought Mariah would find the camera frightening, but I was pretty sure Judge Meiklejohn would order videotape if I refused to agree. It seemed like a decent trade.

I had spent most of the day before trying to prepare her for the deposition, explaining the rules to her: that she should listen carefully to the question and volunteer nothing; that I probably wouldn't ask any questions at all, since I could do that at trial; that she was entitled to finish her answers, and should not let Brant cut her off before she was finished. We rehearsed for hours, with me playing the role of Brant and trying to think of everything he would ask.

She did pretty well, and in the process I learned a few things that I had not known before, for example why Harrison had thrown Mariah out of his house a month after her return from Paris. I thought this information might be useful, especially if Harrison had failed to share it with Jim Brant, which seemed probable. McKay was just the kind of guy to hold something back from his lawyer if it didn't make him look good, and this didn't.

About mid-afternoon, we quit our preparations, and I took Mariah out to the sunshine of the Mall. "Where are we going, Cinda?" she asked. I could see her struggle not to gawp at the Jamaican contortionist, going through his self-knotting routine on a mat in front of the Häagen-Dazs.

"It's okay, Mariah, you're allowed to stare at him. Even in Boulder he's considered an unusual sight. Just don't stare at anyone because they're wearing a safety pin through some body part."

"I know." She giggled. "Lincoln has one in his navel. Not a safety pin, I mean, but a little gold post."

"He does?" I was surprised less by the circumstance than by her knowledge of it.

She nodded, with a small smile, but said nothing more.

"Let's go in here." I steered her into the front door of Solo, a spiffy women's store. "Ordinarily this would be way too expensive, but I think they're having a sale. If you're going to be on videotape, you need to look right."

She looked down at her jeans in dismay. "I don't have any money, Cinda."

"Don't worry," I said. "This is a present from Pike. He asked me to take you shopping, but he's paying."

"He's..." She bit her lip and turned her face away. "Oh, look! Do you think this one would fit?"

The rain started that next morning before dawn, a rare predawn thunderstorm that might have signaled the beginning of the Indian summer monsoon. By the time Pike Sayers dropped Mariah off at my office, it had settled down to a steady clatter. Mariah looked very small again in the formal clothes, the blue suit and silk blouse too obviously new, her feet as wobbly as a colt's in the damp navy pumps.

"All the thunder scared Thelma and Louise," was the first thing she said, creasing her forehead. "I didn't like leaving them, but Pike said we had to because we couldn't do this deposition some other day."

"He's right," I said gently. "Did you have breakfast?"

"I tried." Looking down. "It was hard."

"How about some orange juice at least, before we drive over?" I poured each of us a glass from my stash in the office fridge, and she drank hers slowly while I collected my briefcase and papers.

Neither of us had a raincoat, but I found a pair of umbrellas stuck behind the coatrack. I locked the office door behind us, since neither Tory nor Beverly was in yet, and put my arm around Mariah's shoulders as we shared the biggest umbrella for the walk to my car behind the building.

"You remember your father's going to be there?" I reminded her.

She nodded quickly. "But I don't have to talk to him if I don't want to."

"That's right."

"What about Morgan?"

"She's not entitled to be in the room while you're deposed. But if she's waiting for him in the building somewhere there's not much I can do to stop her. You don't have to talk to her, either. Unless you want to."

She nodded again, her small mouth set firmly to enclose the fears before they flew out and became words.

After shaking hands and introducing himself to the reporter and video operator as though he were looking for votes, which probably he was, Harrison McKay settled into a chair in the corner of the deposition room, next to the table with the inevitable pitcher of water and glasses. He poured himself a glass of water, and did his spectacle-polishing motions again, this time with a very clean handkerchief pulled from the breast pocket of his charcoal-colored blazer. Mariah wouldn't look at him, and he didn't try to approach her. She sat awkwardly in the witness chair at the head of the table while the stenographer's equipment was set up. There was no sign of Morgan. Rain streamed down the wavy glass of the old windows, and at one point a worried-looking woman came in and stuffed a towel along the sash of one.

When I noticed that Jim Brant was trying to have a whispered conference with the reporter and cameraman, I insisted on being included. It turned out he wanted to warn them that the records of the proceeding had been sealed by the court and that they were not allowed to tell anyone about what they saw or heard inside the room. He looked at me as if he expected me to challenge this instruction, but I shrugged. Details about the lawsuit were bound to get out sooner or later, but later was okay by me. This was going to be hard enough for Mariah without the camera-in-the-face routine.

In fact, at first even the unblinking red light on the video camera disconcerted her; she couldn't stop looking at it, even while being sworn in by the reporter. When asked to state her name, she said, "Mariah Suzanne McKay," then looked back anxiously at the light and broke into a coughing fit. I asked for a break to get her some water, and while she was sipping I asked the camera operator, a skinny kid with a mop of black hair, if he could find something to cover the light. He disappeared and came back with a small piece of duct tape, which he smoothed carefully over the red eye. After that, she was fine.

Brant didn't ask her anything more about her name just then, but took her through her early years, leading her through an account of what sounded like a normal, if privileged, early childhood: ballet and tennis lessons, a horse of her own. Then he dwelled for a bit on the accident that claimed her mother's life. I could tell she was unhappy talking about it and wanted to move on, but I understood why he was so interested. No doubt Brant would argue later that any psychological problems Mariah might have now could be attributed to the trauma of her mother's death. And I was sure as well that they would contrast her vivid and fairly complete account of that event with her faulty and hazy memory of the thing they would claim had never happened. I could almost hear Brant's summation in my ears: *Why, ladies and gentlemen, if this child could remember an event as traumatic, as violent, as an automobile accident that claimed her mother's life and nearly her own—why wouldn't she be able to remember this later event in which she says her father harmed her? I'll tell you why, ladies and gentlemen. I'll tell you why.* (Here dropping his voice to excellent effect.) *Because it never happened, that's why.*

It was a good question, and before trial I was going to have to think of a better answer to it than his.

I was relieved that Brant didn't ask Mariah whether she had ever revisited the scene of the car accident. I wasn't eager to relive my poor judgment in driving her to Clear Creek and almost losing her in the water. Instead, he moved on to her troubled adolescence, asking her about the schools from which she ran away and the time in Europe, the drugs she took in Amsterdam and her arrival in Paris. I had prepared her for an inquiry about how she had earned enough money to live in Paris, explaining that she had to answer truthfully, but the question never came. Instead, there was this, as the transcript recorded it.

Mr. Brant: And how did it happen that you left Paris and came back to the United States?
The Witness: I met Kathryn.
Mr. Brant: And who might that be?
The Witness: Shapiro.
Mr. Brant: Was she someone you had known before?
The Witness: No, I met her in Paris. She's an art historian.
Mr. Brant: And what did she have to do with your return to Colorado?
The Witness: She bought me a ticket.
Mr. Brant: Why did she do that?

I had to bite my tongue to keep from objecting. At trial, the question would have been squelched once I rose and said, "Lack of personal knowledge, Your Honor." After all, how did Mariah know what was in Kathryn Shapiro's heart? But at a deposition, there's no judge to rule on objections; the rules of evidence don't apply unless a question calls for the violation of a privilege. No one to hear you scream, I thought ruefully, like in ads for a horror movie.

Mariah considered the question and looked at me uneasily.

"If you know," I said.

"Counsel," said Brant angrily. "I object to your coaching the witness."

"Object all you want," I said. No one to hear you scream either, pal. "She's entitled to know that if the correct answer is 'I don't know,' then that's the answer she should give."

"I don't know," said Mariah promptly.

"What did she tell you was her reason, then?" he said patiently.

"Isn't that hearsay?" She looked at me again, with the air of a prize pupil. Linc, I thought. He's been teaching her the rules of evidence.

"Yeah," I told her. "But that doesn't matter in here, sweetie."

"Counsel," said Brant warningly.

"Let the record reflect I'm trying to get you an answer here, Mr. Brant," I said. "Unless you've changed your mind and no longer want one." I was slightly abashed by my own surliness, but such displays of attitude are more or less expected at depositions, where custom dictates the lawyers should act like small boys who unexpectedly find themselves on the playground without adult supervision. In my small experience with civil litigation, the need to continue these feints seldom lasts beyond the first hour of the deposition, unless your opponent is a real butthead. But in the first hour, they're almost unavoidable, especially for girls who want to make clear they're mean enough to play.

Brant knew this subtext as well as I. He looked at me over the edge of his reading glasses and smiled, signaling the end of the jousting period. "Thank you, then," he said softly. "And now, Miss McKay, will you answer the question, please?"

"I forgot it," she admitted in a small voice.

"What, if anything, did Kathryn Shapiro tell you was her reason for buying you a ticket to go back to Colorado?"

She looked him straight in the face then, and squared her small shoulders beneath the pads of the new suit. "She told me," she said, enunciating every word, "that families ought to be together, that she was sure my father and sister would want me to be at home with them."

I held my breath.

Mr. Brant: And then did there come a time—
The Witness: I'm not finished.
Mr. Brant: That's all right, your answer was fine for me.
The Witness: Excuse me, but I was going to say but they didn't.
Mr. Brant: I beg your pardon?
The Witness: They didn't, sir. Want me.

Harrison McKay stirred uneasily in his chair in the corner, then stilled himself and took a sip from his water glass. Oh, Mariah, I thought, my heart breaking but my mind calculating like crazy. You are going to be a hell of a witness.

She sneaked a quick look at me then, and even returned my smile with a small one of her own. I think she realized that she had scored a small victory there. She couldn't have appreciated, however, that it was only psychological, and not practical: It's unlikely the jury would ever see the parts of the deposition that looked good for us. It would not be admissible at trial unless Mariah contradicted it in her trial testimony, in which case Brant could bring out either the transcript or the videotape to impeach her. Well, I suppose that's not quite right, to be technically accurate about it: If Mariah should become unavailable to testify at trial, we could use her deposition in lieu of live testimony. But it was hard to see how that could happen, or what the point of a trial would be in that case.

Nevertheless, her spirited insistence on finishing her answer thrilled me, and I shot her a quick smile of approbation. And after that turn, she seemed to lose the greater part of her apprehension, to relax and lean into the task of responding crisply to Brant's questions. He had already seen her medical records, at least the ones we'd been able to locate so far, and he asked her quite a bit about the recent hospitalization. But we had anticipated this, and she was ready for him.

Mr. Brant: So, do you blame your father for your recent illness?

The Witness: No. I don't—

Mr. Brant: That's enough.

The Witness: May I finish my answer, Mr. Brant?

Ms. Hayes: Yes. She's entitled to finish, Jim.

The Witness: I'm still trying to understand why I have this problem with food. My therapist, Dr. Kahrlsrud, is helping me. We hope to have a better understanding by the time the case is tried.

Mr. Brant: Is that all, Miss McKay?

The Witness: Yes, that's all.

Mr. Brant: And how did you happen to start seeing Mr. Kahrlsrud?

The Witness: Cinda called him and made an appointment for me. After I got upset when she and I were together one day. I think she was worried about me, and she was right to be. I have an eating disorder.

She was doing beautifully, but I couldn't relax. I needed to be watchful, but my own manic strategizing and fretting were running along a parallel track in my mind, an irritating background monologue, like a radio left on by mistake: *I know exactly why Brant wants to take a deposition this early. He wants to get on the record how sketchy and uncertain her memories are. If she remembers more later, he'll suggest to the jury this is a too convenient return of memory, a result of some manipulation by either me or Andy Kahrlsrud, or more likely both. Too bad I wasn't able to persuade Judge Meiklejohn that she ought to give us more time before subjecting Mariah to this interrogation. . . . Brant's going to try to confuse her, and if she gets confused today, he'll make skillful use of that later, when we get to trial. Our trial date's more than ten months away. It's going to be uphill work to get the jury to understand how Mariah could remember things then that she was unable to remember today. A witness's sudden recollection during trial of things she never mentioned in an earlier deposition looks phony as hell. . . . I hope Judge Meiklejohn allows us to explain to the jury that the statute of limitations problem required us to file the suit sooner than we would have preferred. I should file a motion before trial to get a ruling on that. . . . Assuming she* does *remember more by trial; if she doesn't, we'll probably have to dismiss the case.*

Jim Brant's voice brought me back into the present. He was reading to Mariah from the complaint, his well-trained voice carrying the merest note of ridicule as he did.

Mr. Brant: Now, Miss McKay, let's talk about these memories of yours, these clouded, partial, and to date uncorroborated memories, as your complaint calls them.

The Witness: Okay.

Mr. Brant: What exactly is it that you remember about the event, which is not to concede that there was one?

The Witness: Which event exactly do you mean, sir?

Mr. Brant: I mean the event that caused you to consult Ms. Hayes here and file this lawsuit against your father.

The Witness: All right. My father was there, and so was I. It was night, I'm pretty sure. There were other people there, too.

Mr. Brant: Is that all?

The Witness: No, I'm just thinking a minute. I want to say this exactly right and exactly true. That's what Ms. Hayes told me.

Mr. Brant: All right. Please continue.

The Witness: Someone was screaming. I think it was me. There were rocks. Huge rocks, all piled up. My father was jerking me and grabbing me. Something was keeping me from seeing. Then my father was carrying me away. There were some legs, white legs, uncovered. They might have been mine. There was more than one part of the place where this happened. Some of it was inside, but a big place. Some of it was outside, but that part was harder to see. I was very scared. My father was scaring me.

Mr. Brant: Very well, then, is that all you remember?

The Witness: Yes. I think so.

Mr. Brant: So something was keeping you from seeing?

The Witness: Yes.

Mr. Brant: You could not see, something was covering your eyes?

The Witness: I'm not sure if it was a cover or what. There was some part of the time I could not see.

Mr. Brant: Yet you saw these things you describe, the inside place, the outside place, the rocks, the white legs. Your father.

The Witness: Yes.

I tried to keep my eye alternately on Mariah and on Harrison McKay. He was not looking at Mariah now, preferring to keep his eyes on the vaguely impressionist watercolors that hung at intervals around the walls. Perhaps he really was unconcerned, and interested in art, but I noticed that he looked at each picture for about a minute before transferring his gaze to the next, as though on a schedule. I tried to think what I would look like if I were listening to my child saying such things. I had no idea.

Mr. Brant: Well, did your father hit you on this occasion?

The Witness: I don't know.

Mr. Brant: Do you remember his hitting you on this occasion?

The Witness: I don't remember.

Mr. Brant: That would be a no?

The Witness: Yes.

Mr. Brant: Please answer yes or no, Miss McKay. Did your father hit you on this occasion we're talking about here?

I started to interrupt, to remind Brant, who didn't need reminding, that he was not entitled to insist on a yes or no answer, but Mariah remembered what I had told her.

The Witness: I can't answer yes or no, Mr. Brant, because my memory of this isn't clear. I don't remember that he hit me. That's all I can tell you now.

Mr. Brant: Did he sexually assault you on this occasion?

The Witness: I don't remember.

Mr. Brant: As far as you can recall, he did not.

The Witness: That's right. But possibly I don't recall everything that happened.

Mr. Brant: Well, your complaint says you're trying hard to remember, and that you've had some success trying to reconstruct your memory, is that right?

The Witness: Yes.

Mr. Brant: And are you enjoying any assistance in your endeavor to recover your memories?

The Witness: Yes, from my therapist, Andy Kahrlsrud. But he's very careful not to—

Mr. Brant: Yes, thank you. And anyone else? Ms. Hayes, for example?

Ms. Hayes: Just a minute, Mariah. Mr. Brant, you know better than that.

Mr. Brant: Are you instructing her not to answer?

Ms. Hayes: Unless you stipulate that any answer she gives to this question will not constitute a waiver of the attorney-client relationship in general.

Mr. Brant: Are you saying you'll allow her to answer if I make that stipulation?

Ms. Hayes: Yes.

Mr. Brant: I so stipulate. Answer the question.

Ms. Hayes: You can answer, Mariah. The question was, do I assist you in your efforts to remember?

The Witness: No. I work on that with Andy, you said. You and I work on other things.

Mr. Brant: What sorts of things?

Ms. Hayes: All right, now I am instructing her. You don't have to answer that, Mariah.

Mr. Brant: Well, let me ask you this. Did Dr. Kahrlsrud help you get ready for this deposition?

The Witness: He only suggested some relaxation techniques that I could try if I started to feel stressed-out.

Mr. Brant: Oh, really? Have you had to use any of them?

I thought of objecting, but we had waived Mariah's client-therapist privilege with Kahrlsrud by asking for damages for emotional and mental suffering. I decided to let her answer, even though I didn't know what she would say. I'm glad I did.

The Witness: Well, just one.

Mr. Brant: What was that?

The Witness: He said if you started acting like an asshole I should just imagine you sitting there stark naked, except for your socks. It works pretty well, actually.

I burst out laughing, and I thought I saw the stenographer suppressing a smile as her fingers recorded the exchange. For the first time, I regretted the official seal on the proceedings.

Ms. Hayes: Well, you asked, Mr. Brant.

Mr. Brant: Very amusing, Miss McKay. Did you ever seek to discuss these matters with your father, in order to understand what might have happened?

The Witness: Yes. Once.

Brant has a pretty good poker face, but I thought he might have been surprised by this answer. I had the impression he had to restrain himself from turning to look at his client. For his part, McKay was still engaged in his survey of the wall hangings, and did not appear to be paying particular attention.

Mr. Brant: And when was this attempt at discussion?

The Witness: Not long after I got back from Paris. One night. He and my sister and I were eating dinner, and I started to try to talk about it.

Mr. Brant: What did you say?

The Witness: I don't remember my exact words, Mr. Brant.

Mr. Brant: To the best of your recollection.

The Witness: I asked them what had happened the time I got so scared and couldn't stop screaming. They said they didn't know what I was talking about. And right after that was when they, he, made me leave.

Mr. Brant: That very same night?

The Witness: Later that night.

Mr. Brant: Did any other events intervene between this conversation you've just described and your departure from the house?

The Witness: Yeah.

Mr. Brant: In fact, didn't you steal some items from your father?

I smiled to myself again. Brant had made a mistake here: There's no point in cross-examining a deposition witness the way you would at trial. Moreover, Brant's phrasing made me think his client had not told him the true story about the night Mariah left. I hoped he would pursue it further, and he did.

The Witness: Yes, I suppose you could call it that. Stealing.

Mr. Brant: You took something that didn't belong to you, didn't you?

The Witness: Yes. Well, I didn't leave the house with it. Or not very much of it. But I did take it from where it was in the house.

Mr. Brant: I'm sorry. Didn't leave the house with it?

I was sure now: Harrison hadn't told him what the "items" were. Go ahead, I urged him silently. Ask her. But she was speaking.

The Witness: That's correct.

Mr. Brant: Well, what were the items?

The Witness: I don't remember exactly.

Mr. Brant: To the best of your recollection, please, Miss McKay.

The Witness: To the best of my recollection, it was roast beef. Rice. Pie, I think cherry, but I'm not sure. Ice cream, I don't remember what flavor. Some other food items.

Mr. Brant: You stole food?

The Witness: I ate it, Mr. Brant.

Mr. Brant: You ate it?

The Witness: Yes. Really a lot of it. Then I regurgitated it.

Brant said it was about time for a lunch break. I can't imagine anyone felt much like eating after that last disclosure, but I was glad for an intermission. Mariah looked grateful, too. Brant went over to his client and hustled him out of the room. The stenographer and camera operator left, too, and Mariah and I were alone. For a moment, the only sounds belonged to the storm, which had ceased for a while only to start up again within the last few minutes. The wind hurled drops at the window like Jackson Pollock working on an invisible painting, and Mariah whispered, "How am I doing?"

She looked so fragile and so stubborn, and something turned over in my belly and I thought, Dear God, is this what it feels like to love your own child? I had to turn my face away for a moment, afraid she would see and be frightened. I pretended to cough, and after a moment I faced her again.

"Sorry," I said. "You're doing fine. Better than fine. Great."

She smiled. "I thought so," she whispered.

I held Mariah's elbow as we crossed the building's small parking lot, our umbrellas jostling against each other in a friendly way. "What do you want for lunch?" I asked her, but before she could answer the door of a nearby compact car opened, and Morgan McKay stepped out from behind the driver's seat.

"Drew," she said, but after the smallest catch in her stride Mariah walked on, her small face set and white.

"Mariah!" she cried, and that stopped me. I thought there was genuine grief caught in her voice. I looked back at the figure standing by the open car door, her crisp suit and shapely hair unprotected from the rain. "Don't do this!" I think she called out, but at that moment a bus roared around the corner and hit a puddle of water, drowning her words in the jolt and sizzle of its progress.

"Maybe you should talk to her," I said, dropping Mariah's arm. "She's calling you by your right name, at least."

"She knows my name, all right," said Mariah, putting her hand against my back and pushing ever so slightly until I was walking again. "Let's go."

The afternoon session consisted mostly of questions about Mariah's current circumstances, especially her home at the Sayers farm. McKay seemed to be paying a bit closer attention during this part.

Mr. Brant: This Sayers is some kind of judge, is he?
The Witness: That's right.
Mr. Brant: What kind exactly?
The Witness: Common-law judge is what he's told me. That's hearsay but it's okay, right?
Mr. Brant: What else has he told you?
The Witness: Not very much.
Mr. Brant: Well, you have been a litigant before this so-called judge yourself, have you not?
The Witness: I have if that means I asked him to change my name.
Mr. Brant: And he did so, did he not? Changed your name from Drew McKay to what you are calling yourself today?
The Witness: Mariah Suzanne McKay, yes.
Mr. Brant: And are you aware of where he gets his authority to enter orders and make judgments?
The Witness: No, sir. I'm not a lawyer.
Mr. Brant: And he is a member of a militia, is he not?
The Witness: Not as far as I know.
Mr. Brant: Well, a militia would keep itself secret, would it not?
The Witness: I have no idea.

Mr. Brant: Have you witnessed any of the proceedings of this so-called common-law court?

The Witness: Yes, sir.

Mr. Brant: Describe them, please.

The Witness: One was about a disagreement between two farmers about where their property line was. One was a divorce. In one, a man had borrowed another one's combine and after he returned it, it broke down and cost a lot to fix, and the owner said the man who borrowed it had damaged it. But the judge listened to the mechanic and even looked at the combine, I guess, and thought it had been about to break down for a long time.

Mr. Brant: Are these the only proceedings you've witnessed?

The Witness: I'm trying to think. There may have been another, but I'm not sure. Something similar to those, maybe.

Mr. Brant: Any criminal cases? Anyone being prosecuted for some crime?

The Witness: No.

Mr. Brant: Well, does this Judge Sayers have any criminal jurisdiction?

The Witness: You'd have to ask him.

Mr. Brant: I'm asking you, Miss McKay.

The Witness: I don't know, then.

Mr. Brant: Has he or anyone ever told you anything about common-law trials other than the ones you've attended?

The Witness: I don't think so.

Brant asked for a moment to confer with his client, and while he did I reached under the table to squeeze Mariah's hand. She squeezed back and looked at me, exactly the way I remember Dana would when she and I shared a childhood secret. But there was no secret here, not really, just a silent celebration of our complicity: you and me against the world.

"Hold on tight," I whispered. I thought I knew what was coming; it was the question she'd been worried about. I had hoped Brant wouldn't ask it, but I could smell it coming now. Brant walked back over to his chair and sat heavily down. He was getting tired, too.

Mr. Brant: Now, Miss McKay, please tell me the names of the persons involved in those proceedings that you've attended.

Ms. Hayes: Do you mean the parties to the disputes, Mr. Brant?

Mr. Brant: For starters.

Ms. Hayes: And then do you mean to ask for the identities of others who attended as well?

Mr. Brant: I'll have to see, Ms. Hayes. I'm entitled to know the names of her associates.

Ms. Hayes: For what legitimate discovery purpose, Mr. Brant?

Mr. Brant: To investigate the possibility that someone among them has influenced her to believe that her father harmed her in some way, when that is not the case.

Ms. Hayes: You got this early deposition by representing to the judge that her memory was unreliable, but there's no reason to think she has any trouble remembering the names of the people she's met. I suggest you wait until the proper time and seek that information through interrogatories.

Mr. Brant: Why put it off? Let her answer here.

Ms. Hayes: There's a privacy interest involved here.

Mr. Brant: I don't think the judge will see it that way.

Ms. Hayes: Then seek an order requiring her to answer.

Mr. Brant: You're instructing her not to answer?

Ms. Hayes: That's correct.

Brant didn't quite throw up his hands. He was too self-contained for that kind of gesture, but he managed to pantomime disgust with a collection of more subtle signals: a facial expression, directed at the camera operator, inviting him to share in the affront; and a massaging of his temples, conveying the unprecedented nature of this challenge to his patience.

I thought we'd probably lose this one later, after the judge considered it, but it seemed like a fight worth having. Mariah had told me yesterday that she didn't want to get anyone else into trouble, and was afraid that the people who came to the common-law court sessions might suffer if she named them. It wasn't clear to me that they had anything to fear; the only one who had anything to worry about was Pike Sayers, and he'd already told us he didn't want any effort made to protect him. Still, I couldn't be sure, and in addition I didn't want Mariah to become an outcast, as she might if people suspected her of betrayal. My strategem would probably do nothing but buy us a little time. Still, time is valuable.

Mr. Brant: How about this Sayers? Is she going to refuse to answer questions about him, too?

Ms. Hayes: No, Mr. Brant. She's already answered several, if you recall. You may inquire freely.

Mr. Brant: Thank you, I'm sure. Miss McKay, please tell me about the conversations you've had with Pike Sayers about this lawsuit.

The Witness: We didn't have very many.

Mr. Brant: Please tell me about them.

The Witness: At first, after I saw him doing a trial, I wanted him to be the judge of my lawsuit against my father. But he said no. After that I heard Cinda, Ms. Hayes, talking on the radio about intimate torts and I called her to ask her a question. Later that day, I asked him about whether I should see her and he said it might be a good idea. Since I've gone to live at his farm, he's said very little about it, because he tells me I should talk to Cinda if I have any questions. He says she's a very good person.

Mr. Brant: I'm sure we all admire Ms. Hayes. Now if you could just explain to me, Miss McKay, why Mr. Sayers instructed you not to bring your lawsuit in his court. If you know. Or anything he might have told you along those lines.

The Witness: He said my father wouldn't recognize his jurisdiction, and probably wouldn't appear in his court.

Mr. Brant: Is that the only reason?

The Witness: Far as I know.

Brant pushed his chair out and stepped over to Harrison McKay's corner again, and I scrutinized Mariah's face. It was getting to be almost four o'clock, and I hadn't been able to persuade her to eat much lunch at the little sandwich shop where we had gone at noon.

"Are you hungry?" I whispered.

"Yes!" she said, and my heart soared.

"Shall we go out to dinner after this?" I asked.

She started to reply when Brant came back over and spoke. "That's all for now, Ms. Hayes, unless you want to reconsider your very foolish instructions to your client concerning identifying her associates."

"I don't mind if you ask her who her friends are," I replied. "I just instructed her not to identify those who attend the common-law court session."

"Very well, let's go back on the record," said Brant wearily.

Mariah looked at me with a question on her face, and I nodded.

Mr. Brant: Please identify your friends for the record, Miss McKay.

The Witness: My current friends?

Mr. Brant: The people you are close to now.

The Witness: Lincoln Tolkien. Cinda Hayes. Pike Sayers. Dr. Andy Kahrlsrud. Joe, Ben, Adam, and Hoss Cartwright. And Sparkle, I don't know her last name. She's Ben's girlfriend.

Mr. Brant: Sparkle? Does your client realize she is still under oath, Ms. Hayes?

Ms. Hayes: I'm sure she does.

Mr. Brant: Who is that first person you named?

The Witness: Lincoln Tolkien. He's my best friend, because he's about my age. Pike and Cinda are more like my parents, I guess.

Mr. Brant: Your parents.

The Witness: Yes.

Mr. Brant: That will be all, Miss McKay. Ms. Hayes, may I see you for a moment? Unless, of course, you have questions for your client.

Ms. Hayes: None.

I was still reeling myself from her last description of me and Pike Sayers. I touched Mariah's sleeve to signal that we should sit and wait until everyone else had left the room.

"What does he want to talk to you about?" she asked me after the room had emptied.

"Probably try to find a date for a hearing about his motion to compel."

"What's that again? I know we talked about it but I'm feeling confused right now."

"He's going to ask a judge to make you answer his questions about who attends the common-law court sessions. I'm going to try to persuade the judge this is not necessary and violates the rights of other people, but remember what I said about this? This judge is fair. She cut us a lot of slack by letting the suit be filed under the circumstances. Then she gave your father a break by letting his lawyer take your deposition this early. It's unpredictable, but in the end the judge may say you have to answer. She might even say that she'll dismiss the case if you don't."

"Then what'll we do, Cinda?"

"Let's burn that bridge when we come to it," I said tiredly.

She looked puzzled. "Do you mean cross? Cross that bridge?"

"Yes, cross. Sorry, Mariah. Why don't you wait for me here while I talk to Brant, then maybe we can go out to dinner?"

Almost imperceptibly, she squirmed. "I think I have plans."

"Oh?"

"Linc," she said. "He has the Subaru. I didn't think you'd mind if I let him use it today. He's going to pick me up when I call him from your office."

"Great, then. Hang on and I'll drive you back over."

Brant was lingering in the small reception area, tapping a file folder impatiently against his thigh. When he saw me, he motioned me into an adjoining waiting room, where some decorator had made an attempt, rather misguided in my opinion, at reproduction Victorian furnishings. I sat down uncomfortably on a velvet settee draped with a fringed scarf. On an ornate walnut end table, a modern multiple-line telephone with a couple of its red lights glowing provided a jarring contrast to an ormolu clock, which showed that it was nearly four-thirty. A floor lamp cast out a weak glow through an amber-colored fluted globe.

"I know, I know," I said before he could start. "Do you want to file a motion to compel, or shall I move for a protective order? I'm sure you want this question resolved as soon as possible."

"My client is more concerned about his daughter than about exposing the activities of some ridiculous right-wing sect."

"Oh?" I replied, suppressing numerous smartass comments that leaped unbidden to mind, all of which amounted to *He has a funny way of showing it.* But this was unexpected; I hadn't been looking for a settlement offer so soon.

"Dr. McKay is prepared to offer your client seventy-five thousand dollars in exchange for dismissal of all claims and a confidentiality agreement."

I hated confidentiality agreements on principle, but Mariah and I had discussed this possibility because I had thought it might come up, if not quite this early. I had told her it was up to her.

"She doesn't have a problem with confidentiality, as long as she's still permitted to talk to her therapist."

"Good."

"But what you're offering isn't enough."

He nodded, unsurprised. "I'm authorized to offer ninety. Any more than that and I'd have to go back to my client, and I don't think—"

"It's not the money. We'd have to talk about that later. But Mariah wants him to sit down with her and explain exactly what happened, what it is that wakes her up screaming in the night and follows her around in the daytime. She needs to know, Jim. That's the most urgent thing."

"My client's position is that there was nothing. So how could he explain it?"

I looked at him in the dim light, wishing I had left my glasses on so I could see his face more clearly. "That's the truth, or that's his position?"

Brant rubbed his lower face, checking for five o'clock shadow or perhaps just trying to massage his jaw after a long day of jawboning. "Spare me, Cinda. You know that as far as I'm concerned there is not and could not possibly be any difference between those two. Anyway, that's ridiculous as a settlement condition. He could tell her anything. He could tell her she got lost at the zoo one day and it scared her to death. How would she know whether it's true or not?"

"She thinks she'll know. All she really cares about is the truth, Jim."

"Surely you see this is completely unworkable. Look, Cinda, this man is a person of impeccable reputation, a candidate for the senate of the state. A trial would be painful for him, but only because it would expose his daughter's troubled psyche to so many people. He doesn't want that to happen."

I shrugged. "He may be a man of impeccable reputation, but he's also a man who put his very troubled and nearly friendless child out of her home because she ate too much of his food. His concern about her psyche showed up a little late. If he wants to settle this case, then you figure out a way to make it work. Mariah only wants the truth, and we're prepared to go to trial if that's what it takes to get the truth out."

Brant stood up, his manner more abrupt now. "I don't think you know what you're doing, Cinda. Surely you don't really believe that a trial has anything to do with finding out the truth. It's a contest, that's all. Your client may have scored a few cheap rhetorical points today, but she doesn't have anything that looks like a cause of action and you know it. She's not going to remember anything more between now and trial because there's nothing to remember. And if you or that psychologist is foolish enough to induce false memories in the girl, we will demolish her. I'm prepared to hire Martha Trefusis as a witness if it comes to that."

Go ahead and try, you prick, I thought. I stood up, too, and stepped closer to him than I felt comfortable, close enough for him to feel my breath. "Your threats," I said deliberately, "belie your suggestion that your client cares about his daughter. Now, if you'll excuse me."

I shouldered past him, narrowly avoiding an exit-spoiling

collision with an occasional table, and walked back toward the library, where Mariah waited. I hate that macho shit, but I can do it if I have to.

Mariah seemed in good spirits as we drove back to the office, but whether it was from surviving the deposition or anticipating a date with Lincoln I could not tell. I explained Brant's offer, and she told me again that the truth was more important to her than a damage award. "Except I need enough money to pay you for being my lawyer, Cinda," she said. "I know nobody else would have stayed with me for this crazy case."

I denied it, although it was probably true and not necessarily an endorsement of my judgment. Brant's words had struck me a little harder than I had shown, or perhaps known, at the time. He was a jerk, but what if he was right? I turned on the radio for Mariah, trying not to think about the way she had looked in the hospital bed. Instead my mind summoned up our declining balance at the bank and the landlord's notice that the rent would go up when our lease expired in November.

Linc was waiting at the office when we got back, along with Tory and Beverly and Seamus Kellogg, all standing around in the reception area.

"I did it, Linc!" said Mariah, shrugging off her shoulder bag and moving quickly to his side. He put an arm around her shoulders and threw his other fist into the air. "Yes!" he said. "Vanquished the beast, slain the dragon, returned the heroine!" She beamed at him and I thought I had never seen her look so happy. Some premonition chilled me then, but I thought it was just a renewal of the Impostor Syndrome and my worries about whether I knew what I was doing.

"This is Mr. Kellogg, Mariah," said Tory. "Seamus, Mariah McKay."

I expected the usual ritual of blarney and flattery, but Kellogg shook her hand briefly and said he had to go.

He took my hand as if in farewell, but instead held it as he drew me slightly aside from the others. "You want to be after taking very good care of yourself, Ms. Lucinda," he said earnestly.

"Sure," I said lightly, somewhat mystified by his solicitude. Then he turned back to the others to make his farewells. Mariah's eyes followed him as he thanked Tory for her time, nodded at Beverly with far less than his customary chivalry, and walked out the door.

"Who was that again?" Mariah asked Tory.

"Just a client." Tory smiled. "He used to have a crush on Beverly, but I think he's getting over it."

Tory and Beverly had only met Mariah once or twice before, but they fussed over her, got her a Coke from the fridge, and made her sit down in the reception area. They didn't ask about the deposition, but chatted with her about her goats and Tetanus Booster's upcoming appearances. Before long Linc looked at his watch and said, "We gotta break, Mariah. We're going to Laudisio's for dinner, and then we're supposed to meet Ben and Sparkle to play pool for a while. Okay?"

Mariah came over to where I was leaning against the reception desk and put her head close to mine. "Can I talk to you for a minute first?" she asked.

"Sure," I said, and led her to my office, closing the door behind us.

"Can I talk to Linc about the deposition?" she said. "It really helps me to talk to him." Her eyes were bright, but the ebullience seemed to be metamorphosing into a kind of dazed wonder.

"You can tell him about it, since he's working on the case with me. Just remind him he can't talk to anyone else about it. And you can talk to Andy, of course. But nobody else, okay?"

She nodded, then put her cheek against mine. "I meant it, what I said about you in the deposition," she whispered. "Thank you."

Back out by the door, Lincoln was jangling a large bunch of keys. "Thanks for the use of your car, Cinda," he said to me. "It's a wreck, but it's fly."

I thought it possible this was a compliment. "Thanks," I said tentatively.

"Give me those," said Mariah playfully. "It's my wreck and I want to drive."

It must have been about the ninth or tenth time since the radio show that I'd been visited by the examination dream: the bundle of books, the terrible struggle to remember, the foreknowledge of disaster. But this time a dreadful shrill bell rang in the dream, punctuating my frantic search with a certainty that it was too late, I had failed, failed. The second ring of the bell brought me to a fogged consciousness and I reached for the phone, relief slowly drifting into my mind as I achieved the blessed realization: *It's only a dream.*

The police officer introduced himself by name, Steven Aguilera. He was polite but insistent: Where was the yellow 1982 Subaru that was registered in my name? I stammered out that it had been lent to a friend. When he began to ask me questions about the friend's name, and whether I knew who might have been with her, the terror returned, accompanied by the knowledge that there would be no waking, no deliverance, this time.

"An accident?" I said. "Oh, my God, is she alive? Is he?"

"He's alive," he said. "But in serious condition."

"What about her? How is she?"

"I'm sorry."

"Oh, my God. Where was the accident?"

"Just stay where you are, Ms. Hayes. We're going to have an officer at your house in a few minutes."

"Where was it?" The only picture my mind could conjure was of a car in Clear Creek, upside down as the black rushing waters reflected the circulation of red lights on the bank above.

"Isabelle Road," he said. "And we don't think it was an accident."

God opens his hand, and life flows through it like sand. Tethered as we are to this small, sweet globe, sometimes we do not even realize we are topsy-turvy, and so we imagine the sand is flowing down, that life is flowing out. But, sisters and brothers, the grains of sand are flowing up, higher and higher, to Him and His blessings beyond our imagining. And our confidence that this is so must be our comfort as we consign the earthly body of this beautiful young woman to this blessed ground, with others who belonged to the family she joined so recently.

It was something like that. The preacher was from a church I had never heard of, the Brethren of Our Body in Christ, I think it was. I don't believe he had ever met Mariah, but his voice had a clean, honest sound, free from wheedling or threat, and I believe she would have liked him. Lincoln stood next to me at the edge of the grave that Pike Sayers had dug the night before with his own hands, and when the time came, Linc hobbled forward on his crutches to let fall a clot of brown earth onto the unvarnished lid of Mariah's coffin. Then it was Pike's turn, and I could see the angry blisters on his right hand as he opened it to release a shower of dirt. Marnie and Christopher Covington, led forward by their parents, threw ragged bouquets of sunflowers into the raw excavation. Pike looked at Andy Kahrlsrud, but Andy declined with a minute shake of his head, rubbing one of his big hands up and down on the side of his khakis.

Thelma and Louise, carried here in the back of Pike's pickup, scrabbled around behind one of the old headstones, making some of the loneliest sounds I have ever heard from an animal. Sparkle hugged her bare arms, her hands in lacy black gloves; her dress was black and very short and strewn with jet beads like black tears. Tory and Beverly held hands a little apart from the rest of us, and I think Beverly cried more than anyone. The Cartwrights stood together on the other side of the grave, holding their bluegrass instruments: guitar, mandolin, banjo, violin.

It was a cloudy day, with occasional late-afternoon lightning flickering behind the distant foothills. But the sun held its own for a moment there just at the end, throwing moving cumulus shadows along the ground as the wind shook the rabbitbrush and Joe Cartwright played the opening bars of the song.

I don't know how Lincoln did it. I couldn't have sung even if it would have brought Mariah back to us; my throat seemed to have closed permanently, and my breath came in ragged useless gasps. But Linc turned his face toward the sky and leaned into the crutches to sing, in his clear strong tenor, the words I can never hear now without seeing that place, the roughened white stones, the tender torn-up ground, the line of mountains against the sky, and the little goats, finally silent, grazing awkwardly on the buffalo grass in this patch of earth they had never seen or tasted before.

Away out here they got a name
For rain and wind and fire,
The rain is Tess, the fire's Jo,
And they call the wind Mariah.

We had invited her father and sister to come because we felt we had to, but they stayed away, furious that they had not been permitted to bury Mariah as they had arranged, beside her mother in the plot their family had purchased in Green Mountain Cemetery in Boulder. A "family spokesman" had informed me that they planned to have their own memorial service, private of course. For the disgrace of her burial on this dried-up farm they blamed me, and Pike Sayers, and Lincoln most of all.

It was Linc who, despite his broken leg and concussion, had remembered from his hospital bed to tell me about the envelope Mariah had given him weeks before, as she lay in her own room in Longmont United Hospital. "It says, 'To Be Opened in the Event of My Death,'" he explained. I couldn't stand to look at his eyes, bloody and blackened by the collision between the Subaru and a utility pole. "Look for it on the stand by my bed in the house. I stuck it inside *The Hobbit,* I think. I tried not to take it. I told her she was going to live for years and years." He turned his face toward the wall and his shoulders hunched once.

"Did she think someone was trying to kill her even then?" I asked him gently.

"She thought the anorexia might kill her," he said. "Or that she might want to die because of it. She didn't think someone would *shoot* her. In the face, with a rifle."

"Shh!" I said stupidly. His shoulders were shaking now. "You'll pull out your IV, sweetie. Listen, your mother is outside and wants to see you."

He composed his face quickly. "Cinda? Will you get a wash-cloth and wipe my face off first?"

And then he seemed all right, except for his tortured whisper as I bathed his face. "I should have been driving, Cinda. But I had too many beers at McCabe's."

"Shh!" I said again. "I don't think it would have made any difference, except it might have saved you from your injuries when the car crashed. It wouldn't have saved Mariah's life. Whoever it was wanted her dead. They took perfect aim at her."

He nodded, as if in wonder that one could be comforted by this brutal thought. "Cinda? While we were playing pool with Sparkle and Ben, she told me she was starting to remember more. She asked me if it was too late, since her deposition was over."

"Shh," I said. "It doesn't matter now."

"She told me she thought Seamus Kellogg was there."

"What? Tory's client?"

"That's what she said. Also, she said there was a string of lights."

"String of lights?"

"Yeah. She said seeing Seamus Kellogg reminded her. She couldn't wait to tell Andy Kahrlsrud."

"I'm afraid she was starting to get confused, Linc. That doesn't make any sense at all." I blotted his face tenderly one last time. "Here comes your mom now."

It became clear eventually about the will: She had gotten the idea from a law book that Linc had left behind by accident when he was visiting her at the hospital. I could imagine her easily, a pale figure in a white gown, propped up in her hospital bed poring over the heavy book in the eerie green light. *Colorado Estate Law.* When Tory and I found it later, in our library where Linc had returned it unknowing, a crease in the spine parted it easily and it fell open to this page:

> Ordinarily, a will, to be valid in Colorado, must be signed not only by the testator, but also by at least two individuals who have witnessed the signing of the will by the testator. This requirement may be dispensed with in only one situation, that of the holographic will. A holographic will is one whose material parts are handwritten by the testator, and signed by the testator as well. A holographic will, if established to be in the handwriting of the testator, is valid despite the absence of witnesses.

She must have read some other parts as well; it was a pretty professional document. Her handwriting—printing, really—was beautiful, both graceful and scratchy, like Japanese kanji.

> Being of sound mind, I, Mariah Suzanne McKay, also known as Drew Connor McKay, do hereby make this, my last will and testament, being a holographic will according to the statutes of the state of Colorado. I hereby request the appointment of Pike Gunther Sayers of Erie, Colorado, as executor of my estate, with all the powers pertaining to that office. I further authorize him to make all arrangements for my funeral and designate the place of my burial, asking him to consider my respectful request that he permit me to be buried at some place on his family's property if he should find that agreeable, or if not in some place with a view of the mountains. I further leave all of my estate, whatever it shall consist of, to Pike Gunther Sayers, with gratitude for his love and loyalty.
>
> Signed this 17th day of June, 1994

There had been some confusion, of course. I had told the police officer that her nearest kin were Harrison and Morgan McKay. He had been disbelieving at first. "The professor running for the legislature? He only has the one daughter, doesn't he?" But eventually he phoned in this information, and someone must have awakened the McKays to tell them that their daughter and sister was dead. They tried to claim the body the next day, but an autopsy was necessary, and by the time that was done we had found the will.

Jim Brant went to probate court and tried to get an emergency restraining order setting aside the will on the ground that Mariah was not of sound mind, but by then I had a copy of the deposition videotape, which I was able to show to the judge as evidence of her sanity and clarity. I could scarcely endure the sound and sight of it, and after the judge ruled in our favor and the lawyers and law clerk and court reporter had left the courtroom, I put my head down on the counsel table and wept for that bright spirit erased. Pike Sayers put his steady hand on my shoulder and kept it there until I could lift my head to leave.

Thank God for Sparkle and Beverly, who made tea and coffee back at the farmhouse, and found plates and napkins. Tory had excused herself, looking somehow angry, but I was too inebriated with sorrow to wonder why. After we all ate cake and fresh strawberries, someone passed around a bottle of whiskey. I found myself pulling a long draught from the green bottle, the fumes dizzying me even before I swallowed, coughing. I was surprised how much better it made me feel, and took another large mouthful when it came around again. The Cartwrights got out their instruments and they and Linc and Andy sang Appalachian songs about coal mines and wild mountain meadows and horses that couldn't be rid, and I think I fell into a bit of a sleep. I was aware of people leaving, and then of Pike Sayers sitting in front of me and taking my hands in his. They were roughened and torn, I remember, and neither large nor small.

. . .

Back in my radio days, in college, I studied philosophy. It seemed very important at the time but most of it eludes me now, forgotten like the source of Mariah's terrors. I do remember, though, the closing sentence of Wittgenstein's *Tractatus,* which I took at the time, and still take, as a warning. *What we cannot speak about we must pass over in silence.*

With Pike, it was silent even as it happened, except for our cries and tears. Perhaps it's like that with parents who have lost their child, expecting neither comfort nor pleasure, and yet seeking each other because what else is there? It is sealed in us separately now. And even that is more than can be said.

We breakfasted wordlessly when the morning came, and clasped each other once in parting.

"That," I said into his shoulder, "is not going to happen again."

He merely nodded as he released me, and still said nothing.

There was a lot of evidence, Steven Aguilera told me, but none of it sufficient to identify the killer. Mariah had died of a gunshot wound to the head; the weapon had been a rifle, probably something called a Browning BAR .300 Winchester Magnum. The killer, in a dark-colored van, had apparently been following behind the Subaru for some time; Linc remembered that much after he recovered consciousness. Apparently, it drew alongside in the dark at the stop sign at Isabelle Road and Ninety-fifth Street, near the Pleasant View Grange; they found two cartridge shells in the road there. But the shooter hadn't waited for the Subaru to stop, so the police theorized he was an excellent and confident shot. She must have turned to look at him, because the first shot had gone straight through her head, front to back. The second, nearly as accurate, had struck her in the ear, but it was not needed: The first had probably been immediately fatal. The Subaru had been traveling downhill, and had continued to roll down after the bullets struck. It accelerated under its own momentum, and possibly from Mariah's lifeless foot on the pedal, until stopped by the pole.

Linc told me that he could not remember much, and after his first interviews with the police, he was disinclined to talk about it at all. He came back to work after a week, swinging his weight around on his crutches with a grace that might have concealed the seething anger had I not seen it burning in his eyes. I could hear him banging the keys on the reception-area computer whenever Beverly was not there. I had no idea what he was working on; something for Tory, I imagined.

The police had their theory, of course: Someone connected with the common-law courts or the Brotherhood of Colorado Militia had killed Mariah, because when her case went to trial, or before, she was going to be forced to identify everyone in the community and bring down the forces of the law on them. I didn't buy it. I was certain Mariah had told me everything she knew, and that included nothing more irregular than the conduct of a few mediation sessions accompanied by the superficial trappings of judicial power. Anyway, I believed what Pike Sayers had suggested, that the violent people in the antigovernment community would have welcomed a confrontation between themselves and the government.

Still, I didn't have proof for any other explanation. Only a few shards of evidence that tended as much toward the police hypothesis as any other: a broken car window, a Nazi symbol, a cut-up doll, and the memory of Morgan McKay's voice on the telephone telling me that I had been seen in the company of Pike Sayers. I dug out the Iron Cross from my kitchen drawer to turn it over to Steven Aguilera, and he got the Barbie doll from Beverly. The police didn't tell me what they thought of these items, if they thought anything at all.

For several days, I stayed home and watched television. *The Simpsons* was the best, but I watched a lot of the news as well. You can catch CNN even in the middle of the night, so I watched the local news at six and at ten, using the remote to flip from station to station. They broadcast short, tasteful clips from the memorial service Harrison and Morgan McKay arranged for Mariah. The company was distinguished enough that even the arrival of a United States senator in a black limo did not occasion much of a stir. The newspaper that morning had offered quotations from various friends of Harrison, praising his patience, his fortitude, mentioning the heavy burdens that he had borne since the death of his wife—scholar, teacher, single father, and then political candidate. I watched his handsome grieving face for six seconds, then flipped over to *Jeopardy.*

The capital of Tonga.

The pretty contestant creased her brow, but only for a moment.

What is Nuku'alofa?

The audience applauded, and my telephone started to ring. I ignored it.

He won the Pulitzer Prize for literature twice, both times for books that had the word "rabbit" in their titles.

The other contestant, a bald man in an expensive suit, looked worried. His throat worked but his mouth didn't. Updike, you cretin, I thought savagely. The phone rang one more time and then stopped.

Who is John Updike? The man produced it with a triumphant grin. More applause.

It had been Sam, his voice on the message he left calm and concerned. *So sorry,* it said. *Heard from Beverly... I know you must be... Please let me know... Do you want me to...?*

After midnight, I sent him back an E-mail. *Thanks for... So nice of you to... Not necessary to... I'll be in touch after... Hope all is... Love, Cinda.*

Finally, I went back to work, though without much sense of why. Beverly and Tory's solicitude was too much for me; Lincoln's mood, as dark as mine, made his company easier to take, but he wasn't saying much. So I took to staying in my office with the door closed, reading recent decisions and *Colorado Estate Law.* I walked out one day on my way to the ladies' room and overheard Beverly talking on the telephone to Seamus Kellogg, flirting with him while she told him that Ms. Meadows would like for him to come in to discuss his upcoming trial. Tory had been looking progressively grimmer as his trial date approached. I assumed he had not reconsidered his insistence on going to trial with only preposterous arguments as his defense, but I had lost any interest in discussing strategy with her.

I was reading the latest law reports, or pretending to, one waning afternoon about a week later when a messenger from Jim Brant delivered a package. Tory and Beverly had left, and Lincoln, working in the outer office, directed the messenger to knock on my door. The package contained a brief kind note, and two documents, titled respectively "Suggestion of Death" and "Request to Discontinue Investigation of Grievance." The former had been filed in the district court, and the latter with the grievance committee. I looked through them with a weariness so complete it was all I could manage to focus my eyes. The first was one of the shortest legal pleadings I've ever seen.

> Inasmuch as the only plaintiff herein, Mariah Suzanne McKay, became deceased September 29, 1994, defendant herein makes this Suggestion of Death on the record.

I put it aside, furious. It was my obligation to file this document, since the deceased was my client, but Brant hadn't waited. I supposed I would eventually have to file the proper pleadings to dismiss the case. I couldn't think about that now. I picked up the second sheaf of papers without curiosity. It was longer than the other, and I scanned rather than read it.

> The unfortunate death of the daughter of the complaining party... although the conduct was troubling... giving credit to the possibility that Ms. Hayes may not have understood the extent of her unprofessional... my client does not believe that further investigation of this grievance would serve the public interest in...

My fury grew as I crumpled the document in my fist, then receded as the Suggestion of Death caught my eye again. I tried to summon up a memory of my torts class, what had been said about the death of a party. I knew we had discussed it, but could recall only dim slivers. I'd have to get some sodium amytal, I thought grimly. Or do some research. I rose and went out to look for Lincoln. He was sitting at Beverly's desk, hunched over the computer. The hands that had been trained to play Chopin and Rachmaninoff flew over the keyboard, trying to conjure some truth, or some consolation, out of the ether.

"What are you doing, buddy?"

Headshake, as if to discourage a fly. But when I pulled the spare chair over next to him and watched the screen in silence, he did not object. There was a small box at the top of the screen, which was otherwise full of advertisements for records, books, T-shirts, and airline tickets.

"What is this?" I was whispering, nonsensically, as though that would make my presence less of an intrusion.

"Search engine," he muttered. He typed in a line of text, the click of the keys the only sound in the quiet office: *court common law judge militia Colorado.*

I put a hand on his left arm; his wrist was still wrapped in an elastic bandage. "If the police can't solve this murder, I don't think we can—"

"It's the only thing I can do," he said fiercely, pulling his arm away.

I peered again: *1028 documents found, see 1–10 below.* Hopeless.

"Are you so sure that's where the solution lies?" I said gently.

"That's what the police think, anyway." He started scrolling through the list of documents, most of the entries semi-gibberish, full of *http* and random punctuation and slashes. "Did I tell you I remembered who the lawyer guy was?"

I wasn't really listening. "What?"

"Remember I said I thought I'd heard the name of the lawyer before—the lawyer for that guy who was in the newspaper clipping, the one who tried to hang the clerk?"

"Oh, yeah."

"Tyson Thornhill. He was also the lawyer when Tory's client Mr. Kellogg got convicted of that tax evasion offense all those years ago. That's where I saw the name."

I thought for a minute, but my weary mind shook off this information. It didn't have a thing to do with Mariah.

"That's interesting," I said with an effort. "Did you tell Tory?"

He nodded, still typing. "She got me to try to track down Thornhill through the bar association, but he must have left Colorado. He was disbarred in absentia in 1990 for failing to pay his bar dues for a couple of years. Left no forwarding address, left a lot of clients in the lurch. End of trail."

I'd lost interest already. "Well, when you're done, I have something else I could use your help on."

He looked up. The facial bruises were mostly healed, only faint clouds of yellow like the shadowed skin around a very old man's eyes. "What's that?"

"Mariah's lawsuit."

"Isn't it over?"

"That's what I was thinking, but something just occurred to me. Can you look in the Colorado statutes from there and see what they say about the survival of actions after death?"

He wiped his hands over his face, perhaps needing a moment of darkness to reorient himself to a different task. "Okay. Give me a minute to formulate a search request."

I walked down the hall to the ladies' room. Looking in the mirror, I noted, without especially caring, the way the light brought out the pouches on my face. There was a coffee stain on my white shirt, too, and a clot of something in the corner of my eye. I rubbed the eye indifferently as I snapped out the light. When I got back, Linc had a screen full of text.

"Is this what you wanted?"

I read over his shoulder, then read again. "Can you go to the next page?" He hit a key and the screen broke up and re-formed.

"Here, you take over." He started to struggle out of the chair, reaching for his crutches, but I stopped him with a hand on his head.

"Go on with your research," I said. "I can read this in the hard copy." I went back to my office, pulled down the volume of the red statutes that contained article thirteen, and read. Then I reached for the telephone. I had not spoken to Sayers since the morning after the funeral, and didn't want to, but now he was my client.

"You're probably right," said Sayers. "In Illinois, as I recall, the action belongs to the estate and may be maintained after the plaintiff dies. Except I believe any recovery for pain and suffering would be lost at death. The only recovery possible would be for lost wages, economic loss, that sort of thing."

"It's the same in Colorado. There's not much of that sort of damage we could prove, I guess. There's no evidence Mariah would have earned more money but for whatever her father did to her. But you're the administrator of the estate and that makes you the plaintiff now. You need to decide whether to maintain the case or dismiss it. I can't see it would make much sense, though, if we can't prove any economic damages. Quite apart from any other problems with the case."

"We could seek nominal damages along those lines. If the suit had a different purpose." I thought a question lay behind the noncommittal words.

"Why would you want to do that?" I asked. "I mean seek nominal damages. What would be the point?"

"What was Mariah's point, Cinda?"

"She wanted to know the truth. But now she never will."

"What about you? Do you care about it?" His voice was gentle but insistent.

"I think maybe it was an illusion all along," I said. "The idea that any of us could learn the truth that way. Maybe courts are not the right place to get at the truth."

"*Law is no more?*" he said. "*Law is gone away?*"

"Is that Auden again? Law may still be here, but truth is something else."

"Well, let's think about this. What evidence do we have now that could prove anything about what happened?"

I considered. "Mariah's deposition is admissible in evidence now, since she's unavailable."

Several seconds' pause. "That's true, but I don't think it's enough, Cinda. I saw it, remember, at the probate hearing. She was brave and smart, but she didn't remember enough to allow us to prove anything against McKay at trial. She can't have told Andy Kahrlsrud any more than what she said in the deposition. And there's no chance she's going to remember any more now, is there?"

"No," I said, tears welling up in my eyes.

"How soon do we have to decide?" he asked.

"Once the Suggestion of Death is filed, the case is dismissed if we don't file a motion for substitution of parties within ninety days," I said, trying to control my voice.

"Let's wait, then, since we've got a little time. Until we can think this through. Are you all right, Cinda?"

"Fine," I said, and hung up quickly.

Two afternoons later, a commotion outside made me get up from my desk and walk toward my closed door. I was about to open the door when it flew open, revealing Tory and Seamus Kellogg. Her face was suffused with anger, and his was full of indignation. She actually shoved him into the room—without much difficulty, as she probably outweighed him by twenty pounds. I saw Beverly's startled face behind her desk for a brief moment before Tory slammed the door shut again.

"All right, asshole, this is where your bullshit stops." She nearly spat this at him as she pushed him down into a chair. "You're going to tell Cinda everything—why you hired this office to represent you, what you learned, what you know about Mariah's death, and what you're going to do about it. Talk. Now!"

I was too taken aback to speak. Kellogg looked pretty surprised, too, but the little man maintained some hold on his composure. "Ah, I wondered why you were so eager to have me come into the office. All summer I have to beg every time I want to visit with you for a bit, and now when you finally summon me, it's to abuse me like this in front of your partner."

She's going to hit him, I thought, but Tory retreated to the window and leaned against the sash. "I'm staying away from you so I don't kill you," she advised him. "You fucking *spy!* Who are you working for? Those militia zombies?"

He looked at me and smiled uncertainly. "Ms. Hayes, I wonder if you would excuse us? Since my attorney is insisting I answer her questions, and all of my answers would of course be in strictest attorney-client confidence, I think it would be best if you were not present."

I watched him as if from a great distance, wondering at his poise. Patches of something Lincoln had said were coming back to me, but they didn't explain Tory's behavior. *Tyson Thornhill. He was also the lawyer when Tory's client Mr. Kellogg got convicted of that tax evasion offense all those years ago. That's where I saw the name.* Herbert Gohannon, Tyson Thornhill, Seamus Kellogg, Mariah? My numbed-out brain tried to process this information, but it was useless, like an effort to talk through novocained lips. I couldn't see what possible connection there could be. I leaned back wearily in my chair. "This is my office, Mr. Kellogg. I'm not leaving it. But feel free." I gestured toward the door.

"Oh, no," said Tory. "He's not going anywhere. You can talk just fine in front of Cinda, Seamus. She's my partner, remember? Her presence won't harm your goddamn privilege."

Kellogg was gathering confidence. "Ah, lassie, there's something you're forgetting. She has this other client, I believe, although unfortunately deceased. Her client's interests are not, I can say with assurance, the same as mine. I believe it would be unprofessional for her to accept my confidences. Especially on the subjects you raise."

Tory opened and closed her hands in a way that unsettled me. I spoke quickly. "He's probably right, Tory. If he knows something that he doesn't want to tell me that would help Mariah's estate, he can't confide it in me. Neither can you, buddy. We have to maintain a confidentiality wall between us unless there's some way around the conflict of interest."

She reached over quickly and took an object from my desk into her right hand: the brass paperweight, shaped like a pair of running shoes, that we'd won in the breast cancer footrace. "Tory, no!" I shouted. "Put it down!"

She tossed it up and caught it again, as though testing its heft. "Come with me, Mr. Kellogg," she said, moving toward him. "Let's go to my office for our confidential talk. I'm going to borrow this, Cinda."

I was too benumbed to object, or to reply when he stopped in front of me as Tory was herding him out and took my hands in his. "I truly am sorry for the death of your friend," he said. "It was wrong, what happened."

The law school dream came again the night before I took Seamus Kellogg's deposition. Only this time, as I carried out my frantic room-to-room search, I could look into the classrooms through the small glass windows that pierced their doors. Through each window I saw a professor behind the podium, gesturing, writing on the blackboard, talking, talking, but I couldn't hear what he was saying, and when I tried to open the door, I would find it locked. I was no longer looking for an examination, I think, but for some wisdom, some piece of advice that would relieve the hammering of my heart. I flew from room to room until suddenly I knew, as one does in dreams, what they were all saying, and this knowledge awakened me and kept me awake until dawn. *Never ask a witness a question unless you already know the answer. Never, never, never.*

But I had no more choice about it than I had about *Never get emotionally involved with a client.* It was too late to start observing the rules.

The Reporter: Please state your name for the record.

The Witness: Seamus Daniel Kellogg.

I studied the paper that Tory had given me uneasily as the reporter swore him in. Kellogg himself looked less uneasy than tired and, although uncharacteristically scrubbed and shaven, somehow diminished.

This was the first time I had seen him since the day Tory had pushed him into my office, threatened him, and then taken him off to her own office. They'd finally emerged after being closeted for two and a half hours. According to Beverly, they hadn't been alone all that time. After the first hour, a tall man in a brown suit had appeared and told her he was supposed to see Mr. Kellogg and Ms. Meadows. Beverly was dubious, but when she buzzed into Tory's office, she was told to escort him in. There was shouting at first, she said, and then it got quiet.

I'd seen the other man briefly myself, because Beverly and I were going over some invoices at her desk when the three of them finally emerged late in the afternoon. Kellogg and the tall man, whose features were so unremarkable that I have no memory of them, walked out past us without a word. Beverly's widened eyes followed her erstwhile beau, but his would not meet them. Tory waited until they were through the door, then motioned me to go back to my office. She followed me and closed the door.

"Subpoena the son of a bitch to give a deposition in the McKay case," she told me. "Ten days from now. He'll show up."

"Why? I don't have any questions for him," I said. "I don't have any idea what I should want to know from him."

"Don't worry," she said grimly. "I'll give you the questions. But only right before you start."

"Why?" I asked. "That doesn't make any sense."

"That's the deal," she said. "That's all I can tell you now."

Ms. Hayes: Mr. Kellogg, I see you're here alone today. Are you represented?

The Witness: No, ma'am, not in this matter.

Ms. Hayes: Specifically, are you at present represented by Victoria Meadows, Mr. Kellogg?

The Witness: Not any longer.

Ms. Hayes: How are you employed, sir?
The Witness: Carpenter.
Ms. Hayes: And where do you live?
The Witness: Near Shawnee, Colorado.

I took a sip of water and consulted the paper again. I had no idea what I was doing.

Ms. Hayes: Have you ever heard of an organization called the Brotherhood of Colorado Militia?
The Witness: I attended some meetings of the Brotherhood of Colorado Militia.
Ms. Hayes: Where and when were these meetings held?
The Witness: The first one in a little stone chapel out in east Boulder County, during 1985.

Little stone chapel. I looked at the paper again and decided I hadn't promised to be bound by Tory's script. Hell, if I was going to ask questions I didn't know the answers to, at least they could be my own questions.

Ms. Hayes: Would that be Ryssby Chapel?
The Witness: That is the name of it, yes.
Ms. Hayes: Why did you happen to be at the meeting?
The Witness: I had some interest in the politics of that group, and a friend suggested I might want to attend a meeting.

I looked at the paper, but I wasn't ready to move on to its next question yet, so I asked my own again.

Ms. Hayes: Who was the friend?
The Witness: Man named Ty Thornhill. He had been my lawyer at one time.

I couldn't seem to think fast enough to follow up on this, so I went back to Tory's list.

Ms. Hayes: What was the meeting about?

The Witness: I don't remember specifically, but there was a general idea to put some government officials on trial for their crimes against the people.

Ms. Hayes: Did you attend any meetings of the Brotherhood of Colorado Militia after this first one?

The Witness: Yes.

Ms. Hayes: Approximately how many?

The Witness: Approximately four.

Ms. Hayes: Did there come a time when the group's ideas resulted in any actions?

The Witness: Yes. A trial was held.

Ms. Hayes: Please identify the time and place of this event.

The Witness: September 17, 1985. A farm in east Boulder County. I don't know the owner's name.

A faint buzz, like an electrical circuit just about to make a connection, began to vibrate in my head, then fell silent. I looked intently at Seamus Kellogg, and he returned my gaze expressionlessly. His charm was altogether absent today. Pike Sayers, present as the representative of Mariah's estate, sat still as a stone against the far wall. Jim Brant was sunk in his chair in the corner, not even bothering to take notes. Perhaps he knew what was coming. I still did not. There was only one question left on this side of the paper. "(OVER)," the paper said at the bottom. I asked the last question.

Ms. Hayes: Will you please state who was present on this occasion?

The Witness: I can't remember everyone, but I'll tell you the names of those I do.

Ms. Hayes: Please.

The Witness: It was nearly all men, you understand. The thinking was that women had no proper place in this proceeding. The men I can remember were named Luce, Stark, Gordon, Vandermeer, Gohannon, Larson, Thornhill, McCrate. Smith. Sayers—

What? I looked at Pike Sayers, but his eyes would not meet mine. Son of a bitch! I forgot all about the list of questions.

Ms. Hayes: Mr. Sayers here?
The Witness: No, not this gentleman here.
Ms. Hayes: This was some other Sayers, then?
The Witness: His first name was Gideon.

Sayers's face betrayed nothing; his eyes may have narrowed a little more than usual, but that was all. I was utterly lost, cursing the absent Tory for leaving me marooned in this pointless deposition. I had nothing to hold on to but the damn paper, but when I turned it over there were only five words at the top, printed in Tory's scribbled capitals: NOW YOU'RE ON YOUR OWN. What the hell? While I was trying to think what to ask next, Kellogg spoke again.

The Witness: I didn't quite finish my last answer, miss, before you cut me off.
Ms. Hayes: All right, then, was there anyone else?
The Witness: McKay.

I crumpled the paper in my hand, furious at him, and at myself for not seeing sooner.

Ms. Hayes: What would be the first name of this McKay?
The Witness: Harrison.
Ms. Hayes. Harrison McKay was present?
The Witness: Yes.
Ms. Hayes: Was he a member of the Brotherhood of Colorado Militia?
The Witness: He was involved with something called the Colorado Citizens' Republic.
Ms. Hayes: What was the connection between the two groups?
The Witness: To the best of my understanding, the Colorado Citizens' Republic would issue the orders, and the Brotherhood of Colorado Militia would carry them out. The militia was sort of like the police department, I guess, or the marshal's service. I think many of the men belonged to both groups.

While I was trying to get my bearings, Kellogg spoke again.

The Witness: Then there was a guest, a man who was not a member of either group.

Ms. Hayes: Do you remember the name of that person?

The Witness: Comerford. I think his first name was David.

Ms. Hayes: David Comerford.

The Witness: Yes. He was some kind of judge.

Ms. Hayes: You said he was a guest?

The Witness: Not a voluntary one, I think.

Then I knew, perhaps not everything, but most of it. I didn't know why Kellogg wanted to tell the story this way, at this time, but I knew what his story was. I had heard it before. Twice, in fact, if you count Mariah's telling.

Ms. Hayes: Mr. Kellogg, why don't you just tell us everything that happened that night?

The Witness: It was a trial, more or less. This Judge Comerford and another person, a woman, had been accused of crimes against the people. It was a dispute that had to do with some land and a lien and to tell you the truth I'm not all that clear on the details. I had been hitting the sauce a bit that night. I don't think I was the only one, but I was probably more confused than the others. Remember, I was a relative newcomer. Some of the others knew much more about this dispute. It was very bitter.

Ms. Hayes: Excuse me for just a moment. This woman, do you remember her name?

The Witness: No. But she wasn't there that night.

Ms. Hayes: Why not?

The Witness: I gather they had been unable to take her into custody.

Ms. Hayes: But Judge Comerford was in custody?

The Witness: You could say so. I suppose one way of looking at it is that he had been kidnapped.

Ms. Hayes: Who presided over this trial, Mr. Kellogg?

The Witness: The president of the Colorado Citizens' Republic.

Ms. Hayes: And what was his name again?

The Witness: I don't believe I said it before.

Ms. Hayes: Well, would you say it now?

The Witness: Roswell Stark.

Ms. Hayes: Please describe the proceedings.

The Witness: Well, not much of a trial, I think you'd have to say. No witnesses, or testimony, or anything like that. No evidence, really. Some guys dragged the judge up there to the front of the barn. The place smelled like hay, must have been used for storing the stuff. They had it fitted out like a courtroom, more or less. There was a big pile of rocks in the middle of the barn floor. The poor guy was tied up and they'd stuffed something in his mouth. He was sweating and pale. I remember thinking maybe he had a heart condition. People would take turns standing up and shouting out things against the guy. Finally, Stark recited a bunch of stuff, about the law and the Constitution and such. He pronounced a sentence on the guy. Death by stoning. He pronounced a sentence on the woman, too, even though she wasn't there. Death by hanging. A more merciful death, he said, because her crime was not as great. He went around the room, asking whether everyone present agreed. Everyone did, although folks were beginning to look a little uneasy. Someone pulled the gag out of the judge's mouth and asked him whether he had anything to say, and he started talking in a low voice, trying to reason, you might say, but then while he was still talking one man went to the pile of rocks on the floor and picked up a very big one and threw it at the judge. It struck him on the head. Blood spurted out like it does from a head wound and he sort of crumpled up, and fell. I believe his feet were tied together. Then other people started throwing the stones at him. I left, myself. Not what I'd signed up for. I think a lot of people left, but enough of them stayed to get the job done, I'd say. Next time I saw Judge Comerford he was dead, and some guys were loading him into the back of a camper.

Jim Brant leaned forward at this juncture.

Mr. Brant: Ms. Hayes, I'm going to move to stop this deposition if you can't show me that it has some bearing on the litigation at hand.

Ms. Hayes: I don't believe you're in a position to stop this deposition, Mr. Brant. You don't represent this witness. You're certainly free to leave, if that's your choice. But since you're interested, let me ask the witness this question. Mr. Kellogg, when you named all the people who were present, did you leave someone out?

The Witness: I believe I only undertook to name all the men who were present.

Ms. Hayes: Might a young girl named Drew McKay have been present?

The Witness: Yes. With her father. I remember that she was playing around during most of it, dressing her dolls, drawing in a little book she had, talking to herself. Once, she tried to climb up on the pile of stones, but someone prevented her, got her back to her dolls or some such. We were used to seeing her there.

Ms. Hayes: Had she been to other meetings that you attended?

The Witness: Yes, he often brought her along.

Ms. Hayes: Had she been at other meetings held at Ryssby Chapel?

The Witness: Yes.

Ms. Hayes: The night in the barn, Mr. Kellogg. Was there anything in the scene that could have been described as lights on a string?

The Witness: Yes. I believe the barn did not usually have lighting, and a string of lights, like Christmas lights, had been run out to the barn. In fact, I had been asked to help put up the lights. The little girl pretended to help me. She liked the lights. There were also lanterns.

Ms. Hayes: How much of the proceedings did Drew McKay see?

The Witness: I'm not sure. When the rocks started flying McKay took the little girl out of the barn. I remember that he pressed her head down against his shoulder so she could not see, and she was crying and struggling to get away.

I thought furiously about what Mariah had said about her memories.

Ms. Hayes: Do you know whether McKay threw any of the rocks himself?

The Witness: That's the thing, I believe he may not have up to that point, but one of the others stopped him as he was going out with the little girl. Spoke to him a bit rough. So he put the little girl down for just a moment, and reached over and picked up a stone and threw it. It was awkward, like; the little girl was rubbing her eyes and crying. But his stone found the mark all the same, even though the judge was still trying to move around some. Then McKay picked the little girl up again and pushed her head back against his shoulder, like trying to keep her from seeing anything more, and they went out. But I don't know how much she saw.

Ms. Hayes: What about you? Did you see anything else?

The Witness: I left about the same time myself.

Ms. Hayes: Left? Where did you go?

The Witness: I stayed outside the barn until Mr. Thornhill was ready to leave. I was a long way from home, and he was my ride.

Ms. Hayes: Did you see anything inside the barn that could be described as bare white legs?

The Witness: No.

Ms. Hayes: Nothing at all like that?

The Witness: No.

What now? I asked myself. I knew what Mariah had seen and heard and how it had scarred her heart. The smell of hay, the string of lights, the pile of stones. Her childish eyes straining to see the horror, to understand the trick that made it seem that grown men were throwing rocks until the blood came. Then those eyes covered, blinded by her father's strong hands. All the elements of her memory, except whatever it was that looked like white legs.

I wondered if I would ever find any other witnesses.

Ms. Hayes: Have you now told us the names of everyone present that you can remember?

The Witness: I might have. Did I mention Joe?

Ms. Hayes: Joe who?

The Witness: Not sure. Just called Joe.

Ms. Hayes: Anyone else?

The Witness: Believe that's it, best I can remember.

Ms. Hayes: Do you know where Ty Thornhill is now?

The Witness: (inaudible)

Ms. Hayes: I'm sorry, could you speak up?

The Witness: I couldn't say.

Ms. Hayes: You don't know, or you won't say?

The Witness: I cannot say, Ms. Hayes.

Ms. Hayes: How about Roswell Stark?

The Witness: I cannot say.

Ms. Hayes: Are you refusing to answer, Mr. Kellogg?

The Witness: Yes.

Ms. Hayes: I need a break.

Mr. Brant: Well, I object. This entire proceeding is farcical and—

Ms. Hayes: Object all you want. I'm going to take a break, and after I do I'm going to finish this deposition. Your attendance is entirely optional, but I'd like the record to reflect that you've had every opportunity to attend.

The Witness: May I go outside for a cigarette?

Ms. Hayes: Go ahead.

I took Pike Sayers's arm and steered him into the Victorian drawing room, furious.

"What did you know about this?"

He rubbed his hands over his face. "Nothing."

"Don't give me that crap. Your brother was there."

"Yes, Cinda," he said soberly. "I'm just trying to come to terms with that. Wondering, for example, whether that had anything to do with his suicide."

"You didn't know?"

"I knew of his sympathies, from some of the literature I found around the house. But no, I didn't know he was there. And I didn't know she was there. Do you think I would have encouraged this if I had?"

"What are we going to do now?"

"You said the truth was all you cared about. You've got that now, don't you?"

"It's not enough. This deposition is sealed by order of the court, and it won't be unsealed unless it's used at a trial. Nobody's going to know. This man is running for public office, Pike. And I think he arranged to have his daughter killed."

"Then bargain."

"With what? For what?"

"With whatever you have. For whatever you care about."

I started to leave the room, then turned back. "What do you think the part about the white legs was?"

He shook his head silently, then turned it away.

Ms. Hayes: Let's go back on the record. I don't have any further questions for this witness.

Mr. Brant: I certainly don't have any. This man is either a liar or seriously mentally ill or both, and you may be sure that if you should be so foolish as to go forward to a trial in this matter I will cross-examine him to the limit of the law.

Ms. Hayes: In that case, we can declare this deposition over, and go off the record now.

Tory wasn't in the office when I got back; Beverly said she'd left hours before, mumbling something about coffee. "There was a phone call for you," she added, handing me a slip of paper.

"Marsha Tanner from the *Daily Camera*?" I said. "What did she want?"

"She wanted to know whether you could confirm that the daughter of senate candidate Harrison McKay had filed a suit against him alleging childhood sexual molestation before she died," said Beverly primly. "She said her source told her the court had sealed the file."

"Call her and tell her that if the source was correct about the case being sealed, then I certainly couldn't comment on it, could I?" I handed her back the slip.

"Wait," she said, reaching for her pad, "let me write that down."

"Never mind. Just ignore her. If she calls back, tell her I have no comment. I'm going to look for Tory."

I found her in a booth in the back room of the Trident, nursing the dregs of a demitasse of espresso. I dropped my briefcase heavily onto the opposite seat before going to get a cup for myself.

"You want more?" I asked her, but she waved me away.

"So," I began when I got back to the booth. "You have anything to tell me?"

She looked up. "Didn't you find out what you needed to?"

"Some of it. Most of it, maybe. But not what your part in it was."

She turned her small empty cup around in her hands. "Does it matter?"

"Tory, look at me." She did, her green eyes muddy. "Mariah *died* because she cared so much about finding out the truth. It mattered that much to her. Now there's nobody left to care but me. Whatever you know about this, I want you to tell me, unless it's privileged."

"What time is it?" she said.

"Four-eleven. Why?"

"I can tell you, then. He's gone." And she did. It took quite a while.

Ten days ago, in her office, after she nearly brained him with our race trophy, Seamus Kellogg finally told Tory why he had wanted her for his lawyer. His trouble with the law had started nearly fifteen years ago, when (as Tory pointed out to me) she hadn't even graduated from law school yet. When Seamus followed some of the suggestions that were made at a National Tax Protest Forum meeting, making certain entries on his income tax returns, he found himself in trouble with the federal government, indicted for a federal crime. For help, he went to a lawyer he knew from the group, Ty Thornhill. Thornhill and Seamus's other friends told him he was a hero for making his case a test of their theories about the income tax and phony currency and the privilege against self-incrimination, but when the judge ruled against him, nobody volunteered to go off with him to spend six months in Englewood Correctional Facility. It wasn't too bad there, but after that Seamus was careful to keep his politics out of his income tax returns. Truth to tell, he'd lost most of his interest in politics. But he was a lonely man and he kept going to meetings, including those of the Brotherhood of Colorado Militia after Ty Thornhill invited him.

He never expected the stoning of the judge; he thought all the violent talk was just that—talk. When he saw what was going to happen, he would have left, but he'd ridden in with Ty Thornhill and didn't have a way to leave. When the stoning started, he left the barn and went out behind a shed, where he stayed until it was all over.

Still, it bothered him to remember it. He stopped going to the meetings. After the Gohannon business, the president of the Colorado Citizens' Republic, a man named Roswell Stark, dropped out of sight, and so did Ty Thornhill. There were rumors they were still around, living underground and directing the buildup of some kind of arsenal for the war they were sure was coming, but Seamus didn't know anything about that. Meantime, things weren't going so well for him. He had a bad case of pneumonia, didn't have any health insurance, and couldn't work for quite a while. He looked up some of his old friends from the Trade and Barter Association and the Tax Protest Forum to see if anyone would lend him some money for the hospital bills, but they wouldn't give him the time of day. One of them had done well for himself, and had a new silver pickup; the man said he didn't make a practice of lending money to losers. Seamus drove away from the guy's house in his rusty car and realized he was getting bitter.

He was easy pickings for the FBI. A fellow he'd ended up drinking with several times in a bar in Morrison turned out to be an agent. He knew Seamus's history, knew he was on the skids. Explained the benefits of cooperation: decent pay, his debts paid off, immunity from any small crimes he might have committed that the Feebs knew about. Seamus was down to his last sixty dollars, about to be evicted from his cabin, hadn't gotten laid in four months. He said yes.

They gave him some nice guns, had him hang around patriot bars and shooting ranges, keeping his ears open for rumors and leads. There wasn't much—a few dime-bag drug deals, some penny-ante weapons violations they didn't even bust because it would have burned Seamus. It wasn't a bad life. He was also supposed to be trying to locate Ty Thornhill or Roswell Stark, but he said he hadn't seen them or heard about them, and that was true. Not that he tried too hard. He'd never told the agents he'd been there the night Judge David Comerford died. Far as he could tell, they didn't know what had happened to Judge Comerford, although they had their suspicions. They couldn't prove a thing, and he had no interest in helping them.

Then this summer they told him there was a job they wanted him to do. It required him to get busted for violating the felon-with-a-gun law, they explained, then hire a particular lawyer to represent him. A lawyer named Victoria Meadows.

"That's why he came to you?" I said to Tory.

She nodded. "The little creep. He *used* me. To get into our office, to hang around, to take Beverly out to lunch and to go through our files when nobody was watching. To try to find out what we knew about Mariah and her friends. And I let him. Because I was such an idiot, I imagined he'd wanted me for my special legal skills." I watched her knuckles grow white as she gripped the small cup.

"You mean he didn't really need a lawyer?" I reached over and tried to take the cup out of her grasp, afraid she would break it, but she shook off my effort.

"No way. The Feebs had him all set up with the U.S. Attorney's Office. They were going to dismiss the case at the last minute, say they'd mislaid the guns or some goddamn thing—that's what he finally told me the day I almost killed him in your office. It was all window dressing. The indictment, the trial date, everything."

"But that day when you had him come in. How'd you know that he was shining you on?"

"I didn't know, but when Linc told me that his lawyer had been a guy who was involved with the east county militias, I figured it couldn't be a coincidence. I started thinking about the way he was always insisting on personal consultations in the office, always hanging around, trying to get Beverly to go out to lunch with him. About the time I came back to the office a few minutes after I'd left because I'd forgotten the cell phone and found him in there looking through some files. He claimed I'd left the door unlocked and he was just looking for a copy of the indictment in his case. Stuff like that."

I frowned. "I still don't get it. Why was the FBI interested in Mariah?"

"Just listen."

They told Seamus that a young woman named Mariah, also known as Drew McKay, daughter of politico Harrison McKay, had taken up with some east Boulder County people who were suspected of being involved with the remnants of the Brotherhood of Colorado Militia. This didn't surprise him because he remembered the little girl from the days her father was involved. Some of the stuff those people were doing was bullshit, the Feebs said, some common-law court doing hokey divorces and fighting about property boundaries and grazing leases. But the Feebs thought there might be more to it; they thought Thornhill and Stark might even be out there, underground, living on some farm, biding their time. They were interested in a guy named Sayers, who might be a player, and a Jeremiah Stark, the son of Roswell Stark, who had taken over the family farm when his father disappeared. Mariah knew all of them.

Mariah McKay was going to hire a lawyer, they told him, one she'd talked to on the radio. Some bullshit about her father molesting her. But the girl might let this lawyer get close to her, might talk about the people she knew and what they were doing. This lawyer didn't do criminal defense, but her partner did, and nobody was closer to this lawyer than her partner. Tory Meadows.

He hired Tory Meadows, all right, with the money they gave him, but he never learned anything very helpful. Even the secretary clammed up the time he took her out to lunch and tried to find out more about Mariah and her case. Poor girl, was just about all she'd say. The agents were disgusted with him, said he was useless. They were probably going to cut him off after his case was dismissed, but that was okay with him. He was starting to be disgusted with himself, too.

One of the few pieces of information he'd ever gotten from

Beverly was that Mariah was giving a deposition and was anxious about it. He made up an excuse to come in to the office that day and stuck around, hoping to be there when she returned from the deposition and catch some piece of information about what had been said. So he saw her, for the first time since she was a little girl. He hadn't expected her reaction, or his own. Her vulnerability and affection made him feel dirty, like a worm. But worse, he was sure she had recognized him.

The next day, his control agent called to tell him the girl was dead. Murdered. What did he know? He didn't know anything. The agent told him he was worthless. He knew that. He kept wondering whether he bore some responsibility for her death. He started drinking.

Within days, Beverly called him to say Tory Meadows wanted him to come in for a conference. What should I do? he asked the agent. Go, he was told, and see what you can find out. But don't blow your cover, pal. This isn't over yet.

"You were there for the next part," said Tory. "When I took him back into my office, he spilled everything—about the scene at the farm, the stoning of the judge, the little girl playing with her dolls. I don't think it was because I'd scared him. Seeing Mariah that day had changed him; he was ready to tell what he knew. I realized from what you'd told me—the pile of rocks—that the murder of the judge was the event that had tormented Mariah's memories. But what he'd told me was privileged. I couldn't pass it on to you unless he allowed me to. I was ready to kill the filthy little snitch with my bare hands, but instead I made him call his control agent at the FBI."

"The tall guy who showed up about an hour after you took Kellogg back into your office?"

She nodded. "Bureau hack. Seamus told me he'd get screwed by the Feebs, or the G, as he called them, if he told you anything. So I made him telephone the guy who was running him, tell him he'd better come in or his snitch was going to burn down the whole operation, with me providing the gasoline."

"And you worked out a deal?"

"Correct. Seamus would tell the FBI everything about the scene at the farm, the stoning of the judge, help them locate the place, identify everyone he could remember being there. Then he would fire me. Then he would give a deposition in your case. Then he would vanish. For good."

"Witness Protection Program? Tory," I protested. "He's gone? So I don't have him as a witness if we go to trial?"

"You can use his deposition," she said calmly.

"No, I can't," I said. "McKay's lawyer can object. It's hearsay, remember?"

"Colorado Rule of Evidence 804(b)(1)," she said. "Testimony given in a deposition attended by both parties, when the witness later becomes unavailable, is an exception to the hearsay rule."

"I guess that's right," I said wonderingly. "If I can't find him, he'll be declared unavailable. Why couldn't you just tell me all this before his deposition?"

"That was the Feebies. They needed time to move before anything got out. What's more, you may need to be able to say at some point that when you took Kellogg's deposition, you had no idea he was going to become unavailable later."

"Why?"

"*A declarant,*" she recited solemnly, "*is not unavailable if his absence is due to the procurement or wrongdoing of the proponent of his statement for the purpose of preventing the witness from attending the trial.* Rule 804(a)."

"You told me you never paid attention in law school," I said.

She shrugged. "Some of it must have rubbed off. You'd never be able to use his deposition if you'd known in advance that he was going to disappear after it."

I breathed deeply. The clenched sorrow that had taken up residence in my chest since Mariah's death might have relaxed its grip, just a little. I went to get another cup of coffee.

Tory was sitting up a little straighter when I got back to the booth, still toying with the empty espresso cup. "Do you know who killed Mariah?" I asked her.

"No," she said. "But I think they do. A hired killer, they told me." She shifted slightly in her seat.

"What?"

"I'm not sure you're ready to hear this." I put my cup down so hard some of the liquid sloshed onto the table. "Okay," she said. "Okay! It seems the shooter was working for McKay, even though they may not be able to prove it. McKay took ten thousand dollars in cash out of a brokerage account the day before Mariah's deposition, and he didn't move it to any of his other accounts here in town."

"Bastard," I said savagely. "Having your own daughter killed to preserve your political ambitions."

She was looking at me uneasily. "Well, he may not have intended that exactly. Seems more likely that you were the target, Cinda."

"What are you talking about? I wasn't anywhere near the night Mariah was shot."

"She was dressed like you—blue suit, hair in a braid. She was with one of your employees. She was driving your car."

Bullshit, I thought, my mind flailing away in an effort to resist this information. Bullshit! I made a black cradle of my arms and put my head down into it, trying to escape the roaring that filled my ears from the inside.

"That doesn't make it your fault, Mouse," Tory said gently over the roar.

I raised my head, reluctant to leave the black shelter. "How do they know this?" I asked. I suppose I hoped to find some flaw in the trail of reasons that led there.

"From Seamus. The week before Mariah's deposition, he heard in this patriot bar where he hung out that there was ten thousand dollars for the guy who would off a Boulder lawyer named Lucinda Hayes as an example to other white women who might think of sleeping with a black man. Seamus didn't tell anyone—that's one of the things he's feeling so guilty about."

"McKay wouldn't put that out. Why would he care about me and Sam? He and Sam were friends, sort of."

Tory shrugged. "I'm sure he didn't care, but he probably realized that some of his acquaintances would. For one of them, it might add a little motivation to the ten thousand. I'm sure he thought that without you, Mariah would give up the lawsuit."

"You think McKay sent someone to break my car windows and had that cut-up Barbie doll delivered, to try to scare me off helping Mariah?"

Tory made a little snort of recognition. "That doll. Beverly's still freaked about it. Yeah, I'd guess he did that. I didn't know about the car windows."

"It happened the night I had dinner with you and Linda up at your place. Someone broke the Subaru's window while it was parked in front of my house, and left an Iron Cross behind. Why would McKay hire someone to use a Nazi symbol to scare me? He was trying to run away from his past."

She lifted her shoulders. "I don't know anything about that. But maybe he meant you to think the militia people were behind it. Still might be good for a scare, but you wouldn't connect it with him."

I nodded. "That's what I did think."

"So McKay's contract found a taker," continued Tory, "but not the amateur kind McKay was looking for at first. Looks more like it was a professional, even though he screwed up and hit the wrong target. They don't expect to find him."

"What else is there?" I asked miserably.

"Only what Seamus Kellogg told you today."

I was silent for a long moment. Finally, I nodded and raised my cup slightly. "To Seamus Kellogg," I said.

She tilted the empty cup in her hand slightly toward me. "Confession," she said. "They say it's good for the soul."

"And to you," I said. "Thanks, I guess. What's that saying about knowing the truth?"

"You shall know the truth, and the truth shall set you free?" she suggested, with only a trace of irony.

"Yeah. Except I'm not sure it's about freedom," I said. "Peace, maybe."

She reached across the table and touched her little cup to my larger one. "Peace."

I drove home slowly, wondering what to do with what I knew. With Kellogg's deposition, we could prove what had happened to Mariah. Maybe with Andy's help we could even prove that it had harmed her, cost her some economic opportunities she would have had if she hadn't been so damaged, but any monetary recovery would certainly be small. And by the time we got to trial, the election would be over. Until then, the records, including the depositions, were sealed.

But Marsha Tanner's call made it sound as though the seal had developed some leaks. Moreover, surely Jim Brant had told McKay by now what Kellogg had testified to. The FBI was looking into McKay's bank records. And even if McKay skated through the next few weeks to the election, he knew that his efforts to put me out of the picture had led to Mariah's death. Could he be as indifferent to that knowledge as he had been to her suffering while she was alive?

I tried Pike Sayers's number as soon as I got home. I knew he didn't have an answering machine, so I let the phone ring a dozen times before I put it down. Probably out in the barn, I thought, but I didn't have any better luck at eight or at nine-thirty. In the meantime, Marsha Tanner called twice, and I hung up on her twice.

On an impulse, I pulled out my briefcase and rummaged through the untidy sheaves until I found the material Linc had found for me about Harrison McKay's academic publications. Most of the pages contained bare citations to his various articles, the names of which now seemed more significant than they once had: "The Agricultural Origins of the Conservation Movement." "Term Limits and American Skepticism about the Professional Politician."

There was one longer piece in the thin stack. In 1986, the *North American Political Science Journal* had published a review of a book called *The Tree of Liberty: When Patriots Resist* by Harrison

Pierce McKay. I turned it over in my hands, puzzled; I thought I remembered that the publications section of McKay's CV had shown only articles, no books. The copy of the review Linc had made for me was dim and I had to turn the light up to read it.

I should have read it sooner. The author of the review, a Midwestern professor named Justin Blakemore, began by identifying himself as a former sixties radical turned conservative academic.

> *Perhaps, that is why the True Constitution Press, publishers of this extraordinary volume, chose to send it to me for review. If so, they have misjudged my sympathies. One need not abandon a belief in the propriety of joining Christian politics with religious belief in order to condemn the anti-Semitism found herein. And one need not retreat from the criticism of an out-of-control imperial judiciary in order to find irresponsible the suggestions for amateur adjudication and vigilante justice advanced by Professor McKay. . . .*

I thought I understood then why McKay, having reinvented himself as a mainstream politician, had not claimed *The Tree of Liberty* in his academic credentials. I plugged in Hypatia and tried to find a copy for sale at several Web sites devoted to new and used books, but could not. Harrison McKay's book was out of circulation, like his daughter.

News 4 at ten had a new anchor, a pretty blonde with ferociously blue eyes, to partner the tired-looking male veteran who had delivered the news for a decade. She hadn't gotten the job with her looks alone, though; her delivery was stunningly professional.

"We're following two breaking stories at this hour," she advised sternly. "Both from our Boulder County bureau. In the top story, state and federal law enforcement officers made simultaneous arrests early this evening of seven residents of Weld and east Boulder Counties, including two men who have long been sought by authorities. The arrests were made pursuant to federal warrants issued after the suspects were indicted earlier this week for various federal crimes, including firearms offenses, income tax evasion, and conspiracy to use weapons of mass destruction. Two large caches of weapons have also been seized. A source tells News 4, however, that more serious state charges may follow, including possibly homicide charges related to the 1985 death of a Weld County judge. We'll bring you more news about this story as it becomes available."

Her partner took over then, his deep voice full of sobriety and reassurance as he looked into the camera. "In our second breaking story, a popular Boulder County politician and professor has died in an auto accident. The body of Harrison McKay, who was his party's nominee for the Colorado senate and was given a good chance to prevail in November's election, was taken from the waters of Clear Creek about eight-thirty this evening after his 1993 Bronco tumbled into the creek. Rescue workers say that McKay was dead when they reached him. A motorist who was driving directly behind the McKay vehicle reported that the Bronco veered toward the creek for no apparent reason, and investigators are looking into the possibility that McKay may have taken his own life. Friends have reported that he was in despair over the recent murder of his younger daughter, Drew. Ironically, McKay was driving in this same canyon in 1983 when his car went out of control and plunged into Clear Creek. His wife was killed in that accident; he and his two daughters survived. He was alone in the car today. McKay is survived by his remaining daughter, Morgan McKay."

I called Sayers on and off for the next two days, but never reached him. Then I looked up from my desk on the third morning, and there he was, standing in the door frame. He was wearing a gray suit and a necktie. "You look surprised," he said. "Sorry. I let myself in, and I didn't see your receptionist out there."

"She's, ah, gone to the post office," I said. "What are you... I mean, you look different."

He nodded. "Just rented an office out in Longmont, but I came into the big city to do some research over at the law school's library. Probably see you around from time to time."

"A *law* office?"

"Not all those folks they arrested in my neighborhood are equally guilty. And most can't afford lawyers. I just filed my application for admission to the Colorado bar."

"You're going to represent them?"

"Some of them," he said. "There's quite a hue and cry against them right now, but I expect we'll be able to sort it all out in time."

I smiled. "Always the loud angry crowd?"

"Yeah." A cloud of doubt crossed his face. "And always the soft idiot, maybe. I don't know what I thought I was doing out there. This is better."

I leaned back in my chair. "I've been trying to call you. What about Mariah's estate's case? We could substitute McKay's estate as a party defendant. It's up to you."

He shook his head. "A dead person suing a dead person? Let it go."

"Then what about asking to have the seal lifted on the pleadings and depositions? I still get calls from reporters. It's your decision."

"You know I can't decide that. It would hurt some people I care about, but you'd be within your rights to get it out in the open. Good morning, Cinda." He turned and left, holding one hand up in salutation as he walked out.

"Good morning," I whispered to the closed door. An ache rose to my eyes along with the memory of his back arching over me as he sobbed in completion and sorrow. The pen slipped from my fingers, falling to the floor, and I didn't pick it up for a long time.

FALL 1995

A Timid Similarity

It must have been about a year later, harvest season. The farmer's market was full of pumpkins and squash, the farmers joking and laughing under a sky so blue it caressed your eyes and promised mendaciously never to leave you again. I was just back from a visit with Sam, and Nat and Johnny, in New York.

We'd had a great time together. Johnny had become my best friend a few months before, in the spring, when I told Sam that I wasn't going to be moving to New York to join their practice. I still hope Sam will come back to Boulder, but it's not because he's given me any reason to hope.

On this latest visit, he was tender and loving, as always. The first night, he took a condom from his nightstand.

"It's for you, baby," he said. "To protect you."

"I understand," I said, and I did. I didn't tell him that I had some in my purse. It almost seemed that our bodies together were sweeter for the sadness of it.

Thinking about this, I cruised around the corner by the dried-flower stand on my Rollerblades, concentrating on not rolling into anyone, and there she was. The corn-silk hair and unblemished fair skin, the practiced smile. She must not have known me at first. Rollerblades make a person look much taller, for one thing.

"Hello," she smiled, holding out a flat glossy package. "Would you like..." She knew me then and turned away quickly, but not quickly enough to keep me from seeing the fear in her face. She took a hasty step toward an older couple approaching on her other side. "Hello," she said to them quickly. "Would you like a brochure? I'd certainly be grateful for your vote."

I skated away, no more anxious than she for an encounter. One of the brochures was lying on the ground about halfway down the block. MORGAN MCKAY FOR CITY COUNCIL, it said. QUALITY, COMMITMENT, INTEGRITY. Nice photograph.

I took it home with me and studied it for a while. Finally, I cut the picture out and stuck it onto my refrigerator door, next to one that Pike had given me of Mariah with Thelma and Louise. I looked at the two together. What were they trying to tell me?

It was a gray and chilly day, perhaps three weeks later, that brought Seamus Kellogg's letter in my mail. The envelope was not quite clean, and it was addressed to me at the office, with no return address and a Minneapolis postmark. I slit it open and shook; the first thing to fall out was a copy of the *Daily Camera*'s story about Morgan's candidacy, followed by two sheets of paper. On the first page, he had written:

> *A friend sent me this clipping. By a roundabout route, of course. I'm moving on in a couple days, I told those marshals that Minnesota is getting too cold even for this old mountain man. So no harm done by my writing, it seems to me.*
>
> *The G here tells me they never charged anyone in that judge's death. That's okay with me, I guess. Still, that business in Oklahoma City last April gave me a turn. Lately I've been thinking about how easy it is to become part of something you don't understand, because it gives you a place to stand and belong. I'm not part of anything now. It's lonely, but it's better that way.*

Then this clipping came to put me in mind of something that's been bothering me from time to time. At my deposition, you asked me about some white legs, do you remember? It seemed as though they were very important to you. You asked me if I saw anything like that inside the barn, and I told you no. That was true enough, as far as it goes, and you didn't pursue it. Perhaps I should have volunteered more, but I was scared of the G, and even more of that partner of yours, and they had told me not to volunteer anything. And I wasn't really truthful about Jo, because I did know her last name. Anyway, this is for you, for whatever use you wish to make of it. Please give my fond greetings to Miss Beverly, and my respectful ones to Miss Tory.

Like the letter, it was badly typed and somewhat smeary, but it was certainly a lawful affidavit, composed with a certain care and signed before a notary public in White Bear Lake, Minnesota.

I, Seamus Daniel Kellogg, upon oath and subject to penalties for perjury, do hereby say and depose as follows:

In October of 1994, I gave testimony under oath in a deposition taken in a lawsuit filed in Boulder County, Colorado, named McKay v. McKay. My testimony there was mostly truthful, but it was not complete. I mentioned an event in which persons caused the death of one David Comerford. I acknowledged having been there at the start, but said I had left the barn as the event began. I did not mention that after leaving the barn I occupied myself with a lady apart from the group until it was over.

The lady liked to call herself Jo, but her name was Morgan McKay, and she was with me in the barn at the time those events began. I saw her throw a stone at the judge, then turn away. She seemed upset. She then suggested we leave the barn together, seeking a place to engage in sexual relations. After she and I had been together some time, on the ground in a darkened area behind some outbuildings, we were startled by a flashlight held by the lady's father, a Dr. Harrison McKay, who had come looking for her. Jo was distressed to have been discovered by her father under the circumstances, as she had removed her jeans, and was undressed below the waist. Her younger sister, who I believe was only about nine or ten at the time, was carried in Dr. McKay's arms, and seemed very frightened. I believe she thought that I was trying to harm her sister. Her father said some angry words to me and to Miss Jo, and then took the child away swiftly and rather roughly. The young girl was struggling, and crying, Let me see! or something similar.

I meant Miss Morgan McKay no harm, and indeed it was she who proposed our activities. She was well beyond the age of consent, as I recall she had told me she was twenty-one years old at the time. She and I had often met before, at gatherings of the Colorado Citizens' Republic and the Brotherhood of Colorado Militia.

Further affiant sayeth not.

Signed before the undersigned authority this 2nd day of November, 1995.

I took the affidavit home that night, laid it out carefully on my kitchen table, and smoothed its folds as I looked at the pictures of Mariah and Morgan on the refrigerator door. *She was twenty-one years old at the time.* If Mariah had lived, she would be twenty-one now.

It was one thing Morgan and I agreed on, Mariah had told me, *that we hated our names? We used to talk about what names we'd have if we could choose our own. I always said Mariah.*

Of course. I thought of Linc, singing at Mariah's burial. *The rain is Tess, the fire's Jo, and they call the wind Mariah.*

I made a cup of tea as I thought about Morgan at twenty-one, bereft of a mother, struggling to navigate her small craft in the surrounding sea of her father's ambitions. I pondered her complicity in the death of Judge David Comerford. I considered her possible legal defenses, concluding that she had none. I remembered that there is no statute of limitations for murder. Sipping the fragrant bitter liquid as it cooled, I catalogued in my mind her silences and acts of selfishness. I remembered a few of my own.

For once I found my scissors where they were supposed to be, in the kitchen drawer. I have always been fond of confetti. To the birds scratching around in my backyard, it might have seemed like a parade—or, more likely, as birds have little experience of parades, the first snow of the season. In any event, they didn't like it. They rose from the ground in synchrony, chattering as they wheeled about and took wing toward the south.

As for us, the poet understood. We don't know where or why. We can't compel or fly.

BIBLIOGRAPHY

I learned a great deal about Colorado agriculture past and present from these sources: *Colorado's Centennial Farms and Ranches: A Century of Seasons* (1994), by Michael Lewis; *A Colorado History* (7th ed., 1995), by Carl Ubbelohde, Maxine Benson, and Duane A. Smith; *Colorado Without Mountains: A High Plains Memoir* (1976), by Harold Hamil; *Colorado: A History of the Centennial State* (rev. ed., 1982), by Carol Abbott, Stephen J. Leonard, and David McComb; and *Boulder in Perspective: From Search for Gold to the Gold of Research* (1980) by John B. Schoolland.

The following books were especially helpful in understanding the controversy about recovered memory: *The Myth of Repressed Memory: False Memories and Allegations of Sexual Abuse* (1994), by Elizabeth Loftus and Katherine Ketchum; *Unchained Memories: True Stories of Traumatic Memories, Lost and Found* (1994), by Lenore Terr; *Spectral Evidence: The Ramona Case, Incest, Memory and Truth on Trial in Napa Valley* (1997), by Moira Johnston; and *The Memory Wars: Freud's Legacy in Dispute* (1995), by Frederick Crews.

Marya Hornbacher's *Wasted: A Memoir of Anorexia and Bulimia* (1998) taught me more than I thought there was to know about eating disorders.

And I found the following sources extraordinarily useful on the subject of militias and common-law courts: *Harvest of Rage: Why Oklahoma City Is Just the Beginning* (1997), by Joel Dyer; *Rural Radicals: From Bacon's Rebellion to the Oklahoma City Bombing* (1996), by Catherine McNicol Stock; *False Prophets* (1998), by Dale and Connie Jakes with Clint Richmond; and *The Jubilee Newspaper.*

ABOUT THE AUTHOR

MARIANNE WESSON is the best-selling author of *Render Up the Body.* She is a law professor at the University of Colorado and former federal prosecutor, as well as an essayist and legal analyst for television and radio. *A Suggestion of Death* is her second novel. She lives in Boulder, Colorado.